In every woman's life . . .

In every
woman's life . . .

A NOVEL BY

Alix Kates Shulman

Alfred A. Knopf   New York   1987

THIS IS A BORZOI BOOK
PUBLISHED BY ALFRED A. KNOPF, INC.

Excerpt from the poem "The Heart Asks First
for Pleasure" by Emily Dickinson originally published
by Little, Brown and Company.
Grateful acknowledgment is made to Yale University Press for
permission to reprint excerpts from the poems "A Lesson for
Baby" and "In This Way, Kissing" from pp. 197, 199–200 of *Bee
Time Vine and Other Pieces* (1913–1927) by Gertrude Stein.
Copyright 1953 by Alice B. Toklas.

Library of Congress Cataloging-in-Publication Data
Shulman, Alix Kates.
In every woman's life —
I. Title.
PS3569.H77I5   1987   813'.54   86-46148
ISBN 0-394-55724-7
Manufactured in the United States of America

FIRST EDITION

FOR ANN, FOR MARGARET,
AND FOR SCOTT

I wonder what Adam and Eve
Think of it by this time.
—MARIANNE MOORE
Marriage

ACKNOWLEDGMENTS

My gratitude goes to the National Endowment for the
Arts, the MacDowell Colony, the American Academy
in Rome, and the University of Colorado, Boulder, for
providing me with precious time and space for work;
to my editor, Bob Gottlieb, for his attention and faith;
to the friends who kindly read and discussed my
manuscript: Margaret Fiedler, Vivian Gornick, Ellyn
Polshek, Teddy Shulman, Ann Snitow, Carol Stein,
Anna Tsing, Ellen Willis (who named the rock group),
Susan Wittenberg and Scott York; and to the anony-
mous woman who wrote and circulated the Chain
Letter for Liberated Women. Thank you all.

In every woman's life . . .

At Home

1

IN EVERY WOMAN'S LIFE a time must come to think about marriage. Once, that time was brief, to be seized in the moment, or anxiously borne, or boldly flung away; but now it seems to descend like a recurring dream to vex or tempt the troubled dreamer with secret longings and second thoughts—such are the uncertainties of the times.

Anyone peering into the sprawling East Side apartment of the Harold Streeter family to see Rosemary Streeter wipe her hands on a towel and peek into the oven at another masterly Sunday dinner (something special for everyone), while her humming husband pours steaming noodles into a bowl, would surely conclude that here all second thoughts had long since faded. On the marble hearth a brisk fire crackles. In the kitchen steam whistles in the kettle, duck crisps in the oven, noodles wallow in sesame sauce, newly ground coffee beans yield up their rich aroma. Though the bare branches of trees are not yet black against the pale city sky slowly advancing toward twilight, already in every room lights blaze, and behind closed doors the Streeter children's stereos and tape decks send waves of contrary vibrations merging in the charged interior.

Rosemary Streeter, dutiful wife, carefully closes the oven door. "The duck looks perfect. I just have to finish the sauce, then you can call the kids," she announces to Harold who, to the rhythm of a Verdi tune, is tossing the noodles Mrs. Scaggs made fresh on Friday before she left. But just as Rosemary turns back toward the stove, her nostrils are assaulted by a veiled golden memory that brings on a sudden love attack, raising her momentarily out of this kitchen, this marriage, this family to transport her across town to a top-floor studio off Central Park West where sunlight glints off a gold church dome through a sunny window. She can smell the lantana growing in a clay pot on the windowsill, taste the wine. She catches her breath and leans against the stove until the attack passes. Only then, returning, does she realize that she has left essential ingredients out of the dessert. "Damn!" she cries, almost in tears. "The vanilla! The rum!"

"What?" asks Harold, measuring coffee into a large Melitta. "Something the matter?"

If she acknowledges her lapse, everything may be revealed. In this apartment, large for New Yorkers—big master bedroom and rooms for each of the children, two bathrooms and a half, a spacious living room, a small study, and that rarity nowadays, a separate dining room off the new yellow kitchen—there is no place to hide her feelings except inside.

All her life she's loved two kinds of men: the ones she still desired after she knew they were wrong for her, and the ones she remained tied to long after she lost all desire. Between the two, she believes, she has everything. "Never mind," she says.

Rosemary is not the only one with secrets. Though no one is permitted to open a closed door without knocking, every Streeter feels the need to take certain additional precautions. Throughout the house, objects nestle in locked boxes, sealed envelopes, secret codes, carefully disguised containers. Spider keeps his small collection of skin magazines in the same secret compartment he rigged behind his bed for his collection of precious gems when he was eight. Daisy hides the "speeches" and passionate poems she would be ashamed to have anyone see among the treasured pages of, respectively, Tolkien and *Jane Eyre*. On the hall desk, in the family's bulging red address book, Rosemary keeps certain numbers listed under the names of innocent acquaintances whose association with the fugitives they shield is too slim to make them suspect. Even the spice shelf and medicine cabinets, open to everyone, from time to time house controlled substances disguised as ordinary household oregano or vitamin C. And to Harold, the cylindrical chambers once used for kerosene at the bottoms of the antique lamps mounted on either side of the mantelpiece are a perfect hiding place for the thick rolls of large denomination bills he has been secretly accumulating for purposes of his own.

Sometimes the secrets bursting from the Streeter hearts are too large to be contained within their rooms, too explosive to be safely stored beneath the high ceilings of the comfortable East Side apartment. Then, like certain toxic wastes condemned to be endlessly transported from place to place at ever increasing danger to the populace because there is no acceptable repository for them, the secrets must be taken out into the world in search of an adequate hiding place. The danger of witnesses increases. Lies must be compounded. Acts that seem perfectly acceptable under ordinary circumstances—like standing in line at the post office—may suddenly leave one feeling vulnerable as a rabbit on the highway if one happens to be picking up mail under an assumed name.

Harold piles ice into four tall glasses, then covers the cubes with tap water. "I'll call them now," he says. He deposits the glasses on the table, wipes his hands on his pants, and sets off down the hall.

Spider (*né* Maximilian) Streeter lay on his bed with one arm behind his head and one long leg pounding the floor. The roar of the music left him oblivious of the ravenous roar of hunger waiting to be released with the first rap of his father's knock; his eye was following the intricate pattern etched by cracked paint on the ceiling of his room. He could not remember a time when he had opened his eyes to any other country than the one of which his ceiling was a map. The last time the apartment had been painted he'd cried until they'd agreed to spare his ceiling, it was that intimate a part of him, and the next time it was threatened he would probably cry again. He had allowed his friend Frankie Herschel to name some of the provinces, and sometimes they spoke in codes derived from letters assigned to the mysterious overhead shapes, but he was still king of that land. He would go to dinner, he would fight with Daisy, he would probably get his father mad, and when he returned to his room his country would be carved even more deeply onto the sky of his universe. In his closet was a vast collection of road maps from every part of the United States that had occupied his recent childhood. Earlier, there had been dinosaurs, monsters, rocks, gems, keys, and every Dr. Seuss book ever written, but of these others he'd eventually grown tired, while his passion for road maps had deepened. Daisy got mere miniatures for every birthday and Christmas, while he got something real. Then, when his father left them one summer, he was able to follow his progress west, like a commander charting the movement of his troops.

Inside her room Daisy, squirming at her desk, attacked now her pencil, now her thumbnail, as if the efforts of her teeth could somehow peel open the secret answers to the questions on the blank application lying before her. *Tell us in your own words whatever you want us to know about you.* She knew there were right answers and wrong ones; the questions were traps; but she didn't know what or how much to reveal. The deadline for her applications was approaching, but Daisy could hardly answer the easy questions, like what field do you plan to major in, or describe your academic goals while at college, much less the impossible ones: Discuss the most significant experience in your secondary school years. Pose a question we should have asked on this application to enable us to know you and then answer it. If you could have been alive at any time in history, whom would you most like to have been and why? Justify. I wish, wrote Daisy, I were alive right now and I were myself, living this life, and my applications were finished, crammed from margin to margin with brilliant statements, and you were so impressed by my unusual qualities and first-rate qualifications that you decided to admit me to the college of my choice.

Harold's sharp knock against her door shoved her smack against a terrible realization. Of course! How had it escaped her before? She could not possibly tell the significant experiences of her life from the trivial ones until she knew what was waiting to happen to her; and how could she know what would happen to her until she knew if and where she'd be going to college? How could she divine a cause before she perceived the effect? It was hopeless. Anxiety clutched her heart and squeezed.

"Daisy? Spider? Dinner."

Laying aside the mutilated pencil, she leaped from her desk as if she had suddenly been released from some unjust punishment for an unknown offense. She waited for the violin phrase to end before pressing the off button, then ran down the hall to find the same station on the living room set. Reluctantly Spider swung his other leg to the floor. Upright, he had to pee. The rumble of hunger replaced the bass as he turned off his stereo and prepared to fight if necessary for the bathroom.

"That's nice, darling," said Rosemary, coming in from the kitchen with a large platter. "What is it?"

"Vivaldi, I think," said Daisy.

"Yes—but what?"

"Shh. We'll see in a minute."

Spider arrived in the dining room to find everyone already seated. He skidded to the table and leaped into his seat.

Harold flinched and cowered. "Please, Spider, try to sit in your chair, not pounce on it."

"Harold," cautioned Rosemary.

"Duck! Yay!" yelled oblivious Spider, clapping his hands in a noisy new fashion that proclaimed his ineluctable presence.

Daisy shot a palm in his direction. "Hush for a minute. I want to hear what it is."

"What what is?" Spider looked around, perplexed. "What?" he repeated louder. "Tell me."

"You heard her—quiet!" roared Harold.

Rosemary rushed across the room to tune in the station more clearly before it was lost, only to lose it completely in the moment of truth. Guilt glazed her voice. "Sorry, sweetheart," she said as a restaurant commercial replaced the announcer's voice.

While the duck, noodles, and applesauce are being passed, let us speak of the seating arrangements. For as long as they've lived in this apartment, each Streeter has occupied the same place at table every night and twice on weekends, a place known as "his" or "hers." Harold, whose impressive height sometimes yields half an inch to a trick back that occasionally and unpredictably goes into spasms, occupies the single large orthopedic chair. Periodically Rosemary points out that it is merely this chair, and not outmoded paternal prerogatives, that makes Harold's position appear to be the head of the table, for the table is actually round, with neither head nor foot; but like so many theories, this one is impossible to put to the test. Rosemary sits opposite him in the very spot she commandeered for herself for its proximity to the kitchen when they first moved into the spacious apartment after Harold hit his jackpot a decade before. Though everyone in this modern family participates in getting the dinner on and off, and Harold is responsible for drinks, salads, and certain specialty dishes, it is Rosemary's taste and will, like the sturdy multicolored striped place mats of Mexican cotton, that set the tone at table. Facing the window to her right sits Daisy, dreamily looking out, and to her left, Spider, who sits on the edge of the plastic-coated chair he graduated to from his high chair at the age of three, perpetually tapping his foot against the leg to the perpetual annoyance of his father. (Very soon Spider will be taller than all of them, yet, as youngest, he'll continue to occupy the plastic-coated chair as long as he eats at this table or until a new generation replaces him.)

Had anyone objected to the seating arrangements, or had anyone requested a change, the four would doubtless have arrived at a compromise (as, when guests were present at table, the family put into operation the seating plan they had once in conference hammered out, involving the individual host's seat going to the guest), but no objection ever arose.

Similarly, a tacit agreement reserved for each Streeter a particular cup, color, spoon, part of the chicken or turkey, favorite sweet, bookshelf, turn (at the piano, VCR, telephone), room, role, passion, vice. Now, under the family's vigilant covetous gaze, Rosemary dishes up the initial portions of duck with everyone's favorite piece (except for Daisy, now an ostentatious vegetarian, who gets the heel of the bread instead); she portions out salad to those who hate dressing or dislike onion before pouring dressing over the remaining vegetables and tossing.

When the serving and passing came to an end, a silence, like a collective memory of grace, hovered over the table. Even Spider's tapping ceased. In that instant Harold felt gratitude. He looked at the rosy faces of his children, who had already passed him by and whom he knew he would never truly understand; at the plates laden with delectable food; at the table crowded with trivets and serving bowls that had come into being hardly more recently than the children who had formed them with their own hands; at the parting lips of his wife (in the silence he thought of her still as *wife* though Rosemary sometimes balked at the word), and he felt amazement that somehow, through all the crises and years, he had managed to hold together what everywhere else divorce was tearing apart.

". . . So then she locked herself in the bathroom and exscaped out the window, just like Aunt Jessica said," said Spider.

"*As* Aunt Jessica said," corrected Daisy.

Rosemary put down her fork. "Is that true?"

"Come on, Mom," said Daisy. "*You* know it's *as*."

"No, I mean did Jessica really say she escaped?"

"*Ex*scaped," said Daisy. "Spider said she said she *ex*scaped."

"Jesus fucking Christ, Mom," sputtered Spider, "you should know. You're the one who told me the story in the first place."

"Watch your language, sonny," said Harold.

"But actually," continued Daisy, "that's kind of clever. *Ex*scape is better than *e*scape if you're going out the window."

That Harold felt excluded from the ornate tapestry his family wove before him at the dinner table made him love them no less; if anything, it made him appreciate them more. It was as if they had taken root in a lush garden he was grateful to be able to peek at through a gate. How different were these dinners from those of Harold's youth at which his own father, seated at the head of the table, answered his children's *why*'s with *because-I-say-so*'s and reported on office events to his wife, who fed him questions and courses from the foot, while Harold and his brother in collusive silence kicked one another under the table. This was a different world, and he was a stranger in it. Daisy had been a quiet, reflective child with large brown eyes that looked at him with adoration tinged with fear. Then suddenly one morning he had seen a beautiful busty woman doing yoga on the living room rug in panties and bra. It was Daisy. He still hadn't figured out how it had happened, but he no longer had to be reminded by his wife to knock before entering Daisy's room. Spider, for all the height he had gained over the summer, was still a boy, *his* boy, no man yet. But even Spider seemed shrouded in mystery as he tunneled deeper and deeper toward maturity. Soon he would grow a beard and escape.

"Daddy! You're not even listening," said Daisy, exasperated.

"What?"

"She asked you how come the outside of the glass gets wet too," repeated Rosemary wearily. She supposed she could learn chemistry too, as she had learned the elements of electricity and the rudiments of mechanics, but like so many of her fellow mathematicians who disdain the material world having glimpsed the ideal, she would prefer not to.

Harold cleared his throat, preparing to explain the principle of condensation and so defend himself from their unspoken accusations. They had caught him out being at worst absentminded and accused him of not loving his family. Unfair. Hadn't he, at the very moment they accused him, been thinking of, appreciating, precisely them? He was a respected, even envied man; the educated world quoted what he had written; students wait-listed themselves to be admitted to his seminars; important men invited him to sit on their committees; yet there was nothing he cared more about than his family, his children. He even suspected that he cherished Barbara, his mistress (in her case too his mind still used the old-fashioned word, though his lips had learned to respect her objection, as strong as Rosemary's to *wife;* nowadays, it seemed, women fussed a great deal over words and names), for her mysterious ability to touch the very spot in his heart made tender by the birth of his children. Her energy, her innocence, her adoration were like theirs. Sometimes after they made love, as he drifted aloft among his own cloudy thoughts while Barbara chattered on about one or another of her projects—her studio job, her tap dancing, her quarrels with her friends—sometimes, finding himself suddenly summoned back down with a petulant, "Hal? Are you listening to me or not?" he would be shocked to discover that it was Barbara, not Daisy, accusing him. Shocked and relieved.

"Someone at the Computer Center's been screwing around in my files," announced Spider. "I think I know who, too. They were open security, but now they're protected, and I don't know the password. But that's okay, Herschel and I are going to fix him. We'll slash his juglear."

"Jugular, darling," corrected Rosemary. Daisy smiled.

"Anyway," continued Spider, "we've figured out—"

At that moment the telephone rang. Rosemary leaped at the sound of the bell, as if it were an air raid alarm. "I'll get it," she yelled, dropping her fork to her plate. But seeing that already, before she could even rise from her chair, Daisy and Spider were away, racing down the hall, and realizing that it was after all only the telephone, for a split second she felt giddy relief to have her children gathered around her, safe. When Daisy turned fifteen, Rosemary had stopped worrying about how to save her from the bomb, but Spider still seemed to her too young to be left alone in a nuclear accident, even though sometimes he didn't come home from the Computer Center until long after dark.

Rosemary ran toward the ringing phone. Harold alone remained seated at the table, happy to be released by the bell from that disturbing image of Daisy naked in bed with a lover old enough to be her father.

The Telephone . . .

The telephone sits on the hall desk, the object of as much anxious attention as a newborn: everyone runs when it cries, worries when it's silent. Altogether it seems more necessary to the life of the family than all the stereos, radios, TVs, typewriters, cassette players, minicomputers, air conditioners, and other devices and appliances put together. Even the three thousand–odd watts of electric light, replaceable by daylight and, in a pinch, as summer blackouts proved, by candles, are of less concern than the phone, since some of the hottest conversations the Streeters enjoy are held on wire late at night in the dark.

The instrument in question is a beige console with bold black numbers on square white push buttons. On the dark brown underside, the loud-soft lever is set at the extreme loud end of the continuum for maximum attention. Although affixed to a plug-in wall socket, and thereby portable, this beige instrument is normally positioned on the hall desk where, once the starting bell has rung, any member of the household has a decent chance to reach it from the far-flung corners of the apartment. Though he's the youngest, Spider, with his expert slide, has a slight advantage in any race (especially since the elder Streeters are less practiced racers, used as they are to picking up an extension, plugged into a socket in the kitchen, study, or master bedroom); realizing this, Daisy, who can take the phone into her room by stretching the cord treacherously across a threshold, sometimes neglects to return the instrument to its home base in the hall.

The study—which used to be Harold's, but has become, at least nominally, Rosemary's, ever since she returned to school and laid claim to it on the grounds that Harold has not one but two outside offices, one at Columbia and another at the magazine—the study boasts yet another telephone, a small curvaceous instrument from the 1940s which, though it only sometimes works, is beloved by Rosemary and ignored by the others.

Daisy reaches the desk seconds before Spider, shoots out a hand, and grabs the receiver at the start of the third ring. Spider, undaunted, grabs her from behind and struggles for the receiver. With one concentrated exertion, Spider elbows Daisy in the upper arm and manages to wrench the beige prize from her. "Hello?" he says triumphantly. "Hello? Hello?"

"Give it to me," cries Daisy, making a final grab.

"Too late," says Spider, staring into the phone. "They hung up."

"You asshole! If you'd let *me* get it . . ."

Spider sneers at his sister's delusions of power.

"Who was it for?" asks Rosemary.

"We'll never know," says Daisy. "When they heard *his* charming voice they hung up."

Rosemary consults her watch. "Spider, think. Was there someone on the phone or was it dead when you picked up?"

"That's just what I want to know," chimes in Daisy.

"I told you. They hung up."

"It's not *fair*," whines Daisy.

"Another wrong number?" asks Harold, his voice dripping with irony, when the three return to table.

"Pass the dead duck," spits Spider at Daisy.

Daisy sets her jaw and crosses her arms.

Reaching across the table, Harold glares at Spider while he passes the platter.

Such crises could probably be avoided if the family had more than one telephone line. As the children regularly inform their parents, most of their friends' families install separate lines for the second generation once the children enter their teens. But the high-minded, somewhat puritanical Streeters have always considered such a course, though expedient, an indulgence akin to too much TV. Besides, argues Rosemary, whose master's thesis on infinities makes her see everything as an endless continuum, the more lines, the more calls coming in. She thinks they should learn to share; Harold thinks they should all talk less. Consequently, the smooth operation of emergency signaling systems between Streeters and their lovers is always threatening to break down.

Like most husbands, Harold conducts his affairs when possible on one of his office phones, while Rosemary maps on her mind the location and condition of every pay phone in the neighborhood. She always keeps a large supply of change, ostensibly for Mrs. Scaggs to use in the basement laundry machines, in a jar on the kitchen counter as well as in all her jacket pockets; she is always running out of essential ingredients for which she must frequently dash to the store on a moment's notice.

At this very moment, in fact, she is dialing from a booth across the street from the Hungarian deli where she has just picked up a pint of sour cream. Finding the line busy, she hangs up and retrieves her coin. A middle-aged man in a brown fedora waiting behind her takes a step forward toward the booth, forcing Rosemary to dial again or relinquish the phone. She dials. Still busy. "Hello?" she says to the buzz, "hello?"— until the man steps back. She positions her body in his line of vision and surreptitiously dials again.

Upstairs, Harold is trying to mediate between the two children standing guard at the phone with menacing looks like ballot-box watchers. "Come on now, Spider," he coaxes, "Daisy's expecting a call. You can't tie it up. It's her turn."

"But Pop," whines Spider, hanging up with his finger while retaining his hold on the receiver, "Herschel and I have almost figured out this bug. It's very important. I'll only be ten minutes max, and then she can have it the rest of the night." Nervously he whips the shock cord rapidly back and forth against the desk.

"Stop that!" hisses Harold, asserting his waning paternal authority. "And no she can't, because I have to make a couple of calls myself."

"Okay, okay. One little call. Five minutes. Please."

"Well," says Harold, looking sheepishly at Daisy, "all right. One call. But I'm warning you, Spider, you better make it snappy!"

At last Rosemary gets through. "Thank God. There's someone waiting for the phone and your line's been busy. Did you try to call me at home a little while ago?"

"No. Of course not. Why?"

"Someone called and hung up when Spider answered. I thought it might have been you. I didn't think so, but . . ."

"No, I've been painting since noon. Besides, I'd never call you on a weekend, you know that."

"Yes. But I thought maybe something came up about tomorrow and you were trying to pass me a signal, so I ran out for sour cream." She looks down at the small paper bag from the deli. "We needed it anyway. Is this an awful time to call you?"

"No, baby, it couldn't be better. I was just thinking about you."

Rosemary's uneasiness about the busy wire flies away. She wants to believe. "Really? What were you thinking?"

"I was thinking about what you said Friday just before you left. About the dome? And that got me thinking about your sweet breasts."

Rosemary sighs audibly into the receiver. "That's sweet." It's the same word he used, one of their favorites. It's no longer known which of them started it. For a few seconds they commune wordlessly, listening to each other's breath, until Rosemary senses the fedora moving into the range of her peripheral vision. "Listen, there's someone here waiting to use the phone, and I really have to get back. I wasted a lot of time while your line was busy." (She dares not ask whom he was talking to, but neither can she resist the dig. Not that she doubts him, but this pitch of passion is by nature precarious, and he has not explained the busy wire.) She waits a moment before she is forced to ask, "I'll see you tomorrow, then?"

"You better. I've got a surprise."

She accepts his gift as a rescue and lights up like a child. "You have? Why?"

"You don't know?"

"Should I?"

"You'll find out tomorrow."

"Okay, but now I'll drive myself crazy trying to guess. And I have all these calculus exams to grade—how will I ever concentrate?" She sees fedora's restless, bespectacled eyes peer in at her. "I better go. Tomorrow then."

"I love you."

"I love *you*."

2

As soon as Harold finished fitting the dessert dishes into the dishwasher (the children had done the brunch cleanup and Rosemary, now grading student papers in the study, had done the first course), he wiped his hands and walked down the hall to Spider's room. All weekend he'd been intending to do something special with the boy. But Saturday had slipped by, and now Sunday, with the usual frantic efforts and explosions, and all his best intentions had boomeranged without hitting their mark. He wondered if it wasn't perhaps the enigmatic alchemy of puberty that transformed even the most innocuous suggestions and offhand remarks he offered his son into seeming barbs and criticisms—the same process that had taken his eager little boy who, with nothing but a ball of string, had one Sunday brilliantly transformed his entire bedroom into an enormous spider's web, and given back a tall, mysterious, sulky lad who juggled balls at midnight, chronically overslept, mumbled or shouted with nothing in between, collected dirt on his neck, played trumpet at all hours, and spoke in cryptic codes or whispers through a slit in his mouth when anyone approached his room.

The door, beneath which oozed like stage steam multicolored clouds of billowing sound, was assertively closed. With the music blasting it would be difficult to speak. But Harold resolved this time to risk the consequences of raising his voice over those incurred by asking Spider to turn down the volume. He examined the door for an easy entry, then his fingers closed around the doorknob. Just in time his brain registered the reminder that what the boy did behind his door had recently been ruled a private affair; he released his hold on the knob and instead raised his knuckles to the narrow strip of hardwood that lay exposed between two posters of Lip Service. It annoyed Harold that Spider's striking self-expression, which had erupted as volatilely as the skin on his back, was suddenly permitted to overflow the generous confines of his room's inner walls (excluding neither floor, windows, nor ceiling) onto the public surface of his door as well, defacing the hall; nevertheless, in the spirit of fatherhood, he determined to say nothing of that subject either. He knocked again. Getting no answer, he opened the door and poked his head inside the room.

Spider was once more stretched out on his bed, arms folded behind his head, one foot hanging over the side banging the floor like a drum. His eyes were closed, his mouth open, emitting sounds Harold presumed were of a private musical idiom, like the scat songs of Ella's he had himself once imitated to proud perfection. He was again grateful that their wealthy downstairs neighbor, aging, harassed, and gay, was in no position to complain about banging from above. Never mind; it was still early. "Son?" said Harold, skeptical that the tenderness he always poured into the word *son* could be heard above those relentlessly reverberating lows. "Son?"—as his own father had used the word to alert him to love.

Startled, Spider opened his eyes. His father's sudden appearance set him scanning the day for neglected duties, the house for misplaced equipment—it was so hard to predict his dissatisfactions. Maybe the music was too loud, the hour too late. But this was his room. Spider narrowed his eyes down to mean and folded his arms across his chest. "You wanna back up two feet, Pop, and knock first?"

"Wise guy," said Harold, remembering to laugh. "For your information, I did knock, several times. But how do you expect to hear anything so delicate as knuckles banging on wood when—" He stopped, retreated, started again. "Son . . ."

Spider checked his room for weak borders, preparing to order out reinforcements, when he heard the honorific, *son*. *Son* was usually reserved for formal occasions. Along with *your mother*, *your sister*, and similar nameless locutions, it was a sign that strain was coming, maybe even a lecture. "Yes?" he returned, hitting the rarely used final *s*, as much a concession to formality as a blazer and tie, or as *son* itself. The foot, however, oblivious to these subtle exchanges of tongue, continued to keep the tempo, joined now by a vigorously nodding head, which had replaced the vocal.

Harold had expected when the moment came to know what it was he'd intended to say, even though he'd neglected to form his words in advance. The emotion that had nagged at him all weekend was the same emotion that overcame him on many weekends in the presence of his assembled family, his raison d'être. The feeling he'd come down the hall to express filled his soul like some rich poignant music he heard perfectly in his mind; yet standing there in the mess of Spider's room with that music blaring, he could not even begin to hum the tune of a single theme. Where to begin? Often in this room with clothing heaped in every corner, papers and record albums scattered about the floor, the window shades askew, the stereo blaring, the walls disfigured by obscene posters, and the paint ruined by layers of Scotch tape, the very ceiling, for God's sake, looking like scorched earth—often in this room words failed Harold. Even such ready words as *clean up your room*, were they permitted, would have been hopelessly inadequate against the noise, the foot, the floor. The ceiling. Even with his family he suffered writer's block. "Son," he began again, looking around for a place to light. But there was none. The chair was piled high with sweat shirts, underwear, and rumpled jeans; there was only the bed. "May I?"

Spider sat up. With a sweep of the arm he cleared the bed of a pile of magazines. "Sure. Sit down."

Harold searched for an opening. Every approach he thought of was prohibited. He felt humble, apologetic, innocent—like a child himself. No complaints: that much he knew. Spider was a good boy, the best boy a man could want. Conceived in love. Even the mess was only appearance, a phase. Behind the closet doors were remnants of a soul more orderly than Harold's own: rocks and gems carefully laid out and labeled, road maps from everywhere in some diligently maintained internal order, the complete works of Dr. Seuss. "You're a terrific kid, you know that?" said Harold. He smiled, he blushed.

"Thanks. You too," said Spider.

"I just wanted you to know I feel that way. I'm afraid I don't take the trouble to tell you often enough."

Spider squirmed. He didn't know what was expected of him. Sometimes when his father sat on his bed quietly he felt an inexplicable urge to cry. He looked at his feet, noticed that one of them was leaping wildly, suppressed it, shrugged. "That's okay," he said.

He wished his father would leave the room. And feeling guilty for the wish, wished it again. Caught in a loop. When his Grandma Frieda died, just so had he squirmed at her funeral. Kneeling in blazer and tie, pretending to be sad. Not that he had no feeling about her death; he was deeply sad. But his embarrassment over not properly showing it, over shaming his mother before all the relatives, was more acute at that moment than all his sadness. Then, too, he had looked at his feet, big familiar friends who looked back without malice to comfort him. Weeks later, when Daisy made cookies with Grandma Frieda's cookie cutters, then for a moment, taking the first few bites, he remembered his grand-mother well, felt her presence there in the kitchen, felt his loss. Felt what he presumed he ought to have felt at the funeral. Too late. Besides, there he was eating an elephant made of his Grandma Frieda's molasses cookie dough and enjoying it no less than ever.

Now he crossed his legs, hoping to still the foot during the final crash-ing crescendos.

As the record came to an end, Harold ruffled Spider's hair. Spider, who hated to have his hair touched though he washed it every day, sat rigid, afraid to jerk away or even to move. Which meant he could not lift the tone arm from the record or return the album to its jacket but had to sit there embarrassed, listening to the thud thud thud.

Harold stood up. "Well, isn't that funny. Now that I've finished saying what I wanted to say, you can finally hear me. . . . Ha ha," he added, to make clear he intended no criticism. He wondered why the boy didn't fix the record. Perhaps he'd been moved by his father's visit. Harold hoped so. He hoped that Spider had at least understood him. He thought how much easier it was to talk to Daisy; girls were somehow easier. His own father, he recalled, had sometimes moved him almost to tears with his touching declarations of love. But then his father had been much more remote.

He stood up. "I'm going down now to see if the morning edition of the *Times* is on the stands yet. Want me to bring you back anything?"

"A couple of Mounds bars?"

Harold noted Spider's pimples and frowned. But, as Rosemary would say, it wasn't *his* skin. He nodded, committing himself. "Okay. . . . Don't you want to fix that record? It's bad for the needle, you know."

"Oh, sure."

Harold pulled his wallet out of his pocket. "Here," he said, holding out a bill, "take this. Maybe there's an even louder album you can buy your-self. For my next visit." He laughed.

Spider stared at the bill. "Thanks, Pop." Embarrassed, he crumpled it quickly and dropped it on the table amidst debris. As soon as Harold left the room, he started the same album up again from the beginning and with relief resumed the position on the bed—mouth open, foot to floor—that enabled him to forget how once, long before, his wishing his father gone had carried him away from an interminable, devastating stretch. . . .

From the hallway, Harold poked his head back through the door. "I hope you don't mind a small suggestion. Listen to anything you want, but maybe you could try not to bang the floor any more today? Okay?"

Spider jerked his foot to the bed with a pang of remorse. "Sure, Pop, sure thing."

The Smoke . . .

Usually when he went out, Harold walked three blocks before he lit up a cigarette. But having just come through a heavy emotional scene, he lit up as soon as he hit the lobby. "Evening, Mr. Streeter," said the doorman, tipping his hat. "Get you a taxi?"

"Thanks, Niko, just stretching my legs," said Harold, stopping to get the most out of that first deep drag. Ever since the last time he had resumed smoking, that first drag was the best, so filling his head with the forbidden that it made him slightly dizzy, as it had through the first summer he had smoked in his life, behind the voting booths in the woods, where Edgerton Road ended, when he was thirteen and tall for his age.

At the corner he exhaled slowly, then continued west to Third Avenue and turned. Kids were different then. All of them smoked, though it made them nauseated as well as dizzy. It was the fathers, his own included, who forced them to congregate behind the voting booths to smoke in secret. Now it was the sons. The first time he stopped had been for Rosemary, who dreaded the example for the children. But when he'd begun to backslide last year, it was Spider who'd made the fuss. He never let up on him—hiding Harold's cigarettes, inspecting the ashtrays, holding his nose, opening windows, making ostentatious displays of coughing as soon as Harold struck a match. After a few weeks of such pressure backed by Rosemary's covert aid, on Spider's twelfth birthday Harold formally, ceremoniously renounced smoking "forever," certain that with such a sendoff it would finally work.

That had been more than a year ago—and now he was back up to half a pack a day. He would have preferred to smoke his first post-dinner cigarette at the table, of course, over coffee, but he had been keeping up the fiction too long to go back on his promise now. Spider's trust, already so fragile, was too precious to risk for a smoke.

At the newsstand he reluctantly bought two Mounds bars but skipped the *Times;* the paper would be delivered to their door in the morning, soon enough, and Spider would never think of checking his alibi. Then he sauntered down Third toward Dimilio's, where he could get a Courvoisier and a double espresso to accompany the day's last smoke and where he could make his evening call to Barbara from a phone booth hidden in the basement, discreetly out of sight.

3

Daisy rips another sheet out of her notebook, crumples it up, and heaves it toward the wastebasket, just missing. Like everything she's done this day: just missing. The announcement of the Vivaldi, the last piece of pie, and the phone—Rap's call. (Rap. She shivers at the name.) Maybe her whole life. Everyone says her whole life now depends on her essay. (Plus her SAT scores. But those are over and out of her hands; besides, they tell how smart you are and don't depend on effort.) She fears she'll just miss again, mess up her whole life because she can't think of anything clever or original or true to say.

As she surveys the dittoed list of possible topics handed out by the Counseling Office, she tackles the left thumbnail first, her old familiar, pretending it's off there alone like an island unconnected to the rest and doesn't count. She's promised her father to try to grow them all back in time for the interviews in exchange for ten dollars per nail; but now that she's started, she accepts the knowledge that she'll nibble away at them, one by one, until she has slowly destroyed whatever growth she managed to gain since her first efforts back in summer.

Sometimes it seems to her that whatever she tries to do, she winds up doing the opposite: the day she vows to fast, she eats continually instead. Maybe this is the theme of her life, the subject for her essay. Failure of will. Like now: while she waits for the essay to present itself all she can

think of is Rap. Standing at the bar; under the streetlight; those words—
she could certainly write an essay about him!

A post-Thanksgiving party of her mother's set, big apartment, famous
food. Mostly adults, plus half a dozen kids—friends of the families. She
noticed him right off, watching her from across the room. In the dark green
nubbly sweater her Aunt Jessica had knitted and her tall new boots she
knew she looked good. So did he: long dark out-of-date hair, cool semi-
slouch, long-lashed restless eyes. She assumed he too was someone's kid.

When she let him refill her wine glass at the bar, he started right in
with you-and-me talk, like a coconspirator, a fellow exile banished to
eating at the children's table. This annoyed her a little; she was enjoying
her adult debut. When their first exchange revealed two missing molars
and sloppy speech she wondered if maybe he was a crasher. "Whose kid
are you?" she asked.

He tossed his curls in the direction of the cheese and hors d'oeuvres
table. "That big bearded doctor over there. I'm just down for a week, so
he brought me along."

"Are you home on vacation?" She had a weakness for college boys.

"Yeah."

"From where?"

"Buffalo."

"What year are you?" she asked, relieved.

"Second."

He reminded her of a child actor she'd had a crush on when she was
nine, playing a bit part to his starring role as Peter Pan in a children's
theater production. But that Peter Pan's name was Phillip something, and
even back then when he was twelve his speech had been precise and
theatrical, not glib and slovenly. "You never played Peter Pan when you
were a kid, did you?" she attempted brightly.

"No, but I'd like to learn how. Is it a kissing game?"

"It's a play I was in when I was nine. You look a little like the lead man.
I was crazy about him, but he never looked at me."

"Nope. Wasn't me. I'd a looked at you."

"Not back then you wouldn't."

"Yeah, I would. You were probably the prettiest little kid in the play,
weren't you?"

"Hardly!" She laughed nervously.

"Yeah, you were. And if I'd been Peter what's-his-name, I'd—" He leaned forward and lowered his voice, holding her with his eyes. Running the tip of his tongue slowly over his lips, he smiled.

Daisy lowered her eyes and took a swallow of wine. With his flowing hair he looked like an angel—until he smiled. "What happened to your teeth?"

"Those? Lost them in a fight a couple years back."

"And you haven't had them fixed?"

He laughed. "They're gone, girl. Can't be fixed now."

"But you could get new ones."

"And walk around all day with a mess a plastic in my mouth? Thanks."

Daisy stared at him. What kind of person would willingly adapt to missing teeth? Only someone like Spider—naive, willful, oblivious of the implications. That was it: he was like her little brother, only he was halfway through college and very good-looking.

"Doesn't look too good, huh?" asked Rap, slowly rubbing his jaw.

Daisy was impressed by his singular lack of vanity. "Actually, I think it makes you look kind of . . . interesting."

It was a lie. At that time, she still thought it more appalling than appealing, and seeing her mother walking toward them, she left him standing at the bar.

"Want to stop for a drink somewhere?" he asked later as she was getting her coat.

"I can't. I have to get home and work on my college applications. I still haven't even begun the big essay question. Describe the most significant experience of your life in eight hundred words."

"How do I apply?"

"For college?" she asked, puzzled.

"To be your most significant experience." When Daisy didn't answer, he offered to walk her home. "What about tomorrow, then?"

"I don't know. I ought to have at least a draft by Sunday."

"And I leave on Wednesday. Doesn't leave much time to make love with you."

It was the *with* that got her. She pretended she hadn't heard. (*Had* she?) "You must have gone through this yourself a couple of years ago," she said as he opened the door for her. "What did you write about?"

"I don't know," he said impatiently, drawing his head inside his collar, thrusting his hands in his pockets. "I don't remember."

"You don't remember! If I ever manage to get through writing this, I'm sure I'll never forget it!"

When they reached the first streetlight he stopped, took her shoulders, turned her around toward him, and said: "If I tell you something you swear you won't ever repeat it?"

"Sure. Anyway, who would I tell?"

He tapped her chest with his index finger, narrowed his eyes. "I don't want you to tell anyone. This is just for you."

"I promise."

"Where I go, I didn't have to apply to get in. A judge sent me. Eighteen to twenty-four months, suspended sentence, on condition I straighten out in a detox center. This is my first furlough. If I stay straight they may let me off by Easter."

She felt him testing to see if she recoiled. She held her breath and stood firm. After a while his eyes softened.

"But you know what? If they made me write an essay to get *out*, I'd tell them how much I want to make love with you. Then they'd let me out for sure."

Daisy couldn't speak.

"So what do you think? You mad?"

"About what?"

"What I said."

"Your secret?"

"About making love with you."

She shook her head and began to walk again.

"It's okay," he said softly. "After I go down on you, you won't be mad anymore."

Between two student papers, Rosemary picks up the phone in her study on the first ring while a herd of feet stampedes down the hall. Her heart sinks at the small, young female voice. In her two office hours a week, already this semester she's had two pregnant freshmen and a suicidal's roommate to succor; as the math program's token woman, she has every reason to fear finding another unwanted crisis wrapped in blankets and laid at her door. "Oh, Carrine," she says with relief; then covering the mouthpiece calls, "Daisy—telephone." Daisy picks up in the hall and puts soul in her voice to answer, but hearing the familiar voice switches quickly to matter-of-fact. "Oh, hi, Carrie"—and Rosemary hangs up the extension.

Spider happens to be en route from the kitchen, where he'd gone for a post-dinner snack, at the exact moment Daisy bursts into the study yelling, "Mom! Something awful's happened to Carrie's friend Felice. She was thrown out of—" But the rest is muffled as Daisy slams the door behind her. By the time Spider presses his ear to the door he can hear only the innocuous question, "Can she stay here? I said you wouldn't mind." Before he can be discovered he shrugs down the hall, past the phone lying on the desk off the hook.

Rosemary removes her pencil from her mouth, sets aside her papers. How she longs to be the sort of woman young people can count on, someone so absolutely on her children's side that *no* is purged from her maternal lexicon, someone all her students trust. Unlike most of the others in her department, bemused and aloof, she wants to lace her lectures with compassion, as essential an ingredient of understanding as intellect. "I guess so," she answers, though it's a school night. "What happened? What did she do?"

"Sex, naturally. I'll explain everything later."

Rosemary nods. She's proud to hear the loaded word fall casually from Daisy's lips, proud to be her daughter's confidante, as her own sister Sarah was hers. That the word is applied safely to a friend of a friend and not to Daisy herself cloaks Rosemary's pride in impunity.

"Can Carrie sleep over too? She's pretty hysterical."

Again, Rosemary nods.

Daisy pursues her lead. "And can I invite them to dinner?"

"But sweetheart, we've already eaten."

"I know, but we can make spaghetti. Please. They're calling from a phone booth. On the *street*."

Into *street* Daisy throws the whole year's census of rapes and muggings. She hopes to persuade her mother not only for her friends' sake but for her own. She has a reputation to uphold. Hers is the mom who listens, comforts, keeps secrets, and advises—on everything from bad dreams to birth control—not only Daisy but any of her friends who ask. She's the envy of her friends when it comes to moms—even though, when Rosemary suggests every few months that Daisy be fitted for a diaphragm ("so you'll be ready when you need it"), Daisy, who doesn't pretend to be a virgin, refuses.

"Of course."

"I knew you'd let us. They'll be over in fifteen minutes. You're great, Mom!"—and she streaks down the hall back to the telephone shouting, "She said yes! She said yes!"

Rosemary closes the folder proudly, slips it into her briefcase. When she got it into her head at seventeen that she was probably pregnant though she'd never had intercourse, her sisters, who'd often stayed up nights poring over Van der Velde's *Ideal Love*, explained to her carefully the facts of life. Her sister Jessica, who planned to be a nurse, volunteered to examine her, and her sister Sarah, who until she ran off to Chicago with a married man virtually raised her, offered Rosemary all her money. But none of the five children could have asked their parents' help. In their family certain things were unspeakable, and their parents' task was to see that they never be spoken.

Beneficently, Rosemary returns to the kitchen to start the water for pasta and takes a chocolate Sara Lee out of the freezer to thaw.

"It's you!" said Barbara breathlessly, and Harold could almost see her ebullient face light up. It was wide and bright and flat, with a high forehead and round rosy cheeks framed by auburn poodle fluff. Like the sun, he told her, thinking of the children's early drawings still taped to the kitchen wall. "Moon-face," she retorted with such genuine disgust, or innocence, that he wanted to protect her with love, especially when she lowered her head to bite the knuckle of her index finger and looked up at him past thick sandy lashes out of large childlike greenish eyes. (Hazel, she corrected.) Her words spilled out and bounced gaily through the wires: "At last! I was afraid you were going to be the breather again. You'll never guess what. Kit went home early Saturday and took Ginger with her and they won't be back till after midnight. So I have the whole place completely to myself, I've had it all weekend, but I didn't know how to reach you. Oh Hal," she wailed, "I kept praying you'd call, I made brownies and lit some incense, and I just keep playing my new Paul Winter tape with whale sounds and wolf calls and everything."

Harold looked at his watch. Only seven fifteen. Sundays they ate early. He could grab a taxi, then say he'd decided to stroll down to Times Square for the out-of-town papers or had to go back to his office for his briefcase. He hadn't seen Barbara on a weekend in weeks, and anyway, Rosemary was in the study marking papers.

"All right, baby, but it's going to be a quickie. I'll be down there in, I'd say, about fifteen minutes, okay? I'll ring two shorts and a long so you can surprise me when I open the door." He looked down into his hand. The Mounds bars were softening. He decided to eat one himself for energy and give the other one to Barbara. He'd buy more for Spider on the way back home.

Spider can't take his eyes off the visiting mystery star Felice, who eats her linguini strand by strand in total silence, barely managing to whisper her requests for more apple juice, looking more like a mermaid with her silky black waist-length hair, almost Oriental eyes, and pale, lightly freckled skin, than the criminal she is. Already at thirteen Spider loves strong, enigmatic women, preferably brunette.

Rosemary too wonders how such a shy, breathy girl ever got herself in so much trouble. The top of her shiny head with its black mane barely reaches the top of Harold's orthopedic chair. Her wrists look snappable as toothpicks. Whenever Rosemary, hearing the conversation slurp to a stop, tosses out one of her sensitive, indirect questions, Daisy and Carrie grab it and roll it out of the court where Spider can't intercept it. Linguini, salad, and bread are anxiously gobbled in an atmosphere of strained silence, suspended mayhem, as if a hurricane off the coast were working its way north but no one knows when or where it might strike.

"You've got to tell me now: what's going on?" demands Rosemary between courses in the kitchen as Daisy scrapes the dinner plates into Gorky's dish and Rosemary whips cream. In the dining room, Spider juggles ashtrays for Felice.

"Okay, here it is," brags Daisy, as if she were a hero of the scandal instead of a mere fellow traveler. "They fell in love this summer at music camp and stupidly they've been writing to each other every day. No code or anything. Carrie's mother found Felice's letters and made Carrie confess; then she called up Felice's mother. Felice's mother had a fit and said she was going to kill herself if Felice ever saw or wrote to Carrie again. So Felice packed a bag, took her flute, and came straight down to New York.

She didn't know Carrie's mother knew about it till she called up and Carrie's mother hung up on her."

Rosemary stops her spoon in the bowl, shakes her head. Remembering how Spider's kindergarten teacher once called her in to inform her sanctimoniously that her son had a habit of "touching himself," for a moment she feels sorry for the mothers. But just in time she remembers her principles, her vows: She will *not* muddy her mothering with received ideas or double messages! People should be free to love whom they wish, regardless of race, creed, gender, or even age. "Why can't people just let each other live?" she observes didactically, beating cream. "Go on."

"So then she spent the night riding the subway. Can you see it? Felice from New Hampshire?" Daisy dries her hands and takes down five dessert plates.

"Not for me, sweetheart. I'm not having any. So how did they finally get together?" asks Rosemary, placing a square of thawed Sara Lee on each plate, then spooning on whipped cream.

"Felice remembered the name of Carrie's music teacher. Lucky for her Carrie takes her lesson on Saturday. She waited on the steps of the music school till Carrie came out. Pretty smart, huh? Now she hopes to earn a living playing flute on street corners. But she doesn't have any money yet, she has no place to stay, we're the only people she knows in the city, and she can't go home. Her father called her an animal and said she was sick and—oh, you know."

"Yes," sighs Rosemary, who knows all about the price of passion. If it isn't pregnancy or disease it's harassment and shame. She hands Daisy the creamy spoon. "As if every human being weren't born bisexual, as if love in any form weren't—"

"—beautiful," chimes in Daisy. "I *know*, Mom, I've heard it," she snaps impatiently before licking the cream off the spoon. "Now the big question is, what are you going to tell Carrie's mother if she calls up here?"

On her index finger Rosemary collects the cream still clinging to the bowl, then licks the finger thoughtfully. "Yes. Well, we'll have to discuss that, won't we? Because you know I can't really lie to Mrs. Johnson if she asks me outright."

Daisy pops her eyes. "You *have* to. I promised them you wouldn't tell. You can't *do* that!" she cries, waving the spoon in the air. Gorky, finished with the plate scrapings, leaps at the spoon.

"All right, now, don't get excited. We'll talk about it," says Rosemary, free spirit but mother too. She wants to display the courage of her convictions, but as often happens, she's uncertain which of her convictions are being challenged.

"I should listen to my friends," grumbles Daisy. "Everyone says, never tell your parents *anything*."

Fleeing from the crowd of parents, as she once fled her own, Rosemary invokes reason. "We'll discuss it. I'm sure together we'll all be able to figure out what to do. Down, Gorky. That's all. Go away."

"But you don't understand, Mom," moans Daisy. "Felice is a senior and she's missing school. They could kick her out. Carrie too. And if we start a big discussion, Spider will find out. He's already snooping around."

Theoretically, Rosemary thinks Spider has as much right and need as anyone to know the facts of life. How will the world ever change if children are barred from the truth? Since before they learned to read, Rosemary has been conscientiously evenhanded in feeding both her offspring the same books and talks on the nature and beauty of sex, the varieties of human love. But practically, she fears Spider's of an age that prefers snickers and street taunts to her own exacting lessons, and Daisy has reason to mistrust him. Once again, Rosemary is uncertain where her duty lies; once again, secrecy offers a partial comfort. She follows her impulse to reassure with an encouraging "Don't worry," and, moved by the example of her daughter's fierce compassion, places the bowl on the floor for the pleading dog.

4

Harold tiptoes into the dark apartment a little before eleven and trips over two bodies stuffed into sleeping bags like giant sausages.

"Who's that on the living room floor?" he asks his wife, who is upright in bed surrounded by books and papers. "I almost broke my neck."

"Shush," says Rosemary. "They're completely exhausted. They've just gone to sleep." Hastily she begins to clear the papers from Harold's side of the bed by moving them to the floor on her side. "Just a sec." She returns to her notebook to jot down one concluding equation before closing it for the night, then rests her reading glasses on the night table and returns Harold's pillow from behind her back to his side.

"But who *are* they?"

"One of them is Carrine Johnson—remember? Daisy's friend Carrie— and the other is the girl she . . . a friend of hers from music camp who's suddenly come down from New Hampshire and swears she's never going back home."

"So she's moving in with us?" asks Harold, straight guy, who's adopted the stance that nothing will surprise him now that his children are teens. He leans over the bed and kisses his wife's cheek. "I go off to my office for a couple hours' work on my P.C. and my family doubles. Population explosion."

Rosemary shushes Harold with a finger to the lips. "It may be truer than you think. Now that Felice is in New York, Carrie may have to leave home, too. But don't worry, I promised Daisy only one night's sanctuary here. And I got Felice to swear she'll let her parents know first thing tomorrow that she's safe."

Harold stands up. First it's Rosemary's students, now it's Daisy's friends. "You mean her parents don't know? Now we're running a safe house for runaways? What's the story?"

"In our day it was pregnancy that did it. Now it's other things. It seems there were some intercepted letters—oh, Harold, why are people so intolerant?"

"Aha," says Harold, "they've touched your bleeding heart. What are they up to, smuggling cocaine?"

"They're lovers."

"Lovers!" Into his head pops an image of a famous painting of two Renaissance ladies demurely pinching one another's small hard nipples. "They certainly start young nowadays, don't they? And in our living room!" He pauses before the gravity of his next question. "How did Daisy get involved in this?"

"Come on, Harold. Carrie's her *friend*."

As he hangs his clothes across his chair, Harold tries to imagine the precise meaning of *friend*. Ever since Spider's voice began to crack, Harold has often searched his heart for its response to the prospect of his son's somehow turning out gay. And whenever he does, there in every chamber he finds fear and shame swimming around like plump water rats. He knows better than to admit to such feelings, knows that the pendulum of reason has swung against them; and in certain calm moments he regrets his fears, even confronts them with a litany of his own liberal shibboleths, hoping he'd have the character at least to love his son no less for it, though much more fervently he hopes his love will never be put to the test.

But his daughter—he has never even tried to imagine such a fate for her. His whole being rejects the possibility. What troubled him when her innocence was suddenly transformed to immodesty there doing yoga on the living room floor—what troubled him was the thought of a penis anywhere in her vicinity. Esau's hairy form against her silken one. No, the treacheries lurking in his heart when he thinks about Daisy are not visible rats on the surface, but creatures that swim the depths, invisible to his scrutiny. Now, suddenly, for the first time confronting the prospect of a Daisy dyke, as he draws his turtleneck up over his head he comes up blank. For her friends on the living room floor he has an archive of images, but for Daisy, as he turns off the light and lightly kisses the top of his wife's head, he has not a single one.

Spider wakes to giggles from the living room. He turns on the light. After two, and a school night; how come they're allowed to stay up and not he? On pretext of a pee, he sneaks off to the bathroom where he can listen at the door. Three voices, not two, from the living room. Unfair.

Back in his own room, he puts a blank cassette in his recorder, straps the box around his waist, cuts a small hole in his pj pocket where he cleverly hides the small mike, runs the wire through the hole, and attaches the mike to the box. On top, his bulky robe hides all. He takes two candy bars from his stash for an offering and tiptoes down the hall toward the party.

Outside

5

NORA KENNEDY opens her eyes to see her new sheepdog pup push his nose into the bedroom. Ruefully she watches the last scene of a slippery dream disappear behind his wagging tail. Buster scrambles onto the bed, strokes the headboard with his large silky paws, whimpers wetly, and begins pulling the corner of the blanket. Nora parts his thick white fur to enjoy his eerie eyes, one brown, one blue, then checks the clock. It's barely dawn; an hour before the radio is set to go on with the news. Deciding Buster can wait to be taken out, indulgently she grants herself permission to spend the hour reliving last week's triumph.

Would you mind repeating that—slowly? she'd asked with contained fury, pushing her small tape recorder closer to Keith Prescott's side of the table. She allowed him gracefully to retreat, thereby revealing herself to be a worthy adversary, tough but gracious.

She stretches with satisfaction, sits up, snaps up the window shade on the dawning sky, congratulates herself on having brazened through the entire two-hour interview and seduction undaunted.

She feeds the pup and fills the kettle. While the water rises toward a boil, Nora pours bath oil stolen from the hotel in Santa Fe into the tub and runs the bath. Very hot. Like the one they took together. Though he's a new type for her, elegant and blond, still it's always possible he may be the one.

She tests the water with a toe and gradually eases herself in. She prides herself on being able to stand it burning hot; she likes to think she's able to stand anything. When she's finally in, she wrings out a washcloth and lays it steaming across her eyes, submerges slowly to her neck, and finally, when she's almost flat, launches her monthly breast examination. She begins with the left, following instructions by starting at the nipple, then letting her fingertips slowly, gently feel their way outward in small concentric circles to the outer rim. But all she can think of is Keith. His delicate eyebrows and mustache, indubitably—shockingly—yellow, make it difficult for her to decide if his thinning hair is blond or white. White, she concludes, making him the first white-haired lover of her life. A powerful, courteous man—like a Bergman hero or a Swedish ambassador. Maybe powerful enough to do the trick.

Nora is famous for her interviews with high-ranking politicians and world-renowned statesmen who, amazingly, make confessions to her that shake their power once she puts them in print. Why do the mighty so foolishly expose themselves? Because she's persistent, she thinks. Having lived in seventeen different towns before she fled home (her father was a military man), she knows how to assert herself and doesn't back down. But according to her reputation, it's because she's a shrewd witch who, with her masses of thick wavy hair (usually called blond, though actually brown with blond highlights) and large, blue-black kohl-rimmed eyes, can trick the truth from any man.

This reputation troubles her. She despises tricks, she believes in truth. She asks only direct questions and tries to get the answers down on tape. There's no trick at all, she likes to explain. People are only too happy to defend their own points of view—that's why they hold them. Otherwise, they'd never have achieved their positions. *All the ways of a man are clean in his own eyes:* Proverbs 16:2. All I do, she explains, opening her eyes wide, is ask them what they think and simply record their answers. Nora is fond of saying to anyone who asks that to her, *shrewd* is a synonym for *sound,* which, along with *honest* and *brave,* are traits that earn her highest praise. Still, she can't deny that when she books herself into the major trouble spots of the world, unlike other reporters she gets her interviews. Nor can she turn off the current that usually flows between her and her subjects. Surprised by her courage, disarmed by her directness, and eager to impress the beautiful—they will say blond—woman with the sharp chin and piercing eyes leaning across the table with brow knitted in concentrated attention, even the powerful straightforwardly answer her questions.

On the right breast, bottom right quadrant, her fingers hesitate. Something new among the familiar swells and thickenings that come with the new moon? When she searches again, whatever it was that registered in her preoccupied mind has disappeared. She sits up, tries again. A graininess here, a slight thickening there—but what she thought she felt before feels more like a soft cyst. She goes to the mirror, holds out her arms. Her breasts look normal to her, feel normal for this time of month, but she decides to see her doctor anyway; her checkup is long overdue.

While the coffee drips through, Nora dresses. Her clothes are few but select. She always wears a work uniform of good boots, silk shirts, severely tailored, elegantly cut jackets in rich tweeds of linen or wool. Her only frivolities are her snappy hats, her only extravagance the ornate Indian jewelry she has begun to collect on her trips out west. Her vices: hour-long baths, chain-smoking, and living alone. She puts on three silver rings and the turquoise necklace she got in Santa Fe—with him—as the news snaps on.

She fills the watering can and moves from window to window, listening to the news, moistening earth, pinching off dead leaves, checking the weather below. Though her day's work is all laid out, she fears that today she may have trouble concentrating. She's relieved to hear the familiar radio voice report no new "terrorist acts" or "police actions," no international incidents to disrupt her plans, only the usual outrages and exposés. Returning the watering can to her tiny sink, she grinds coffee again, forgetting that a fresh potful stands waiting on the stove. Afterwards, when she's ready to go out, she can't find her keys; and when she does finally find them, she can't remember what it was she'd intended to do outside first thing this morning. Instead, she remembers how all through the interview he had stared at her with his pale blue eyes unblinking and his lips pursed in a half-smile so intense she almost thought it insolent.

As she sharpens her pencils, thoughts of him keep bubbling up, then quieting down, only to be charged up again like seltzer by the sudden infusion of a new thought, until her agitated mind can no longer contain the bubbles but sloshes them over the sides, spilling entire conversations into her ears, sending hot blood bubbling up into her cheeks, and causing her keys to disappear again. Once more she searches through the bottom of her bag and in all her pockets, but the keys are in none of them.

Docked for Love . . .

Nora sits down at the table with a cup of coffee. Love and work. With two urgent deadlines, plus the ever-pressing book, she's reluctant to indulge this unworthy distraction. It's all very well for people with salaried jobs to lose themselves now and then: they can clock in and out at the regular time, allowing the office team to carry on while they go through the motions of doing their tasks and still collect their pay at the end of the week complete with lunch breaks, coffee breaks, and fringe benefits; but those who've carved out for themselves free-lance lives are simply docked for love. She prides herself on living a life so disciplined that weekends mean nothing special to her; seven days a week are hardly enough for the work she's charged to do. Her instincts tell her that this entire adventure may be a mistake: her lover lives in New Mexico, she in New York, and he works for the very government she opposes. Yet—her eyes keep glazing over at the most unexpected moments as she turns a corner in her mind to find the tall, pale, courtly man stretched out on the bed of Room 24, his thinning hair mussed, quietly waiting to repeat a phrase that has already caught her in the stomach half a dozen times; and no sooner does her stomach recover from its sudden plunge than she's assaulted by a wave of excruciating embarrassment (how she'd answered him!) and, worse, of shame. Shame to be so shameless, shame to be swept along like an ordinary woman by those voluptuous waves of longing that keep her rising and crashing like surf, rising and plunging like a child pumping dangerously high on a swing. All right, perhaps, for a child, but what's to be said of a grown woman with two pressing deadlines (plus the nagging book) taking time out to pump herself high up on a playground swing during working hours?

As for the work, her famous work—the mass of notes and clippings carefully sorted and spread in dozens of irregular piles among the open books and government reports lying face down on her Queen Anne work table suddenly seem to her, as she searches among them for her keys, like so many mulching leaves in a windswept meadow awaiting the rake and the rains, notwithstanding the neat bouquet of freshly sharpened jonquil pencils in the small blue vase beside her typewriter. Disorder is ever ready to erupt.

Nora pours another cup of coffee and listlessly attacks the mail. Two requests from her agent for permission to reprint, one invitation to speak, one to participate on a panel, the usual pack of announcements of conferences, benefits, and books, and three real letters from friends in Denmark, San Francisco, and Paris. Nothing from him. She decides to postpone the moment when she must settle down to work by taking care of "business," as she calls reducing the pile of mail. Then she'll turn off the phone and correct the overdue proofs of her newest piece on nuclear waste.

But what was it she'd intended to do first thing this morning? She flips through her tooled Italian leather engagement book (Lex's annual gift) searching for a sign of the forgotten task. Not a clue—only the densely documented record of a strictly structured life. Mornings blank as she labors at the word processor; frequent lunches with Lex; interviews and research starting in the late afternoons, a riot of engagements in restaurants, conference rooms, theaters, cafés. . . . She heaves a sigh as experience warns her that her rich book of hours may be the first structure of her orderly life to crumble before the destructive onslaught of new passion.

The truth is, despite the independent image Nora sends into the world as an advance guard to distribute her challenges broadside and sweep away the pity that collects around single women over thirty, privately she is as vulnerable in love as any. Her work is under control; her friends—even those who call her driven—admire and envy her discipline; she's never abandoned a piece in the middle or backed down under attack. But the love game with its subtleties unnerves her, coyness confuses her, and sexual acrobatics put her instantly on guard. She prefers her passion, like her politics, candid: straight and direct. Her approach to love is Spartan, generic: even in bed she wants no frills. Those who prefer more amorous arabesques and more cunning calculations she dismisses as dishonest with a wave of her hand—thus confirming the adage that everyone gets the mate he or she deserves. She keeps her flirtations bold and obvious: her eyes glitter, her cheeks flush, her voice drops; instead of coy she grows contentious, like boys pulling pigtails, and parades her desire till she finds her pleasure. She firmly believes that if two people are drawn to each other, they must proceed on course until they connect. And when their ardor cools, they must, however wrenchingly, disconnect. The operative word is *free*. Unless she badly miscalculates, it seems to work in most cases well enough: she gives what she promises and gets what she wants.

Or so she tells herself. She knows that her long-term connection with Alexander Levy, a passion that defies all her principles, is bad for her, as a crutch retards recovery; but she's prepared to throw it away as soon as she's well enough. She's already composed her Dear John. Maybe, she comforts herself, this new love is the miracle drug to effect a cure.

But Buster is waiting to be taken out. Half the reason she has the dog is to force herself outdoors—to breathe the air, feel the sun—before starting work; otherwise, it might swallow her up. (The other half, unacknowledged, has something to do with loneliness.) While she engages the studded collar with the leash, Buster's disproportionate tail energetically wags the fluffy body back and forth—a crude image of her state of mind. Resist! she counsels—and is rewarded by discovering her missing keys, miraculously suspended from the keyhole, as she opens the door. Of course! When she went down for the mail.

She pockets the keys and releases the leash. The pup plummets head over tail down two flights of stairs toward the entrance hall; she takes it for a sign of the terrible danger she's in. Oh God! here come all the schmaltzy songs from her youth and all the love poems she ever memorized welling up in her ears, and worse, the greats are gradually replaced by the sleaziest fragments from college anthologies. Mostly Romantics, full of exclamations: Alas! Glory! Ah! Sleaze and romance: the return of the repressed. She's in for it now. For a moment she's blinded by light as she grabs the leash and pushes open the door.

• • •

Rosemary keeps her eyes closed while Harold tiptoes around the room trying to dress and slip off without disturbing her. It's somewhere between six and seven a.m.; she doesn't dare turn over to see the clock. It's all she can do to stay on her side of the bed and periodically force her eyes open a slit to catch him at something, she doesn't know what. Through the slits she sees ambiguous sights: something slipped into a pocket from a drawer; too much clothing squeezed into the attaché case; papers mysteriously shuffled; ominous stolen glances toward the bed where she lies feigning sleep.

At any moment it can go either way, this marriage of Harold and Rosemary. Like every marriage nowadays, it's held together by sheer will, a substance so strong that a web woven of it, though nearly invisible, is capable of withstanding the struggles of even the most formidable or subtle enemies, at the same time so fragile that the web can be instantly obliterated, like even the most powerful dream. Every single day the spider risks his world, spinning his artful edifice; so each morning Rosemary and Harold open their eyes determined to preserve the gossamer net of their marriage for the rest of their lives, but uncertain whether it will last out the day.

Rosemary drifts into sleep for moments, only to wake again at Harold's stealthy sounds. He puts on his favorite shirt, thinking she won't notice. Like all those other signs—the secret phone calls, the evening walks for no reason. There was once a time when she would not for anything have read a note addressed to someone else or listened at a door. Not out of prissiness but pride. And here she was, spying on her husband, feigning sleep, laying traps, noting discrepancies, even searching waste baskets, for God's sake! What a long way down.

She sleeps again, watching Harold the double agent slip in and out of doorways, run contraband across the city in an attaché case, steal state secrets from bobbed vamps with ruby lips who'd rather turn him on than in.

Rosemary believes in her dreams as other people believe in stock market reports. They are both cause and effect. Her dreams come like urgent dispatches from home, conveying in her native tongue crucial intelligences of which she might otherwise remain ignorant. Even bad news is welcome if her life depends on it. The bastard, seducing anyone he can with leftover insights scraped from his wife's last night's dinner plate. He'll be impotent the second time, blood on his penis. Maybe she should warn them. Harold the bureaucrat meeting contacts on country roads at dawn, keeping his family safely out of it. Then gunning down Daisy for a spy—Daisy!—a hunting accident. Couldn't save her. Why did he get them in so much trouble?

She starts; every time Harold opens a drawer she wakes again. Her heart pounds as it might discovering a prowler in her room— atatatatatatatata, as Spider would say. Harold is poisoning her with those small, potent doses of adrenaline.

At last she hears him reset the alarm for its next shift: seven thirty: time for her to wake the kids. He's careful with the details of his duties, so she can have nothing on him. Then he dons his overcoat and pauses fleetingly before the mirror—the tip-off. Even reduced in size by the square of the distance from the mirror to the bed and viewed through a single squinting eye, his face in the mirror looks culpable. Go! she thinks. Get out! Never come back! But says sleepily as he lifts his attaché case and places a hand on the doorknob: "When do you expect you'll be home? For dinner?"

"No, tonight I'm staying over in New Haven, remember? It's the Fellows' Meeting. But I'll call you. Sorry I woke you, hon. Go back to sleep now, it's only twenty after six."

As soon as she closes her eyes, Rosemary creeps to the top of the stairs and looks down to the front door. There stands her sister Sarah in her good traveling suit, holding her two bags. Rosemary signals to her sister to run upstairs, but it's too late: Sarah's gaze is fixed on the hall, where their mother's heavy step approaches from the parlor.

Their mother, a short stout woman who has borne seven children and raised five, strides like a giant into the hall. She wrings her hands, cocks her head, closes one eye, and juts her chin to ask, So how was your trip to Chicago, Miss Sarah?

Rosemary clutches the balustrade at the sarcastic *Miss*.

Would you mind if I put my bags down first?

Their mother takes a step toward Sarah. Don't sass me!

I'm not.

You know how I know about your trip to Chicago? Your sweetie's wife called up crying to me, that's how.

His wife?

Oh? You didn't know he has a wife? You didn't fool her like you thought you fooled me. So what was I supposed to say to this woman?

From on high, Rosemary pulls a string and Sarah takes a tiny step backwards.

Not enough you go off on a train to Chicago with a man, but a married man! Slut! Homebreaker! Whore! She steps toward Sarah with her arm raised. Clasping her elevated hand with the other to form a pointed roof of clenched fist above her head, like a mourner she begins to bow and wail.

Sarah stretches her arms toward her. Mama, Mama, please.

Their mother pulls herself back abruptly, as if one touch from her daughter's hand will defile her. Don't give me please! she shouts. You think you can carry on like this and live in the same room with Rosemary, a baby? Well, you can't!

She's not a baby, says Sarah. But if you want me to, I'll leave.

Leave then! Yes! Go with that husband! Get out! Never come back! Their mother's eyes pop and her jaw is like carved stone.

6

For all her scoffing at romance, Rosemary is the one who, as soon as she leaves a note on the table for the children, dabs perfume between her breasts and slips out of her house at four o'clock this sunny Monday, and proceeds briskly toward the Budapest Bakery, the glory of her neighborhood, praying it's not closed on Mondays, which would force her to look for someplace else when she's already late.

Of course Peter would understand if she arrived empty-handed: usually they meet on Tuesdays when Harold is teaching his seminar at Yale and Mrs. Scaggs comes in to clean. But Rosemary wants every meeting to be perfect. Not adequate or forgiven but perfect. Her standards have shot up like an amaryllis in winter since the casual, weedy sex of her college days; now every detail must be cultivated for maximum pleasure. Special food, the right wine, real espresso, and of course "their" music. If they can't have at least three hours together, she's said a dozen times, she'd rather not see him at all. It's okay with her if they talk on the phone or meet somewhere for coffee; but if they are to make love, she insists on those minimum conditions. And the sheets clean, and the light right: not glaring (sometimes they pull the shutters partway closed), but light enough for each to see the other's face bloom. In her other life Rosemary prides herself on being the most accommodating of women, so flexible that Harold accuses her of being flighty; but here everything must be just so: only at times when Harold's away; only when they won't feel rushed; only when the children don't need her and there's no chance of being seen—only, in short, when she can truly forget about everything in the world but love. Otherwise, how will their affair be different from any sordid romance or long-term marriage, with everything taken for granted? As soon as their love begins to resemble either, she says, it will be over.

The three fat sisters who run the bakery greet her with knowing smiles. She deliberates over the cakes as if something important rides on her selection. Sometimes it's the cheesecake that catches her fancy, sometimes the linzer torte, but today she wants one of the chocolates—the mysteriously light torte made without a grain of flour, or the black devil layers glazed with icing that shines like crystal and teases sweetness out of the bitter essence beneath, or his favorite, the chocolate truffle cake. Yes. "That one, please," says Rosemary, pointing to the darkest one. For him.

The second sister lifts the cake from the case and slides it into a box. Watching her raise her plump muscular arm for the overhanging string to wrap round and round the box, Rosemary thinks of the day Spider renamed his life with a ball of string.

"And half a pumpernickel, please."

Down the counter the first sister tosses a large black loaf to the second, who cuts it in half with one slash of an enormous knife. "Slice it?"

"Yes," says Rosemary. "I mean no." This double life: for her family she has it sliced, since they gobble it up in a day, but for just her and Peter she usually takes it whole. "Half sliced, half not." With Peter, she's the one who eats the heel, while at home Daisy gets it. As a lover, she's the extravagant one, the tardy one arriving breathless and laden with packages at the last minute, while at home, compared to Harold, she's frugal, prompt, a rock. She winces as the bread rattles its way through the slicing machine.

Seeing her crosstown bus just pulling away, she sends up a prayer, steps into the street on the flashing red, and hails a taxi. In the backseat she feels relatively safe as they cross Central Park, but once the cab merges into West Side traffic, on the same side of town as Columbia, where Harold teaches two days a week, her adrenaline flows again. Not for anything would she humiliate Harold. She pays the driver and readies her keys. Then, without looking up, she begins the most compromising act: mounting the four stairs of the stoop to the familiar green entrance.

The next-door super's son rolls a toothpick between his teeth and tips his chair back against the brick building as she fumbles with the key. The lock keeps its secret. Embarrassed, she tilts her head away from him, hedging with a smile that she hopes is ingratiating but fears is of the sort called guilty, and welcomes the distraction of a clutch of noisy school-children dashing past.

At last the lock yields. She slips inside. She hurries past the mailboxes, with their suspiciously familiar names, across the neat marble foyer where her footsteps echo ostentatiously, up two flights of carpeted stairs, and down a short hostile hall with its peepholes of spying eyes before she approaches the privacy for which she weekly submits to this humiliating ordeal. Two more keys, and suddenly, like that moment in a dream when a secret door appears, she's safe inside.

Love Nest with Dome . . .

From their futon on the carpeted floor Rosemary gazed past Peter's back-lit ear, beyond the pot of lantana on the windowsill, up through one window at the gilded dome of an Orthodox church. The gleaming dome, so unlikely on the gentrified Upper West Side, made her feel continents and centuries from her real life instead of only blocks and hours. Though they might have opened the sofa into a bed, they preferred the spacious floor beneath the dome.

The other window was filled with the branches of a large flowering chestnut tree growing in the garden of the house next door. In summer shapely green leaves on the swaying branches cast voluptuous shadows on their naked bodies. In autumn they'd watched the leaves fall one by one. In winter they'd sometimes awakened to see the bright light of moonlit virgin snow on the dark branches or lay for hours watching wet snowflakes glide slowly past their window. No street sound ever penetrated, no neighboring window threatened their privacy there in that bright top-floor studio. Secluded, secure in their nakedness, the most they knew of the world was the occasional sound of music coming from some nearby house, which they were free to drown out with music of their own.

"You didn't tell me you were getting your hair cut," Rosemary says, running her fingers across the soft remnants of curls perched above the newly shorn, sinewy neck.

Shyly Peter turns his head. "I held off as long as I could for you, but really, it was way overdue. My fares were starting to take me for an *art*ist."

Rosemary draws back and scrutinizes him. Though by now his face is as familiar to her as her son's, a haircut is always a bit of a shock. She apprehends his ears and temples in a new light, as she sometimes does the rest of him, catching sight of him unawares or on those rare occasions when she hears his name on someone's lips. His precious hair. Often when they're making love, she likes to bury her fingers in his silky chocolate-colored curls, the more the better, to keep more of themselves in contact and assure her that he plans to continue; if she has to think about his stopping she might not be able to let herself go. That's why she prefers the sixty-nine position, where she can give him the same pleasure he gives her and never worry that he might be growing tired—even though sometimes, concentrating on the feeling, she gets so carried away that she's the one in danger of stopping, at least of slowing down, on him. Every part of his body has grown precious to her—his graceful, talented hands, the sharp, cleft chin, the worry lines, the disparity in size between his two dark dreamy eyes, the slight droop of one shoulder, the curve of his spine as he curls around her, his secret underarms, the hollow beneath his ribs, his three different voices, the trail of freckles on his left flank, the hair on his chest and knuckles, the way he tilts his head when he asks her questions, the way his mouth falls open and all his muscles tighten when he's ready to come. And though she regrets sacrificing a single cell in that erotic field that is his body, she supposes people do have to get haircuts.

"You still look like a birthday cake to me. Only without the goopy frosting. Probably more delicious. I like it," she lies.

.   .   .

Rosemary's diaphragm slides in easily; her juices have been flowing since the first touch of Peter's lips. She seldom bothers with jelly now, remembering how men have sometimes objected to the taste; and though she believes Peter when he professes to treasure all her tastes and smells, even the artificial ones, because she knows how she treasures all of his, she avoids the jelly all the same. She walks toward him stretched out on the futon, long and naked, arms folded behind his head, staring off beyond the ceiling to a private image she presumes she will one day see materialized on one of his dark, mammoth canvases.

Actually, he's thinking about maybe driving his taxi an extra shift, if he can get someone in his garage to agree, so he can buy one more bottle of the good champagne he's got chilling in the fridge. It's their anniversary: three years; nothing's too good for them. Before he can win her away, he knows he's got to get himself a decent gallery and some steady work. It always comes back to the same thing: he's not ready to be a family man.

As she stretches out beside him, head to foot, she rationalizes that with teenaged children she's probably no longer even very fertile. The music is perfect, the light in this sublet magical. They take each other in their arms and mouths, arranging their limbs in the way she has come to count on, and begin the long lyrical climb to their secret room.

Nora watches Bianca's pretty, motherly face tense with concentration as she carefully palpates Nora's breasts. Nora thinks that of all the doctors she's ever had, Bianca is the only one who would stay after her last appointment of the day to examine her when there's clearly no emergency. Bianca looks tired; she must think Nora's really scared. She's not, but having got less work done today than she'd intended, she's glad she called Bianca anyway.

"You can get dressed now," Bianca says with a reassuring smile. Though Nora knows there's nothing wrong, she's suspicious of the smile.

When Bianca announces from behind her desk that all she feels are the usual insignificant, benign cysts, that the new one in the bottom right quadrant is probably nothing to worry about, Nora feels foolish and guilty for having kept her after hours. "If you're going home now," she says, only partly for penance, "why don't we stop for a drink together? We haven't really talked for a long time."

Bianca looks at her watch and declines. She may have to deliver a child tonight. Nora rises to leave, but Bianca stops her to say that she wants Nora to have a mammogram—"because after thirty-five I think it's a good idea to have one every five years, especially women who haven't nursed babies."

Nora's confused. "Right away?" she asks, seeking a clue.

Bianca crosses her legs, shakes her head. "No rush, but I see no reason to put it off, either. Might as well have it checked. Here's the name of the specialist I want you to use. He's a bit of a grouch, but he's really one of the best. Call him at your convenience." She writes something on her prescription pad and hands it to Nora. "And have a sonogram too, while you're at it. Then after your next period I'll check you again."

"Bianca, dear," says Nora, reading the name and address, "I believe you are the only doctor I've ever known whose official handwriting is perfectly legible." She folds the paper and buries it in her pocket.

Bianca laughs. "Look, let's have that drink soon. It has been a long time. For the next couple of weeks I'm working nights at the hospital, but after that it should ease up. I want to hear what's happened to everybody. What a time we used to have. I hate to lose touch, but now, everyone I know is having babies, and all I do is work. You too, I gather."

Nora rolls her eyes. "Work yes, babies no."

"I want you to know I read you every chance I have, but it's not the same as talking, is it?"

Despite years of publication, Nora can't suppress a rush of pride that she's read by her physician; despite the mammogram, she leaves the office elated. One good talk with Bianca, or any of her strong, hardworking women friends, is worth five shrinks for giving courage.

"Give me a call when you have some time and we'll set up a sauna together, okay?" Nora throws back from the door before hurrying home to work.

7

Harold thought the pontificating professor not much older in years than he himself. His hair had only a smattering of gray, his voice was smooth behind the youthful smile; but judging by the smug way he sat in the carved high-backed chair pulling on his pipe and shaking his head over the sorry state of Yale and the world, he might as well have been an ancient. "In my day it was different. Nothing like this," he was saying, as if it were news. (They'd expected the world as it was when they were young to go on forever and deplored every sign of change.) He puffed the same tobacco he had always puffed. "When T. S. Eliot came here to lecture in '54 when I was an undergraduate, the entire student body turned out to hear him. People returned the books they borrowed from the library in those days and handed in their papers on time."

Harold could not remember the fellow's name. He felt more comfortable with the junior faculty, who wore sweaters beneath their tweeds, ate natural foods, married women who did things outside the home, and played Frisbee on the beach. His own seminar was popular, he'd been told, not because he was a celebrity—there were dozens of celebrities at Yale—but precisely because he embraced the changed and changing world. He listened to his students and gave everyone he could an A. He thought the turmoil back in '68 and the addition of female students were ultimately good for Yale; but in a deeper sense, Yale was still, would always be, Yale. At the bimonthly meeting of the College Fellowship, the Fellows drank sherry before dinner, respected rank, engaged in disparaging banter, and did not bring their spouses except on specified nights.

True, the younger faculty also deplored the state of things, but they deplored a different state of things. A good article in here somewhere, Harold thought, though he knew his problem was a lack not of topics but of time. The lean, bearded assistant professor of political science in the rusty cashmere turtleneck standing before the fire was announcing in a newer style of smug, one that looked to the future instead of the past, "In my utopia the state would take the child at eighteen months and return him to the parents at eighteen years."

"Thanks a lot," said Pippa Powell, a sexy woman who wrote novels. "You just deprived me of the best thing in my entire life."

"Oh, come now."

"It's true."

The assistant professor looked surprised but undaunted. "If women weren't ghettoized, though, you might have something better to call the best."

"May I ask you," said Pippa, clenching her sarcasm between smiling teeth, "do you happen to have any children of your own?"

Harold's pulse responded to her pluck but he never got to hear the answer. "Come now, we've been summoned," said the full professor, pulling on Harold's sleeve. Harold carried his sherry glass, still half full, down a flight of carved stairs into the airy college dining hall, tall, Gothic, and oak, where the Fellows joined the students in the food line. "It used to be," explained the full professor standing behind Harold in line, "that we were served our dinner upstairs in the Fellows' Hall. But that was years ago. Then the war and the inflation . . . well, you know. After that we came down here—waited till the students had all cleared out and the staff could serve us. Damn nuisance, but better than now. Now, as you see, we serve ourselves and stand in the same line as the students, and I'm told that some of them resent our presence among them. Quite a comedown, isn't it?"

"Why do they resent it?"

"They say we take up their places in the line. If you ask me, I think we ought to go ahead of them, right up to the front. Some of us have other work to attend to after this dinner—meetings, whatever. But the Master won't hear of it. He wants to keep the students happy. A committee of students actually complained about us to the dean last year. Can you imagine that?"

"About what?"

"About anything that comes into their heads. First they objected when we followed them into the hall. Then they objected when we preceded them. Then they objected to our eating together off by ourselves. I'll tell you one thing, if they had stiff enough assignments, they'd be too damn busy to concern themselves with the mechanics of the Fellows' Dinners. Now it's all we can do to get one big table for ourselves and sit together. Imagine! They say we take up too much room. And the food nowadays . . ." He was piling his tray with every offering, from curry to fish sticks to chocolate pudding. "The only good thing is we still have decent table wine. They haven't managed to take that away yet."

Harold was glad to see his companion stop at the salad bar, allowing him to escape. He hurried ahead to the Fellows' table.

"Mind if I join you?" said Harold, placing his tray down in the middle of a heated argument between Kermitt Fox, the Shakespearean, and Pippa Powell, the winner of a literary award that earned her Harold's lust and an invitation to teach a Yale seminar. They were debating the merits of a recent proposal to the English faculty to prohibit any more dissertations on living authors.

"That's outrageous!" sputtered Harold, whose own writings, he'd been told, had already spawned several dissertations at obscure universities. "All the authors I assign my students are living."

"But you teach journalism, Harold," said Kermitt with a wave of his hand. "That's different. Our question concerns literature."

Harold took umbrage, forcing it down with several forkfuls of curried lamb. It was not the dismissal of journalism that offended him. What could you expect from a Shakespearean? It was the revelation that Kermitt Fox considered him a mere teacher rather than a writer whose work might one day itself merit a Yale dissertation. In fact, his celebrated book on terrorism in the Western world was on the syllabus of at least two courses on this very campus.

"And I write stories—is that different too?" said Pippa. Harold watched her execute one of those daring arabesques of duplicity for which women were famous: flashing a combative eye at Kermitt and a conspiratorial one at Harold, all at once. "Don't take it personally," she shot at Harold sotto voce as he swallowed his wine. "They'd rule out most of the writers I assign, too. And your work is much more important."

Modestly, Harold demurred. If it were true that his work was important, then he ought to be back in New York working on his next volume instead of commuting to New Haven every week to teach a seminar whose twin he also taught at Columbia. The deadline for his book contract had long since passed. Sometimes he wondered if, had he published three big books by now instead of one, he'd find it easier to turn down the honors and invitations that continued to come his way; but with only one, however celebrated, he was afraid to be forgotten or dismissed as a "mere" journalist should he dare to refuse. On the other side, he wondered if it wasn't precisely to avoid working on the next volume that he spread himself thin, immersing himself in so many outside activities. (It was well known that after the kind of success he'd achieved with *Terror!*, the critics would be gunning for him.) Grateful to Pippa for her vindicating avowal, he imagined spreading himself even thinner.

Kermitt touched his napkin to the corners of his lips. "We're not talking about course assignments, only about thesis subjects. Besides, even if we were, you'd still have plenty of people to assign. The human life span is fairly short, remember."

"Right," said Pippa. "All the wild writers who OD or die in car crashes. Thanks a lot, Kermitt."

Now it was Kermitt who, assuming the kindred soul, smiled complicitously at Harold.

Harold refused the invitation and winked at Pippa. "So you can do Kerouac, who's dead, but not Ginsberg, who's alive? O'Hara but not Updike. Isn't that kind of silly? Won't it inhibit thorough research?" The only qualm he felt at taking Pippa's side was over Barbara, to whom he owed his extramarital fidelity.

"It's true," said Kermitt, "some people argued for an inclusion principle based on a cutoff birth date instead of the accident of mortality—say, only people born before 1900."

"Then for my course on women novelists, my students have the grand choice among Austen, the Brontës, the Georges, and Woolf." Pippa sighed. "That's progress."

"It didn't pass, though," continued Kermitt. "Someone pointed out that they'd have to keep changing the cutoff date and it was bound to seem arbitrary. And others thought too much had already happened to justify ruling out all of twentieth-century literature."

After *Terror!* had been published to furor and applause a decade ago—particularly after the record paperback sale, the book club selection, the European splash complete with major reviews in *Le Monde* and the *Times Literary Supplement*—for one long sweet moment Harold imagined that he might slip sideways into literature. He was giddy, of course, over the unexpected riches that kept pouring in; he was transported by the attention and respect with which even his enemies began to address him; he was jubilant at being invited to teach in the prestigious Columbia School of Journalism, though he'd never got his B.A. But when the first flush of fame wore off and he began to feel at home with his success, his slide began. Slights and barbs he'd never experienced before were aimed at him from every side. Even his friends started treating him differently. And when the attacks began to appear in print, in editorials, letters, op ed pieces, and a rash of snide references in others' reviews, he would have dived deeper than writer's block straight into depression had Rosemary not been there to buoy him up. It was then he began to dream of revenge through a steady stream of breakthrough books, each more important than the one before, and for his next—why not?—a Pulitzer. But his next had not (yet) appeared, was still "in progress." No wonder that over the years Harold had grown extrasensitive to the callous laughter of posterity carousing without him in another room.

"If you're going to define literature as what's dead, then frankly," said Harold, glancing at Pippa, "I'd rather be a journalist. Better company. Livelier."

"I'm getting us some more wine," said Kermitt, rising, "so drink up, all."

Pippa pushed back her tray and, gazing up into Harold's eyes with her chin in her palm, sighed. "Thanks. I usually have to carry this ball all by myself. It's so depressing. What a relief to have you here."

Concluding that she was flirting, Harold inched his hand over hers and squeezed.

Pippa popped up. "I'm going to get dessert and coffee. Shall I get you something?"

"No thanks, I'll come too."

"But you haven't finished your curry."

"I've had quite enough, thank you."

When they were back in the cafeteria line, Pippa confided, "I feel so isolated here sometimes. Except among my students, of course. Commuting up here every week from the city, knowing no one in New Haven except the dinosaurs in the English Department. How do *you* manage here?"

"No better than you do, I'm afraid. I commute too. I don't know anyone either. This is only my third Fellows' Meeting."

"If you're going back tonight, do you want to share a taxi to the train?"

"I'm not going back. My class isn't till tomorrow morning. When there's a Fellows' Meeting, I usually drive up the night before and stay over. But if you have any time before your train, why don't we get out of here and go someplace for a drink?" He panned the environment to see who had heard. He didn't yet understand the politics of Yale, sexual or otherwise; he didn't even know if it was really okay to smoke in the dining hall.

"Oh yes, let's!" said Pippa. "Thanks. Then I'll tell you about the conversation I had in the Fellows' Hall just before dinner. You won't believe it. Around here either it's still the 1950s or we're in the midst of a revolution. Try the devil's food cake if you like chocolate. It's Yale's secret weapon—especially if we get some ice cream to go on top of it." When she dimpled over the chocolate and used her conspiratorial *we*, Harold thought of Daisy and decided that the fastest way to learn the mysteries of Yale politics was through experience.

8

Daisy was closer to the desk when the phone rang, but Spider with his long legs overtook her, and with his long arms outgrabbed her. An umpire might have judged that Daisy's hand closed over the receiver first, but they were alone in the apartment, and Spider's hand, strengthened by years of precision exercise on piano, trumpet, and video games, managed by a timely digital maneuver of press and squeeze to usurp the receiver before the third ring.

Incensed at the injustice of Spider's claim, Daisy picked up the nearest book, a volume, as it happened, of Oscar Wilde's *De Profundis,* and whacked Spider on the back of his head, causing him to drop the phone back into its cradle, where Daisy grabbed it.

"Hello? Hello? Hello?" said Rosemary. She covered the phone with her hand and whispered sternly to Peter, "Not now!"

Obediently Peter left off kissing her breasts and lay his head in the soft hollow of her belly, between her protuberant hip bones, where he could listen to the mysterious rumblings of her insides.

"That does it," said Spider. Now anything he might do would be justified. He twisted Daisy's arm behind her back until she had let fall the book and the phone. "Hello," said Spider in a grim, breathless voice.

"Hello? Spider? Hello? What's going on?"

"Oh, hi, Mom. Nothing. Everything's fine."

Peter lay still, watching Rosemary's face. The smile she reserved for her children was already beginning to spread through her whole body, altering her features, her muscles, her voice. The voice announced her departure toward that intimate plane where she met her children, issuing in a timbre, a register, that never failed to arouse his longings. Peter turned his head and kissed her belly lightly.

Daisy reached out. "Is that Mom? Let me talk."

With his palm, Spider pushed air toward Daisy, spiriting her back.

"Spider? Is that Daisy too? Have you been home long?"

It was not exactly jealousy that Peter felt, or even resentment, though from the start she'd made clear to him that her children "came first." Half of what he loved in her was her completeness: her energy, her worldliness, her accomplishments and finesse that created around her a heaven with two radiant centers like twin stars, one her children, one herself. It was longing Peter felt. No matter how generously she revealed herself to him, he was always startled to hear the woman she was when the mother surfaced. Here, with him, she was a certain woman—independent, voluptuous, unpredictable—hardly reconcilable with the soft, efficient, ferociously protective woman on the telephone. Whenever she spoke of her children at any length, her eyes grew more animated, her imagination played like moonlight on water. He envied the selfless attention she showered on the child at the other end of the wire whom he'd never been privileged to know, and desire transformed his envy to longing. Slowly he rubbed his lips back and forth across the straight top boundary of her dark pubic hair.

". . . Look, Spider, honey. I won't be home in time for dinner tonight. But you can manage for yourselves. There's still some turkey left, you can make sandwiches."

"Again?" whined Spider. When it was his turn to get dinner, he usually ran out for pizza, while Daisy, when it was hers, made salad and brownies or chocolate meringues. "Jesus, Mom, I'm sick of turkey sandwiches."

Peter covets Rosemary's rich, wide-ranging life, but how can he possibly claim it for his own? The banalities that bombard him from the backseat of his taxi, the pitiful parade of female fares with their whining kids, demonstrate daily how impossible it will be ever to find another woman like Rosemary. That day he picked her up at MOMA, a madonna in a white dress with two beautiful kids yacketting on about Matisse, he knew he was ruined for anyone else. If only he knew how he'd landed her he might figure out how to keep her. He knows he's not who she thinks he is. Even ten years from now, when he'll have lived longer than she has now, and his paintings are selling well, and he can finally afford a family of his own—even then, hers will be the family he longs for: charmed and ready-made.

Rosemary reaches down a hand to still Peter's head but lets it hover at the outer halo of his chocolate curls, and it registers that she loves him. She loves him—she swears it every day. A miracle. She calls his body beautiful, his paintings accomplished, his spirit free—she, whose spirit has created a little masterpiece of amenities that she risks every day for him! If he dared ask her why, she might discover what he has so far managed to conceal: that his talent is shaky, his future unsure, that he's had only two other women since he left art school—both young and limited, like himself.

"If you don't give me that phone," said Daisy, "I'm going to tell you twisted my arm."

Spider covered the mouthpiece with his free hand, leaving only his feet to work with. He kicked out toward Daisy, just missing her thigh. "You tell and I'll tell," he said. "What'd you say, Mom?"

"I said," said Rosemary, crossing one knee over the other, squeezing Peter away, "if you'd rather have hot turkey, take out the leftover gravy, it's in a big peanut butter jar, heat it up over a very low flame—you better use the Flame Tamer—and then put the turkey slices in the gravy for a few minutes. But don't let it boil or it'll get tough. There's cranberry sauce left and brussels sprouts, if you like. Daisy can have salad, too, and there's ice cream in the freezer."

"Gotcha."

Peter ran his fingers gently down her thigh, across her instep, up the other side of her leg. He wanted her to yield herself up to him right then and there, but he contented himself with inhaling the strong fragrance of afterlove.

"When'll you be home?" asked Spider.

"I don't know. Say around nine if anybody calls."

Peter checked the clock. If she made it nine thirty instead, then after dinner when they made love again they wouldn't have to hurry. He held up nine fingers, followed by the sign for half, but she turned abruptly away, cradling the black receiver against her white shoulder.

In the three years they'd been lovers, he and Rosemary had charted and colonized an entire country, complete with its own language, laws, literature, maps, cuisine; but the land where she lived, the country to claim the best of her, lay on the far side of a border he was not permitted to cross. Sometimes she allowed him to follow her up the craggy mountain that divided her family's vast lands from the small protectorate she shared with him and win a glimpse beyond the border to the lush fields and towns, rich and various, stretching to the far horizon; but never was he permitted to accompany her down the other side of the mountain. If he crossed the border, she warned, he could be turned to stone; the children might become brambles fixed in the earth; she would probably be taken captive by border guards; certainly they would be separated forever. He was free to look; she would tell him everything he wanted to know; but he could not trespass or touch.

"What about Daddy?"

"Daddy won't be home till late tomorrow. Remember? Tonight's his night at Yale. If you think you'll need help with dinner, ask Daisy. Can I talk to her now?"

Peter couldn't even try to dissuade her. When he took her home late at night, she insisted that he walk a few paces behind her, in case someone saw them on the street. He found this humiliating and absurd, but if he challenged her ridiculous behavior, she grew defensive, even hostile, as if he'd made a sneak attack. Her other life was strictly her own, and on no account, she said, would she put it at unnecessary risk. Because of this, many pleasures were barred to them. Walks in the park were out of bounds, as were evenings with friends, parties. They couldn't sit together at movies or show each other their favorite restaurants. On the other hand, when they were together they were complete, with a secret land of their own, and no need of the world. Or so they said.

"Here she is. Well so long. More dead turkey for dinner," Rosemary heard him say.

"Spider!" she cried; then, minutely altering the pitch of her voice, crooned, "Hi, sweetie," trying to make things better.

Peter pictured Daisy smaller than she was and younger, the perfect girlchild, whom he'd met only once, in his taxi, three years before.

"Spider's going to get the dinner tonight. I told him exactly what to do."

"Yeah? I bet I wind up doing it anyway."

"If he complains just tell him I said it was his turn," said Rosemary.

Daisy smiled snottily at Spider and dripped "Thanks, Mommy" into the phone. With its backup troops and a high court to adjudicate, *Mom said* was the most potent weapon in the sibling war. "When will you be home?"

"I'm not sure. The meeting's just starting and there's a lot to do. Why? Do you need me for something?"

"Just this stupid essay."

"Don't worry, sweet. You're so imaginative, it's just a matter of choosing a focus. It'll come, I know it will."

Peter fancied taking them to his studio, to Coney, to the aquarium. He would teach them how to draw, show them the Palisades where he grew up, present them with another sort of model than their callous, calculating father.

"Anyway, we can talk about it tomorrow, okay? And Daisy? I know it's his turn, but please—help Spider if he needs it."

While Rosemary pared asparagus, Peter squeezed lemons and separated eggs for the hollandaise, then laid a large red snapper in the broiler pan, rubbing it with cut lemons. As she watched him sprinkle it with mushrooms, shallots, and herbs, her feelings for him swelled. She was always touched by the slight but significant differences in their cooking techniques. He chopped vegetables, even garlic, on a chopping board, while she did it in her hand as her mother had; he sliced onions and carrots the long way, she the round way; he pulled out and discarded a small round of soft bread from the center of a hard roll before piling in the filling, whereas she spread it flat. Her husband's kitchen innovations generally irritated her, but every time her lover revealed another of their culinary differences she wanted to hug him. Their meals were revelations of each other, savory intimacies, each dish from their other lives a secret confided, a caress, part of that long, slow disrobing that was their love affair.

How they'd redefined the transgressions! Playing house had become an integral part of foreplay. Rosemary had initially hesitated to rent a place of their own, reluctant to commit her feelings for more than two weeks ahead and leery of returning weekly to the scene of a recurring crime. But when she saw the announcement at work of the perfect sublet—a young anthropologist off to Borneo for a year had a "charming studio on quiet block, one block from crosstown bus"—at a price her teaching salary could absorb and directly across the park from where she lived, she couldn't resist. And now she was already mourning the passing of their precious months. She loved their hideaway with its books and textiles and tasteful furnishings, its shuttered windows and eat-in kitchen, the garden below. She loved the wind chimes and the covered teacups and the Indonesian woodcuts in bamboo frames. She loved the way they had turned the spacious room into an intimate chapel dedicated to love. It took her back to her own carefree days, before the children came, when she and Harold lived like free spirits on air and hope and nerve, when Harold seemed like an artist too, when everything looked possible. Peter pointed out how much safer it was than the risky places they'd sometimes gone—hotel rooms, borrowed flats, empty classrooms, even once on a train; safer to light their own candles and eat at home than risk being seen out. On the other hand, the old way they could plead that they never planned to take such risks, that it was sudden desire that swept them into recklessness. Here, it was clear they came for no other purpose than to make love, signing a lease to ensure they could go on doing it. Flagrant, unrepentant voluptuaries.

Peter set the timer and led Rosemary to the couch. While the fish baked and asparagus steamed, he ran his fingertips lightly around her neck from the nape down into the hollow of her throat before following with his tongue.

She felt it in her nipples. "It's happening. It's starting already, it's going to happen again."

"What?"

"You know." Why was it, she wondered, that whenever she felt this happiness coming on, felt as if she would burst like a pod and cover the room with a thousand silky umbrellas of happiness, the next moment she invariably thought of death? Was it because death would preclude a comedown? But by now, after three years of feeling it every week, she knew it would come back again. Could it be simply because there was nothing left beyond such happiness but dissolution?

The timer rang. Peter pulled her up. "Smell it! I'm getting really hungry." They walked in lockstep to the kitchen.

Spooning hollandaise sauce over the asparagus, Peter thought of yellow bedsheets over an orgy of thighs. He lifted a bottle of champagne from the fridge and opened it deftly with hardly a pop.

When Spider, his hands sheathed in potholder mitts, tried to lift the peanut butter jar full of gravy off the Flame Tamer, he was abashed to see the sides of the jar pull away from the bottom as neatly as if he had unscrewed it. The gravy oozed down through the burner all over the stove.

Too late he saw that he ought to have transferred the gravy to a pot before trying to heat it. And now—what a mess! Shameful as jism on the bedsheets. He ran for paper towels and spread blame. First to his mother, who hadn't bothered to tell him; then to Daisy for bugging him while he was getting directions. She should come into the kitchen this minute and clean it up. But even as he fumed he realized that no matter who was truly at fault, he was the one who would be held responsible. Condemned again as careless or slack or stupid. Every time he tried to be a hero, or even just do his duty, somehow he failed—as if his enemies were keeping special watch on him in order to mess him up. While he sopped up gravy with paper towels, he consoled himself that at least the turkey was safe, at least the jar hadn't shattered. (Though if it had shattered, he realized, he might have pretended he'd dropped it, leaving him just as open to the charge of carelessness but at least not of foolishness.) Mopping up the mess, he wondered what it was about him that caused these things to happen with such systematic regularity. Why was it his account on the DEC 20 that was invaded? Why his trumpet the one that got left behind on the band bus? His father accused him of being scatterbrained, of not paying attention, but it wasn't true. He paid scrupulous attention to the minutest detail of the things that mattered. Who else could recite the entire table of atomic weights, or the distance of every planet from the sun, or the capital, population, and area of every state? What other member of his family could recognize every constellation or recite pi to sixty places? Who in his school knew more about UNIX than he did? These feats, he assured himself, were not the result of inattention.

To see him now, a spindly gangling youth, fast, long-necked, long-limbed, one might suppose that his nickname was a metaphor for his appearance. It suited him so well that no one meeting him ever forgot his name. But in fact, the name was given years before to celebrate a precocious act accomplished when his small body was as compact as a beetle's, long before anyone suspected how puberty would stretch him into the lean sapling that astonished his mother and made his father brood upon his own lost, fragile youth.

When he has finished off the last of the paper towels, Spider calls Gorky from under the piano. "Here you go, boy," he says, pointing him to the pool of gravy collected under the stove.

They'll have sandwiches again after all, and tomorrow Mrs. Scaggs can clean the stove. He takes the turkey from the fridge and two slices of bread from the bakery bag. If Daisy finds out about the gravy and tells, he has plenty on her to threaten, things she doesn't even know he knows. Like the soppy letter he recently found hidden in the third chapter of Tolkien; what a stupid hiding place! And the pack of cigarettes in the back of the record cabinet. He'd always believed her when she said she didn't smoke, and since smoking is hardly forbidden, he wonders if they aren't funny cigarettes.

By the time he's piled the rye bread high with onion, lettuce, Swiss cheese, mustard, sour pickle, and turkey, he's no longer sorry about the gravy mishap. He pours himself a glass of milk, spoons cranberry sauce onto his plate, and is all ready to plunge in when the phone ringing in the hall reminds him that he has neglected to make up a plate for Daisy.

He whacks the side of his head with the heel of his hand in a TV gesture as he hears Daisy tear down the hall. Quickly he gets one more plate out of the cupboard and takes out two more slices of bread.

9

Resolutely, Nora drops two envelopes into the mailbox before she can change her mind. One is the corrected proofs of her piece on nuclear waste; the other is a short, witty note to Keith, rewritten twice before she found the right tone, twice more to make it fit to print. Bullied by indecision, she'd sealed the letter, stamped it, opened it up, changed the crucial last sentence, printed it out again, and resealed it, all the while berating herself for the lost time, the energy.

And now Buster, though barely trained, pulls Nora headlong through the street, stopping at every second tree, already a creature of habit. Like herself: every significant love affair she's ever had, the inappropriate ones no less than the suitable, has followed the same trajectory—from the first raptures, to the developing joy, to the risky temptations, to sudden surrender, to the predictable, decisive end.

At the thought of the end Nora hardens. Endings are bleak: the moment of fear, the self-contempt, most of all the waste. Like the end of the world she labors to forestall. She has been seriously in love five times, including twice with married men (was married herself once, briefly, in her youth), has had countless quick encounters with seductive men whose eyes respond swiftly to her direct approach and allow her the illusion that she started it. But always the moment comes when—possessed or embattled—she must ask herself: why am I doing this? Sometimes she has an answer. Occasionally after completing a difficult piece she celebrates with a fling at love even though her work is its own reward.

This time she thinks it's to help her shed Lex. Or is that merely an alibi? The more avidly she searches her soul, the less certain she is. Can her motives be anything more than presumptions and conjectures? Can anyone's? Particularly when her passions are involved, the different versions of her life begin to crowd each other like rush-hour riders, so that just as she's ready to accuse one sly passenger of straying hands, he disappears in the crowd, leaving her suspicious of someone else, until she doesn't know whom to accuse.

Either way, no matter what her motive for seeing Keith, she hasn't the slightest intention of stopping. Not even of trying to stop. She's glad she can't retrieve the letter. As for the wasted time—she'll cancel her lunch for tomorrow, work straight through till dinner, call her editor in the morning to see about an extension and tell him she still has the flu.

Peter drained the bottle into their glasses, raised his glass once more, and pressed Rosemary's knee with his. (They always sat catercorner to each other at table instead of opposite so they could face each other and still go on touching.) "To the next three," he said, clicking her glass three times, once for each year they'd been together.

Rosemary drank. In those three years each of her children had been promoted from one school to another, Harold had won tenure, she herself had taken her master's degree, and still she and Peter, passion undiminished, had hardly missed a week. Tipsily, almost smugly, they congratulated each other on having managed for so long to put it over on the world.

Peter held up the empty bottle. "What do you think—shall I run out and get another? It's still early."

"I'll come too," she announced on a lark. She was usually the more vigilant of the pair, but it was their anniversary.

They cleared the table quickly. (As usual, Rosemary's plate was clean but for a small neat heap of tiny bones along the edge, while Peter's was strewn with asparagus ends, swirls of hollandaise, bones, skin, and squeezed-out lemon.) Then they left the building separately and walked on opposite sides of the street until they turned the corner and teamed up again.

How dangerous, how delicious seemed the crisp city air laden with the sharp aromas of frying chiles, ripe fruit, and the ubiquitous garlic from upstairs windows; how voluptuous their voices mingling with the soft din of music and conversation; how confident their carefree step, as if they were people without a secret—until suddenly, at the second corner, standing at the curb on the other end of a leash from a sheepdog pup, was Nora Kennedy.

Frantically, Rosemary kicked Peter away with the toe of her shoe. He swiveled around to stare, guilty and engrossed, at the flashing Christmas window of a hardware store. "Nora!" cried Rosemary, louder than she ever intended, smiling gaily to cover up. "What in the world are you doing here?"

Clutching a towel to her naked torso, Daisy answers the phone. "Oh!" she cries and slithers down the wall onto the floor in the corner of the hallway. "Oh. It's you."

"Yeah. It's me."

"I thought I told you not to call."

"So—should I hang up?"

"No!"

Rap laughs. "Did you finish your college stuff?"

"Yes," Daisy lies, winding a lock of her long silky hair around an index finger.

"Great. Then how about you meet me tomorrow?"

"When?"

"Soon as you get up."

Daisy is silent. She unwraps her hair from her finger and begins again. "Well?"

"Tomorrow's Tuesday," she says.

"So? . . . You gonna meet me?"

"Not till after school."

"Three thirty then."

"Okay. Where?" she asks, holding her breath. Her voice keeps diminishing with every word; soon she'll be inaudible.

"Should I come up there?"

"*Here?*"

"Yeah."

She looks at her body, covered with towel. "Oh no! Not here!"

Rap laughs, a short staccato laugh. "I get it. Okay. Then meet me at that Benno's Pizza on Madison, we'll leave from there."

"Where are we going?"

Don't you worry, girl, I'll find us a place."

After she hangs up, Daisy paces the whole apartment, clutching her towel. With every breath, she blows out gusts of air. Tomorrow's so soon—what will she wear? Remembering her bath waiting, cooling, she hurries back. The water is tepid; she turns on the hot and gets out the razor, the conditioner, the shampoo. She bathes hastily, abandoning her plan to soak, needing to stay in motion. Before the tub is empty, she turns on the shower to rinse her hair.

When he hears the shower running, Spider runs to the phone to dial April Waters' number. He keeps a finger poised over the button all the time it's ringing, ready to hang up at the sound of a wrong voice.

Someday he knows he'll have to come out and speak to her openly, but first he's allowing himself a long period of apprenticeship. In this practice he maintains high standards and strict discipline. If April answered, he permitted himself to listen respectfully for as long as she stayed on the line, but if any other member of her family answered, he hung up at the first reasonable opening. Unlike Herschel, who takes delight in asking provocative questions in the most shocking language he can concoct, Spider has no desire to frighten, shock, or provoke. Especially not April. He's nothing like the breathers his parents complain about; he's a suitor, not a pervert. Not that he's a prude either: he's as happy as anyone to play computer sex games with willing partners or to answer ads in the skin magazines—as long as April isn't dragged into it. When he and Herschel constructed their computer list of the best phone numbers for several categories of calls, he refused to allow April's number on any of them. Nor would he permit himself—much less Herschel!—to attach April's name or face to even the least voluptuous *Playboy* body.

Spider is disappointed when, on the fifth ring, Mr. Waters picks up. He chose a time to phone when he presumed April would answer, but evidently he miscalculated. He waits politely while the irate man delivers his threats; then, at the first break, he quietly severs the connection with a slight pressure of his index finger and runs back to his room before Daisy is out of the shower.

Daisy, having finally got her call, couldn't care less about the phone. Now she's busy flossing her teeth and creaming her face. Back in her room she tries on every sweater in her drawer, looking for the right one. If only the sweaters Aunt Jessica knits for her would fit, but they are always slightly off, enough to ruin them, each in a different way: arms too long, neck too wide, bodice too loose or tight. Except the green, but he's seen it. The white? Dirties too fast. Distressed, she pads down to her mother's room prepared to search the closet and drawers, as if she didn't already know by heart their exact contents.

Though he had been given the use of a guest room in one of the ivy-covered buildings, Harold knew it would be imprudent to take Pippa there, even though she was clearly not a student. Instead he took her to the Hotel Taft in downtown New Haven, ostensibly for a drink.

What chemistry combines these two? For Pippa, who's been raising a child on her own, writing nights and those weekends when her ex has Lolly, copyediting free-lance to make ends meet, and for recreation occasionally collapsing over dinner with her women friends—for Pippa, who seldom meets anyone anymore, it's the Spell of a Man. A man: one who comes to her rescue, orders her drink, guides her by the elbow, allows her to relax. A man who, far from fighting her (though he towers over her by nearly a foot), seems content to let her color their conversation like the water clouding her Pernod a milky green. For Harold, studying the jaunty nose and tiny feet, it's part birthright, part reward: doesn't he deserve the appreciation of a peer?

Now she stands beside him at the desk looking up at him through her long lashes past the fringe of her long bangs while the clerk records his credit card number. When the clerk returns his card, Harold tears up the receipt and drops the pieces in an ashtray beside the elevator. Not that he believes Rosemary checks his pockets, but having long since traded the romantic life for the obligations of family, he prides himself on his discretion.

"What really amazes me," says Pippa, as they wait for the elevator, "is how novelistic this is."

"Novelistic?" Harold laughs nervously. "How do you mean?"

"You know—tall, dark, glamorous writer picks up divorcée at party, takes her to hotel—"

Harold fears she's making fun of him. For a brief while after the publication of *Terror!*, he no longer felt his nose was too big, but now he's again unsure. Women are such a mystery—he can't tell if it's he they like or who he is. Except his wife, who knew him when, who's not impressed. If only he could consult Rosemary, who's so savvy about matters of the heart. She'd see what's going on and protect him. But about this one thing he's barred from her advice and comfort. In this he's on his own.

"—just like the hero of all those romances. In fact," warns Pippa, dimpling, "I might use you in one myself. Unless you object."

Flattered, Harold looks down at Pippa, petite and effusive, offering to lift him out of journalism into literature. Though he balks at the idea of being displayed in a book where someone might recognize him, he has never been able to refuse anyone anything. Least of all himself.

As he takes her elbow to usher her into the elevator, suddenly Harold feels strong and lusty and immortal.

Peter returned to their love nest seconds after Rosemary, wondering as he climbed the stairs if this was the moment it would all end—on their anniversary. "Who was that?" he asked breathlessly, before he had even closed the door.

"That," said Rosemary, taking ice from the freezer, "is Nora Kennedy."

Embarrassed not to recognize the name, Peter covered with concern. "Really. Is this very bad?"

"Bad! A journalist! My luck! And she lives in our neighborhood."

"Is she dangerous?"

"You don't understand. She's a *reporter*. A professional blab."

"But does that necessarily mean she'll tell?"

For comfort, Rosemary invoked Streeter's Theorem of Possibilities, the pivotal principle she'd derived from her years of experience, along with its contrary, her Theorem of Association: *nothing necessarily goes with anything else*, and *anything can go with anything, no matter how unlikely*. All the same, her voice glided up toward the hysterical registers as she explained it was not treachery she feared so much as carelessness, first of all her own. "How could I have walked openly in the street with you?" In fact, she said, pacing the room, it could hardly be worse. Nora was a hardboiled, fast-talking, chain-smoking reporter of the old school who had it both ways because she was a ravishing blonde. Nora was the only woman

she knew who'd had her tubes tied in her twenties. She specialized in
exposés. She'd made a name for herself getting powerful men to hang
themselves by saying what they really think, and then publishing it.
"She's a colleague of Harold's. She reviewed his book. She knows everyone I know."

"You think she noticed me, baby?" asked Peter, twirling the bottle in
the ice-filled sink.

Whenever he called her baby, Rosemary suffered a pang of shame:
Peter was younger than she, a puppy. She reached over and began unbuttoning his shirt. "A man like you? You?" Despite her agitation, she
couldn't hide a certain satisfaction. Her smile softened. "Of course she
noticed. Look at that incredible face."

When they were both naked again, Rosemary bared her teeth and growled,
"Okay, now fight me."

She wants their bodies to connect in every possible way. She adores
that feel of flesh on flesh on flesh. They square off, squatting in opposite
corners of the futon. She narrows her eyes, readies her arms, letting him
know by the glint in her eye that she means business. She's tall but he's
taller; he's strong but she's foxy. Her muscles tense with determination.
To win.

She begins by falling toward him, clutching his arms in a tight embrace. They snake and twist, now to one side, now the other.

The first time she challenged him to wrestle he laughed at her. She
argued, pleaded; finally, angry, she leaped on his back and twisted his
arm with all her strength until he began to resist. Now when she
challenges him he doesn't laugh; but even after three years he doesn't
know quite how to respond. He wants to please her, but how? She's
so unpredictable. She says she loves him for his gentleness, but she
means to win, really win. Should he try to pin her or not? Wrestling
turns her on.

He follows her lead, gradually letting her work herself up with her
sudden lunges. Then, when her cheeks are red and her skin glistens, he
starts to resist, till her excited squeals turn into grunts. Slowly he presses
forward, meeting her spurts with steady, even force until she begins to
fall backward, inch by inch. The more seriously he fights, the more he
admires her fearless turns. On he presses, his own lips now curling in

anticipated triumph. He could kill her with a snap of her neck. Her delicate body. He feels himself getting hard.

For a few seconds their strengths are matched in perfect equilibrium, force against force, love against love. Then, at the crucial moment, when Peter is about to topple her, Rosemary turns aside, letting him fall forward, and like a weasel leaps on his back.

This is the moment she's been waiting for. She presses herself against him, her cheek against his shoulder, her breasts flattened against his ribs, her pelvis tight against his haunches, her thighs clasping his thighs. Panting with effort, she pulls his shoulders back with all her strength until he is up on his knees, clutching her arms, clawing her hand from his throat. Like this they struggle for a long time, until they enter their secret place. *S*, they call it, hoping to convey much more than merely *sex*. Sex, secrecy, stomach, where she always feels it first—and also shame, though they never mention that.

At last, with a sudden jerk he flips her onto the mat, splat, flat on her back, and, straddling her, pins her shoulders. Refusing to concede, she goes on struggling, heaving up against him with her pelvis, then with one shoulder, then the other, thrashing her head from side to side until—she can't help it—she begins to laugh.

Now they're both laughing, laughing and panting. "Say uncle," says Peter.

"Never!" shouts Rosemary.

"Say lover then." He presses his weight against her.

She goes suddenly limp. "Lover," she says. Panting for breath, she reaches up with her arms and legs and pulls him to her.

"Again," he says, becoming a different man.

She wraps her arms around his shoulders and her legs around his buttocks. "Lover."

He slips inside her and presses his lips against her lips.

So they begin again.

Confessions

10

IN THE MIRROR Nora saw Lex on the bed watching her kohl her eyes. He looked puzzled or annoyed or possibly hurt, she wasn't sure which. He was usually the one to tear himself from the bed and leave her behind—for the theater, where she could never accompany him, or his family. It was her apartment they used, her hours that were flexible. But today she was the one to watch the clock and leave.

For a moment she considered forgoing the makeup for another ten minutes of love. But there was never enough time anyway; and whenever Lex looked at the clock she felt betrayed. Let him feel it for a change;

soon, she hoped, she would be free of him. She would spend the ten minutes dressing.

Nora had always made up her eyes, even during those severe days a decade before when political purity proscribed makeup. A cheap dash of purity, since they were all in their twenties then and hardly needed to make up. But Nora, already divorced, had felt obliged to call attention to her large, blue-black, passionate eyes, almond-shaped and by consensus her best feature. Besides, though she had felt the pressure to eschew makeup, she could never bear the hypocrisy of acting under pressure. That was probably why she'd taken on governments and armies, the ultimate hypocrites, the ultimate bullies.

Rosemary, of course, had worn no makeup at all. Married, with kids, Rosemary had been involved in day care, where how you looked hardly mattered. But Nora, a spokesperson, an advocate, was often judged by appearances. Now a decade had passed; they were both shamelessly older; different standards applied. Just as Satan argued that Job's loyalty to God could hardly be put to the test while Job prospered, so Rosemary's rejection of makeup hardly counted when she was young, beautiful, and married. Nora wondered if Rosemary would be wearing makeup today.

"I wish you hadn't made the date for three," said Lex. "It cuts out half our time."

Nora turned her darkened eyes from the mirror to confront him straight on. "Our time?" she asked sharply, making short black marks against him in the air with her kohl stick. "Your time, you mean. It's your life that cuts into our time, not mine."

His deep-set eyes, all but hidden in the high-ridged bones of his craggy face, seemed to sink deeper and glaze over under her attack. Tough, independent, high-spirited, brainy woman attending to the mysteries in bra and pantyhose: she was bound to leave him eventually. If only he could give her what she wanted, but he could not. He would have liked to tiptoe away when she accused him, but instead he tried to placate her. "I know, darling. But our afternoons are so short. Couldn't you have met her for dinner instead?"

"You think you're the only one who prefers to eat with your family? Rosemary has to get home to her kids too."

Lex rolled up onto an elbow. "Rosemary has kids?" he asked, letting pass Nora's polemical choice of the word *prefers*.

At the mention of kids, Nora felt a bond form between Lex and Rosemary that excluded her. If she and Lex happened to be driving behind a van of waving kids, Lex's waving back was a statement. If she waved too, she'd seem hypocritical; but if she failed to wave she'd appear heartless. She was neither. She could appreciate children as well as anyone, but Lex had one and she didn't. And probably wouldn't. Her impetuous consent to having her tubes tied after a youthful abortion made her a monster to the world, a tragedy to her family, and to him, she feared, irrevocably flawed. She was convinced that was the reason he no longer talked about leaving his wife. It was hopeless: every night he lay snug in bed beside his wife—though he claimed they no longer made love—while Nora silently endured self-doubt, resentment, and sometimes, when she dared admit it, loneliness. How long had it been since they'd slept together an entire night—three months? Four? He went to three plays a week, always without her. Any actress in town claimed more right to him than she had. She felt the clutch in her throat. How she longed to find someone else, someone single, someone free! How she wished she could replace every instance of Lex in her life as easily as she could use the Universal-Search-and-Replace on her word processor! But her makeup was half done, she wouldn't allow tears to smear it and make her late.

Seeing her agitation, Lex tried to appease her. "I guess we're just insatiable. We always need more time together, don't we? We'll never get enough."

She removed his birthday earrings from her ears, now stinging with his thoughtless irony. When she had replaced them with the long silver ones she'd brought back from Santa Fe, she turned to him and began her dissent. No, she proclaimed, it was not sex she needed. From her earliest brush with it, she had considered it a danger, a liability, a thrill, an asset, an expedient, a game, a joy; but never, she insisted, a necessity. She wanted it, but in its place. As a solace or a satisfaction, but never a priority. Although she couldn't claim to have hung back often when she felt its pull, still she was proud to have said no in her life and counted her interludes between lovers as feats akin to losing ten pounds or giving up smoking. The longer they lasted, the prouder she felt. Once, she boasted, just before she met him, she'd gone for a year and a half without desire. (Her reward, she believed, had been the prestigious Petersen Prize.) She counted it her strength that she could take it or leave it, her weakness that she nevertheless chose to take it.

She brushed back her hair from the sides and fixed it with two large silver and turquoise combs. Next time she was tempted to fall in love, she said, reminding Lex there'd be a next time, she would try harder to resist, seeing how easily it fouled up her work, her life. "In my utopia," she proclaimed, dabbing carefully at the corners of her eyes with a tissue, "people will be free of desire whenever they choose." *Free*. A word she esteemed even more highly than *brave*.

Lex reached over for his pipe. He wished he knew how to calm her. He'd happily recite whatever she wanted to hear, but he feared this was one of those times when anything he said would set her off, when the more he agreed with her, the more she'd resent him. He wished he could give her everything she wanted, including his whole self, but he hadn't the resources or the stamina to leave his wife.

While he filled his pipe, she wrapped herself in a robe and walked to the kitchen for seltzer and cigarettes to calm herself down. A week or two after they broke up, she said, returning to sit briefly on the bed, she might not even remember his face. Sooner would she remember the smell of his pipe tobacco. Even now, after all this time, she said, lighting a cigarette, she was quite sure that if Lex were suddenly to disappear from her life—she handed him the glass, clasped her knees, and blew a smoke ring toward the ceiling—she would probably be relieved.

Lex slowly stroked her foot, enduring her grief without protest. Hearing her frequent declarations of independence was the price he paid for remaining married. She'd been saying this piece for years, half plea, half threat, more reflex than truth, one of those lies she needed to tell herself, and he had come to accept it as his punishment for having two women when he could barely afford one. For the sin of living beyond his means. Once he realized she didn't mean it, it stopped making him afraid or even sad, only guilty. She was right: if something happened to them she'd be relieved. Still, he knew they were far too enmeshed to be anywhere near finished with each other. They saw each other every day, were best friends. Once, when they lay on the bed after one of their long flights, their limbs barely untangled, and she began her complaint, he replied that she depended on him as much as he depended on her, whatever she said.

"Don't be too sure," she warned him now, secretly placing her bets on her new blond lover. "I love you, but I don't need you. All I *need* is my work. One of these days—"

He smiled. Of all the women he'd known, Nora was the most earnest, the most passionate.

"In fact," she continued, "if Sheila found out tomorrow" (Nora was no longer as scrupulous as she'd once been to avoid mentioning his wife and son—even though each time she did she risked hearing again his tiresome litany of how, when, where, and why he could not leave them), "I might be sad for a little while"—this much she would offer him—"but mainly I'd be glad it was finally getting settled."

She slipped on her bracelets and dabbed on perfume. Sometimes in the aftermath of lovemaking they got carried away and allowed themselves to follow their fantasies wherever they led. Usually they started slowly, first imagining living together in his place (after his son was grown), then in her place, then both keeping their own places, alternating where they spent their nights, and, finally, finding a large place, new to both of them, where they'd have plenty of room to mingle their separate lives. Sometimes they imagined leaving the world behind, moving to the country, to an island surrounded by beach and seaweed, to Mexico or Greece. In those fanciful, passionate flights Lex never mentioned his family, nor did Nora speak of her work. Invariably, he would grow hard again, and she would feel herself begin to float out dangerously far on those misleadingly calm waters buoyed by nothing but a flimsy hope-filled raft.

Discriminating critic, he watched her dress with the same admiration he felt at a first-rate performance. Some of his theater friends were on their third, fourth wives. The ones who envied him the fawning actresses and his biweekly by-lines didn't see that the one thing in this world he most longed for he couldn't have. If he had a fraction of their money, he would give Sheila whatever she asked and take Nora off forever. But on his salary he could barely manage to do right by one family, much less two. Whenever he'd tried to explain it to Nora, she heard only weakness and refused to understand, claiming she could support herself or live on nothing. He knew better than to try again. She was a woman, and free, without the slightest idea of what it meant to support a family.

Nora buttoned her shirt, adjusted the collar in the mirror, then held up Lex's silk paisley scarf, the lilac and blue one that set off her eyes, looking for permission.

"Take it," he said, pained by the nagging knowledge of how little he could give her, and watched her tie it deftly around her neck. "I'll walk Buster for you if you like," he added in conciliation as she put on her coat. "Have fun."

"Thanks. I will. Rosemary's sure to present me with another amusing portrait of married bliss."

On her way to the door she kissed Lex good-bye. She would prefer, of course, to end it fast and clean, but she's still stuck in her hopes. From Santa Fe, high on her new conquest, she wrote to Lex: "I'm poised on a highwire I can get off in several ways: If you're willing to risk it, if you care enough, we can do it together, step by step, feeling the thrill as we cross to the other side. Or else I can simply step down into the safety net woven of my own satisfying life. Either way, I'm not going to crash." She was still waiting for his reply.

11

Rosemary's briefcase was too stuffed with tests to close properly. Feeling foolish, she carried it into Lido's cradling it in her arms like a baby. (Or a monster: this semester she'd been given two sections of Calculus 125.)

Of course Nora had suggested they meet at Lido's, *Nouvelle's* newest discovery, with its rubbed oak and tile, its glassed-in sidewalk terrace, a magnificent antique mahogany bar with its elaborate Cruvinet, and some of the best wines to be had by the glass in New York City. And of course, though they were only two, Nora would manage to nab the largest window table, where Rosemary found her blowing perfect smoke rings toward the light. "Am I late?" She dropped her briefcase on an empty chair and bent to kiss Nora's cheek.

"Not very," said Nora, pecking the air.

Each time Nora raised the cigarette between manicured nails to her matching red lips, five silver bracelets fell jingling over the bones of her slender wrist. Her thick hair, swept off her cheeks by a pair of sculptured combs, shone like the silk of the paisley scarf tied artfully at her throat. Her very bones were on display. Noting Nora's masterly makeup, an art Rosemary had abandoned years before in a rush of honesty, she concluded Nora was a man's woman.

Rosemary had had no trouble phoning to make this date, but how would she ever present her embarrassingly personal request? She seated herself, removed her gloves, her coat. Glittering mirrors behind the bar doubled the high-ceilinged room with its pale pink decor, its polished woods, its high-color art and low-voiced vitality. Trim young waiters with naked necks and narrow hips hurried back and forth to the kitchen, releasing irresistible smells with every swing of the swinging doors.

Nora looked curiously at the overflowing briefcase, Rosemary's scrubbed rosy cheeks, her smart tweed suit. "So tell me," she said, tilting her head at the briefcase, "what are you doing now? It's been a long time, hasn't it?" She vaguely remembered Rosemary had once done some kind of editing; maybe those were manuscripts she was lugging around.

"I'm teaching at Gotham Community College," said Rosemary uneasily, though not without a certain pride. She had labored hard to be able to produce this decently respectable answer, so much sounder than her former, inadequate "mother," but she still doubted her own credibility. Despite her hard-earned M.A. and several hundred students behind her, her job was too precarious to feel real. Nor did her recent meeting with her dean encourage confidence.

"Oh? What do you teach?"

"Math."

"Really!" said Nora. "I would never have dreamed you'd be doing math." As soon as she had spoken she regretted her words, which seemed disparaging. Her unconstrained tongue that served her so well in her work often botched her private life. "But that's terrific!" she rallied. "You're teaching math. Times have really changed for us, haven't they?"

"Maybe less than you think. I'm teaching now, but I never know from one semester to the next if I'll be hired back, even though there's a critical shortage of math teachers all over the country. I know I'm a good teacher, and I'm the only woman they've got in the entire department, so you'd think they'd want to keep me on, wouldn't you? The women math students have a hard enough time with no role models, no one to talk to, no encouragement from their professors—I could tell you some real horror stories. But they still won't give me a regular job."

"Do you have your Ph.D.?"

"No, but with the shortage of math teachers, this job doesn't require a Ph.D."

"Then why . . . ?"

"I wish I knew. Sometimes they tell me it's a matter of funds, sometimes they say I haven't published—but I don't see how I can be expected to publish with the number of students I have, plus being mother-confessor to the freshman class, plus taking care of a family of my own. Hardly anyone in the department publishes. You need months of clean, uninterrupted time for that, and where am I supposed to find that kind of time?"

Nora fingered the bracelets on her arm as if each one were a shackle she had luckily escaped.

"I'm a really good teacher," Rosemary concluded, "everyone says so, but that doesn't seem to impress anyone except students, who don't count. The better a teacher you are, the less time you have for the other things that do count."

"I know," said Nora. "A few years ago when I was working in Washington I gave a course at the Center for Policy Studies. I had only twenty students, but all I managed to write that entire semester was a couple of reviews. Preparing my lectures and working with the students threw my whole work schedule off. I'm pretty well disciplined. If I don't produce a certain number of pages every day, I administer horrible punishments to myself. But that whole semester my writing was a complete failure. And I wasn't even that good a teacher, either." She shook her head and lit a cigarette. "Some people can do it with ease. Harold, for instance. He manages both jobs, doesn't he? But me, it doesn't matter how hard I drive myself, I still have only so much creative energy."

"Yes! That's what it takes, creative energy. Too often I tell myself that if I just had enough will or discipline I'd be able to do everything. But I think you've hit it. Creative energy. We each have only so much, and mine goes into my kids."

Nora was baffled that Rosemary could possibly think kids and intellect took the same creative energy. It was probably that very insidious idea in the minds of the faculty that deprived Rosemary of a regular appointment. Kids took away your time and maybe even your judgment, but creativity? With so many women her age now rushing to have babies as if the world were coming to an end, Nora was glad she'd long ago settled the matter for herself with surgery. (She could always adopt if she changed her mind.) All the same, calling on her vaunted discipline, she held her tongue.

"When I went into math," Rosemary explained, "it was because I loved the precision of it, the abstraction, the clarity. I never gave a thought to the politics of academe. I shouldn't complain, though. I'm grateful for my job, even if it is more about kids than equations. I'd probably hate most of the math jobs out there—in insurance, or computers. . . . But I didn't call you up to dump all this on you. Tell me what's going on in your life nowadays."

Nora thought: *breast.* She remembered that Rosemary knew Bianca— they had worked together years before on an abortion project that Nora had written about. She resisted spilling her fears by returning the conversation to Rosemary's court as she signaled a passing waiter for menus. "Nothing special. I'm free-lancing, working on a book. But you did call me up about something. What is it?"

Rosemary's pulse speeded up. She was mortified to have to turn the conversation so soon from work to her sloppy private life. Particularly with Nora Kennedy, whose life seemed a model of control. But if she didn't do it now she was afraid she'd lose her nerve. "Look," she blurted out, "I have a favor to ask you. Since I saw you on the street, I've worked myself into a real state over this."

Nora leaned forward. "Oh? What can it be?"

"I know you're a friend of Harold's and I hate to put you on the spot, but I have to ask you please never to mention to anyone that you saw me with . . . a man."

Half offended, half amused by this newest evidence of obsessive human self-centeredness, Nora pursed her lips like a lawyer. As if she had nothing better to do than observe the vagaries of random couplings or gossip about the peccadilloes of colleagues' wives. Rosemary's small mouth tensed in a nervous smile, her bright, wary eyes darted furtively over the room, her restless fingers picked at one another. Again, Nora judged her a dabbler—careless, undisciplined, probably weak. "You know, Rosemary, the way you sent that man off when you saw me made it rather obvious it wasn't the sort of thing to mention. He's quite attractive. Who is he?"

Nervously Rosemary opened the menu. Never had she revealed her lover's name. She had a superstitious fear that once their secret was out he would disappear in a puff of smoke. She waved a hand casually. "No one you know. . . . Have you ordered yet?"

Nora tapped her nails against the table. She had built a reputation getting her questions answered. Powerful men yielded up their secrets to her; she would not be put off by a cheating wife.

Reluctantly Rosemary relented and watched her lover's name step onto the brightly lit stage of her lips for the whole world to desire. "His name is Peter Valentine. I told you you wouldn't know him," she said, momentarily glad his work was still unrecognized. Then she leaned forward earnestly and said, "Believe me, Nora, I hate dragging you into this. It's just that we're bound to bump into each other now and then since I usually meet Peter in your neighborhood."

"Oh? He lives near me?"

Rosemary didn't want to go into the real estate if she could avoid it. "Not exactly."

"He's married, I suppose?"

The way Nora paused over the word *married* invoked a long line of shabby little affairs doomed to secrecy and sham. Rosemary began picking the border off the doily under the sugar bowl and shook her head.

"Then why . . . ?"

"The point is, *I'm* married. I think I'd die if anyone found out."

"By anyone, you mean Harold?"

"No. Anyone. Peter is the absolutely perfect lover for me. It would kill me if I had to break it off."

"If he's so perfect," said Nora cattily, unable to restrain herself, "then why would you want to break it off?"

"I'd never jeopardize my family!" said Rosemary, drawing herself up so righteously that Nora couldn't let it pass unchallenged. She blew a perfect smoke ring and drawled, "You must have the perfect husband, too, then, if you'd choose him over the perfect lover."

"Well, yes. Harold's wonderful."

"As long as no one knows about Peter."

"Right. As long as no one knows about Peter."

Nora wouldn't let it go. "The perfect lover, the perfect husband, but not, evidently, the perfect marriage. Too bad," she said.

"It works."

"As long as no one—"

"Believe me," interrupted Rosemary, "open marriage doesn't work."

Nora couldn't understand how Rosemary, having just made the ultimately damning confession, could sit smiling smugly across the table. She was just like the Guatemalan general who, having confessed into her tape recorder to unspeakable crimes, thought he had pulled off a PR coup. Not even after the published interview created an international sensation would he understand what had happened. Bewildered, he'd blamed the incident on her.

Nora tipped her chin on her long neck to signal a passing waiter.

"What's good here?" asked Rosemary.

"Everything. The wine, of course, and the pastry, I hear. Me, I usually have six shrimp in their special mustard sauce, and Perrier."

But Rosemary, who sat in bars too seldom to know unhesitatingly what she wanted, continued to study the menu. Not since the children had been born had she had time to sit through an afternoon leisurely talking with a friend. Given her life, it was the sort of outrageous extravagance with time that she lumped together with afternoon movies or skiing weekends—luxuries of the single or the young, not available to someone with as dense a life as hers—a life she would not, however, trade with theirs for anything. "Café Royal? What's that?"

"Our double-strength coffee with our house brandy," said the waiter with pencil poised.

"Sounds good. Okay. Café Royal."

"With or without whipped cream?"

"With," said Rosemary, because, though she had no particular craving for cream, it was a minor sin, and if you're guilty anyway, you might as well get everything you can. "Tell me," she said, looking slyly at Nora—for now that she finally had a confidante despite herself after her three-year forbearance, she longed to speak her lover's name, hear it sing, see it dance—"what did you think when you saw Peter and me together?"

"I wouldn't say I saw you exactly *together*. Really, Rosemary, all that skulking around on street corners—you'd think sex was still a wicked activity women had to hide from the world."

"I can't afford to be open about it. I'm married. You're not."

"I should say not!" said Nora hotly, leaning forward across the table toward Rosemary with that eye grip for which she was justly famous in journalistic circles. She struck the table and her nostrils flared. "Marriage! Thank God that particular brand of bondage is dead. That's one mistake we'll never have to make again."

Rosemary was bewildered to find that her seemingly innocuous remark had provoked such an encompassing outburst. What could she possibly say? If Nora had pounded the table and proclaimed God dead, she might have perhaps offered condolences. But the death of marriage? Ever polite, she looked for some way to withdraw the offense, despite her suspicion that if anyone ought to be offended, it was not Nora but she herself, who had called this meeting precisely to protect her marriage, who had devoted half her creative efforts of recent years to preserving her marriage for the future like fragile summer berries preserved in jars against the sudden frost of shaky times. "Maybe that's true for you," she said finally, "but I've been married over eighteen years and have two children to think of."

Nora's eyes darted purple sparks. "What in the world have children got to do with it?"

Rosemary cocked her head incredulously. "With marriage? What do you think marriage is all about?"

"I always thought," said Nora, holding firm in the face of Rosemary's wide-eyed opacity, "it was supposed to be about love."

Rosemary was surprised to hear a sophisticated woman like Nora speaking innocently of love. She waited until the waiter had placed their orders on the table before asking, "Exactly what do you mean by love?"

"Oh come on. You know perfectly well what I mean. Love. Passionate sexual attachment."

"Passion?" said Rosemary, beginning to lose patience. Some people went to all the trouble of separation, divorce, custody arrangements, and remarriage in order to appease the god of passion. She had been tempted in the early days herself, before she knew how the children would suffer, but she honored efficiency too much to be seduced again. All that agony and action only to wind up with another husband and another set of lovers? "You call that love? Are you serious?"

"Of course."

"But you're confusing marriage with a love affair. They have nothing to do with each other."

"Really?" said Nora, leaning back. She smiled archly. "What's it all about then?"

Rosemary leaned forward. "That's easy. Marriage is about family. It's about raising children. It's an economic arrangement. Passion has nothing to do with it, except maybe to get it started."

Nora tamped out her cigarette. "That's disgusting," she said, looking Rosemary unflinchingly in the eye. "That's prostitution. A woman who enters into marriage with that in mind deserves everything she gets."

Daisy jumped up, nearly spilling her coffee, when Rap put his hand on the back of her neck at the counter of Benno's Pizza. "Ready?" he asked. He lifted her right hand with his left and plunged them into his pocket.

"Where are we going?" she asked. Her hand, nestled in the lining of his short black leather jacket, lay inches below his heart along his ribs.

"I'm taking you home. Come on."

Retrieving her hand, Daisy clung to her mug. "Don't you want something to eat?"

"There's food at home. There's everything—music, booze. Come on. My dad's at the hospital till late; the place is empty."

Stalling, she lifted the mug to her lips.

"Come *on!* Leave that. Or take it with you. But let's *go!*" Rap grabbed the mug and replaced it decisively on the counter. Half an hour to get there, another half hour to open her up, another half to get her home. Never enough time. "Zip up, girl. We're taking a ride."

"Where do you live?"

He waited till they were back on the street before answering. "In Riverdale."

"Riverdale! But that's—"

"Don't *worry*," he ordered.

They stopped before a large black Harley. He handed her a helmet, adjusted his own, and seated her behind him for the ride uptown. When they finally reached the highway, he shot into the center lane and opened it up all the way. Daisy's heart pounded wildly. She clung to Rap's back, terrified, half hoping they'd crash and bring everything to a fast, neat end.

Feeling Daisy lean her cheek against his back and cling tightly to his waist, Rap imagined her legs wrapped around him, her hair spread out on the mattress, her fingers squeezing his as the Jagger pumped into her. Why was it always such a hassle just to get to make love? The way he saw it, sex should be as easy to come by as water to drink or a place to piss. But no, there was this conspiracy to keep it scarce. Women were supposed to pretend they didn't want it when you could tell from the way they walked and smiled and breathed that they were dying for it; and men were supposed to pretend they were really interested in every little thing except that. Like the cream Mercedes edging him out of the fast left lane.

When Rap shot off to the right to fly along parallel to the shoulder, Daisy prayed: if they have to crash, let it be going home, or, better yet, after she's told Carrie.

At last they arrived. She avoided the eyes of the doorman and in the elevator shrank from the woman in fur boots balancing two bags of groceries on her hips. Not a word from Rap, either, until, crossing the threshold into his apartment, he lets out an animal howl, picks her up, races into the bedroom, and dumps her onto a king-sized bed. Breathless, he falls on top of her, covering her with his body, hand to hand, arm to arm, thigh to thigh, mouth to mouth.

"There," he says, coming up from the first long kiss for air. "Man, I haven't thought of anything except this since the first second you walked into my life in that green sweater. Do you have it on?" Unzipping her coat, he scans her body. "Let's get outa these *clothes!*"

She lets him push her coat off her shoulders. Straddling her on his knees, he begins tearing off his jacket, his sweater, his shirt, until, by the time she's lifted her own sweater gingerly over her head, he's out of his pants too, stripping off his socks. Free, he turns to help her, tugging her jeans down over her hips. She wishes the sky would turn suddenly dark, as she once saw it do at the onset of a spectacular afternoon thunderstorm.

"Beauty," he whispers, kissing her breasts. "Baby. Lover."

When the first round of shouting comes to a halt, Rosemary and Nora stare speechlessly at one another across the table.

Nora, lips pursed, is appalled at Rosemary's marriage.

Rosemary, jaw slack, is amazed at Nora's makeup.

Each one, convinced there's been a misunderstanding and ashamed of her outburst, prepares to explain again.

"But don't you see, the secrecy is half the reason it's so perfect with Peter. Secrecy makes us accomplices. And what could be more voluptuous than a secret affair?"

Nora pushed up her sleeves and bracelets and leaned forward on her elbows. "Not being able to see each other whenever you want? Not even being able to walk down the street together? You call that perfect? If you excuse me, it sounds rather"—she searched the rubble for an inoffensive word—"limited."

Rosemary nodded eagerly. "That's just the point. That's what keeps the passion high. The limitations keep us yearning, and since we only see each other once a week, when we are together we can devote ourselves totally to love. No distractions. No conflicts. No children interrupting. No money problems or work or dirty socks or taxes. No worries about the future. We can accept each other just as we are."

"Accept?" said Nora, allowing a smile to adorn one side of her face. *"Accept?"*

A couple came through the door holding hands. As they searched out the farthest table, Rosemary recalled that just so had she and Peter sometimes managed to steal whole afternoons to meet in an out-of-the-way café. But after they'd accepted that they were lovers they always met at places where they could use their limited time most efficiently.

"Maybe secrecy's an acquired taste," said Rosemary, backing down a step, "like hot chile peppers—something you have to experience often to appreciate. Or even to tolerate."

Nora leaned back in her chair and lit another cigarette. "As a matter of fact, I speak from as much experience as you do. It happens that I've been trapped in a secret love affair for a number of years. As you say, the effect is like hot chiles—it's left me with damaged intestines and a permanently bad taste for secrecy."

Glimmerings of enlightenment colored Rosemary's face. In a voice as soft and comforting as a bosom she asked, "Why secret? Is he married?"

Nora frowned. Rosemary's tone, mushy and pitiful, struck her as patronizing, as if her involvement with Lex compromised her instead of him. How annoying: he, not she, was the hypocrite; he, not she, deserved pity. She sees her lover's marriage as a sort of character flaw, like a weakness for drink or gambling, which she must reluctantly endure, his personal failing, which must not be held against her. If you asked her, she would say without the slightest hesitation that the only honorable course for Lex would be to leave that wife tomorrow. But no one asks her, least of all Lex. This is one of the things they no longer discuss. In the early days, when she hoped her love would give him the courage to do it, they discussed it constantly; but it's one of many subjects that has long since slipped out of bounds. Now, in fact, it is she who needs courage—to end the affair. She's tired of living what she calls half a life.

She removes a comb and resets it in her thick hair, then lowers her voice to the throatier register to deliver her reply. "Yes, he is. And he has a son, too. But it's okay, Rosemary, no need to worry, I'm working on it. Very soon I expect to be free."

"Free?" breathes Rosemary. A foreign word.

Nora stares at her. As ardently as Rosemary wants to prolong her duplicity, Nora longs to end hers—though so far her efforts have been unsuccessful. But she's not without hope. When she remembers how she's managed to escape what had been in store for her by constructing out of work and imagination a life of her own design, her resolve springs back. She can't but pity Rosemary, living out an endless compromise. At moments like this, Nora sometimes wonders if it's really an accident that she falls in love with "inappropriate" men; sometimes she wonders if any man could ever be "appropriate."

She blows another smoke ring and says, "It's a long story."

Rosemary consults her watch. "We have time. Today Mrs. Scaggs will get dinner started, and my kids aren't expecting me till six."

"Then what happened?" asked Daisy, dipping her spoon back into the half gallon of Rocky Road ice cream Rap had brought back to bed with a tall glass of water and two long spoons.

"Then I went to junior high school and learned about life."

"But I mean," pressed Daisy, propping herself up against the pillow and covering her breasts with the sheet, "how did you get started?"

"My dad's a doctor, so it was easy. I lived mostly with my mom, but I'd go to my dad's on weekends. There was all kinds of stuff just sitting around in boxes, in the cupboards, the drawers, everywhere."

"Like what?"

"Demerol, codeine . . ." He rattled them off like a salesman. Daisy scanned the room for evidence. It was a sumptuous room, starting with the bed, the biggest bed Daisy had ever seen, so big that her fingers nowhere reached the edge of the mattress when she stretched out her arms. The subtly patterned wallpaper matched the comforter beneath them—a design of voluptuous vines and tropical flowers that looked like tongues in open mouths. The pattern was so rich and intricate that she wondered if it ever repeated. Pleated silk draperies, a huge armchair, thick rugs, plants in fancy pots—but no sign of drugs.

". . . even prescription pads—everything you could want. Man, it was so easy."

"Were you selling it too?"

"Sometimes. Sure. To my friends."

"How old were you?"

"Let's see. I was in the eighth grade."

"Eighth grade!" Daisy gasped.

"I had this friend, see, a ninth grader who lived in our building. His dad was a doctor too. We'd get high together. He taught me everything—even how to meet girls. It was great for about a year, and then the school found out we were doing drugs and suspended us."

Daisy presented a spoonful of ice cream to his lips.

"I really wanted to stay in my school, too, I liked school, I was doing all right. But Dad found this place to send me, like a military school. It was bad. The only way I could stand that place was to stay high all the time."

"Didn't you tell him you didn't like it there?"

"Tell him! I ran away twice. I hated it there." I begged him not to send me back. But I don't know, he had a new girlfriend, I guess he didn't want me around."

"And you really don't do it anymore?" asked Daisy skeptically.

"I've been in some pretty serious trouble, you know? I lost a lot of time. Now that I'm straight, I'm gonna stay that way."

"You don't take anything anymore?"

Rap lit a cigarette. He placed his arm around Daisy's neck and pressed his thigh alongside hers. "I'll tell you the truth, girl. I wouldn't shoot anything into my veins, never again. And I wouldn't take anything I didn't know exactly where it came from and what it was. Prescription drugs only, nothing off the street, strictly guaranteed material. But then, sure, if I can sniff it or smoke it or swallow it, and I can pay for it, sure, I wouldn't turn it down."

"But . . . why?"

"Why?" He laughed. " 'Cause I love it. 'Cause it *feels* good. Same reason I want to be with you. Three things I love in this world. Music, getting high, and your pussy." He set the ice cream down on the floor abruptly and rolled on top of her. "Okay, girl. Get ready. Now you're in for it."

12

Nora's Story . . .

"It all started years ago, just after a series of articles I'd published on disarmament in a small international journal won me my first journalism prize and suddenly doors started opening for me. People who had always rejected my work began inviting me to write for them. But one of the best things that happened was I was invited to go on a four-week trip to China with a group of other professionals, and the man in question—let's call him Lew—was one of them.

"First, you have to understand I never wanted to get involved with a married man. It just happened. We met on the plane to China; our real lives were remote. What was his wife to me? He never even mentioned her name, only said sometimes in passing *my wife*, or *my son*. I paid no attention—I didn't want to marry him, I only wanted to love him for a month. I was really ready for an affair. It had been a long time since I'd been in love, and now a month-long trip in an exciting place like China— why not? I was up for it.

"The first instant I saw Lew I liked him. He was standing at the airport newsstand flipping through a book on China, so I figured he was on our trip. I liked the way he looked—not like your usual run of hard-nosed, hard-drinking macho journalists. He had a warm, open face, craggy but soft, and the kind of lean body I like, almost boyish. The way he was standing, one hip raised, looking down at the book from under a funny hat, he reminded me of that beautiful Donatello statue of David in Florence—you know the one? When I saw him getting on our plane I was very pleased.

"When we met, he seemed just as pleased as I was. The first thing he said to me when we were introduced was how much he'd admired my series. He started to tell me why, but people were lined up behind him waiting to get through to their seats, and we couldn't talk then. Later, in the Manila airport where we stopped to refuel, Lew and I got together immediately, as if by prearrangement. And when we boarded again I sat in the empty seat next to his.

"It was a long flight from Manila to Tokyo. We never stopped talking for a minute, but even so, we barely managed to get acquainted. There was so much to say, and believe me, no mention of wives. When we landed for the night in Tokyo, he and I slipped away from the group and went off sightseeing by ourselves. We wound up in the old part of town where the houses are made of paper, and the streets are too narrow for cars, and we saw geishas riding through the streets in sedan chairs. We sampled all the strange wonderful foods sold by sidewalk vendors, like eel and sweetbreads and delicious things broiled on skewers we never managed to identify. By the time we boarded the plane for China the next morning, it was pretty clear that we'd teamed up for the trip.

"Now, if you think our affair began then, you underestimate the Chinese. I understand it's different now, but in those days absolutely no hanky-panky was permitted. We were each assigned a roommate of our own sex. Even if our roommates had offered to let us switch for a night now and then, it wouldn't have worked. Our guides patrolled the hotel corridors and enforced lights out. And if we'd managed to defy the rules, the rest of our group would have disapproved. We were guests of the Chinese government, we were ambassadors, and we took our obligations seriously. Anyway, there was hardly a free moment; when we weren't traveling in our private bus or touring a commune or factory or school or hospital, we were having group meetings or meals. Lew and I always sat and walked and ate together. But nothing more than that. We were never alone for more than ten minutes at a time.

"Can you imagine what it felt like? Completely wrapped up in each other, together eighteen hours a day in that amazing place, exploring an entirely new universe together, but unable to touch. Now I know what it must have been like in the old days of chaperones, and the meaning of love at first sight. By the time the trip was half over, I was—we were both!—in a state of constant arousal. We'd meet in the morning before going down to breakfast to make sure we'd be able to sit together, and the erotic sparks would begin to fly. When we touched knees under the table we could have burned down the dining room.

"At that point in the trip, believe it or not, we had never spoken of an affair. Lew was married—and to a woman he hinted was rather sick. He had a teenage son he was greatly concerned about, and, as I told you, the last thing I wanted was to get involved in a messy affair with a married man. Not only for the principle but the hassle. Oh, if we had been able to manage it for the duration of the trip, that would have been fine with me, I think anything goes when you're away from home; but the Chinese saw to that. For the rest, I had no interest in planning to meet secretly after we returned to the States. I consider myself a free woman. Adultery offends me.

"But then we arrived in Beijing for a five-day stay, and suddenly everything changed. For the first time, we found ourselves with an hour alone together. Our hotel was directly across the street from a large park where swarms of people gathered at dawn to do their Tai Chi exercises—like joggers around Central Park. The first morning in Beijing, Lew knocked on my door at six, and we walked in the park for an hour before we had to be at breakfast. It was like a slow-motion dream, walking together alone in crowded Beijing Park surrounded by Tai Chi. That evening, as soon as dinner was over, we went back to the park and discovered that here and there among the families and old people on benches and kids singing or playing ball were couples walking along the paths holding hands or hiding among the shrubs. We'd discovered the local lovers' lane! When we were sure no one had followed us, Lew and I—strange, middle-aged Westerners with our outrageous Western clothes and enormous feet—found a bush of our own where we finally managed to kiss.

"From then on, each night after dinner we'd disappear into the park. We were both so wired after those weeks of not touching that our hands groping in the dark were enough for us.

"By the time we left Beijing a few days later, everything had changed between us. Now we talked constantly about us. I still insisted that we not see each other and ruin everything after we got home, but Lew was just as determined to change my mind.

"We had only one more opportunity for physical contact before the trip was over. It was on a spectacular overnight train ride across the Yellow River, through craggy mountains filled with caves in the heart of the Chinese continent. The train itself was a relic of European colonialism: four bunks to a compartment, with a lamp on the side table topped by a lacy pink, ruffled Victorian shade—a romantic anomaly. Lew and I used all our ingenuity planning out the details of that journey. We spent hours maneuvering to wind up in a compartment with the two other reporters we thought most likely to look the other way if we happened to spend part of the night in a single bunk. Even though crossing the heart of China by train in daylight was one of the high points of the trip, we couldn't wait until the day ended and night fell. Dinner seemed endless that night; the dining-car staff put on a special banquet just for our group, complete with talks and toasts, every word said twice, once in each language. I thought bedtime would never come. Eventually, though, the bunks came down, we all got into our beds, the lights went off.

"I was below Lew. As soon as it seemed to me that the men directly opposite us were asleep, I climbed up to Lew's bunk. With the others only feet away, ever so quietly we made love under the sheet, as we had in Beijing Park, with our hands. By then he knew exactly how to touch me—pretty rare in my experience. And he whispered the magic words at precisely the right moment."

"You mean *please? Thank you?*" quipped Rosemary.

Nora cocked her head and gave her sly laugh. "*I love you.* I'm still amazed at our recklessness, and our ability to fool ourselves—actually believing that the others didn't know what was going on right in front of them. And the risk! Just think if one of our guides had happened to look in on us, in bed together right there before The Press! Lesser breaches had created international incidents.

"Well, that was the last opportunity we had to touch in China. As the end of the trip approached, despite my hard-line position on married men, it seemed out of the question that we part forever without consummating that month-long passion. Finally, we agreed on a compromise: we would spend one night together after we hit the States before going home. All the way back across the ocean on that two-day plane ride we huddled together in our seats under an airline blanket and planned our strategy.

"As soon as we landed in San Francisco, where the group dispersed, we postponed our connecting flights home till the following day and checked immediately into a hotel, barely stopping to say good-bye to the twenty people who'd been our intimates, our family, for a month. At last, we were completely alone with a whole night before us."

Nora lit another cigarette and signaled the waiter for refills. The bar was beginning to fill up and the Cruvinet machine was working steadily.

"Do you think," continued Nora, "that after a night like that one we could have stayed apart? It would have been physically impossible. For a while we pretended that we would stop seeing each other after another week, or another. But soon it was obvious to both of us that we couldn't end the affair, not in a week or a month or a year." She sighed. "That was almost exactly five years ago."

"Five years!" exclaimed Rosemary.

All at once Nora's whole demeanor changed. The familiar half-sneer returned, and the gentle lilt in her voice gave way to resignation tinged with bitterness. "So now you see why I hate secrecy. Years of clandestine meetings, last-minute cancellations, lying, sneaking around, holding back, living apart—all because he believes in the so-called sanctity of the family. There's no question that I'm the one who makes him happy, the one he loves—we're not only lovers but colleagues, collaborators, best friends. But we can't make a life together because his wife clings to him. She's a parasite. And the son I gather is a mess too. And together they blackmail him into staying in a moribund marriage. Everyone is miserable."

Nora's shoulders slump as she rummages in her bag for a fresh pack of cigarettes; and suddenly Rosemary sees before her the embodiment of everything she's always feared when she thinks about divorce.

When the fresh drinks arrive, Rosemary can't resist observing, "As I hear it, your whole story only goes to prove what I've been saying all along. It's probably secrecy that's kept your affair alive all these years."

"That's ridiculous," sputtered Nora. "Secrecy has kept it crippled. It's passion that's kept it alive. Alive though limping."

"Crippled? You mean because you have a hard time managing to see each other?"

"Not at all. Except on weekends, when he's stuck with his family, he comes to my apartment almost every day—either at lunchtime or on his way home. And for your information, our passion hasn't diminished one bit over the years—so much for the hackneyed theory that time deadens passion."

"Every weekday for five years?"

Nora nods.

"And that's not enough for you?"

"Of course not!"

"What is it you want, then?" asks Rosemary, to whom the arrangement sounds ideal.

"Why, everything. To be able to mention his name, go to the theater with him, let him meet my friends. Share our lives and get on with our work. Is that so unreasonable? I'm thirty-eight years old. I'm tired of living half a life."

Rosemary stares at her. She too longs to have everything, preferably all in one. Who wouldn't like to be able to swim through air, breathe under water? But life has taught her to respect the boundaries between one thing and another, never to soak the gossamer veil of fantasy in the disintegrating wash of reality. She knows that pursuing one desire usually means endangering another, perhaps sacrificing a third. Better to add them cautiously, one at a time, to see if the mixture holds.

"Then if he did leave his wife eventually, you'd get married?"

"Married?" thunders Nora. Her face is like a wild animal leaping at its cage. "Married!" Her cheeks grow once more flushed, her eyes animated by glorious ruddy rage. Her lips pucker, her nostrils flare, her eyes glisten. Pulling herself up abruptly, shoulders square, bosom heaving, neck erect, chin doubled back on itself, she practically rises from her chair to repeat, "Haven't you heard a word I've said? I want a simple open relationship between equals so I can have some satisfaction and do my work. A life of imagination. Not marriage!"

"Sorry," whispers Rosemary.

Could a stranger—say, that rather chic bobbed bony brunette in the voluminous cape at the next table who seems to be listening in— possibly make any sense of this odd quarrel? Could anyone? From shared premises the passionate adversaries seem to draw opposite conclusions—like two marbles aimed at a single spot, coming together only to fly apart.

They agreed that marriage was anathema to passion—to solve which, one would eliminate marriage and the other would supplement it.

They agreed on the incomparable joys of sexual love—for the sake of which one longed to incorporate it into, but the other dared not burden it with, daily life.

They agreed on the futility of vows of lifelong fidelity—causing one to feel confined by them, the other to feel released from them.

They agreed that marriage was an economic and familial arrangement— which led one to excoriate it and the other to celebrate it.

They agreed that family life promoted mutual dependency—deemed infantilizing by one, maturing by the other.

"How can you mature when you're cooped up with children for your most productive years?" interrupted Nora, at the end of her patience.

"How can you *not* mature when you have to put others' needs before your own?" returned Rosemary so loudly that a balding man at the next table turned his back to the pair, rattling his *Journal* in protest.

"I'm talking about the death of *passion.*"

"Passion!" spat out Rosemary. "When other people's lives depend on you, passion may be a luxury you can't afford."

To which Nora smiled and crossed her arms to rest her case.

Harold was in the bathroom counting out his cash. Mrs. Scaggs had left, and now he was adding several thousand dollars to his secret stash, amassing funds as fast as he safely could for his next meeting with Angus Bacon, a financial genius he'd met at a party at the Vineyard who had undertaken to advise him.

After years of dull or deleterious investments, including two disallowed tax shelters and one failed bank, he'd finally got smart. Under Bacon's imaginative guidance and with the help of certain books available to anyone, like *How to Prepare for the Coming Crash*, *Tax Shelters for the People*, and *The Pros and Cons of Swiss Banks*, he was finally adopting a rational plan. To start with, in place of the pot-luck money-market accounts and mutual funds he'd bought when *Terror!* unexpectedly began to climb the best-seller list, he was preparing to divide his assets between the only truly safe investment, gold bullion to bury on the Vineyard property, and a numbered Swiss account and Bacon's winning speculations.

The problem was, where to keep the money in the meantime so Rosemary wouldn't find out. Bacon advised dealing strictly in cash and had told him how to withdraw small enough sums from his accounts to pass unnoticed. For though Harold wouldn't think of making an important decision without consulting his wife, wouldn't publish a word she hadn't read (as he freely told the world on his dedication page), he was no longer willing to discuss finances with her. Not only because to her the ideal investment was the savings account, but because she had taken an immediate and intense dislike to Bacon. A full decade after their sudden elevation to prosperity, she still liked to pretend they were just getting by and never responded to money talk without irritation. Even clothes, which she couldn't help but love and wear with flair, she could not buy without spasms of indecision when they cost more than she deemed they should.

At first, he thought she might be jealous of his success, but now he thought it more a matter of liberal guilt. Not that she didn't appreciate their opulent apartment and their beach house at the Vineyard and the excellent schools; but her enjoyment seemed exactly balanced by her discomfort. He suspected that this was the reason she insisted on working, though it was obvious to him that teaching math at Gotham Community College took far more time and attention than she had to spare, time and energy she could better have spent at home. But that was Rosemary—protector and coach for every insecure female math student in the school, champion of returning students' rights, wet nurse to every pregnant or miserable girl who stumbled into Calculus 125. And for a pittance. As long as she insisted on her job, he urged her at least to have Mrs. Scaggs come in every day, but she refused, claiming the family would benefit from taking turns at chores.

Harold taps the bills into a neat, even pile. At first he had stored the money in empty tape boxes among his jazz collection; but the boxes were too small and no longer felt safe. Any day Spider might go through his tapes looking for something, or one of Daisy's boyfriends might get interested in jazz or opera, and then? Locked up in his office, the money would not be safe. He supposed he could rent a safe deposit box to keep it in, but after those shaky few months with some Texas CDs, he no longer trusted banks. And suppose he should die? When he'd gone through the contents of his father's box after the final heart attack, he had come across two pictures of Kaye Wokowski, his father's longtime secretary, hidden at the bottom. He did not suspect until many months after the funeral that they'd been lovers, and even then, it seemed unlikely. His straitlaced, quiet, Midwestern father? Still, he'd somehow known to slip the photos into his pocket while his distraught mother was blowing her nose. (He, at least, would never be caught out like that. All suspect photos were stashed in the college yearbooks in his office, as if Lois or Barbara meant no more to him than any other former student, and Pippa's picture smiled out from the jacket of one of her books.)

For the time being he seals the bills in two envelopes, rolls them tight, and hides the money back inside the secret chambers of the antique lamps.

All Daisy's feeling is concentrated in those two points of erectile tissue, her nipples. They have been compared to rosebuds, to cherries, but to her they are nothing like these. If they are like anything other than themselves, they are like the inside of her navel or the tender bottoms of her feet. She wants him to caress, kiss, suck, perhaps even bite her nipples. She longs for his fingers, his lips . . . *there*. She wants him to find her breasts the center of the universe until the feeling is diffused upward and downward through her entire self. She thinks he would like it too—aren't men said to worship breasts?

But she can't bring herself to ask. What words can she say? As soon as she tentatively formulates a phrase, he smothers it in a kiss. Her body, tense, tender, yielding, still hopes. She loads his fingers with messages as their lips meet, but he doesn't read her, nor can she bring herself to guide his head.

Finally she conceives a plan. She will maneuver his hand beneath the sheet where the hard nipple will shout its invitation. Her blood pulses through her temples as she prepares to execute the willful, lustful act, so much more difficult for her than, say, to take his penis in her hand or guide it inside her. Why? Because every time she touches his skin and organs it's for his pleasure, but wishing him to touch her skin and organs is for her own. Easier, she thinks, to place his penis than his hand between her legs, though at this moment the hand is what she most desires: his mouth on her nipple, his hand between her legs.

This is her fantasy of marriage: her wedding night, a night of confession and consummation, when she can freely guide her husband's lips and hands to all the secret places of desire.

"Well, so do I," insists Rosemary, half sorry she asked for the whipped cream. "Who doesn't want everything? But you seem to think that just because I'm married, just because everything doesn't come wrapped up in one neat package, I should have to settle for less."

"It isn't less I'm talking about," says Nora. "It's more."

Rosemary opens her arms. "I have my family, work, security, love—what more is there?"

Nora narrows her eyes and voice to deliver the coup. "Freedom." The great god of refusal, whom she's worshiped all her life, to whom she has made all her offerings, all her sacrifices: *freedom*. For freedom she refuses to be bought or sold, coddled or kept. To freedom she gave her firstborn, aborting herself on her wedding day. For freedom she had her tubes tied, exorcising temptation. In freedom she's managed to create a proud if difficult life for herself, risky and brave. And for the joys of freedom she is willing if necessary to endure loneliness, slights, slander, even scorn— but not without a fight.

"Freedom to do what?" asks Rosemary. "I do everything I want. More than I want. Harold and I are each so busy that, between our work and our kids and everything else, we hardly see each other. What couple could be freer than *that*? Really, Nora, you seem to think I suffer by being married. But actually, marriage frees me. I refuse to give up anything that matters to me."

Nora knows the price of Rosemary's so-called everything. As Camus says in a passage Nora has typed and taped to her wall, "Freedom is the right not to lie." She leans forward, trying to temper her contempt as she asks, "And integrity?"

"Ah, integrity. It's fine for you to talk about freedom and integrity, you, with no one to answer to but yourself. But it's different when other people have to suffer whenever you feel like exercising your so-called freedom."

"Like who?"

"Like—okay, let's forget about the mothers, whom you seem to expect to make all the sacrifices. Let's just talk about the kids. No matter what the parents do, the children hardly deserve to have their homes disappear from under them and their families break up whenever someone happens to fall in love!"

"The kids! You're not going to bring *them* up again! I thought that line went out with Anna Karenina," snaps Nora, lighting another cigarette.

Rosemary catches the combat in Nora's words. Why? Why, she wonders, if marriage was so terrible, did married people turn bitter only after they split up? Why was single Nora the bitter one, while she, Rosemary, hoped to stay married to Harold for the rest of her life? Who was Nora, anyway, to speak of marriage, having tried it exactly once, ages ago, for less than a year? As if the perpetuation of the species, life's hidden agenda, could be left to the quirks of attraction or the lies of romance. Of course, the final argument, the wild card, the unanswerable reason for staying married was the children. The next generation.

"But I have to bring them up, don't you see?" says Rosemary, sounding an urgent note approaching entreaty. "Children are at the heart of this. And they're innocent."

The Noise . . .

Daisy was suddenly aware of an unearthly noise crouching at the bottom of her throat, waiting to emerge into the room and betray her shame. Though she'd never heard it, she knew it would be a sound she couldn't stand to hear. It lay inside preparing to leap out and humiliate her at the last minute, like her bladder when she was a small child, threatening to let go before the entire world. Those shameful, uncontrollable functions. Hips longing to move; the awful animal howl. Abruptly she concentrated all her attention on stopping the noise before it began, before Rap could see what a wild, shameful, uncontrolled creature she was.

After a great effort, finally she knew she was safe; the sound along with something else had passed. No point going on. Anyway, it was time to get up and dress: her mother would be expecting her for dinner; Rap's father would eventually come home.

Letting her stand-in, her stunt girl, march on stage and cry out while she took a break and safely watched them do it, she moaned a low, breathless moan, thrashing her head and arms back and forth as a signal to Rap that he was free to finish. How did she know? She just knew: better these artificial cries she could control than the real one waiting to humiliate her before this stranger and herself.

When he was done, Rap gave her a long passionate squeeze that rearranged all the organs in her body; then he picked up the carton of Rocky Road, now a melted multicolored swirling goop, and handed her back her spoon.

Nora and Rosemary, eyes blazing and voices raised, are oblivious of the after-work crowd now filling the bar. At the smaller tables in the larger room, waiters have already begun to recite tonight's unlisted specials to early diners. Just beyond the windows of the heated terrace a dry snow, lit by streetlights, falls like a scrim, shielding the actors inside from the notice of pedestrians rushing home.

NORA: If you had your way, you'd condemn everyone to the bondage of the past. People should only be together because they want to be.

ROSEMARY: But if they happen to want to stay married for any reasons besides romance, you won't allow it.

NORA: Nonsense. You can't stop people from being together if they want. But if marriage were abolished, at least they wouldn't be punished for it. They'd be free to choose.

ROSEMARY: If marriage were abolished people would bootleg it. If it didn't exist they'd invent it. Look at them, marrying and remarrying in droves. It's what people want, it seems to satisfy some ardent need.

NORA: Sure, like the need for tranquilizers or alcohol. In a better world they wouldn't need it.

A momentary hush cloaks the room as a flaming platter is borne aloft to a nearby table, and it suddenly strikes Rosemary that beneath Nora's tough exterior lurks the soul of a dreamer. Tenacious, hardheaded Nora Kennedy is a closet utopian masquerading as cynic, a visionary singing the song of realpolitik. "Do you really think," says Rosemary, trying to soften her question, "the world is going to change according to plan if certain people just decide to change it?"

"Don't you?" asks Nora, who finds it frankly quite unthinkable that her efforts to change the world are doomed to fail. Opposing madness, murder, corruption is what makes her life not only tenable but joyous. Not that she can't see as well as anyone how chancy are the results, she who spends her days watching plowshares turn into bombs. But her pride demands that the worse things get, the harder she try. "It's certainly worth a try."

"Really, Nora, you're such a romantic."

"*I'm* romantic? *You're* the romantic!"

A new waiter, scrubbed and shorn, approaches their table and asks if they'd like to see the dinner menu.

"Dinner! My God, I'm late!" cries Rosemary, leaping up. "Everyone's probably home waiting for me." She checks her watch and groans. "And I have all these papers to grade."

"Do you really have to go? Too bad," moans scrappy Nora, always quickened by controversy. "This conversation is just getting good."

"We can meet again next week," offers Rosemary, donning her coat and gathering up her briefcase. She too is eager for another chance to make herself understood. She was not, after all, in favor of marriage the way Nora was against it, on principle. Her life was simply something she wore like a favorite old coat. It served her well enough season after season; and if it was a garment somewhat out of fashion, still it was comfortable, pleasingly familiar, one with which she was prepared to make do for as many seasons as it lasted. And if one day perhaps it gave out, at that time she would reluctantly, but, she trusts, graciously, replace it with another one which she hoped would suit her as well and last as long.

Nora comes round the table and embraces Rosemary. Like dancing, their quarrel leaves both of them high and breathless. Having each once rescued herself from the claws of unconscious choice and the summary judgment of men, suddenly in one another's presence each sees the other as the court in which she must justify herself. That night, each will lie awake, mind racing, till after three. If love is ninety percent attention, as Rosemary is fond of saying, you might almost say they are falling in love.

While the adversaries embrace, the waiter writes out their check and holds up five fingers to the captain.

Beached

A LESSON FOR BABY

What is milk. Milk is a mouth. What is a mouth.
Sweet. What is sweet. Baby.
A lesson for baby.
What is a mixture. Good all the time.
Who is good all the time. I wonder.
A lesson for baby.
What is a melon. A little round.
Who is a little round. Baby.
Sweetly Sweetly sweetly sweetly.
In me baby baby baby
Smiling for me tenderly tenderly.
Tenderly sweetly baby baby.
Tenderly tenderly tenderly tenderly.

—GERTRUDE STEIN

13

AFTER HER BREASTS began to swell in pregnancy, each morning when Harold left for work Rosemary stripped before the bedroom mirror. Her surprise turned quickly to pleasure as she lingered to inspect and admire those full, round, voluptuous orbs she had always considered small in the great divide between the buxom and the flat. Startling and volatile, they grew larger every day. For the first time in her life she dared to wear dresses designed to show them off. A roll of heavy, multicolored striped silk that had long stood in her closet, too gorgeous to cut, finally went to the dressmaker accompanied by a sketch of a cloudlike dress, calf-length and flowing, distinguished by great puffed sleeves and a deeply plunging neckline. She took delight in the smooth white bulges above her maternity bras and the deep new recess between her breasts into which, for the first time, her gold locket settled. (And so it should, for though it had once contained a picture of her mother and later a picture of her husband, henceforth it would hold a picture of her laughing child, whose claim to her breasts was unassailable.) The startling sight of her naked, gravid body with its newly glistening surfaces aroused her lust; exploring its unfamiliar contours with her hands, she felt such pleasure as she had felt before only at the hands of certain lovers.

In labor she shed all vanity. Her body was a dynamo of shattering power, a heaving, grunting, shuddering conduit through which forces beyond her will or understanding did their immense, foretold work. Even after the violence, when the small, squalling animal that emerged from inside her had been snipped off and laid in her arms, the forces possessing her continued to work. Not until they shook her again, squeezing the afterbirth out of her womb with powerful contractions, did she enter that deep restorative sleep wherein she could try to repossess her body, now forever transformed. Waking, she ran her hands inquiringly over her torso, once more unfamiliar, and was thrilled to find an almost flat stomach and mountainous breasts. Breasts so firm and full the nipples barely protruded. She rang quickly for the nurse. "Where's my baby?"

When her infant's mouth, perfectly matched in size, color, shape to the aureolas of her engorged mammaries, clamped onto her nipple to suck out the first drops of that deep, lemon-yellow fluid colostrum, rich in protein and antibodies and mysterious as her baby's eyes, she felt her womb contract in sudden, piercing waves—too painful for pleasure, too ecstatic for pain. In those first moments, each sucking contraction of her baby's lips was matched by an equal and opposite contraction deep in her womb, electric ripples shooting through her wired body, orgasmic yet unbearable, as if a giant penis were endlessly thrusting home. With each contraction of her womb she winced with pain and pleasure until the steady rhythm of her infant's sucking lulled her, and her body was becalmed.

She worried only that the billowing breast would smother the child whose breathing apparatus seemed buried in flesh. Modesty and shame, in which she had always clothed herself, no longer fit. With the fingers of her left hand she pressed back the white flesh surrounding the aureola and thrust the nipple deeper inside. (Soon she'd get the hang of it; like sex, it took technique.)

When her baby's sucking slackened, she wrapped her fingers tenderly around the smooth mini-arm that clutched at her hair and cheeks, then slid one hand beneath the small rump nestling in her lap and swiveled the baby around to the other breast. As the lips approached her nipple, again she felt the strange, thrilling clutch of her womb.

Half an hour later the round baby belly is full, and a satiated sigh passes across first one, then the other face. Fingers relax, mouths shudder and sigh, the nipple slips out of the lax lips, leaving a thin trickle of what can only be milk seeping down the tiny chin.

Then gradually the stomach empties, the diaper fills, the baby screws up its face into a tight red shrieking knot, milk surges again into the ready breasts, the womb contracts—and once more the two beings merge until both sets of eyelids flutter closed; and sleep, with its haze of contentment, releases mother and child, both dreaming the birth of love.

14

In the beginning was the fall.

But who started it? This question is regularly dragged out of the closet, sniffed, and aired in the Streeter household, like hand-me-downs come spring and fall, whenever the quarrel goes back to first things. By now Rosemary and Harold have grown so deeply attached to their own versions of Genesis, each adamantly insisting that the other was the first to fall, that each one's automatic denial seems a gratuitous affront. Over the years so much bitterness has collected in the seams of these old clothes with each airing that husband and wife are increasingly reluctant to bring them out; nevertheless, each serious quarrel leads back to that primal one.

One thing is sure: she at least never planned to be unfaithful. (Neither did he, if we, like him, discount what happens with strangers out of town.) They married for love, assuming they would be faithful to each other for the length of their marriage, which they vaguely hoped would last till their deaths. Young and inexperienced, they thought of the future as of the stars—mysterious, inconceivably distant, benevolent, steady, visible only under certain conditions. If she imagined it at all, she pictured the future arriving in the guise of her parents' lives—only different, of course. She and Harold would perhaps have children, then a larger apartment, absorbing jobs, adventurous vacations, money enough; the clothes would all be forever changing, and in time, no doubt, both of them would turn gray.

Others, they acknowledged with the smug smiles of newlyweds, might go bobbing along in the choppy seas of open marriage or let themselves be beached on the shifting shores of wait-and-see; but *they* understood that love was a matter of will. Chemistry? Of course. Economics? Naturally. But underneath everything, will. Blind, free, unreasoning, ungrudging, unconditional, voluntary will.

This early, repeated conversation took place rarely in bed or at the table, but rather on the living room sofa of their first apartment, with wine and French bread, a ripe cheese, and some juicy tropical fruit spread out before them on the cocktail table, so they could kiss occasionally while they ate and talked of love. Everything at once. How impatient they were.

And how delighted with their discovery. How satisfied. Will explained everything—passion, palpitations, hesitations—and allowed everything, all their audacious claims. Will: what the old books called surrender and the new ones called commitment. Including desire, of course, said Harold. And trust, added Rosemary. They agreed that romance, ephemeral and shaky, was not what they had in mind. They meant something firmer, something finer, something that depended, ultimately, on nothing but themselves, the only creatures in the world they could truly trust.

And so they married. For love. Assuming they would be faithful forever.

But someone started it. Who?

Harold traces his wife's betrayal all the way back to the eve of their wedding when Rosemary heaved one of her monumental sighs and asked out of nowhere, "What will you do if you come home one night and find me in bed with another man?"

"Is that what you think will happen?" said Harold, a romantic, feeling his stomach sink under the sudden threat of doom.

"No, no, no!" she insisted, regretting the question as soon as it was out. It was meant neither to wound, warn, cajole, nor threaten; it was theoretical, hypothetical—he was taking it the wrong way. The point was, she didn't know what would happen. In her single days, she had seldom forgone an adventure; what if "the paper," as her friends called marriage, should fail to transform her from one sort of person to another? For some reason, love, which she'd never before doubted was a matter of will, suddenly appeared to her as a powerful outside force, a gale that could swoop down without warning and demolish all one's resolutions. Or an illness for which there was no known cure but to wait it out. Or a deep pit one carelessly stumbled into. Not an action undertaken willingly but a passion passively suffered.

Or perhaps her question was a last-ditch warning, a rebellious act unwittingly but coyly intended to put her fiancé on notice that, married or not, she was not to be taken for granted. If so, it had backfired. The time for coyness was over; to banish coyness and its entire retinue of petty retainers was at the heart of her very desire to marry. She wanted to stretch out on the luxurious bed of matrimony, relax at last, lean back, sink deep into the comfy cushion of trust. With her ice-blue lace wedding dress laid out on the bed and a case of good champagne on ice, what could have possessed her to ask such a harsh and untimely question, particularly when she longed for fidelity and worried only about what she would do if *he* should begin to stray? "I'm sure it won't happen; I was only asking *what if?*"

Harold sprinkled the hurtful question with camphor, labeled it, and buried it at the bottom of the grievance chest.

On her side, Rosemary's counterconviction that Harold did it first was grounded not only on hypothetical questions or general principles (who didn't know the opportunities that fan out before a journalist with the merest flick of his pen?); she believed she had hard evidence. If called upon, she could evoke the precise moment his treachery was revealed to her. Even now she can describe exactly what sweaters they were wearing, which sycamores had put out the first buds, what song was blaring from the cars cruising past the playground that Saturday morning in early spring when Rosemary and Harold sat on a park bench watching two-year-old Daisy attempting the small jungle gym. "Tell me, Rosemary," queried Harold, allowing his attention to slip from Daisy to the sex life of college girls, a subject he had recently broached more than once. "*You* slept around in college; what does a young woman see in an older man?"

In that instant Rosemary's skin was scalded by consciousness. Though to this day Harold too insists that his curiosity was merely hypothetical, Rosemary is convinced she knows better. Such a question as his was far too specific to be free of fact. Seeing innocent Daisy potentially fatherless even as she risked the unknown with every step, tears welled up in Rosemary's eyes. Harold, her heart called out, look what you're doing to us! But Harold folded his arms over his chest, silently denying everything, and she turned away before he could see the first anguished tear slip down her cheek.

15

In the Beginning . . .

Rosemary rubbed more lotion on her skin and watched plump little Daisy laboriously fill her pail to transport sand from one side of their blanket to another. As futile as her summer. With Harold on assignment in Mexico and Daisy barely three, everyone thought Rosemary ought to be content, even grateful for the chance to spend the summer at the shore instead of sweltering back in the city. Indeed, she was ashamed to complain. The four other adults, and their children, with whom she shared the small clapboard beach house in the rundown section of New Hampton Cove, could hardly be nicer: it was into Rosemary's eyes that Priscilla's husband, Robert, reported the news from the city when he arrived on the 5:48 on Fridays, as if she were the one true urbanite among them. Priscilla and Robert's children, Nan and Billy, though older than Daisy, were tender companions for her child. Robert's old college roommate Seymour, and his lover, Chet, adopted the conceit that Rosemary was their fag hag, their moll, their true love, their beard, and encouraged a giddy three-way flirtation. And even Priscilla, whose life was a slow disapproving burn, fussed over Rosemary as if she were another child, appreciating her creative salads and desserts. Leaving their distant city lives packed away like winter boots, the householders worked at fun, silently agreeing to think no further ahead than the weekend coming up. Eager to intensify their lives by pooling them, anxious to recapture the carefree summers of their youth (for they were now all past twenty-five and adulthood had silently overtaken them), they thought they could contain their ragged lives for a season in a neat summer envelope.

But Rosemary was not content. In the sultry salt air surrounded by half-naked bodies, with nothing to do but daydream and finger old wounds, how could she be? The house she lived in was full of lovers—clandestine and complicated—and the beach with its whining families and bitter wives sent her restlessly searching for someone to spark her fantasies. Poised between guilt and desire, wherever she was she wanted to be elsewhere; whatever she did she dreamed of doing something else.

Still, she did not plan an affair. Aside from the practical impediments imposed by her shadow, Daisy, and by sharing a house with her husband's closest friends, she liked to consider herself above affairs, pointless little couplings that, if she had one, would only expose her imperfect resolve. Even after she discovered the Swallows' tall piano player Woody Blake she thought herself safe; otherwise she would have had to acknowledge the supremacy of desire, that pitiless pulse that made her hands damp and her breath short and directed her feet to the Swallows every day, ostensibly for real Italian espresso.

She spread the lotion in long slow strokes, first on her shoulders, then on her arms and legs, prolonging the feel of fingers on flesh. "Me too," said Daisy, squatting down on the blanket beside her mother. Whatever Rosemary did, Daisy wanted to do. Put oil on her skin, polish on her nails, eat olives, go to bed at midnight.

"Okay, a little bit." Rosemary coated the pudgy arms with lotion and asked opportunely, "You getting ready to go to the Swallows?"

Daisy pouted. "No."

"You don't have to come with me, you know. Priscilla will watch you. You can stay and play with Nan and Billy. Wouldn't you like that?"

Daisy shook her head.

Rosemary was not surprised. "Well then, if you come now you can use the candy machine. Think about what kind of candy you'd like."

"Jelly beans!" shouted Daisy, popping up on her plump legs. She started up the beach, swinging her pail.

Of course it would be jelly beans. She always chose jelly beans. But every day Rosemary asked her to reconsider because she longed to have her daughter know that life held other possibilities.

Rosemary dropped her sandals into her straw bag and wrapped a skirt around her waist. *People in bare feet or bathing suits will not be admitted to the dining room*, said a sign in the Swallows window. She decided to leave her blanket behind, knowing they'd be back soon enough. Probably too soon. She shook out her sandy hair, now bleached by the sun to almost the exact shade of gold as her tanned skin, tied up her straps, and started off after Daisy.

. . .

Through the open doors of the terrace Rosemary could see inside to where Woody Blake sat bent over the keyboard, his dark forelock bobbing over his eyes as his left hand kept the beat and his right wove sweet arpeggios in the higher registers. Jazz, pop, sometimes Chopin. In the two weeks she'd been coming here she'd worked up quite a case over him, considering they'd not yet spoken. As he caressed the keys, she imagined his fingers, expert and swift, moving down her spine and up the inner surface of her thighs.

Daisy pressed her knees and thighs to the flagstone floor and, pulling her heels back to her dotted swimsuit, leaned forward, hoping to confine her body, limbs and all, to the single irregular flagstone on which she sat surrounded by all her possessions. An ant scurrying past to a neighboring pinkish stone tried to tempt her out of her cell, but Daisy clung to her heels, resisting. That was his house, this was hers. Above her, her mother's long legs, which stretched from the blue chair on which she sat to the red one she had positioned opposite her, formed a partial protective roof for Daisy, leaving her striped half in sunlight, half in shade. If her mother would move her legs a tiny bit over—just there!—the shade would enclose her like a real roof. Then, with her mother's sandals for one wall, her stones and doggie for another, her pail for a window, shovel for a door . . .

"Daisy! You're tickling me!" cried Rosemary, jerking her legs suddenly and placing her bare feet firmly on the floor. She never sat in the bar but always outside on the terrace where no one could guess why she came and Daisy could play on the sunny floor. For all anyone knew, she might have been a budding pianist herself, or a clam freak—for if she came late in the day she ordered clams and white wine, as if she were just out of college traveling down the coast of Italy, suddenly free and seething with desire.

Daisy's lips puckered, poised on the verge. It was a shock to see anew that her mother's legs belonged to her mother. Like her mother's hand, in which she curled her own as they walked side by side along the beach, or her mother's strong arms that held her afloat in the cold blue water or carried her seated on her hip when her own legs buckled. Like her mother's lips that pressed her neck with tickles and spread into rippling smiles when she was pleased but pursed like the maws of ferocious beasts when she was angry. Or her mother's eyes that looked at others besides herself. People told her mother, Daisy has your eyes exactly, and you two have the same laugh. But Daisy was coming to learn that they were not the same eyes, the same laugh.

Rosemary stroked Daisy's arm and searched for a worthy distraction to avert the impending crisis. On an impulse she wrote a song request on the back of her cocktail napkin and held it out to Daisy. "There are some peanuts on the table in there. Why don't you go take some, and on the way back give this note to the piano player for me, okay?"

Daisy looked at her mother, then at the strange dark room beyond the glass doors, then at the napkin, and clung to her spot on the floor.

"You won't? Not even for peanuts?" Rosemary called over the waiter, ordered another espresso, and casually sent off the note. It was an innocent enough request, but the way her pulse beat as she watched the waiter's progress betrayed her intentions. Hers was not a generation that worshiped virginity or disapproved of sex. Raised after the war, hers was a generation that valued daring, a generation of women who, armed with the pill, secretly sowed their wild oats like men before settling down. Self-styled free spirit, like thousands of others, she had run off to Europe that summer after college, with her graduation money and her hoarded earnings, to learn about "life." On the night train from Naples to Geneva, she had attached herself to a young stonemason traveling north to seek work and taken him to her bed. In Venice, knowing only what she felt in her heart and saw with her eyes, she had ignored the warnings about Italian men and lingered for two entire weeks—forgoing Florence!—to make passionate love with her devoted dark-eyed guide. In Paris, she had teamed up with two painters, one Parisian, one Basque, who lived in her pension; for a week and a half, alternating nights, they had fervently dwelt on their "predicament" until it was time for her plane to leave. Only after she had come back home, found a lucky job in publishing, met the savior of her dreams (handsome, gracious, promising), and given birth did she bury that hungry, seething part of her.

Woody Blake held a long trill while he took the note from the waiter, then drank from the tall blue glass he kept on top of the piano. Rosemary's anxious longings sprouted around the room like mushrooms after a heavy rain as the trill gradually became "Tonight."

Daisy saw two walls of her house disintegrate as Rosemary slipped her feet into her sandals. Daisy's lower lip trembled, her brows rose, and tears splashed from her eyes. She let out a wail: The house! The house!

"Sweetheart! Don't cry!" cried Rosemary. She swept her pen and sunglasses into her bag and stood up. Daisy clasped her tightly at the knees and squeezed. "Come on, sweetie, let go. We're going back to the beach now. Pick up your things while I pay the check. Let go now." She unhooked Daisy's fingers one at a time and gently pulled away. Daisy began dropping the remaining walls of her house—her shoes, doggie, shovel—into the red pail.

"Leaving so fast?" said Woody Blake as Rosemary walked slowly by the piano on her way out. "What's your name?"

"I'm Rosemary. And this is Daisy."

Daisy swiveled herself around Rosemary's leg to hide. Woody switched to another key and played "Rose Marie" and "Daisy, Daisy" in quick succession. Rosemary laughed as Daisy began to push her toward the door.

"Do you have to go?" asked Woody.

"I promised her we'd go back to the beach before dinner."

"Which beach?"

"Just the little beach at the corner of our street, Emory Lane."

He did a few bars of "Memory Lane" and said, "A perfect place to catch the meteor shower that starts tomorrow. Will you be there for it?"

"What is it? Where?"

"It's all over the sky after dark. How about I meet you down at your beach after work, okay?"

She was ashamed of how clearly he had understood her. "Okay," she said recklessly, for the next day was Friday and the men were coming out from the city. "If I can." Promising herself she could always change her mind. But she knew from the feeling inside her that it was already too late, she would not change her mind. Harold should never have left her alone for the summer in a house full of couples where nothing ever happened from one weekend to the next, where from Monday to Friday the future like the past whistled across the beach coating those who remained with a fine dry powder of discontent, where only the children, whose desires reached no further than sundown and for whom bed, ocean, and sand encompassed the universe, could rush headlong into a Monday morning (forgetting again and letting the screen door slam) as if any day held all the promise of life itself.

Seymour, dressed in clean black chinos and a satin-piped white cowboy shirt, was humming a Cole Porter tune as he mixed martinis in an iced pitcher. Friday—at last! All day the air was charged with excitement: the men were coming out on the 5:48. Since breakfast, all up and down the block stores of food had been laid in; bottles of beer and wine were squeezed into packed refrigerators; bedrooms had been swept clean of sand and children made to pick up their toys; the mothers, anticipating guests or sex, were shampooing their hair and dressing up.

Rosemary looked up from where she was arranging crackers around the perimeter of the largest tray and justified her plan by noting for the first time the added hollowness of weekends. Chet was coming back to Seymour, Robert to Priscilla, another couple, lovers, had been invited out for the weekend, but no one was coming back to her. Like the center of the tray she now left free for the pâté, cheese, or other delicacy Robert would be bringing for a treat, the weekends held for her more promise than fulfillment. She wiped her brow with the back of her hand. "I'm going up to get dressed now, Seymour."

Seymour turned off the water and lifted the ice tray from the sink. "Do me a favor? Wear the white dress with the gathers—you know the one. I'll find you an outrageous flower, maybe a zinnia, to wear in your hair."

Gratefully she kissed Seymour on the cheek. A quiet, bespectacled young man of slight stature and boyish charm, he provoked the maternal in Rosemary, despite their flirtatious pretensions. "Here," she said. "Let me open the freezer for you. I'd hate to see you spill any of Priscilla's frozen mousse."

"So that's what's in there. Sin. Raspberry, I take it, a well-known aphrodisiac. Smart woman."

Daisy stared at the outline of bikini etched in negative across her mother's bare skin. She peered down her own sunsuit to compare, but all she saw was the white skin inside, stretched over her smooth protruding self.

"You want to shower with me?" asked Rosemary.

"Shower!" cried Daisy, stepping quickly out of her sunsuit, leaving her clothes in a heap on the floor.

Rosemary wrapped each of them in a terry robe. "Come on then."

The water trickled down in a thin, irregular stream. Rosemary stepped aside to let her daughter get wet. Daisy giggled as Rosemary bent to soap the small body with a singsong naming of parts; then she reached up to touch her mother's white swinging breasts.

"Don't, sweetie." Quickly Rosemary stood up. "Now get under the water and rinse off before it turns cold."

It was a ramshackle house, half a century old, that had let itself go. The roof leaked badly when it rained, the furniture smelled of mildew, the freezer built up frost in a week, the fuses kept blowing, and there was never enough hot water. But the house was set on a decent street adjacent to a not unfashionable beach, enabling them to play the parts they wanted for the summer. The rent was a bargain for the area, and there was a screened-in sleeping porch, a roomy kitchen, and enough bedrooms for Priscilla's dream collection.

"Nan says Daddy's coming back tonight," said Daisy as Rosemary patted her with a towel.

"Oh no, darling. Nan and Billy's daddy is coming; Robert is coming. But your daddy won't be here for quite a while."

"When?"

"I told you. Another month or so."

"Can Daddy shower with us too?"

"Of course he can."

"Go get him."

"I told you. He's in Mexico. He won't be back for a month."

Daisy's face clouded over. "I want Daddy to shower with us *now*."

Rosemary felt the familiar stab of pain, then of anger. What good was his glamorous job if it took him away from her? It got harder and harder to remember that Harold's working as a stringer for *Time* magazine had once seemed half a reason to marry him, had promised an adventurous life to come, when now all she felt was abandoned.

"He can't come now. He's in Mexico. But if you want, after dinner we can write him a letter. You tell me what you want to say to him and I'll write it down. Okay? Right now, though, we have to hurry and get dressed so we can be all ready when everyone gets here."

"Don't want to get dressed," pouted Daisy, wriggling out of the towel and tearing out of the bathroom.

After Rosemary vigorously toweled her hair, she heard Seymour playing a fanfare on his clarinet. The car had arrived, then; Robert and Chet would be wanting to use the shower. She went down to her room to put on the white dress. She dabbed perfume on her wrists and between her breasts just as if her husband hadn't gone off for the summer leaving her alone, and fastened around her neck a string of bright amber-colored beads.

. . .

She sits on the low wall separating the street from the beach, sets down her tumbler of chablis, and looks up. The sky is spectacular, with so much stardust that the planets themselves seem to glow less brightly, and the whitecaps on the water are as clear to the eye as to the ear. Rosemary listens to the whisper of the sea but is not much interested in the stars. She sips her wine and sighs. The truth is, one night feels like the next to her as she marks time till her husband returns, when she will begin to mark time till he leaves again.

"Rosemary?"

She starts up so suddenly she sloshes wine on her leg.

"Is that you?" Looming over the wall, Woody sits down beside her. She brushes off her skirt and hopes there will be no stain. "Hi," he says. "You made it. I wasn't sure you would. I'm really glad." He slips his arm around her waist. "Well—are you ready for the big shower?"

Rosemary looks up to check the sky. She knows her desires, as she has always known, at the first touch; the difference, now that she's married, is that she can dispense with all pretense. There's no reason to hesitate, no time to be coy: the summer is already mostly over. "Yes," she says, leaning into Woody's arm with relief. "I'm ready. Bring it on."

"You sure you want to do that? Remember how easily you burn," said Priscilla, frowning, as Rosemary untied the straps of her top and rolled the thin cloth down to her nipples. Priscilla was a squat fastidious woman with slow ways, a thin, high voice, and only a pair of glittering eyes to belie the sluggish metabolism that made her seem dumpy and prissy beyond her two childbirths and thirty years.

Rosemary wished Priscilla would come out and admit that she was concerned not about Rosemary's skin but about her own. "Don't worry. I put on plenty of lotion." Rosemary recognized that even with the straps tied Priscilla was embarrassed by Rosemary's spare Italian suit, thinking it too skimpy. As she thought Rosemary's skirts too short and her hours too erratic and her eyes too restless for a married woman—especially a woman married to her husband's oldest friend. Rosemary wished Priscilla would say it straight out to her face instead of by insinuation and innuendo, as if she were not her friend at all but her child.

"But what if you have to jump up suddenly and grab Daisy, then what will you do?" Priscilla persisted.

"Oh, come on, Priscilla," said Rosemary, "you think no one on this beach has seen a breast before?"

Breasts were definitely on Priscilla's mind. That morning, while braiding Nan's hair, Priscilla had noticed for the first time the unmistakable beginning of a breast beneath her daughter's striped Lycra suit: a small puff around the left nipple. Examining it she found a knot of flesh, like an angry pimple. It was hard for her to think of nine-year-old Nan as pubescent when it seemed she had only recently come sliding head first into the world. Yet the time had slipped by. The war had ended, Robert had switched into publishing, they had moved from the one-bedroom apartment in Brooklyn next door to the halfway house, which, though safe enough for an infant, seemed unsafe for a growing child, to the rented matchbox duplex with the back garden where Nan, and then Billy, could be left to play in the sun, to, finally, their first real house—a two-story, two-bedroom brick with window seats in the living room windows and a lawn in front—too modest and small to hold onto for long, but their own and within walking distance of the second-best public elementary school in Brooklyn. She resented being forced to object to Rosemary's thoughtless behavior, but with puberty about to descend on them like a thunderstorm, she could not afford the luxury of leaving the windows open in the name of "freedom," of turning her back on every sort of indiscretion.

It amused rather than annoyed Rosemary to be cast in the role of *femme fatale* when Daisy never let her out of her sight. She had no doubt that among the several dozen mothers sunning themselves whose husbands were away during the week she was not the only one having a summer affair. "Want me to do your back?" she offered.

Priscilla produced her little dismissive smirk and handed over the tanning lotion. She had already turned such a deep bronze that anyone who didn't know her might take her for a member of some hedonistic sun cult rather than one of the guardians. She resented Rosemary's thinking her a prig. What prig would ever have assembled such an interesting houseful of people, including Seymour and Chet, who shared a bedroom, for the summer? She was happy to live with gays, thinking Nan could benefit from knowing the variety of people in the world. But adultery was something else. Every instance of it threatened her—indeed, threatened all married couples—but she was confused as to why. She was offended that

Rosemary, who pretended to be her best friend, also pretended that she and the piano player at the Swallows were nothing more than friends. Hoping to gain Rosemary's confidence, broadmindedly she proposed, "I was thinking you might like to invite your friend from the Swallows over for dinner some time. It might perk things up a bit between weekends. And maybe he could give Seymour some advice about getting a gig. Would you like to?"

When she had invited Rosemary to come out for the summer, she had expected her to spend her days on the beach or in the kitchen, instead of chasing after men—and men who were completely inappropriate. She would never understand how an educated woman like Rosemary, who could identify by key and number all the symphonies of Beethoven, who had a membership in MOMA and a B.A. from Vassar, who in one year at the finest publishing house in New York had managed to grab for herself the most interesting manuscripts and then quit—she did not understand how such a woman could walk across the beach like a slut, allow herself to get sloppy drunk, let her child run wild, and practically throw herself at anything in pants while her husband slaved away in Mexico.

Rosemary retied her straps before sitting up. She was uneasy about bringing Woody home, where it would be harder to hide their true relationship, but she found Priscilla's invitation irresistible. In fact, sometimes she thought she had started her affair partly to tantalize Priscilla, for whom nothing was more interesting than people's sex lives, not money, crime, politics, affairs of state, fashion, food, or even epidemics. No wonder she wanted to invite Woody to her house. (Though everyone split expenses, they all thought of the house as Priscilla's, since she had assembled the sharers for the summer and her husband Robert had signed the lease; in the winter she lived in a real house with a real family, whereas the rest of them lived in makeshift quarters or relationships, as if they were still in college.) "I'd love to, Priss. When?"

"Whenever you like. Tonight. Seymour's cooking chowder. It's easy to stretch."

Rosemary stood up. "Okay. I'll go ask him right now."

Daisy ran to her mother's side.

"Why don't you stay here, Daisy?" suggested Rosemary; but seeing the shadow pass over Daisy's face she quickly changed her mind. "Come on then, monkey, get your doggie. Time for jelly beans."

. . .

Down on the beach the wives were talking. Rosemary had heard on the radio that back in the city the recent electrical storms had caused a fire so terrible that a twenty-three–block chunk of midtown and the heart of the financial district were completely without power for more than eighteen hours; two major jetports were shut down, and train service from the city to the northern suburbs was at best intermittent. With the weekend still far off, such news caused only complacent smiles or a mild stir among the summer wives. Thank God they were out of the city. Here at the shore, where the only news to penetrate was strictly local—Fourth of July clam-bakes, weekend bashes, vandalism by the teenaged renters who had taken over the West End, the price of lobster at the Swallows—here the storms had done nothing more than upset children and excite grown-ups as they sat on their porches with nightcaps, watching God's fireworks light up the blackened sky. The city and their husbands were remote. Inside the house, the wind banged the loose shutter and piled up sand in the corners of the slanty rooms, the musky smell of mildew penetrated a little deeper into the closets and mattresses, that was all. While the smaller children cringed at thunder and sucked their thumbs, the mothers smiled. Storms were good for gardens and gossip; eventually, they said, sunshine followed.

Monday. The husbands are back in the city, dictating memos, dialing suppliers, coming out of meetings, crouched behind the wheels of their cars, hoping to make the next traffic light before the yellow turns red. . . . The mothers are back on the beach covered with lotion, their straps rolled down, hoping that this week their children's squabbles will diminish, certain their charges will drown should they dare to open a book. . . . While the older children chase each other along the beach shrieking to the sky, the younger ones squat at the edge of their blankets moving sand from one place to another as if the world had been made for this alone. Little Daisy piles sand on her mother's legs, shovelful by shovelful, hop-ing to bury them so deep in the sand that she will never be able to leave her.

16

"You'll never guess what," said Priscilla, hanging up the phone. A satisfied, slightly malicious smile animated her prim mouth as she said in the clipped voice she reserved for reproaching the children, "A cable from Mexico. Harold's flying home."

"That should liven things up around here," said Seymour, spreading jam on his toast and raising it to his lips. "When?"

"Sometime this weekend. Tonight or tomorrow."

Seymour returned his toast to his plate unbitten. "No! Without any notice?"

Priscilla passed him the message she had taken down verbatim from the operator. "Read it yourself."

Seymour glanced at the paper, then looked urgently around the room. The dirty dishes on the counter, the *Times*, the morning sun streaming in the back door gave away nothing that he could see. Still, there were bound to be clues, trouble. He shook his head. "Somebody's got to tell Rosemary right away. Where is she?"

Slowly Priscilla raised her brows and lowered the lids of her dark eyes. "She doesn't tell me where she's going, and I don't ask. But I can make a pretty good guess."

"Isn't Daisy with her?"

Priscilla shrugged. "Daisy doesn't seem to interfere with anything Rosemary wants to do, haven't you noticed?"

"Oh come on, Priscilla. Daisy's a baby. She doesn't know what's going on."

Priscilla silently sipped her coffee.

"I'm sure they don't do it in front of her, Priscilla."

"When they're together they can hardly keep their hands off each other."

"So what? You and Robert 'do it,' as they say, just down the hall from where Daisy sleeps. So do I with Chet."

"That's different."

"Why? You're just upset because Harold's coming home."

"Well, aren't you? You should be, Seymour, because from the minute Harold comes through that door, everyone in this house is going to have to cover for Rosemary, including you. God, it's going to be one long hideous charade. And you'll have to play it too." Priscilla's face was beginning to glow in the light of fresh scandal. It was for this she had assembled her sharers to start with.

Seymour took a gulp of coffee and stood up. "I'll go to the beach and find her."

"I'll call Robert at his office. Oh God."

"I love charades, actually," said Seymour, downing his coffee and moving to the door.

Tonight or tomorrow? Rosemary felt joy and panic at once. "Where did you get this, Seymour? It doesn't look official."

"Western Union phoned it in. Priscilla took it down. Unless it's an inside job, it's probably real."

She'd hated Harold's leaving them, but once he was gone she hated to have him return. For his first foreign assignments, before Daisy was born, she'd quit her job at the publishing house to go off with him. Even when *Time* sent him to the Dominican Republic to cover the aftermath of the Marine invasion, they went together, piling up adventures. But after they had Daisy, Rosemary stayed behind with the baby when Harold traveled, and when he was home she tried to keep the baby quiet for him. Life was smoother when he was away, like motion in a vacuum; indeed, sometimes almost empty. Aspiring youths, they'd hoped for the best of life and put first things first: he work, she love. But whose love? She might, like some, have resented the baby for compromising her marriage; instead, she followed the more traditional path and put her child first, turning all her resentments against Harold. She knew they were lucky he got the assignments, for they were both ambitious and poor; yet each time Harold left, the old lonely panic returned and something buried inside her surfaced to wonder if this would be the time he failed to come back, until she almost wished it would. And when he did return, ready to take over where he'd left off, her resentment would be raised to precisely the level of her relief. Had she missed him? Yes, but she had managed very well without him too, thank you. Did he expect to leave them for so long without consequences? Look! Daisy barely recognizes him! She wondered if he'd been unfaithful; she assumed he had; she didn't care to know. At least this time, she consoled herself, so had she.

Seymour stood waiting for orders. "Will you stay here with Daisy for a bit? I've got to tell Woody. I've probably already missed him and he doesn't go on again till five. But I have to try. Here. Take her for ice cream. I'll come back as soon as I can. Do you mind?"

"Darling," said Seymour, lowering himself to the sand, "I'm yours."

She strode across the beach past the sunning mothers and digging children, the message in her hand, until she hit the hard sand of low tide, where, she couldn't help it, she began to run. She had to take the news somewhere, act upon it. She hoped to stem her panic long enough to do what she had to do. Kindly, sparely, cleanly. But if Woody wasn't at the Swallows she might simply have to tell him on the phone.

An hour ago she was caught up in the delicious conspiracy of summer love, eagerly planning the next clandestine scene in their passion play. They'd wooed each other with music, not words, inventing the harmonies they needed; now she would rush ahead to the last bar, with no coda, no finale. She didn't want to hurt him, but Harold's wire made pain as irrelevant as pleasure. Her family was the circle within which everything turned, with Daisy the fixed point. Her affair was already extraneous, parenthetical, *extramarital*, as disconnected from her real life as this beach, this summer. Harold would be back in a day or less; she had to close the curtain on her audacious performance before his entrance, clear the stage, swear the audience to secrecy, burn her costumes and props, and be at his return exactly as before. Otherwise . . .

Already she was half transformed as she pushed herself faster, leaning forward, flying on the balls of her feet. Otherwise was unthinkable. Several times a week at low tide she waded in the tidal pools to gather mussels and periwinkles, which she prepared for the household in glorious bouillabaisses, spectacular salads, classic pilafs, pastas, stews; but come September she would go back to the supermarket and the recipes from the *Times* as if foraging wild food were something she'd merely read about in a magazine or dreamed in a dream. Come September, the feel of Woody's arms and those erudite fingers that teased amazing melodies from her instrument—these too she knew would return to the dream in which she had discovered them.

She ran up the stairs into the bar. The piano was closed, just as she'd feared. She picked a cocktail napkin off the bar and fumbled in her bag for a pen.

They had known from the start that their connection would end abruptly—with the expiration of the season or with Harold's return, whichever came first. She had seldom even mentioned Harold's name, referring to him only as "my husband" or "he," though sometimes, lying with Woody on the sand in the moonlight, she had found herself imagining that he and not Harold was the one with whom she would be returning to her winter life. But that image always vanished in daylight when Daisy woke.

Harold's coming home so I'm afraid tonight's off. I'll try to catch you later. Otherwise—

Otherwise . . .

She bit the pen and looked out once more across the terrace to the sea. There it was again—*otherwise*, like a suspicious boat reappearing on the horizon. For the first time since they'd become lovers she recognized she might have to end the affair without a final night of love. Her body winced. *Otherwise I'll try to get in touch with you tomorrow. Don't try to call me.* She wanted to tell him she had hoped they'd have another month, two more weeks at least; but already, turning back into Harold's wife, she knew better than to put such regrets in writing.

She took the napkin to the piano, folded it in quarters, slipped it under the lid of the keyboard at middle C, and closed the lid.

17

Rosemary feared the conversation in the car when Robert, who had left his office early to handle the emergency, drove Harold out from Kennedy. Not that she didn't trust Robert to be discreet. No one in that house would tell, she could count on that; by now they were all too deeply implicated. And if one of the children made a slip, the grown-ups would cover up. Yet, as the rest of them waited like conspirators in the motley living room, drinking iced tea or beer with the music playing loud, she felt certain that he would find out anyway, if he didn't know already. How could he possibly look at her, how could he sleep beside her again and not know?

For this reason Rosemary leaped from her chair and headed for the back door the instant she heard the car turn into the drive.

"Rosemary! Get back here!" hissed Priscilla, interrupting the preparation of her own smile. "What's the matter with you?"

"I thought I should get Daisy."

"Sit down!"

"Oh God," sighed Rosemary, sinking back into the rattan chair, throwing her head back and gripping the arms.

"Courage, darling," whispered Chet. He tipped up his trimly bearded chin and raised his glass to her in a valiant effort to disguise his own agitation. "Courage," echoed Seymour.

And here was Harold, coming through the door, dropping his two battered bags, opening his arms, and shouting jovially: *"Buenas tardes,* everyone."

In the moment of his entrance Rosemary thought with alternate rushes of relief and alarm: Those aren't our suitcases. Robert must have picked up the wrong party.

Smiles circled the room. Harold looked quickly around. "So this is what I've missed. God, am I glad to see you."

Fearing hysteria, Rosemary forced the image before her, those smiling eyes, to merge with the image in her memory until she was shocked to see in the approaching figure the same tall genial man who had once gallantly saved her from herself by whisking her off to married life, but not her familiar enemy and husband. *Who is he?* He had grown slim again in Mexico, more angular than her husband, his eyes more quizzical; there was less confidence in his voice—did he suspect? She did like the way he looked—yes, as much as the first time, the small, deepset pale-gray eyes, the broad forehead, the silky hair the color of maple bark, the thin, delicate lips set in the square jaw, the slight stoop that made him seem always relaxed, the smooth, luminous shaven skin that turned darkly shadowed by night, even the long neck. Who could he be?

She put down her glass and leaned forward. She was afraid she would be unable to speak until she had figured everything out. Were they all watching her? If she sat there scrutinizing him another minute she'd give everything away.

His eyes caught her eyes. To avoid them she stood quickly and with six steps was in his arms.

"There's my girl," said Harold, all but lifting her in the air.

Yes; that's what she'd loved in him from the start, now she remembered: he was large enough to treat her like someone small, to raise her right up off the ground. The proportions were finally right. Yes: her tall, shaggy, glamorous husband. She kissed his mouth familiarly, then rested her head on his shoulder, appreciating the tender curve of his long neck, remembering with her whole body that until she'd met Woody a month before, Harold was the only man she'd ever known who was truly tall enough to make her feel like a woman instead of an impostor, tall enough to satisfy her.

Chet rushed him a glass, Priscilla rose to kiss him. Feeling Harold's shoulder beneath her cheek, Rosemary wondered why he hadn't been enough. There's no such thing as enough, she'd told him once. About cherries! No? he'd said, we'll see. And for her twenty-second birthday he had bought her an entire case of large Bing cherries, eighteen succulent pounds of them, stacked four-deep in perfect rows, their dark shiny burgundy skins glistening invitingly. And if these don't satisfy you, said Harold, I'll get another case. They had taken to bed for the whole birthday weekend, where they'd made love, told each other "everything," and fed each other cherries whenever they got hungry or remembered. And by the end of the marathon she'd had to concede that she'd finally been satisfied. Priscilla had predicted she'd never want to see another cherry, but the truth was, it only made her love them more.

"Where's Daisy?" asked Harold, squeezing Rosemary's waist. "I brought presents for everyone."

"I'll get her," said Rosemary, once more grateful to Harold for rescuing her.

Harold watched them come toward him like an image in a movie: Rosemary carrying Daisy on her hip, supporting with one arm the smooth back where one sunsuit strap, having slipped down from the small shoulder, drooped limply; Daisy clinging loosely to her mother's neck. Like koalas, thought Harold, the romantic, melting with love at the sight of them. His occasional youthful fantasy of himself as a family man had included freckled boys, even sulky sons, ball games and camping trips, checkers and picnics, with a smiling woman waving from a distant door, but never the round long-lashed sloe-eyed laughing girlchild, riding on her mother's molded shelf of hip, who pulled her ear and sucked her lip and rubbed her hair and seemed to adore him. Seeing the white skin beneath the loose strap, he caught his breath. Sometimes, finding himself alone among women—in the brothels of Mexico City, on the beach in Key West, in the hotel bars of San Juan, all the places where journalists congregate—he took comfort in this image of wife and child. Other men kept snapshots in their wallets and framed on their desks to prove their place in the universe; but Harold kept his in his memory, where it showed him not only his wife and child, timeless, extraordinary, sanctified, but his own best self.

"There's Daddy," said Rosemary, spilling Daisy to the ground and heading her off in his direction with an encouraging pat.

Like a reflection in water smashed by a stone, the image breaks—first in two, then ten, then ten million. Each hesitant, tentative step Daisy takes is another break, returning Harold back into his ordinary self, now crouching on the floor to receive her, arms wide, lips spread in a mighty grin. He expects her to roll to him like a bowling ball heading for a strike, while the others stand cheering on the side; but instead, Daisy hesitates, stops, reaches back for her mother's hand, and rubs her face shyly against her mother's thigh.

"Go on, honey," says Rosemary with another encouraging push, "that's Daddy!" But Daisy only buries her head deeper in her mother's skirt.

"I don't understand it," says Rosemary with an embarrassed shrug as she pats Daisy's head. "She asks for you all the time, she dictates letters, she wants you to shower with us."

"Aha!" says Chet, arching his brows. *Now* we understand."

Priscilla cluck-clucks at Chet, then pronounces her diagnosis. "Well. Two months is a long time to be apart at that age. She'll have to get used to him again." Priscilla sends a proud look to her husband, Robert, that says, At least our Nan and Billy know their own father. "Come on into the kitchen, darling," she invites, stretching a hand to Daisy and sliding her voice up to high maternal. "I'll give you a cracker to eat and one to give your daddy. Wouldn't you like that?"

But Harold has beaten Priscilla to it and is blocking the way, holding out to Daisy the large package wrapped in shiny red gift wrap and gold

tinsel ribbon he has retrieved from an airport bag. "Look, Daisy"—he
beckons. "Come see what Daddy brought you from Mexico."

Daisy watches him suspiciously, looking from him to the package and
back again. Then, to everyone's relief, she relinquishes her mother's hand
and moves cautiously toward the package. Harold holds it fast and close
until she is practically upon him and settles for a modest, face-saving kiss.
As she clutches the box and backs away, Harold returns to the bag with
a smile of largess and showers on the assembled company presents for all:
bottles of tequila, brandy, more boxes of chocolates, silver jewelry for the
ladies (the best for Rosemary), all well wrapped in the same red airport
gift wrap.

"Get the glasses out of the freezer, will you, Chet?" directs Priscilla,
but softly, for this is Harold's show.

"Wonderful!" says Harold. "You knew I was bringing tequila so you
frosted the glasses for margaritas."

"No, we frost the glasses for martinis every night," says Robert. "We're
very civilized around here."

"I'd forgotten. Now you'll see how it pays. If you bring the salt, Priscilla,
and a couple of limes, I'll show you the right way to drink tequila."

"At three thirty in the afternoon? Really?" says Seymour. "And I
thought *we* were decadent."

Daisy has taken her box to a corner, where she squats on the floor.
After painstakingly removing all the ribbon and paper, she tries vainly to
pry the top off the box. She tries and tries.

"Shall I help you, sweet?" asks Rosemary, stooping down beside her
and cutting four invisible Scotch tape seals with her thumbnail. "Now
try it."

Daisy pulls at the red satin top till it flies off, revealing underneath a de-
luxe, lavish display of assorted chocolates. Each sits in its own frilled cup,
a jewel in a setting. Some are individually wrapped in colored foil, some
lie naked and brown. Daisy looks over the vast array with astonished eyes.
She studies them row by row, then piece by piece, gingerly poking one
piece here, another there, observing their vast variety. From near the center
she plucks a large white milky ball flattened on one side and presses it with
two fingers against her lips into her mouth, then with a clamp of teeth
bursts the center. It is sweet and soft and chewy: like nothing she has ever
known. Steadfastly, cowlike, she chews and chews, exploring the effect,
and looks across the room to the large laughing man from whom it came.

. . .

She had been thrilled when the tall man let her ride all the way across the beach to where her mother spread their blanket. Daddy. She kept repeating it proudly: Daddy, Daddy. But after he set her down he seemed to forget all about her, as if he were perhaps not her daddy after all, or a different one from the one she remembered. She took her pail to the water's edge, filled it with dampened sand, and returned at a sprint on her short legs to unmold the pail close beside her mother, then back to the shore to fill up again.

"So tell me. What's been going on here?" asked Harold.

Rosemary's pulse gave warning. Was such a question possibly innocent? Coolly she looked her husband in the eyes and said, "Nothing. Why do you ask?"

Harold laughed nervously. "You don't seem too glad to see me."

Every time he left it was a wrench; every time he returned it took several days before she could accept him back. Though they were on to it, had even learned to joke about it, it seemed they still had to go through decompression to avoid the bends.

"Of course I'm glad to see you," snapped Rosemary, turning her back to Harold and busying herself with Daisy's sunbonnet. For the first time since Harold's return she felt Woody's long fingers on her skin, his tongue in her mouth; the image was so vivid that she feared Harold would see it by the light shining in her eyes.

"Okay, okay, maybe it's me. Maybe it's jet lag."

Her summer affair, which had seemed so tame, was strutting around in the middle of her marriage like a menacing cur. Watching Harold stumble and grope before it like a blind man, she wondered if it wouldn't be kinder to acknowledge the beast just to reassure him of how harmless it really was.

Daisy felt suddenly lonely. "Mommy," she said, flinging down her shovel and pulling at her mother's arm. "Mommy?"

"Sweetie?"

Daisy glanced surreptitiously at her father. "Bury me," she whispered to Rosemary. She wriggled a declivity in the sand and sat with her legs stretched out before her, surrounded by many small conical piles of sand.

Rosemary began absently piling on sand. Maybe he wasn't a blind man at all, she thought, maybe he saw through her. That would explain why he sat on the sand as if it were concrete, not sifting it with his fingers or stroking it with his toes. She had learned as a child, conspiring with her sisters, to deny everything. But if he did know something, perhaps she ought to switch tactics and reveal the mere truth before he could confront her.

Daisy was growing impatient. "Here," she said, pointing to a piece of shin that had reemerged.

"Here?"

"No! *Here!*" She reached out impulsively to guide her mother's hand. "Here, Mommy, here!"

"Daisy," said Harold sternly. "Your mom and I are talking now. See if you can't play by yourself for a while and let Mommy be."

Daisy's chin puckered up; Rosemary moved sand rapidly. "That's all right, Harold. I told her I'd bury her. I can listen to you too." It seemed to Rosemary that when Harold was away Daisy was hardly ever cranky. Alone, she and Daisy were a smooth duet. Rosemary resented his interference—implying he thought it okay to leave them to cope by themselves for months at a time, inventing entirely new rhythms, and then move back in and take over as if he had never left them at all. Did he think life stopped for them while he was gone?

"Sure, you can do ten things if you want to. But there's only one thing you should be doing now. Honestly, Rosemary, I haven't managed to get a minute alone with you since I've been back."

"Tonight. After dinner everyone's going to the movies. We'll stay home and talk." Rosemary remembered how, when they were first married, Harold had liked to come up behind her and slip his arms around her waist while she was doing the dishes, then cover the back of her neck with kisses. If he got his way and they wound up making love, the next morning the dishes would still be waiting to be washed.

Did everyone suddenly stop talking when he walked into the living room, or did it only seem so to Harold? "Why so quiet?" he asked with, he hoped, a hint of irony. Let them take up the defensive.

"Not quiet, mellow," said Chet. "After a dinner like that . . ."

"Not mellow, decadent," amended Seymour. "Chet's wine, but your brandy, Hal. Want some?"

"Thanks. Not yet. Where's my family?" It was a word he pronounced with a certain surprised pride, as though to have one of one's own were a considerable accomplishment, at the same time acknowledging that it was an accident of fortune to which he was not, as yet, completely reconciled.

Priscilla sent a glance to Robert, cleared her throat, then held up her glass to Harold and said, "Upstairs with Daisy, I think. You know, Harold, if you'd come a week later, after Chet's vacation, you wouldn't have seen how truly decadent we really are around here." She swirled the brandy in her snifter and ostentatiously inhaled the aroma.

"That's right," said Robert. "They claim they dine on franks and spaghetti during the week, to bed by eleven, up by seven. But I don't believe it."

Seymour put on his offended pout. "You doubt us? I'm here to testify it's true. Too true. This place is like the refrigerator. As soon as you close the door on us on Monday morning our light goes out. Come Monday, this town reverts to a children's camp. Poor Rosemary. Always trying to organize some fun for these lazy fuddy-duddies, and nobody willing to go along with her."

"I did," said Nan, with her hands on her slim, boyish hips, defending her daring. "Me and Daisy and Woody walked all the way to the end of the beach wall, remember?" She shot a challenging glance at her mother. "Even though it was late at night."

"Oh, smarty," said Seymour, sticking out his tongue and flagging his ears toward her. "Well, of course, *kids* are lots of fun, and people who live in other houses. I meant in our house." He looked at Harold and pouted. "Like me, for instance. You give me a sunset and I don't want to do anything but sit there with my thermos and watch it till it's all gone away and then toddle on home. Same sunset up here as the one at the end of the wall."

"It wasn't sunset, it was full moon. That's why we went," said Nan.

"I thought you went in order to stay up past your bedtime," said Priscilla archly.

"I'll get that," said Robert, jumping up on the phone's first ring. Everyone tensed.

"Sit still," said Harold, who was standing nearest the kitchen and the phone. But before he could even turn around, Robert was pushing past him. "That's okay, Hal, don't bother, I'm expecting a call."

"Oh, Harold," cried Priscilla, in her slightly hysterical voice, "come sit by me and tell me about Mexico. Of course we all read your stories, but it isn't the same. I want to know what they edited out. We haven't had a moment alone since you came back."

"I haven't had a moment alone with anyone. This house is one long party."

"Nan dear," said Priscilla, leaning toward her daughter, "be a love and run on up and tell Rosemary that everybody's waiting for her?"

"No, she doesn't need to do that, I'll go myself," said Harold, turning. Robert, carrying two logs, returned from the kitchen. He stepped back abruptly as Harold made to pass him. "You're going out?" asked Robert, startled.

"Just upstairs. Was that the call you were expecting?"

"Yes, it most certainly was," said Robert.

Seeing another sly look pass around the room from eye to eye, Harold began to feel decidedly uncomfortable. Something fishy was going on, though he couldn't pin it down. No longer could his doubts resist the evidence. When he reached the top of the stairs, he stopped to listen to the voices below. He could make out Priscilla's squeaky sounds, but either they were too high to carry the words up to him or they were telling secrets. Then Robert said something too low to hear, followed by Chet in the clear resonant tones of a singer, advising firmly, "Now is not the time to discuss it." After that, someone switched on the stereo and he heard nothing but Schubert floating up the stairs.

There was only one thing he could imagine: His wife had been sleeping with one of them while he was gone. What else could it be?

Which one?

Rosemary kneeled beside the tub with her hair tied back and the sleeves of Harold's blue shirt rolled up. "Press this cloth against your eyes, sweetheart," she said, handing the folded washcloth to Daisy with one hand and holding the baby shampoo poised over the child's head with the other. Rosemary tried to ease their weekly ordeal-by-shampoo, now with distractions, now with promises, now honesty, now bribes; but always at the moment the shampoo touched Daisy's hair, all her strategies dissolved in Daisy's tears.

Daisy trustfully took the cloth while Rosemary held the fine baby hair on top of Daisy's head and said, "Tell me when you're ready."

"*There* you are," said Harold, pushing into the bathroom. Rosemary jerked guiltily at the unexpected sound of Harold's voice, sending a stream of shampoo cascading over Daisy's head, eliciting an astonished wail of betrayal.

"Christ!" cried Rosemary. "You scared her to death! *Now* look!"

"I'm sorry." Harold sat down on the toilet lid.

Rosemary quickly began rubbing up a lather on Daisy's head while Daisy, shrieking, struggled with her mother's hands.

"Something funny's going on around here," said Harold. "People are whispering, Robert won't talk to me. Even you—" Assaulted by a sudden hypothesis, he threw a question to his wife: "Is it something between you and Robert?"

"Don't be ridiculous," said Rosemary. But already her heart was pumping hard. "Priscilla's my best friend." For once Rosemary was grateful for Daisy's intransigence, giving her breathing space. What was the matter with everyone? She'd have to speak to Robert. Someone would have to contact Woody, too, before he committed some irrevocable indiscretion. Woody: she was puzzled by how little she felt for him now. Harold's telegram had abruptly pulled the plug on her feelings, sending them all rushing in a whirl down the drain.

"Anyway," said Harold, "I need to talk to you."

She sat back on her heels and turned to Harold. "Can't you see I'm busy now?"

He crossed his legs and folded his hands in a gesture of patience. "Sure. Sorry. . . . Look," he said after a while, "would you like me to finish the bath?"

Rosemary sighed. "Thanks. I'm almost done." Trying to ignore Harold sitting there, Rosemary attended to Daisy. Having lathered her hair, she now faced the problem of rinsing it. Postponing the tense moment, she soaped the cloth and ran it gently all over the smooth little body—the plump arms and legs, round belly and buttocks, the touchingly narrow back—all the while keeping up the running chorus of reassurance that accompanied their never-ending duet. When she was done, she wrung out the cloth, folded it in four, and held it out to Daisy. "Hold this over your eyes while I rinse."

"This time, Mommy," said Daisy, once more pressing the cloth tightly against her eyes with both hands, "wait till I say 'ready.' "

"Okay." Rosemary tested the temperature of the running water against the surface vessels in her wrist, then filled the cup from the tap. "Ready?"

"Not ready."

"Ready now?"

"Not ready."

Rosemary strained to maintain patience as she helped Daisy collect her courage. "Now?" she asked. She sat back and waited. "Tell me when."

Harold could not believe, watching Rosemary bathe their child with such patience and finesse, that this woman, his wife, could have betrayed him in the house of his closest friends. How could he have made such a grievous mistake about her? He wanted to reach out, stroke the familiar pear-shaped backside as if it were still his, until he felt reassured. But he was afraid she would snap at him again, feeding the worm of doubt, already fattening on his hesitation, eating away at their trust, until he was sick with suspicion. Then all his forbearance would be wasted, for he would have to ask her anyway. He tried to frame a question that would not irritate her. (To stimulate and irritate came to the same thing, after all, the gesture was the same, only the spirit was different.) But to ask was to accuse—and to risk her answer.

"Okay, Mommy," said Daisy, marshaling enough resolve to fill her lungs with a reserve of air and blurt out bravely, "Now." She sat firmly in the tepid tub, pressing the cloth hard against her eyes, pursing her whitening lips, hunching her shoulders against the spray, as Rosemary began to pour cupfuls of rinse water on Daisy's head. Two, three, four—

Is it trust, sheer faith, that keeps Daisy sitting there silent through the wet ordeal? Harold's silence is powered by the opposite: suspicion and fear. Helplessly he sits on the toilet lid, opening and closing Daisy's potty with his foot, waiting for his turn for attention.

"There," said Rosemary, grinning. "All done. You were wonderful. Now would you like to stay in and play for a while? Want your dolphin?"

Harold was vexed. Couldn't she see he'd been waiting for her? Never mind: Daisy was clutching the edge of the tub trying to climb out.

"Hand me that big yellow towel, will you please?" Rosemary lifted the glowing child from the tub and stood her on the bath mat that said Palm Court Hotel. She draped the towel over Daisy's head, rapidly rubbed the scalp, then wrapped the squirming body in the towel. "Okay. Run along and get into your pj's, then I'll brush out your hair."

As soon as Daisy was gone, Harold rose and took Rosemary in his arms. He wanted to tell her how grateful he was to her for giving him so much, how the sight of the two of them together, his family, always filled him with love, how alone he felt without her, how sullied by other women;

but what came out were only the usual inadequate phrases: wonderful mother, beautiful child, love.

For a moment she nestled against his shoulder, comforted. Then, remembering, she kissed him quickly and knelt again before the tub. "Have you ever seen anything like it? Really, for one small body," she said, scrubbing the dark ring, "that child picks up one helluva load of dirt."

"Have you said anything to Harold about . . . you know?" said Rosemary, confronting Priscilla in the kitchen.

Priscilla's hand flew to her open mouth. "Me? Really, how can you even ask that?"

"He seems to know something. He keeps asking me what's going on."

"Well of course. He's not a crack reporter for nothing. We both know he's one of the smartest men in the business. But believe me, no one here has said a word. My God, if he knew we were all in on it . . . You'd have to think we're crazy as well as disloyal."

"Still, he's acting so funny. I don't understand it."

"Maybe because *you're* acting funny. Try to relax a bit."

"Relax! He leaves us for the whole summer, then he suddenly reappears without any warning and expects everybody to drop everything and act as if he was never away. I don't see how I can be expected to relax!"

"Look. If you don't want to seem like a—"

Rosemary's face jumped. "Hush! Here they come."

"I'll put her to bed now," said Harold.

"No. She never goes to bed this early. Besides, her hair isn't dry yet."

"What's her bedtime?"

"Whenever she wants."

"Since when?"

"I told you. Everything's changed."

"Now I'm home it can change again. Come, Daisy, Daddy'll put you to bed."

"But Harold, you don't know the routine."

Daisy looks from one to the other, twirls a lock of hair around her forefinger. "Book!" she shouts into the gap in their conversation and clasps her mother's legs. "I'll read you a book," says Harold, but when he bends down to pick her up, she pulls back.

"What's wrong, baby?" asks Harold. She clings to Rosemary's thighs, half hiding behind them. When Harold picks her up a storm of tears breaks. "What's the matter with her?"

"Nothing. Maybe she's just not used to sharing me."

"Well, she'd better get used to it. I'm back to stay," he says, carrying her toward the door. Her cry sounds desperate, pathetic, as she stretches her arms toward Rosemary.

"Harold, don't! It's nowhere near her bedtime. And her hair's still wet. I told you." Then fiercely: "Come. Give her to me."

18

Daisy's hair is combed and dry, her teeth are brushed, her bladder is empty, her blue doggie is in her arms, her bed, a mattress on the floor, has been moved, now that Harold's back, from Rosemary's room to a corner of Nan's room, and Daisy has finally, reluctantly, settled into bed. Harold and Rosemary have each read her a story, Rosemary has tucked her in twice, the music box has run its course, the night light has been turned on, the door has been left ajar. At last the parents are ready for the homecoming scene they have been avoiding all day long.

Harold gets his cigarettes off the dresser, grabs one with his lips, and, postponing a little longer his big push to quit, deposits the pack into his breast pocket. Rosemary, who almost never smokes, asks Harold for a cigarette. Armored thus, busy in hand and mouth, they lie down together on the less-than-double bed, where two will now sleep in place of one.

A strong wind has suddenly risen; it blows the curtains at the open window and sets a shutter banging at the back of the house. As she hears the ocean beat the shore Rosemary wonders if she ought to check Daisy's window; knowing how her concern will annoy Harold, she drops it. "So," she begins, exhaling long. "How was it? Tell me. How come you came back so soon? What happened in Mexico?"

He shrugs off her questions with a pointed, "Why don't you tell me what happened here instead?"

"You see it all. The beach, a few excursions, Priscilla carping at my swimsuits, drunken feasts on weekends . . . But Daisy. She's the main thing. She seems to have taken the most incredible leaps since we've been here. Do you even recognize her as the same child? And another thing. She seems to have fallen madly in love with Chet, almost like an adult. Honestly, she flirts like crazy and follows him around—maybe she'll stop now that you've come back."

"That's really interesting. Because Chet's the only one in this house who doesn't just clam up and start passing looks whenever I walk into a room. How come?"

"Don't ask me."

He could see by the angle of her limbs that she intended to resist his probings. Even on this bed, too narrow for two, nowhere were they touching. Her legs were crossed at the ankles, her arms were stretched over her head, when she spoke she looked not at him but at the ceiling, straight up, to where the smoke rose. She was surrounded by an invisible aureole, in some places no wider than a fraction of an inch, which he could no more easily cross than if she were inside a closed coffin.

"It's been pretty boring here. After dinner Seymour usually goes off to practice his clarinet, and Priscilla complains or reads magazines. No one's willing to do anything different. I tried to get up some weekend excursions—looking for new mussel beds, seeing how far we could go on the beach without getting stopped, the strawberry festival on the North Shore. But when it comes right down to it, no one's ever game."

"Nan said you followed the wall to the end one night."

"Yes. That was fun."

"Who's Woody?"

When Rosemary was done coughing, there stood Daisy in the doorway, eyeing her parents on the bed, her large eyes, unglazed by sleep, alert and trusting.

Rosemary swung her long legs to the floor. "What is it, sweetheart?"

"I'm thirsty."

"Come then. We'll get you a drink." She took Daisy by the hand to the bathroom and handed her a half-filled glass of water.

Daisy held it in both hands, tipped it up, and swallowed the water glug by glug. "More," she said, holding up the empty glass.

"Don't you think that's enough for now? If you drink too much you'll have to pee again. Now it's time for sleep." She picked the child up in her arms and pressing the shiny cheek against her own, carried her back to bed. "Try to sleep now, sweetie," said Rosemary, kneeling to kiss the curled-up little girl on the forehead. She stood up, trying not to disturb the quiet air of the darkened room. She turned the key on the castle-shaped wooden music box until a tinny lullaby tinkled through the room, then placed it once more on the floor beside the mattress and tiptoed out, leaving the door ajar at the precise angle required.

The Quarrel . . .

By the time they were four years married, the quarrel of Harold and Rosemary had already taken root in the soil of their love, taking precisely the nourishment needed to flourish there. Like their lovemaking, their quarrel and reconciliation followed a familiar, private pattern they had come to rely upon, though they would have been at a loss to describe it had anyone asked. As reliable as their shorthand for love was their short-hand for hate. From the first accusation to the final kiss they knew the steps, precise as a formula; they would go exactly so far, no further, and took comfort in knowing they could count on one another, the most important thing in marriage.

Harold watched Rosemary lift herself onto the bed beside him, taking bets with himself as to whether this time she would allow their bodies to touch. In order not to leave the verdict to chance, he let his right leg lie slightly over the center mark toward her side. For an instant her hip pressed ever so lightly against his—so lightly he didn't know if she even knew—but the next moment she avoided his thigh by crossing her ankles carefully. In the early years they had slept with one of her legs thrown over one of his, their bodies curled together. He wanted to cut through their trouble, take her in his arms, forget about the past. But he knew they had first to complete the process they had started.

Lying on a strange bed too narrow by half, Harold turned halfway onto his side, leaned on his elbow with his head in his hand, and asked, "What was I supposed to do then? Pass up the chance to cover Mexico? Did you really want me to do that?"

"Of course not!"

"You could have come with me if you'd wanted to. I never told you to stay home."

"Oh sure. Boil Mexican water for the baby in a hundred degrees of heat while you run around. Great."

"You think I liked it there without you? Think about it. Horrendous heat, impossible traffic, no one to talk to, alone every night."

"Alone every night, sure! That's like saying—"

In their quarrel each imagines the worst. Why, he wonders, does she pull back her hand every time he reaches out to touch her? What's she thinking? And another thing: she treats him like an intruder in his own home who might harm his own child. As if he's contaminated. He suppresses his impulse to set her straight, in case he has misunderstood. He wants to ask her what's going on, demand that she come out with it. How ungrateful, how perverse she is to treat him one minute as if he's never been away and the next like a visitor who's overstayed his welcome.

She sees him set his jaw in that injured stance that accuses the world. Bad enough he left them alone to fend for themselves for a whole summer when she begged him not to, warned him what might happen, but then for him to return suddenly without warning, disrupting everything, expecting everyone's schedule to accommodate his, wanting to take over as if nothing were changed, as if he'd never been away. How could he be so insensitive? It had taken her weeks to accept his absence. She couldn't switch back so quickly; it would take time.

But there is Daisy in the doorway once more, twirling her hair, looking up sheepishly.

"Daisy!" says Harold sternly. "What is it this time?"

"I'm thirsty, Mommy."

"But sweetheart," says Rosemary, "you just had a whole glass of water."

"I'm thirsty."

Rosemary and Harold pass a look. Neither believes the child can still be thirsty, but there their agreement stops. Harold believes Daisy is fibbing in order to stay up. He believes that such tactics, though understandable, should not be encouraged by indulgence and prepares to oppose them with firmness. You've got to set limits, he says.

Rosemary sees the problem differently. Her daughter is a growing flower, opening up, bending to the light; her "thirst" is not a fib, not even a tactic, but an effort to control whatever fear is keeping her awake. What she needs is reassurance, not opposition.

Rosemary reaches out for Daisy's hand. "All right, sweetie, come along, I'll give you another drink. Maybe it will help you get to sleep. But this is the last time." Over her shoulder she says, "Right back."

Harold lies on the bed and waits, counting clues. The whispers, Nan's remark about someone named Woody, Rosemary's smoking. Is she trying to evict him from his own family? Unfair! For them alone he labors, only to wind up squeezed out by—but he can't complete the thought. Pain, fear, rage tumble together like free-form wrestlers on a mat. He pushes in to blow the whistle, break them apart, keep control. Maybe he's imagining everything. Better to brave her out, ask her to state her grievance so he can demolish it.

She's careful not to touch him when she returns to the bed, careful to leave him plenty of room lest her burn reflex betray her by jerking her body from contact with his. They need a wider berth.

Bewildered and angry when she pulls away, he wants to reach out, grab her wrists, force her to acknowledge him. What kind of welcome is this? His whole summer, all his sacrifices—never sure from one day to the next how the peso will hold up, if his story will come off, no security, no companionship, no Xerox or comfort or company, the impossible heat—are wiped out by her tormented look. He watches her tucking her hand into her armpit as if her arm were a folding wing and wonders whether her chief crime is heartlessness or blindness. Then he remembers: it's always like this when he's been away, reentry blues. Again, he resolves to be patient, to try to make allowances—though part of him thinks that as the chief beneficiary of his efforts, she ought to be the one making allowances.

"I can't understand it. This is the first time all summer she's had the slightest trouble going to sleep," says Rosemary. She hopes he gets the message.

"Oh?" says Harold with a hint of sarcasm. "Why, do you suppose?"

Rosemary simply shrugs, afraid to escalate, afraid of confrontation.

Her refusal to answer is too much. Harold raises himself on one elbow and reaches over to clasp her shoulder. "Why are you avoiding me?" he asks. "What's been going on in this house? Who is Woody?"

No matter how wildly her heart pumps adrenaline through her veins, nothing will save her now. She sees her sister Sarah at the bottom of the stairs with their mother coming toward her, hands on hips, calling, "Slut! Homebreaker! Whore!" Already the blood is rising to her cheeks, betraying her. Now it's her turn—only, unlike her sister, she has no one to run off with, no one to help her, and a child. The worst has happened. "Was it Priscilla? Did she tell you? Couldn't she even wait one day?"

"Rosemary!" says Harold in a whisper. He can't believe what he's hearing. He was only looking for a way to stir the pot, not cause an explosion. Now, in excruciatingly slow motion, he sees everything in his life rise up abruptly, tumble over and over in the air, then plunge back to earth. Not one but a whole series of explosions, all connected, and eerily without sound. He's weak, faint, the blood has drained from him till his head is swimming. He pulls his hand back from her shoulder, glad he's lying down. He can't bear what he hears. "Rosemary!"

She looks at her husband's pale, expressionless face. His eyes are closed; she can't tell if in anger or anguish. His silence is terrifying, forcing her to imagine the worst. If he could leave them for a summer he's capable of leaving them forever. If he leaves them . . . The rage that gathers whenever he leaves comes charging into her as she remembers every story she ever heard of abandoned wives and fatherless children. "I told you not to leave us," she cries.

"Who is he?"

"No one. Just someone who plays piano around here."

"Piano?—" Harold looks at her with hope, then returns to his painful questions. "Just tell me one thing. Did you sleep with him or not?"

She scrutinizes his face to find out how she should answer. Her instinct is to deny everything, but if he already knows the truth her lying will make it worse. She remembers the conversation they had centuries before, on the eve of their wedding, when they were two free people in love. No history, no children. *What if you come home one night and find me in bed with someone else?*

"Look who's asking," she says, stalling. "Every time someone approached you in Mexico I suppose you pulled out your family photos and refused?"

Everything she says is another wound. He winces at each remark. He's sinking in quicksand; each question he asks to pull himself out drags him in deeper. She's trying to compare Mexican whores with betrayal. He leans over her body, a hand on each shoulder, his lank hair falling in strands before his narrowing eyes. "I asked you a question. It's important. Now answer me, please."

Rosemary is absolutely unable to choose an answer, when suddenly she sees Daisy once more, standing in the doorway, her eyes open wide, watching them. "Daisy!" she cries and sits upright. "What are you doing back here?"

"I'm thirsty, Mommy."

"Thirsty. That's impossible. You've had enough water to float a ship."

"I'll handle her this time," says Harold and rises abruptly from the bed. Threateningly he tosses back his hair and knits his brows. "Enough nonsense, Daisy. Now you get back into that bed and stay there."

"I'm thirsty."

"That's a fib, Daisy. Now tell the truth. You're not thirsty. You just want to stay up, don't you? . . . Don't you?"

Daisy watches her father's face puff red, his eyes beam. Her lips quiver; she doesn't want to cry. But she's terrified of this large red-faced angry man beginning to shake her.

"Okay, if you want to stay up, you can stay up. You can stand in the corner all night, or until you tell me you're ready to get in bed and go to sleep."

"Harold!" cries Rosemary from the bed. "You can't punish her for being unable to sleep. She's only a baby!"

At this signal, Daisy begins to bawl.

"You stay out of this!" Harold calls back, roughly grabbing the screaming child in one arm and striding with her from the room.

Rosemary flies to the door after them, then stops. If he has come back to be the father, she must allow him this. After he's calmed down, then she'll go comfort Daisy. Even seeing him at his worst, she can't bear the thought of their living without him. He is Daisy's father—better than none. She closes her eyes and counts the seconds, the screams. By the time Harold returns she has numbed herself.

"I don't think she'll be asking for any more water now." The proud father's chest heaves; his breath is short as if he has just been in a strenuous race; the expression in his eyes tells that he's won.

"She's in bed?"

"In her room. But she won't come out again."

"Did you wind up her music box? She needs—"

"What she needs is a little firm discipline, that's what she needs."

Hearing no screams from the hall, Rosemary resigns herself. Yesterday's frivolity seems so long ago. Maybe Harold's right. Maybe what Daisy needs is a father. Nothing matters to her now but to re-establish their family. Otherwise the next twenty years of her life will be a tragedy.

"Now . . . where were we?" asks Harold, settling down once more beside Rosemary on the bed.

She looks at him pleadingly and allows her thigh to outline his. How can it matter where we were, she wants to ask; it only matters where we are now. But he has an agenda to pursue. Pride demands its question. "Tell me the truth. Did you sleep with him?"

If Priscilla has betrayed her she'd better ask for mercy. She closes her eyes and nods slowly, hoping he can see her remorse.

Harold lets out an anguished moan combining all his unasked questions and clutches his belly where he's been hit. Pain distorts his face, tears fill his eyes. When they spill over the lids, he covers his eyes with his hands, turns his head away, and curls his body around his wound.

"Harold," says Rosemary touching him at last. She strokes his shoulder, his hair, kisses his neck, whispers into his ear. "It was nothing. And it's over now. I'm sorry."

But Harold stays curled into himself, afraid to speak, afraid he will go too far.

And she—she wonders, will he leave her? Now it's hard to know who's more frightened.

Soon he will strike back with harsh, well-aimed blows. He will tell her about the whores who welcomed him every night he was in Mexico, the one who called him Guapo and the young girl who traded a rich man for him. Relentlessly he will paint the scene until she too cries for him to stop. Their cruelty will take them into new quarters they have never before explored; they will enlarge their house, build closets and entire wings to house this knowledge for years to come, their passion will furnish nurseries for the new additions to their family.

"Whores!" she sobs. "If you'd fallen in love with someone else, a reporter or someone, I could understand it. But to go to whores, who mean nothing to you, to *whores*, as if—"

"For you to carry on with someone openly, right here in the middle of my family, in front of our daughter, instead of having the grace to hide it—"

But isn't that always the way? What hurts is not the general but the particular: *this* betrayal, *this* disgrace, *this* deceit. And if Harold had fallen in love, then how unacceptable, how terrible *that* circumstance would appear to Rosemary.

God's Trick . . .

When they are both sobbing in pain, terrified that this time they have delivered the fatal blow, the one from which they will never manage to recover, the one that will orphan their child and leave them each alone, evicted, bereft, when they are both ready for any relief, when they are quits and sorry, when their pasts are destroyed leaving them ready to begin their lives anew, then they turn to each other with a passion they have not felt since the days of their honeymoon when in a rented bed they tried to pound their two separate lives into one.

God's trick, Rosemary has come to call this passion: God's trick to perpetuate the species, which he readily abandons once his purpose is fulfilled. It had worked very well, producing first their marriage and then Daisy. But once she was on to it, she thought she would indulge in passion again only on her own terms: with strict limits, only when safe, with birth control. Rosemary underestimates God.

She knows the steps, precise as a metronome, between the first kiss and the last cry; it comforts her to know: what she needs most of her husband, has always needed, is to count on him.

At first he moves slowly, entering each of the secret rooms inside her, as she holds herself ready. One at a time, she opens the doors. Gradually he slides into the living room, made cozy and comfortable over the years, where he sinks in the rocking chair with a sigh, removes his shoes, gratefully accepts the warm tea her body offers, then rocks and rocks and rocks.

His rocking soothes her, it is just what she needs. That he comes home to rock before her fire, that she knows she can count on him, comforts her. Like a reliable old metronome she needs only set and start—this is exactly the measure of her love.

And hate. For he is seldom on time. He comes home too late or too soon. He falls asleep just when she needs to talk. He leaves her for weeks at a time, for a whole summer, to tend the fires herself. He drives too fast; he claps his hands and calls for passion; he admires flash and recklessness, he flirts with the waitress in front of her, he insists upon driving and paying the bills, he suddenly changes his rhythm without discussing it with her. He goes to whores. He cooks up more hope than they can possibly finish so that she must throw some out, and then he takes her forgiveness for granted.

The corner where her father sent her to stand smells musty and rank. She feels suffocated, but he's forbidden her to turn around until he comes back. Where is he? Where is her mother? When no one comes she cries, she stamps her feet, she pounds the wall. Nothing happens. After a while Daisy hangs her head and waits, letting her chin rest against her chest while tears of shame stream down her cheeks, splashing against the floor.

Sand is heaped in the corner and underfoot. She moves her toe in slow circles against the baseboard, trying to clear a spot in the corner, but the shame, like the sand, remains. It's everywhere, oozing from her corner into the rest of the room, pressing hotly against her cheeks, inside throbbing against her temples, spreading in hot shivers across her skin.

When her sobs have subsided to a soft rhythmic pulse and she's able through the blur of tears to see the familiar pattern of flowers on the faded wallpaper, she leans her arm against the wall and rests her head on it. So tired. She wants to sit on the floor, but he ordered her to stand in the corner, not sit. Slower and slower drags the time; maybe she's been so bad they'll never come back. The corner is her house, her cave. Here she will stand for the rest of her days, breathing the hot, damp, musty air, feeling the grit of sand packed in the cracks between her toes, hearing the low whine of the refrigerator through the wall, seeing the faded flowers— blue, purple, pink, red—on the peeling wallpaper which mysteriously ends at the corner of the room.

To pass the time she begins to trace each flower with her fingertip, losing herself in the patterned rows. No two seem alike, yet she wonders if across the room the same flowers turn up again. If only she could leave the corner to see. But still no one comes.

One by one she touches the flowers near her, saying the color of each as if they are wooden beads on a string. She tries to concentrate on the order, but suddenly remembering her punishment and shame, she forgets the colors and has to begin again. Useless. She'll never find out if the pattern repeats. She's trapped there. As her eyes blur again, she tries to listen for the voices of her parents coming from another room, but all she can hear is the distant sound of a shutter banging and banging against the house. It's no use: as surely as she's forgotten the colors of the flowers, her parents have forgotten her.

Rosemary reaches up to Harold's neck and covers his face with kisses, kissing his eyes, his tears. He clasps her hands in his, weaving their fingers together and once more moves on top of her. Their passionate sighs put everything in balance: the past, their pain, even the future is born of this compelling now. The shutter bangs and bangs, but they take as little note of it as of Rosemary's diaphragm, boxed and powdered in the bedside drawer.

19

Red, orange, and purple leaves, mainly maple and oak, collected in the park by Daisy for the first time in her life, are held to the refrigerator door by magnets. Leaning against the leaves on the open door, Rosemary drinks a whole pint of milk in a draught. The summer is far behind. Her breasts have begun to swell again. She feels her womb grow, harden, spread. Her navel, that other mysterious declivity, begins to alter its shape. Her nipples darken, harden, enlarge. Sometimes she eats a carton of ice cream at a sitting. Her blood supply increases by twenty percent; she feels it course faster through her vessels like swollen rivers bubbling with the winter's runoff. Sometimes she can see it pulsing in her wrist, just beneath the skin. The tiny purple pulse is alive, like an insect rhythmically scurrying back and forth, like the new creature swimming in her womb.

She is body. No less than the spider spinning out its life in the elbow of the porch railing, she is body.

When Harold leaves for work, she pours herself a cup of coffee, adds milk, and spreads Limburger cheese thickly on a hunk of French bread. The tang is rich, smelling vaguely like vomit, like insides. She takes big bites, licks her fingers, sniffs the cheese, chews vigorously. For the first time she is aware of the path the food follows, going down to nourish her and the other. She is body, and the bounty of other bodies and growing things nourishes her as she prepares to nourish them. The great chain of being. She remembers the pleasures of the breast.

She piles the breakfast dishes in the sink, then strips off her nightgown for her bath. While the tub fills, she admires her body in the bathroom mirror. Her flesh shines out from beneath its pale familiar surface with a glow so new she can hardly claim it for her own. The belly is rounded, planted between hipbones barely visible beneath her ribs. Once again her breasts are large, high, round, full—larger than she remembers, larger than she ever imagined they could be. She feels herself come suddenly, throbbingly alive. Her left hand cups one of her new breasts, she rubs her palm lightly across the nipples, first one, then the other, then back again, while her right hand touches her soft wet centerfold. She is as wet as a newly hatched chick. Mysterious, dormant muscles are entering the race; new organs are forming. Never has she felt stronger. In seconds, her pulse is pounding, throbbing in triumph. She presses her wet fingers to her nostrils and breathes in deeply, smiling into the mirror.

The torrential sound of the water changes. It has reached the trap. Quickly she turns off both faucets and slides down carefully, immersing herself up to her neck. Her breasts float on the water, independent of each other, of herself. Washing them, again she fills with lust.

It comes to her that if it's a boy, she'll name him Max. Maximilian: emperor of the world.

Anatomy Lessons

20

"ALL RIGHT, sweetheart," purrs Rosemary, pulling the rocker up beside Daisy's desk, "how would you describe yourself?"

"I don't know. Medium tall, I guess, musical, hyper, a chocolate freak."

Since Daisy's nursery days, Rosemary has been everything from artist to umpire, mechanic to nurse, and welcomes each new role. Now she leans forward eagerly, college counselor. "I mean, how are you different from other people your age?"

"I do a hundred pushups and an hour of yoga every day, I take dance, and I'm a vegetarian?"

"Yes! That's good!" says Rosemary, resuming Mother. "Why don't you write about that? Maybe about *why* you're a vegetarian."

Daisy pouts. "Because I don't know *why* I'm a vegetarian, that's why," she mocks, sticking out her lower lip as she's done from birth.

"You don't? Really. I thought you did."

"Well I don't!" she snaps, swamped by equal portions of gratitude and guilt that blend like sugar and butter in a batch of fudge. How they might be transformed into something good is beyond her. Better overdone than raw; better to snap than to cry.

"Then maybe you should try to figure it out," says Rosemary, rising. "Ask yourself: Who are you? What have you done? What do you want? What does it mean? I'll be in the study if you need me."

Two hours later Daisy triumphantly enters the study, hands the two typed yellow pages to her mother, and leaves smiling.

The Most Significant Event in My Life

The most significant event in my life happened the summer I turned nine, at Martha's Vineyard. Toward the end of the summer, Sharon Snow, the thirteen-year-old who lived next door, broke her leg wind surfing. She had to wear a cast from her foot to her hip and stay in bed for a month with her leg raised up on the footboard.

Everyone lined up to sign her cast. While I was waiting my turn to sign, I noticed something dark flashing above the plaster whenever Sharon raised her nightgown. I was shocked. There were always people in her room. Why didn't she wear underpants?

When my turn came, I signed quickly and ran home. The next day from my bedroom window I saw Sharon's older brother and his friends sitting out on the Snows' back porch drinking soda and listening to the ball game. The Red Sox were beating the Orioles. For some reason I still don't understand, I took off not just my underpants but all my clothes, pulled a chair up to the window that overlooked their porch, and climbed up on the windowsill, pressing myself flat against the window, holding onto the frame with my fingers. I stood there as long as I could keep my balance (not very long), terrified they might look up but also hoping they would. I don't know if they did or not. I do know it was one of the most significant, scary, mysterious events of my life. Afterwards, I was so ashamed that I pretended to be sick and stayed in my room for five days, until it was time for us to leave the Vineyard for home.

I think about that day every time I sit down to write my college essay. Maybe writing this essay is a similar act: stripping naked before strangers, exposing my most shameful secrets, taking a dangerous risk to get your attention.

If some miracle were to get me into your college, I believe I would like to study psychology, to find out why the most significant events of my life so far are those I can't begin to understand.

Beaming with pride, Rosemary hands the yellow sheets to Harold. Harold puts on his glasses and reads down the page; then he slaps the paper with the back of his hand and says, "She certainly can't submit an essay like this. Can she?"

Rosemary, who weekly battles to defend her handful of female math students against blind male scorn, is ready to take on Admissions too. "If I were on the committee," she says, "I'd be very impressed by her honesty. Honesty like this is rare in any teenager, but especially in a girl. Any college that doesn't recognize courage doesn't deserve Daisy. Why, even the writing is excellent—no wasted words, and notice how well she uses the subjunctive."

"You mean you think this really happened?"

"Don't you?"

Harold lays his glasses on the coffee table and squares his shoulders. "I'm going to go ask her."

Standing in the doorway of his daughter's room, Harold clears his throat and says in his most engaging voice, "Your mother, who loves you, claims to be charmed by this essay; but what I want to know is, did anything like this ever really happen to you?"

Daisy reaches for the paper. "Oh, Daddy. If it did, do you think I'd write about it?"

"Frankly, hon, I can't think of any other reason to write this sort of thing. What's your point, if I may ask?"

"Miss Mannheim says it's more important to write a good, imaginative essay and say something original that will make us stand out than to stick to what really happened."

"You'll stand out all right if you send this in! How the devil did you ever think up a thing like this?"

Daisy's index finger glides to her mouth. "I don't know. It's what doing this application feels like to me."

"I see," says Harold, rubbing his chin. "Well, I can't believe this is the sort of thing your teacher had in mind. I'd advise you to get another opinion or two before you send it in."

"Oh, Daddy," says Daisy disdainfully. But when he closes the door again, she rips the essay in two and drops it among the Reese's and Heath Bar wrappers piled in her waste basket, then flings herself on her bed.

She's fourteen. Her breasts are small, her period still feels new. At school she's known for piano and dance, at home she's a force, but here at the edge of the ocean where she's come with her best friends, Diane and Carrie, to sell hot dogs and soda at Diane's parents' concession at Hunter's Point, here she's a hunter, a cannibal.

Each of the girls works at the hot dog stand four hours a day, alternating shifts: nine to one, one to five, five to nine; the rest of their time is free. Daytimes when they're off work they lie on the beach, ears glued to their radios; after dinner the two off duty wander the boardwalk looking. At night, the three girls lie in the dark gossiping on their narrow bunks in the musty sand-strewn room they share, while flies buzz at the screens or circle slowly near the ceiling. Daisy and Carrie giggle, egg each other on to tell more malicious jokes, more delicious lies, while smart Diane, ambitious, disciplined, respected, listens silently. Never does a secret or slander cross her lips; no one has anything on Diane. Daisy wishes she could be like her, but she knows she never will. Her yearnings are too strange, her curiosity too strong. Her unspoken goal is to do everything there is to do, see everything there is to see. Starting now. This summer she hopes to experience for herself the forbidden and awesome acts she and Carrie so carelessly pin on absent members of their set.

Every day she searches the beach and boardwalk for someone to test her theories on. Weeks pass. No one appears. Finally, when there are only three weeks left of summer, when she's all but given up, at last she finds what she wants. He comes for a hot dog and orange soda during her one-to-five. He wears cutoff jeans, a straw hat, no shoes or shirt. He is husky and square-jawed, he has large muscular arms and legs covered with fine dark hairs that lie flat on his limbs but on his chest curl voluptuously from his neck down into his jeans. His toes and fingers are long and slender, darkened by dirt. His face is still downy. From the very first time she sees him, the thought of him sends her stomach diving and turning like a dolphin going under, makes her catch her breath for breathing under water. She hasn't exactly willed this feeling. It was there as soon as he threw back his head and tipped the bottle to his lips and again, stronger, when he grazed her fingers paying in tickets.

Each day she waits for him to return, each night she schemes about finding him. She offers to work all the middle shifts, hoping he'll show up again at the stand, but the other girls refuse and he never does. Before and after work she wanders the beach, the boardwalk, even in drizzle, but she can't find him.

She wishes she could confide in Diane and Carrie, but she knows better: Diane finds boys disgusting, vowing she'll never let one arouse her, and next year Carrie may be someone else's best friend. She could sooner tell her mother than these two, who know nothing but gossip and giggling when it comes to boys; at least her mother would understand what she's feeling. But her mother's far away; she's on her own.

At night in bed she can hardly wait until Diane and Carrie fall asleep so she can be alone with him, watch him tip the bottle to his lips with his long fingers, see his Adam's apple move in his throat. The room is damp; sand piles up in the corners; the wind bangs a shutter across the hall. When she's absolutely sure no one's awake, stealthily she calms her excited body with her barely moving finger. But her touch only strengthens her desire and coats it with shame.

She looks and looks. Then one day, at the farthest end of the boardwalk, she sees him selling tickets in a booth. The next day, after her shift, she washes her hair, irons her prettiest dress, the red and white candy stripe with the string straps, and presents her card to him for her employees' discount on four strips of tickets. Don't I know you? she asks. Didn't I sell you a hot dog and soda a week ago?

He punches out the tickets without answering. Brazenly she asks his name. Vince. I'm Daisy. She tells an elaborate story to keep him away from the hotel where Diane and Carrie would pry, and then goes on talking. He lets her do all the work. His shyness makes him safe, makes her want him more. Why not ask him to meet her? Diane and Carrie won't find out, and after next week she'll never see him again.

The next day after work they meet on the beach. The evening is perfect: half moon, slight breeze, even phosphorescence on the waves, and the water has never been warmer. They run in holding hands but don't get past the shallows. At knee depth she falls into the water and pulls him down with her. He understands. They kiss. He sets her on his knees in the water; it laps at her waist. They sit and float in the water kissing until she begins to shiver.

Hand in hand they run back up the beach to where their sandals wait on his blanket. The beach is not quite empty, but no one can see them in the dark. He wraps her first in his towel, then in his arms, rubs vigorously. I'll warm you up, he says, spreading his body on top of hers, but she's afraid; she rolls over and pushes him off. He follows her lead. Now they're lying side by side. They kiss and nuzzle—face, ears, neck, shoulders. When she's warm again, she notices that the bow at her neck has come untied, letting her straps hang loose.

As he begins to stroke her breast, she crosses her legs tightly. Only on top, she whispers. Whatever you say, he says. She throws back her head as he squirms down the blanket to kiss her breasts.

Though she feels the bulge against her leg, he doesn't move his hips. His word counts. She forgets everything except his lips sucking gently at her nipple, his hand slowly caressing her other breast. When she closes her eyes, she sees the orange bottle at his firm lips and the long expanse of his thick muscular neck.

21

The Haven . . .

Nora and Rosemary, who have begun to feel really comfortable with each other lately, even close, are stretched out at the Haven side by side on white chaise longues, sipping ruby-colored aperitifs, naked down to the skimpy white terry towels draped over their hips. Between sips, they steal curious glances at each other's breasts.

Nora, who has taken half a year's trial membership in the club, resolving to give herself the full treatment at least once a fortnight plus every time she feels blue, has grown comfortable with the casual nudity of the place. Listed under Health Clubs in the Manhattan Yellow Pages, the Haven is much more, though it has all the necessary facilities—hot tubs, sauna, cold plunge, pool, tanning tables, exercise room, masseuses: from its spacious rooms the appraising male gaze is strictly barred. Though the price of half a day at the Haven is commensurate with the price of a night in a first-class hotel in New York or London, the patrons consider it good value. Sometimes, in those high-arched halls, decorated entirely in stark black and white except for the garishly colored parrots and parakeets and lush air plants and bromeliads that inhabit the moist, semitropical air— sometimes the ubiquitous nudity strikes Nora as chaste.

To Rosemary, a newcomer to the Haven, the cats gliding along the black-tiled paths, the birds preening on their high perches, the swings hung from vine-covered ropes above the free-form pool, even the chaises, arranged in intimate groupings among the mirrored pillars, render the atmosphere too exotic to relax in clothed, much less nude. Her first glimpse made her think of voluptuous brothels of an earlier time, harems, Parisian pleasure palaces. Not until she finally understood that no man, not even a eunuch, would ever appear did she recognize her error. To her, nothing is sexy here, only chic, even unto the French receptionist. No need to be on guard.

"Your breasts," says Nora, who has made a career of speaking her mind and has had breasts on the mind ever since her mammogram, "your breasts are terrific, you know. They're really in fine shape—for women our age." She says it plainly, objectively, for the sake of honesty, and only incidentally to put her guest at ease.

Instantly Rosemary crosses her arms over her chest. "Oh, no! They're awful!" A passing black cat with white paws takes advantage of Rosemary's distraction to leap onto her chaise.

"How can you say that?" cries Nora, truly shocked.

As the cat curls up purring in the curve of her waist, Rosemary releases her arms to pet it and looks down. "They were great when I was pregnant, but as soon as I stopped nursing Spider they sort of shriveled up, and now they sag and the nipples pucker. Let's face it, their day is past.

I shouldn't complain, though. They did their work well enough." Stroking the cat philosophically, she lets herself look straight at naked Nora for the first time since emerging from the dressing rooms. "You're the one with the beautiful breasts."

How many times have the slim, silent attendants in white terry sarongs who glide along the tiled Haven paths emptying ashtrays, replacing magazines, collecting empty glasses and discarded towels, heard this conversation? Too big, too small, too pendulous, too high, too pointy, too flat, lopsided, hairy, wrong. Nora has finally begun to comprehend and even appreciate the vast assortment of breasts and bones and body types, various as faces, on display in this female-only club; yet a lifetime under the scrutiny of men has left her as obsessed as the next woman by her differences. "Don't be crazy," she orders. "Mine'll be down to here in another few years. One is bigger than the other—see? I know, I know—you probably find them voluptuous, but I hate them."

In these months of growing close, the two have been able to talk about many things: books and politics, dreams and fears, money and sex, now even their naked breasts. Nora longs to tell Rosemary how odd they look flattened this way and that against a photographic plate. Of all her friends, Rosemary is the one who she knows would come through in an emergency. She'd see the cheerful side, know how to comfort her with a smile or a touch, witness her fear without judging her, and refuse to leak her secret no matter what its gossip value. Not that having a mammogram is incriminating by itself. But Nora's afraid that once she starts talking, she might not stop. It's part of her code, learned the hard way, that, except in extremis, she may not lean. Otherwise, her whole independent edifice might weaken and collapse. This is why she hasn't told even Lex.

From their breasts, Nora and Rosemary move on to compare and disparage other aspects of their bodies—skin, weight, veins, muscles, hair—growing more insistent and trusting with every remark, until Nora suddenly claps her hands, sits up sharply, and shouts, "Will you listen to us? My God, you'd think we were models or something, with nothing but our bodies to peddle. Let's stop this insane talk—right now! We should remember how lucky we are to have the kinds of work and lives that only improve with age. Who cares about skin! We should take a lesson from George Sand. She told Flaubert: The day I resolutely buried my youth I grew twenty years younger."

Rosemary stares at Nora. She's not ready to bury her youth, not yet—

not with midterms coming up and integrals still to cover; not with Daisy's graduation looming and Peter talking about a trip. To do everything she's promised to do she'll need all the energy and youth she has.

"Anyway," continues Nora, "I've got a lot worse things to worry about right now."

"Like what?"

"Like—" Again, Nora resists the temptation to speak of her breast and instead spills her newest dilemma about whether to testify at a House subcommittee hearing on nuclear waste. "Should I speak up and tell them what I think of their sneaky plan to dump waste in the middle of a Chippewa reservation, which they probably don't even realize is practically on top of the headwaters of the Mississippi River, or should I just work on my story and wait till I'm subpoenaed and then refuse to testify? My editor doesn't want me to blow my story before it's published, and my sources will be terrified if I talk, but I'm tempted to stand up in front of that crazy committee and tell them just what I think. The Mississippi River!—can you believe it? What would you do?"

As always, Nora wants to do what's right, what's brave. But she can't be sure which of her choices fits the bill, which of her ears the devil is whispering in. As for Rosemary, who remembers how just before his book was published Harold was threatened with jail for refusing to turn over certain of his files on terrorism, prudence rules. He was prepared to go to jail to protect his sources and prove a point, but Rosemary, with no income of her own then and two dependent kids, felt constrained to protect her family. Heroism always arouses her suspicions. Just as she's about to counsel prudence in whatever form and so plunge the friendship into yet another scalding bath of combat, an attendant with a clipboard approaches her.

"Ms. Kennedy? Excuse me, but there's room in the sauna now."

Saved, Rosemary points at Nora.

Nora nods her thanks, then turns to Rosemary and explains, "She took you for me because you're the tall one. They always assume I'm tall because of my big mouth. Ready?"—and leaping up she lets her towel fall to the chaise, revealing firm flanks beneath two obtrusive hipbones, a flat stomach, a small, perfect triangle of light brown curls, and beneath them all, short, skinny, slightly bowed calves.

"You see?" cries Rosemary triumphantly. "You've got no tummy at all, and nice trim hips—but look at me. All fat." She's small on top, her shoulders are square, her arms firm, her ribs and even her hipbones show, though it's true her hips, stomach, and thighs are padded and rounded like a seventeenth-century nude's. But you know women. When she stands, she must force herself to fold her towel over her arm instead of wrap it around her waist.

"Last week," says Rosemary, "I realized why they say it gets much harder to lose weight after a certain age."

Nora opens the sauna door. "Why?"

"Because after a certain age you no longer care."

They're still laughing as they enter the room and the hot air assaults them. Rosemary feels as if she's in a strange, new medium, breathing under water. Gradually her senses adjust until she makes out five naked bodies on three tiers of slatted wood in the dimly lit wooden room. Nora points Rosemary to a corner place on the bottom tier. "You should start down here where it's not quite so hot, get used to it gradually. I'm going up." On the empty top tier, Nora folds a towel into a pillow, lies down, and closes her eyes. But Rosemary, fascinated, sits staring into the room until her eyes become accustomed to the dim, hazy light and her ears to the buzz of hot stone and the low conversation of women.

Before she feels herself going limp, Rosemary moves up a tier to join Nora. "Peter wants us to go away over my spring break. There's a math conference in Rome I could use as an excuse. I don't know if I should go."

Up here the women are so relaxed that they neither gasp nor recoil when their bodies accidentally touch.

"Why not?" asks Nora.

"First of all, Harold's bound to be suspicious. If it were a teachers' conference there'd be no problem, but those mathematicians will almost all be men, and Harold knows how alien they make me feel. It's one thing to be the token woman in a department where my students need me, but it's something else again to willingly subject myself to the insult of an international conference." Beginning to sweat, she drops her towel from her shoulders to the bench. "Besides, three weeks is awfully long. Peter and I have never spent more than three days together. I'm afraid it might wreck what we have."

Nora, who relishes her clean uncluttered life yet still believes she'd like to live with Lex, shakes her head wistfully and says, "I'll never understand why, if you're so crazy about Peter, you don't want to spend more time with him. If I were you—"

"Ah, but your time is your own, you control it yourself. In my life, one afternoon a week is all I can afford. Anyway, if I were living with Peter I know he'd start to be like a husband instead of a lover. The last thing I need is to wind up with two husbands."

"I buy *that!*" announces the plump, jovial woman with a mass of thick red curls, pink cheeks, and long pointed breasts seated below Rosemary. "We're really quite protected by marriage, aren't we? It lets us have our love life on our own terms: don't call me, I'll call you."

Rosemary welcomes an ally. "Exactly! I like to see my lover once or twice a week, very intense, then nothing but talk in between."

"Not me," joins in a small blond woman stretched out on the bottom tier. Her voice is a husky contralto; she's somewhere in her fifties and probably bleached, but her body is firm and well tended. Even nude she seems chic. "I once had a secret affair—meeting in motels, the whole thing. I couldn't take it. It lasted about three months and then I thought, it just isn't worth it. I was always terrified I'd be caught in my lies, always anxious, saying I'd be here when I was really going there, lying to the children. And suppose I had a car accident and they found me on the highway? What was I doing on I-91? And then they'd *know*."

The plump redheaded woman laughs. "Don't listen to Estelle. She's got a kinky taste for monogamy."

"No, really," says Estelle in her deep voice. "I couldn't take it. After my divorce it was much better. No more lies."

"Me, I'd never make it without adultery," says her redheaded friend. "Married sex is so *boring*." Righteously, from opposite sides, both Nora and Rosemary nod.

"Even so," says Estelle, "I can't imagine how any relationship built on deceit can possibly last."

"Really?" chimes in Rosemary, as if any marriage could be safe, even her own. "I can't imagine a lasting relationship without it!"

Rosemary's rosy-cheeked ally laughs and sits up. "Absolutely right. Look at me: I've been married for twenty-two years, and it's a perfect marriage," she says proudly.

"Perfect?" asks Nora archly. "How interesting."

"Go on, Maggie," urges Estelle. "Tell them your secret. Tell them why you think it's perfect." Even her giggle comes out husky.

"It's easy," says Maggie, smiling through reddened lips that perfectly match her hair. "My husband's a TV producer, he works mostly on the

Coast or on location, so we only get to see each other once or twice a month." As she rises to leave, sweat drips from her long breasts, glistens on her heavy pink thighs. "If he were home more we'd probably split up, but this way we have everything."

"If you ask me," adds Rosemary, making points before her team disperses, "the thrill is over as soon as you start living together."

"Who's talking about living together?" chides Nora. "We were talking about a three-week trip to Italy."

"I'm not sure I can leave the children even that long. Their vacation starts after I leave, and Daisy will be hearing from colleges then. She needs me." Rosemary senses something else is going on with Daisy, she doesn't know exactly what, but something tells her she ought to be around, just in case. But if she tried to explain, Nora would accuse her of being overprotective. "And Spider . . ." Her voice trails off in a reverie. How can she leave Spider? "I know what you're going to say, Harold can take care of them, but his cooking—"

"What about Mrs. Scaggs?"

Rosemary shakes her head. She's learned through years of experience that it's not a matter of cooking. The more help she has at home, the more indispensable her own unique presence. She's a hands-on mother. "Mrs. Scaggs can only come in three times a week. Anyhow, she does everything, she can't be mother to the children too."

"Children! I don't see why you call them children. They're practically grown up."

Rosemary looks at Nora pityingly. "Because they're my children," she says softly. "That's what they are. They'll always be my children."

"I have to confess," says Rosemary as the two women approach the pool, "I almost called you up to cancel today. I even dialed your number—then changed my mind. I'm so glad I came, though. I had no idea places like this existed."

Nora, who thinks Rosemary's hesitance had something to do with nudity, pauses beside one of two dainty swings hung over the pool by vine-covered ropes and issues the challenge, "Why? Why in the world did you want to cancel?"

"Because," says Rosemary, sitting down on the wet black tiles to dangle her feet in the white-tiled pool, "this amazing thing happened to me

Sunday night. I was grading the week's problem sets when I saw a brilliant deduction on a student paper. It was a proof of an ordinary problem in differentials, but it was done in a very peculiar and interesting way, a way I'd never seen before. I was puzzled, because the paper belonged to one of my poorer students. I went over the problem again, and when I couldn't find anything wrong, I started to get really excited. I thought of all the stories I'd ever read about unheralded genius—Einstein flunking his exams, Woody Allen getting kicked out of NYU. And—especially since the student was one of my girls—I thought maybe I'd been suddenly offered the privilege of grooming a new math talent for the world. I read the problem through again with great excitement, trying to figure it out, until the third time through I realized that all my agitation was over nothing but a pair of careless mistakes—first the student's, then mine. She'd misnumbered her work sheets so that I was reading a solution to an entirely different problem from the one I thought, and a faulty solution at that.

"At first I was crestfallen, until I realized that even if my student wasn't onto anything special after all, maybe—just possibly—I was. Because that mistake started me thinking along certain lines I'd never considered before. Maybe no one ever had. Anyway, what does it matter where an idea comes from? Penicillin began as an accident too, right? And there in a dumb mistake in a student's problem set, I discovered a startlingly new approach to a problem I'd been tripping over since I'd begun my thesis. Maybe a whole new kind of proof. I closed the door to the study and without even finishing grading the paper went straight to work. I worked half the night and again most of the next day. Hours biting pencils, pages of equations."

Nora sits down beside her. "What happened?"

"Nothing . . . yet. But—" Rosemary watches a green parakeet land on the swing. Her eyes glitter and her voice prances as she explains excitedly: "Since I began teaching, I've almost forgotten how thrilling it is to sit alone for hours struggling with a difficult proof, calling on everything you know, with nothing between you and the light but your own concentration and effort. God, it felt so good. It was like slowly turning a beautiful abstract kaleidoscope, watching all the shiny pieces fall into place in fascinating new patterns—intricate, startling, symmetrical—while all the trivial daily distractions just vanished away."

"I think I know what you mean," says Nora. "For me, most of the time it feels as if my ideas come out only with great effort, like sausage out of a meat grinder. Or else they come too fast for my words, so that by the time I'm done writing down one idea I can't reconstruct the next without an enormous effort. My mind and my fingers are out of sync. But sometimes, on certain rare occasions—and I can never predict when this will happen—sometimes the sentences begin falling into place as soon as I form my ideas. If I'm very lucky, I'll get a whole day or maybe even a string of days like that, when it feels as if all I have to do is open up my channels and the ideas will enter from out there someplace and flow through me in perfectly formed, even elegant, sentences, spilling out of my fingers straight onto the page. As if I were simply a medium, an inspired medium. When I'm working like that I get so carried away that my building could be burning down and I wouldn't even know it. You know me, Rosemary, I don't believe in that mystical crap, but when the prose is flowing that way, with so much grace and ease, it's like hearing some glorious new song."

"Yes. Me too. Though for me, it's not the ease but the effort I love. The challenge. Like a strenuous, exhilarating workout." Rosemary sighs with pleasure. "I get so high. There's nothing like it in the whole world."

Two women climb out of the water, wrap themselves in towels, and walk away, leaving the pool empty. Nora, who has taken two vinyl caps from a passing attendant, hands one to Rosemary and tucks her long hair into the other. "So what happened with your proof?"

"That's why I almost canceled—I'm still working on it. I don't expect too much, but even if it finally comes to nothing, I'll still have made certain connections I never made before, seen certain things. It's not the proof that counts, it's the effort, stretching the mind, those timeless leaps."

"Speaking of leaps," says Nora, lifting herself onto a swing, "watch this." Sailing slowly, gracefully through the air with her head thrown back, she works up a certain momentum and then, as the swing flies out, leans forward and lets go, splashing down into the deep water. "Now you," she calls up, wiping her eyes.

Rosemary catches the swing on its return and after one short arc drops into the pool.

"We really are lucky," she says when she reaches Nora's side.

"You mean this place?"

"Yes. And the work we do."

"I know," says Nora.

"I almost missed it, too. I almost let it go. It was that close."

Not me, Nora thinks. I would never have let it go. But quickly, before the proud words can slip out, she swims away.

They float on their backs in the tepid pool. A parrot's repeated squawk echoes above them. "Tell me honestly," says Nora, paddling close to Rosemary, "would you really rather stay home with your kids than go to Italy with Peter?"

Rosemary fills her lungs and blows out air—a water sigh. "You seem to think being with my children is some sort of sacrifice. Actually, I think I'd rather be home with them than almost anywhere. I'm sorry, but it happens to be true. I'm not proposing it as a model or anything, I'm just being truthful. They come first. The reason I'm happy is that I know what's important to me and I have it."

Nora can't stand the bottomless smugness of Rosemary's response to her cozy little life. How can she fail to respect the ever-encroaching disasters or acknowledge the misery in the world? Whole countries are enslaved, people everywhere are under siege, at this moment the world is preparing to self-destruct, and Rosemary is *happy*. That very morning while walking her dog, Nora came upon another journalist walking his, a man she scooped on her first trip abroad twelve years before, a man she's never much liked but whom she respects for his deep skepticism about the touted virtues of this imperfect world. She debated whether or not to greet him, for despite the mundane pooper-scooper in his left hand (mirroring exactly the one in her right), he seemed lost in profound thought. At the precise moment they passed each other, he looked up and recognized her. But instead of commenting like most people on the banal virtues of the day, he had the good manners to restrict his greeting to a curt nod and the grace at least not to smile.

"And the reason I'm miserable," returns Nora, "is that I know what's important to me and I don't have it. I don't come anywhere near it. And I wish this heartless world would take notice and change so the rest of us could get a crack at what we want, too!"

When they were done with their sauna, hot tub, cold plunge, sun treatment, swim, massage, and shower; when they'd made free use of the body lotion, shampoo, setting lotion, hair dryers, and makeup; after

Rosemary had made her daily contact call to Harold from one of the small decorated phone booths, and Nora had phoned Bianca's office to see if the mammogram report had come in, they decided to stop someplace for a quick bite. As usual, Nora wound up ordering Perrier with lemon while Rosemary studied the menu.

"I'll have a glass of chablis and—"

The Salad . . .

"What's in this Salad Primavera?" Rosemary asked the waitress.

The waitress raised her pencil from her pad to recite: "It has arugula, Bibb lettuce, watercress, feta cheese, olives, tomatoes—and I think some other veggies."

"That sounds good. Please bring me that, then." Rosemary turned to Nora. "I'm starving. You sure all you want is Perrier after all that heat and exercise?"

"I'm afraid," said Nora, shaking her head, "I'll never be able to eat a regular meal again."

"Why not?"

"I've been dieting for weeks and I can't seem to lose any weight. All I do is eat one ordinary meal, not even anything particularly fattening, and I gain two or three pounds. And then I have to starve myself for days just to get back to where I started. I'm afraid something has changed in me. I used to be able to eat anything I wanted, even desserts, and at least one big meal a day. But now it feels as if I can't eat anything at all."

Rosemary thought Nora looked as slim and beautiful as ever, but she knew better than to say so. When her salad came she ate it guiltily, even though it was only salad.

22

"Rosemary," says Harold sternly, poking his head into the study. "The music's stopped in Daisy's room and the door's closed." His brows meet in a troubled V.

Rosemary welcomes the interruption. For days she's been working on the same difficult proof and getting nowhere. On Tuesday in the middle of the night she woke up with a luminous inspiration. She thought she saw in a flash the proof that had hitherto been unprovable, one that would redeem all her recent efforts. It contained an idea she'd dimly glimpsed while writing her thesis on infinities, then had dropped, then forgotten. In the dream she saw the solution colorful and whole. Harold rushed pencil and paper to her in bed so she wouldn't risk forgetting and the next day helped clear their calendar. But now, after filling three legal pads with her scratchings, she's once again ready to give it up as a mistake derived from a mistake. A pity: she knows her support is vital to certain of her students, who may lose her if she fails to publish. Yet she's also aware that her very devotion to her students has raised suspicions with her dean about her commitment to math. Sometimes she wonders if the suspicions may not be justified. She'll go down fighting the relentless insinuation that women can't do math, but that other cliché, about youth and genius, has started to get to her: she may be just too old for original mathematical work.

She lays down her pencil and looks up. "So?"

"So it's midnight. What do you suppose they're doing in there?"

"Homework," says Rosemary.

"Suppose they're doing—something else?"

Rosemary closes her eyes. When her children were little, she tried to protect them from Harold's well-meaning discipline, as her sisters had protected her; now that they're in their teens, she feels she must protect them from a more insidious intent. Since before they learned to read, she has dutifully fed her children appropriate books, articles, and talks on the nature and beauty of sex, life-giving and rosy like the sun, and on various types of birth control—far better, she thinks, than prohibitions. Yet even now, despite the advent of the pill, the revelations of the sixties, the hysteria of the New Right, the discrediting of the double standard— despite all this, she is still required to police her children's private lives. Even Harold, who she knows would do anything for his children (but who, she recalls, managed to check his puritanical tendencies when he was courting her), expects it. Well, she won't. She will present her children with every conceivable option and pray she'll have the courage to let them decide for themselves. "Okay," she says, prepared to take on Harold and the whole world. "Suppose they're in there kissing. Is that so bad?"

"Oh, come off it, Rosemary. You know what I mean." Harold stalks off to the window, tugs his crumpled pack of cigarettes out of his pocket, then shoves it back in again.

"Harold. Honestly. I doubt very much if they're having sex in there. But even if they were, wouldn't you rather have them do it here at home than God knows where? At least they're safe here."

"She's too damn young for sex."

"I was the same age. I turned out all right."

"And that boy."

Rosemary never feels stronger than when she's fighting for her children. Once a huge drunk followed her and Spider down First Avenue muttering threats. At first she was frightened, but when the man began to tap Spider's shoulder she wheeled around in a rage, placing her body between him and Spider, and began shouting, "Get your hands off that boy! Don't you dare touch him!" growing fiercer and fiercer until the man backed off and left them. "What about the boy? What's the problem?"

"I don't know anything about him. That's the problem."

"He's a kid in her class. But really, Harold, Daisy's old enough to choose her friends now."

"Who says? Anyway, it's after midnight."

He begins to pace; she turns vainly back to her proof. She notes that a generation ago she might have been arguing the other side of this question. He notes that a generation ago the situation would never have arisen.

This time when Harold pulls out the cigarettes he lights up. He pulls deeply on the smoke. "Just how late do you think he should be allowed to stay in there?"

"We've never set a curfew for them as long as they're home when they say they'll be home. And they've always been good about it. So I don't see how we can suddenly start imposing curfews now. Especially here."

"I'm not talking about a curfew. That boy can't stay in her room all night."

Rosemary clears away his smoke with a wave of her hand. "I doubt they plan to spend the night together, if that's what you mean. They have school tomorrow."

"Then I think it's time he left," says Harold decisively, moving toward the door.

Rosemary marshals reason. "Look, Daisy's a high school senior. How can you start telling her what time to go to sleep?"

"I can damn well tell her what time to clear that boy out of my house."

"That's absurd. She's going to college next year. She'll be able to sleep anywhere she wants with anyone she likes and you won't even know about it. Don't be ridiculous."

"I know I have no say about what happens outside this house. But goddammit, I still have something to say about what goes on under my own roof." He snuffs out his cigarette, hides the butt in his pocket, and starts off down the hall.

"Harold!" calls Rosemary, her voice dashing after him. "*Please* don't go in there. Let's talk about it first."

He turns, lifts his chin. "As far as I'm concerned, we just talked about it." Nevertheless, Harold's shoulders slump, his mouth droops, and slowly, trailed by his wife, he detours into the living room, where he pours himself a brandy. Already he's wishing he'd taken Rosemary's position, so much more liberal than his own. Possibly she's right. She often is. But he's unwilling to sacrifice his children to some questionable idealistic principle. Even if Rosemary is theoretically right, he knows what boys do to girls. All he wants is to protect his children, and girls have curfews.

He gulps his drink. Fortified, he tries one last thrust. "What if Spider had a girl in *his* room with the door closed? I bet you'd make pretty damn sure *she* went home at a decent hour, wouldn't you?"

Rosemary sees he's got her. She can be as daring as she likes with her own children, but hardly with someone else's. She remembers the exact moment when she had to decide whether or not to banish her children from the bathroom before inserting her tampon. Precocious Daisy was trying to teach Spider the alphabet by stacking letter blocks against the bathtub. Rosemary stalled as long as she could, yielding to every prudish, lazy, cautious impulse; but in the final crucial moment she somehow managed to cling to her faith and proceed with her toilette unabashed. In a triumph of principle, she casually inserted the tampon as if it were as ordinary an act as brushing her teeth—at the very moment when the blocks came tumbling down. Teary Spider ran to her knees. Fearlessly, she rinsed off the cardboard insertion tube and presented it to him—the perfect toddler's toy.

Harold looks at his watch, sighs. "I'm turning in now. Do whatever you want."

. . .

Back in the study, Rosemary stares vacantly at her proof. Sex, sex! Once it had seemed her very ticket to freedom, her Niña, Pinta, and Santa Maria, her Declaration of Independence and Bill of Rights. But in the end, it was mostly trouble. Generation after generation: guilt, shame, the monthly pregnancy scare, cystitis ("the honeymoon disease") with its wake of pain, incontinence, and bright orange pee from the peridium pills. Sometimes the pleasure she touted to her kids didn't seem worth the trouble. Even when, mellowed by wine in their darkened hideaway, she finally lets her hips go with Peter, it's always without memory. She can recall the image of her joy—the twining of their arms and legs, the music on the stereo, even the fantasy rolling slowly through her mind— but not the feel of it. How disappointing to find that after all her liberated pretensions, her deepest secret is still, after all, sex.

She turns out the lights, content to have averted disaster for another day. How she longs to protect her children from the ravages of shame, wishes she could teach them everything she knows; but despite the upheavals of the past decades, it's still impossible to speak truly of sex. As impossible as it was to speak as a child of the thrill of seeing two dogs copulate. No matter how hard she tries, all she ever finds in her mouth are the same pristine or sugared words she's heard all her life, the safe mouthings of motherhood. The day she announced at dinner in preachy tones that henceforth condoms would be kept on the bathroom shelf beside the tampons for anyone who wanted them, the whole family roared. And when she retells her sisters' cautionary tales, the children grow bored with the distant past. As for the shuddering thrill she feels when Peter's cock fills her mouth and he rubs his lips and tongue across her swollen vulva—these secret joys she may never acknowledge, much less describe. Tiptoeing past Spider's room, she listens to him sleep. The best she can hope for, she decides, is to get Harold and the world to leave the children alone on the improbable chance that they can learn the secrets for themselves in time.

After flossing his teeth, Harold empties his pockets of butts and watches them swirl down the toilet. The record in his mind repeats: *too damn young.* He thinks he genuinely believes that the problem is only a matter of age, that even his darling Daisy will someday reach an age when sex is perfectly acceptable.

But when? What age? Like that fiction *the present*, the acceptable age for sex seems always to be slipping away or not yet arrived.

Adolescence? A prime contender, at least for boys. But Spider slouching past the peep show on the way to school, hands in pockets, head lowered, eyeballs sneaking sidelong glances at the spread thighs of giant women in shiny black boots, or the open red mouths of swan-necked panting blondes with heads thrown back, of redheads holding up red-tipped breasts, is painfully embarrassed, even before the ticket seller.

Daisy, heavily schooled in sex ed, knows that everyone is born bisexual, nothing is dirty, desire can be beautiful and childbirth painless. But she also knows the world thinks otherwise. She hopes that once she gets to college people will be as enlightened as she thinks she is. She dreams of orgies in dorms, wild parties with throbbing music, masquerades. But until then, though she hardly pretends to be a virgin, she still refuses her mother's urgings to get a diaphragm.

Lovelorn Rosemary is sometimes shocked to see herself, an instructor in mathematics and twice a mother, carrying on like an adolescent, and each time it happens she's shocked anew.

As for Harold, the best candidate, a man of power and maturity, this very morning when he saw his lined stubbly face and the worrisome roll of flab squeezed up over his belt when he buckled it, and he flashed the plump unlined face of his laughing mistress, Barbara, across his mind and realized he was approaching fifty, a phrase popped into his head that made him suck in his gut and skip breakfast for the first time that month and forgo his precious morning cigarette: *dirty old man*.

Sex, sex. It was done in the dark or behind locked doors, with parts of the body no one mentioned. The unshown culmination of a scene, the unspoken punch of a joke, the hinted meaning of a glance, the unmentionable disgrace, the unspecified longing. Its secret name: *it*. Doing it; making it; getting it. Unnameable, indescribable—like the secret name of God.

You can say:

They rendezvoused in a certain bar in Santa Fe; seeing his white-blond hair as he came through the door, Nora wished she had worn the dark blue one instead of the mauve and had shaved her legs; too late now. They talked nervously for exactly as long as the Sports Roundup lasted, then had a nightcap in the hotel bar. Eventually, when he thought she was ready, they walked to Room 24; they double-locked the door. He kissed her and cupped her breast in his hand. She wondered: Is his hair blond or white? I've never loved a white-haired man before. She said: Please, I need to go slow the first time, okay? I'm nervous. I'm not used to this.

Don't you want to? he said.

Oh, I want to, yes, oh I do, but I'm a little scared. Just go slow with me, please. Staring at the phone, she wondered what time it was in New York and if Lex was waiting for her call.

Look, he said, we can have another drink if you like. I have a bottle in my suitcase. Shall we?

Oh, yes! Let's do, I'll get us some glasses from the bathroom, she said, grateful for the chance to leave the room.

On the bathroom sink are two clean glasses, covered in paper cases that say Sterilized for Your Convenience. A similar paper message covers the toilet seat. Modern woman knows that in passionate affairs it is important to urinate immediately before and after sex (and to drink quantities of liquid, preferably cranberry juice) to prevent or ease cystitis. Quietly Nora closes the bathroom door, breaks the seal on the toilet seat, lifts her skirt and relieves herself before he can occupy her premises. She wonders: While she's in here, shall she wash herself too? Unlike some, this bathroom doesn't celebrate the body: there's no bidet for cleansing, no Jacuzzi for stimulation, only a standard tub with shower and a single sink. No, she decides. She's too embarrassed to wash, afraid to seem either calculating or overfastidious. If only it could all be accomplished without dragging the body into it. But now it's too late for such scruples: once she flushes the toilet everything will be known to him.

She rises, flushes, picks up the glasses, kicks off her shoes, and returns to the bedroom, smiling cheerily.

He too has removed his shoes and is lying, clothed but with shirt unbuttoned, on the bed, which he opened as soon as she left the room. The bottle, a half pint of Dewars White Label, is on the night table. She thinks: How considerate of him to have brought us something to drink. But as he pours them each a hefty inch, she wonders if he brought the bottle for her or for himself. She sits on the side of the bed in her dress and pantyhose (why has she kept them on?) and toasts, *To us*. He looks at her with his intensely blue, unblinking eyes and repeats, *To us*.

These are familiar words and phrases. The other ones that tell of longing, lust, greed, ambivalence, helplessness—what of them?

He brushes the hair from her temples, letting his fingers and palm linger on her cheek. She removes her silver rings and turquoise combs. He places his glass on the night table and kisses her lips.

It is 12:21 a.m. Just as Harold passes by Daisy's door on his way to bed, Daisy and a thin young man carrying books emerge from her room into the hall. They are neither glowing nor disheveled. But instead of feeling relieved, somehow Harold feels humiliated. The young man is insultingly unattractive. Harold balls his fists and nods at the pair, trying to hide his disgust.

"Good night, Mr. Streeter," says the awkward young man, offering half a smile. Grudgingly Harold mumbles good-bye.

"Going to bed, Daddy?" Daisy lays her head against her father's shoulder. As she kisses him sweetly on the cheek, his clenched hands unfold like tulips.

Good night.

23

Tears streamed into Nora's ears when she opened her eyes. Why? Where was she? Lying on a bed in a large, barren room. As she turned her head groggily to the side, she gradually became aware of a terrible pain suffusing her from her right shoulder to her waist. With the back of her hand she wiped her tears only to feel the pain pull together to punch her full force in the right breast. She moaned; her ears filled up again. As the sharp pain subsided and diffused, a nagging nausea took its place. She wondered if she'd been shot. She had to throw up.

"You can use this if you like," said a very young, dark-skinned nurse, handing Nora a stainless steel bowl. "It's just the anesthesia. You'll feel better in a bit. You're coming along just fine." She had large unwavering liquid eyes, intricate corn rows, and a comforting voice that inspired confidence. Gently she held back Nora's hair, laying one hand lightly against her cheek.

Nora's throat was dry and her nose felt swollen, as if she'd been vainly trying to breathe under water. "Where am I?" she asked, feeling foolish.

"In Recovery," said the nurse without removing her hand.

Cher, read the name pinned to the white uniform. *Cher.* Nora thought Cher the kindest person she'd ever met. She tried to throw up, but nothing came. Then she closed her eyes.

When she opened her eyes again, it was nearly dark outside. The pain. There was a woman asleep in the bed beside hers and another across the room. Nora thought about her mother, fearful and mystified by her daughter's life, and was glad she hadn't told her about the operation. If the biopsy says it's cancer she'll have to tell her—and disappoint her yet again. Her poor mother, thinks Nora, beginning to cry again, living in Miami with her third husband, a retired broker, not even Catholic, and her only daughter dead.

Cher wheeled her bed out of Recovery, into the elevator, down the hall toward her room. Nora felt better now, but for some reason the tears kept running from her eyes into her ears as if she had sprung a leak.

"Still sad?" asked Cher. "What is it, dear?"

She'd be strong later. "The pain," she said.

When Cher leaned over and kissed her forehead for no reason, Nora was overcome with love.

"You're still here!" cried Nora, seeing Rosemary peek in through the door of her room. "Did you spend the whole night here?"

"I went home after we killed our second bottle of champagne last night, don't you remember?" said Rosemary, picking up a fat cork from the bedside table. She sat down beside the bed and adopted the patient tone she used with her children. "Then I came back around ten this morning, remember? As soon as they took you up to surgery I ran over to Bloomingdale's and still had plenty of time to check on Buster with your neighbor. I got back about half an hour ago." She handed Nora a Bloomingdale's gift box. "Now tell me, how do you feel?" It was with trepidation that she asked, for though she knew surgery was never a breeze, she was shocked by Nora's red eyes and chalky face.

"What's this?"

"Open it and see."

Nora untied the ribbon and eased off the lid. Slowly, like a child, she pulled aside the tissue paper flaps, then lifted out a puff of pale-peach-colored chiffon. A delicate, classic negligee with flowing sleeves, fine lace trim, and narrow satin ribbon ties. "Rosemary!" she cried, holding it up. "Rosemary!"

"Do you like it?"

Though Nora's eyes had started to leak again, she couldn't stop grinning.

While the doctor's in the room speaking to Nora, Rosemary hunts down a sandwich and a telephone. As Nora's only confidante for this surgery, she wouldn't think of leaving until they kick her out; but now she needs to talk to Harold. Hospitals do that to her: one whiff of death and she must count her children, go running home for comfort.

The old trade-off: if she were the one in the hospital instead of Nora, she couldn't possibly keep it secret. How she admires Nora, clinging to her independence even in the face of death. In her place she knows her phone would already be ringing, her room filling with visitors, no matter how unwelcome, she'd have to put on a smile and start playing hostess the minute she came to.

On the other hand, Harold would be there for her—handling the children, holding off the relatives, running interference with the doctors and the bureaucrats, sneaking in her favorite foods. Now, too, when she's not even the patient, she wants Harold to comfort her. They do that for each other, no matter what else is going on between them: it's their right. In sickness and in health, whatever might befall them, the children must be considered first. This is the necessity of family; also its luxury.

Rosemary saw a man sitting in the bedside chair in a dapper tailored overcoat twirling a hat between his knees. Nora, decked out in the new negligee, face tipped to the light, was making up her eyes.

"I forgot," said Nora, looking up. "You two don't know each other, do you? Lex—Rosemary. She brought me in here last night and stayed most of the day."

Lex leaped up. His face was lined with worry; when his labored smile ended, his ruddy cheeks were hollow. He looked sad and tender at once. Rosemary decided she liked him. All the same, she took Nora's hand to protect her from the tension filling the room like gnats. "Sit, please," she said.

But Lex continued to stand. He was relieved to see Rosemary instead of a man. For months now he was sure he had a rival, and though he was too delicate (or cowardly) to question Nora, knowing how happy she would be to pelt him with justifications and details, he was grateful for any reassurance, however indirect, circumstantial, or speculative. The empty champagne bottles in the bathroom, the open gift box beside the bed, which made him envious and guilty, were probably from Rosemary.

"Nora didn't tell me anything about this till a few minutes ago," he tried to explain, full of apology. "I grabbed a taxi right over, but I'm afraid I can't stay. There's an important opening . . ." The irony of his remark showed up in a tortured grimace as he waved Rosemary to the vacant chair and pulled up another for himself. "But at least I'll be able to take her home tomorrow."

"Tomorrow?" said Rosemary, confronting Nora. "Really? Tomorrow's my teaching day. I thought you weren't going home till the day after."

"I know," said Nora, laying down the mirror. "But the doctor said if there was someone to stay with me, I could go tomorrow. So"—her voice dropped in what sounded to Rosemary like defeat—"I called Lex."

Rosemary felt paralyzed by equal and opposite pulls. For a moment she even considered canceling her classes. But, remembering the midterm coming up and the crisis conference she'd scheduled with one of her boys whose girlfriend is probably pregnant, she understands she can't. It may be a part-time job but it's full-time crises. Nora at least has Lex; her students have only her. Besides, it's too late now: Lex already knows. Seeing him quietly watching Nora, Rosemary offers herself in alliance. "I'll come over as soon as I can. I'd like to dismiss my last class early, but—"

"Oh, no," said Lex, "there's no need for that. Tomorrow I can stay all day. It's only tonight . . ." He rubbed his fingers over his watch but refrained from looking at it. That Nora hadn't told him in advance about her surgery was bad enough, but that she had summoned him so abruptly that he hadn't been able to stop for flowers was insupportable. If he couldn't act like a husband to her, at least he should come through as a lover. She was forcing him to bungle, forcing him out.

"If they're letting you go tomorrow, does that mean they know the result of the biopsy?" asked Rosemary eagerly.

Nora watched her two visitors leaning forward on their chairs, intently awaiting her answer, and felt the tears well up again. Why was she suddenly so vulnerable to tears? "The surgeon says it's almost certainly benign, though Bianca told me we won't have the final lab report for a couple more days. The tumor was as big as a prune."

Rosemary's jaw dropped open; Lex shook his head. "Really!"

"Yes. They never give you the measurements, they always tell you in fruit. He said it could have been growing since I was thirteen years old, but we could only feel the very tip of it. Isn't that scary? You never know what's going on, even inside your own body."

When Rosemary reached over and squeezed her hand, Nora turned her head away. Before her body could betray her again with tears, she eased herself back on her pillows, smoothed out her negligee, forced a smile, and began: "But let me tell you about this beautiful nurse named Cher."

After unexpectedly losing at three separate games, one more sophisticated than the next, Spider conned Herschel over to Ms. Pacman, where he had once been champ, "for old times sake." Now he flipped the joystick till he got the fourth power pill, instantly turning Inky, Pinky, Blinky and Sue into blue monsters. Out shot a cherry, worth a hundred points. Now to take it!

"Beware of flashing monsters which are about to change back to the dangerous colors," intoned Herschel, in the Mickey Mouse voice he'd recently adopted, just as Ms. Pacman approached the cherry. Spider cracked up. Herschel, who walked around in strange glasses and an old coat disguised as a nerd but could do a perfect imitation of every teacher they ever had, knew just how to distract him. Sure enough, before Spider could compose himself, he missed his turning and Inky gobbled up Ms. Pacman. A lousy 40,820 points.

"Now will you come on?" said Herschel in almost a whine. He tugged Spider's arm out of the pocket he was reaching into for another coin. "You said one more game, and that was it."

Spider obeyed. It was late. His parents didn't care what time he left the Computer Center, they said, as long as he didn't come home after dark. He never deliberately broke the rule; he hated waiting in the dark for the bus as much as his parents hated to have him wait. It was just that when he entered the world of UNIX he got carried away, losing track not only of time (hour, date, month, year, decade, century, epoch), but of space too (city, state, country, planet, galaxy), and even sometimes of his very identity. Sometimes he worried that if Herschel weren't with him keeping track of time, he might get locked in and blank out who he was, like those guys in the old movies, and never get home at all. And then his father, who had used his faculty pull to get access for his school to Columbia's DEC 20, would be exposed, and all their accounts would be revoked.

"You sure you can't talk your dad into picking us up?" asked Spider, though Herschel had already asked and been turned down. "Can't you?" Herschel replied. Spider shook his head. His dad had picked them up twice that week already, and since they'd logged out of their accounts and were now in the basement just fooling around with games, he didn't want to impose again. Though his father always said he'd be happy to pick them up any time he could, his mother thought it wasn't fair to ask him to get the car out of the garage and put it back again when they could just as well come home on the bus. Spider could see the logic of that, but he thought she ought to give him money for taxi fare instead. He thought it absurd of her to insist that they take the bus when everyone knew his father had written a best-seller. But his mother was like that, always cautioning him and Daisy that just because they were lucky enough to have money was no reason to go around spending it. She seemed to think buses built character.

As if by telepathy, at that moment Harold, driving down from the bridge, suddenly thought of Spider needing a lift. He was as proud to be a transporter as a provider. The rose in the sky was fading fast as he hummed down the drive, planning to go inside and surprise his son. He planted Spider's happy, astonished face on his retina and stepped on the gas. If he'd already left (it was almost dark now), he would cruise past the bus stop and follow the bus route home.

Herschel got behind Spider and, sending a tire screech out a small opening in the left side of his mouth, leaned forward, pressed his head into the small of Spider's back, and pushed. Spider added his voice, turned up his toes, and leaned back. Down the hall they skidded.

Spider knew anyone else would be tempted to let go and let him fall, but not Herschel. They were perfect partners. Herschel: weird, wicked, wacky, squat, clever; Spider: sensible, serious, tall, talented, determined. Not for them the P.C.s everyone used with little idiot programs; nothing less for them than the biggest computer at Columbia. Together, he and Herschel already knew five entirely different languages, and Herschel was well on his way to perfecting a program to beat roulette. If they ever got it working, they planned to spend their earnings on taxis home. Spider wasn't quite sure how roulette worked, but he knew how Herschel worked; he was ready to lay money on any number Herschel said because he was ready to lay money on Herschel.

They screeched their way past the guard through the outer door, into the freezing air, and continued their skid to the street. A car at the curb gamely added a honking horn to their sound effects.

It was Harold honking. Just as he'd pulled up to the curb and was getting ready to open his hood to avoid a ticket while he ran inside, out came the boys. "Dad!" cried Spider, shooting upright. "Hi, Mr. Streeter," said Herschel, snapping to attention.

"Dad," repeated Spider, full of admiration. "How did you know we were coming out just then?"

Instead of explaining, Harold smiled a mysterious, omniscient smile that warmed him through. "Hop in, boys," he purred, reaching back to open the door.

Discoveries

24

ORDINARILY Rosemary took no notice of the fire-side lamps. She thought of the ornate antiques mounted on either side of the mantelpiece as belonging to Harold, who had bought them without consulting her shortly after they'd moved in. But having just wiped from Mrs. Scaggs's newly polished marble mantel the smoky traces of last night's fire, she happened to look up and see the graceful glass shade on the left hand lamp dangerously askew. Rosemary reached up to fix it.

The Fireside Lamps . . .

They are fancy and French. Each contains a central cylindrical chamber designed to hold kerosene from which swivel into the room on gracefully curved arms two small porcelain lamps, each crowned by an etched glass shade. The lamp to the left of the fireplace is painted with a pastoral scene; the one to the right shows a hunt.

Harold fell in love with the pair at an auction in Connecticut. Topping the highest bid, he bought them, along with four silver decanters in a mahogany case, as a gift to himself, and after having them appraised, polished, and wired, presented them to Rosemary. She liked them well enough but would have preferred to be consulted about such commanding and valuable objects, which from their dominant hearthside perches would probably be noticed every day for the rest of their owners' lives.

Aware of his slight duplicity and detecting his wife's hesitation, Harold allowed the lamps to sit in a closed box in a corner of the living room, to Rosemary's mild annoyance, until one rainy Saturday he got out his tools, tuned in the opera, and to the strains of *Don Carlo* undertook to replace two nondescript sconces with the elegant new fixtures. During the long intermission he disconnected the fuse a final time and connected the wires to a dimmer he installed on the wall.

Throughout the operation Rosemary, afraid Harold would either drop the lamps or electrocute himself, wrung her hands and moaned, forcing Harold at last to banish his unhelpful mate during the final stages of installation. As the curtain was rising on the last act of Verdi's masterpiece, Harold summoned Rosemary to a demonstration of the dramatic range of lighting effects they could henceforth achieve at the mere touch of a knob.

Now, reaching up to set the shade aright, Rosemary notices something white protruding from beneath the top of the hollow kerosene chamber. An envelope? When she tries to remove it, she finds it so tightly wedged in place, like a map in a mailing tube, that she must climb onto a chair to get a good enough grip to extract it. No wonder—it's stuffed full. Tugging at it, she accidentally rips a corner of the envelope and sees poking out the unmistakable green of cash.

Carefully, Rosemary rolls the envelope tighter and lifts it out. It's money all right, a fat wad of bills, but how much? And whose? Her hands have already begun to sweat. To count it she'll have to open the envelope, and then whoever it belongs to will know she knows.

Rosemary replaces the top and swiftly carries the envelope into the study.

Thousands of dollars! It has to be Harold's. (Unless, knock on wood, one of the children is dealing drugs.) But why?

A sound. The elevator. She stuffs the money back into the envelope and shoves it in a folder in the bottom desk drawer, then runs back to the living room and with trembling hand begins rapidly swishing the cloth over the mantelpiece, waiting for a voice.

Why this money? All she can think is he's planning to leave them. What other reason can there be? You read about it all the time: husbands' secret bank accounts, impoverished wives, mistresses living in luxury. The children!—the children are far too young!

Sometimes she thinks Harold's riches are a curse, making their lives not more but less secure. How easily he could leave them now. Sometimes she wishes they still lived in the Village and struggled for their luxuries; then her own earnings would count, and the children would grow up knowing the truth about the world, and no one would have to be guilty.

She waits, listening, rubbing the marble. Nowadays he's away so much—where does he go? Her head is hot, her knees weak. She thinks of her students with their shy faces and sad stories of broken homes: stepmothers hardly older than themselves, fathers who ran off one night and never returned, mothers embattled or mad or dead. If he leaves them, what will she ever do?

Gradually, anger replaces fear. At least she has a job, has Peter. Maybe she should keep the money, say nothing, use it for a trip with Peter to Italy. That would show him! Rome, Florence, down the coast to Naples—let the owner inquire if he dares! Or maybe she should sit right here in the dining room till Harold comes home, confront him outright with her find, demand to know what's going on, see how he answers then.

She listens. Nothing. She walks down the hall, checking every room. No one home except Gorky, lying on Spider's bed, pulling clumps of fur out of his right flank. Everything is coming apart—she'll have to take him to the vet.

She returns to the study, retrieves the money from her drawer, seals it in a fresh blank envelope, and with thumping heart replaces it in the lamp. When she's confident she's still alone, she pulls a chair over to the other lamp, removes the top of the kerosene chamber, peers in, and once again strikes pay dirt. Another envelope, as fat as the first! Eagerly she lifts it out, slits it open, and begins to count.

25

Nora was driving too fast, like someone without children. She had rolled down the window for Buster, who was enjoying the breeze in the backseat, oblivious of his master's hair blowing against his face or the cigarette ash she flicked after every puff. Great white luminous clouds fled before them. Nora took the curves like a skier, with a slight lean. Her mood was ebullient. It was an unseasonably balmy day, and that morning when she stepped on the scale she found she had not only not gained after her recent spree but was actually down two pounds—an undeserved bonus which she considered investing in a two-day fast instead of Italian food. "What do you mean, he's the perfect lover? You mean like a perfect dance partner? Hold on," she warned, coasting into a curve.

Rosemary suppressed her protest and induced calm by pretending she was in an airplane, passive and powerless, with Nora the invisible, trusty pilot. It was for her benefit, after all, that they were transporting a cartonful of secrets to Nora's country retreat. A three-week trip abroad was too long to risk leaving suspect souvenirs locked up with the linens or indiscreet documents zipped into pockets of unused purses—especially after Harold discovers half the money gone. (Half seemed fair to her.)

"Sort of," she answered. "Not exactly. I mean, our bodies are in tune. He knows exactly how to touch me and how long. By now, for us every caress is an end in itself. Absolutely nothing's out of bounds."

Nora disagreed. She remembered a lifetime of odd caresses she'd been asked to perform or suffer that she considered out of bounds. And whether she submitted or refused, they always upset her until that notorious dinner with some of her friends when Bianca insisted that you don't ever have to do anything that makes you sick, and they all decided that just because you do something once is no reason that you have to do it again. "Perfect technique? Is that what you mean?" asked Nora, trying to hide her disdain.

"No, not exactly. In fact, I'd guess that anyone watching me and Peter make love would probably find our sex boring, if you're just talking about technique. Because by now we usually do roughly the same things in the same order. But that's part of what's so wonderful: I can count on him. I know he won't get bored or decide to stop. It's like music: half the pleasure is in sensing what's coming and getting it."

"Not for me," said Nora. "I hate to know what's coming. I never know with Lex. And Keith—I haven't any idea what he's got in mind. That's part of what attracts me. You know—the old thrill of the unknown."

"For me the thrill's in the known. That's what I have with Peter that I never had before. Trust. Our bodies trust each other. Completely."

"You don't have that trust with your husband?"

Rosemary snorted. "By now our sex, such as it is, is just an extension of a snuggle."

"But trust. What about trust?"

Rosemary watched Long Island racing by. Once Daisy was born and she needed Harold, trust was the first thing to go. Dependency killed trust by making it too risky. Rosemary wondered if maybe marriage wasn't a substitute for trust, an attempt to supplant it with something surer, something enforceable and lasting. "Maybe we take each other for granted, but that's not the same as trust."

"If I take anything for granted I get bored," said Nora, "and then it's over for me. At this moment I don't even know for sure if I'll see Keith again."

"Don't tell me you're one of those women who's attracted to cads!"

Nora laughed. "I suppose you could put it that way. I do like to feel a challenge." She tossed out her cigarette, rolled up the window, and went into overdrive to pass two trucks, while Rosemary clenched her teeth.

"Hold on," said Nora, enjoying this challenge too. Speeding was so seductive that not once but twice she had gone sailing past border guards (once between Switzerland and France, once between Yugoslavia and Italy) to be halted by drawn guns. She always managed to laugh or sweet-talk her way out of each predicament, relying on her press card only when necessary. The helpless-little-woman routine was beneath her dignity, but she had no scruples about the one-of-the-boys approach— one of the boys with a difference. God, did I really do that, officer? Believe me, I had no idea. I don't know where I was: off in another world. But look, officer, I'm on a story—give me a break, okay?

"Challenge!" said Rosemary, letting her foot up off the imaginary brake. "Not me. If I smell a cad coming, I run. I think I'd even prefer a wimp to a cad."

Cads and Wimps . . .

"A wimp!" said Nora, taking her eyes off the road to stare at Rosemary. "Really!"

"At least with a wimp you know where you stand; you don't feel so powerless."

"For me," said Nora, "as soon as I feel I have power over my lover, I lose interest. Without a challenge, I find it dull. I'd never be able to . . . to . . . *surrender* to a wimp. If I knew I could control what was coming, if he did whatever I said, if it was too easy, I'd never even get turned on."

"Don't get me wrong," said Rosemary, rushing to defend Peter. "It's not power I want either. I need to surrender too, just like you. But if I can't trust my lover to really mean what he says, if I'm not sure he really loves me, then I won't *be able* to surrender, because I'll always be on guard. If I'm guarded, if I'm not sure of him, my body won't let go. It just won't work."

"And it won't work for me if I'm too sure of him. I start to wonder if he's worth it."

"I wonder if he's worth it if I have to work too hard. Try this out," offered Rosemary after a pause. "I have to conquer and you have to be conquered."

Nora considered. Finally, she shook her head. "No. I need to conquer too," she was explaining when she suddenly saw her exit going by. She swerved sharply from the center lane onto a second ramp, cutting off a Cutlass. "Damn! I always do this. I get so wrapped up in our conversations. . . . But we get a second chance at this exit. Now, close your eyes and pray."

This time when Nora switched lanes Rosemary slammed back against the headrest, clutched her bag, and obediently sent up half a prayer. When she opened her eyes, they were braking on the access road and she had a flash of insight. "Maybe it's like this," she said when her voice returned. "If it's going to work, really work, we both need both: total control and total surrender. Maybe everyone does, including *them*. But if we have to sacrifice one of them, you'll sacrifice control for the sake of surrender, and I'll sacrifice surrender for the sake of control. Because I know I can't surrender if I'm *not* in control, while you know you can't surrender if you *are*. So we each take a risk. But I take my risk from one side, while you take yours from the other."

"Yes!" said Nora. "You're willing to risk losing interest, I'm willing to risk getting hurt. In order to make it work."

"Right," said Rosemary, excited. "We each choose the lesser of two evils, but we see different evils as lesser."

"That's why I get hurt and you don't," said Nora after a pause. "I'm ready to take risks."

"Wait a minute. So am I," said Rosemary, ready to take offense. "Just different ones."

But Nora felt her risks in love were greater than Rosemary's. She lived her whole life at risk, making it up as she went along—that was the thrill of it.

"So then maybe," said Rosemary, seizing the conciliatory moment, "the difference between us boils down to a matter of taste."

"Temperament," amended Nora. "Or as Lex calls it, toilet training."

By the time they'd finished laughing, Nora was turning up a narrow winding dirt road at the end of which one small gray shingled saltbox cottage looked out to sea—a loner like Nora herself.

"This seat's saved," snaps Spider, ready to fight if necessary with an immediate elbow to the ribs. But when he turns to follow through, Spider finds himself looking into the pale, broad, dimpled face of April Waters.

"It sure is. This is my coat. I've been waiting on line since eight thirty this morning. Stupid!"

Spider stares at the purple plaid coat folded on the floor beneath the seat in question. Blood rises unbidden up his body to his scalp, engorging his tongue and palate in a wordless stammer. April curls her lip at Spider before ostentatiously whipping her attention around to her bony friend Lisa on her left; she gives Spider her back until the lights dim and six spangled musicians, volume maximized, storm the stage—leaping, cavorting, feigning death amidst shrieks and wails. Time stops for Spider— until the band, launching into a frenzied rendition of "Stolen Kisses," suggests a plan.

The Kiss . . .

He hides himself in the stomping crowd while secretly tracking the rhythmic rise and fall of April's jeans, inches from his own. In the corner of his eye he catches her fists pounding the seat in front of her, sees with each leap how her thick glossy hair bobs against her shoulders, how her breasts bounce inside her sweater. Slyly he matches his own calculated leaps and lunges to hers, echoing each of her moves.

Spider feels himself an instrument of some imperative force of demonic will. The song is a sign. Crouching like a forward, awaiting the perfect coincidence of high frenzy with one of April's upward leaps, Spider aims his spring to bring his lips against her cheek on her downward plunge.

The music screeches its crescendo. April does not so much as turn her head or brush her hand across her face; still, an incontestable kiss has registered itself forever on Spider's lips.

Not a note of the last set does he hear—only the beat of bass and heart that holds him captive in his chair until the final crash of the last encore releases him. Flushed and triumphant, Spider bursts from the auditorium, looking for Herschel.

The cottage, off on a gothic bluff with no access but a blind dirt road, was essentially one spacious room dominated by a flagstone fireplace and the sea. At one side was a kitchen area, at the other side were the sleeping couches, and in the center was a large oak table, half of it covered with books. Rosemary took off her coat and an imaginary ten pounds, projecting herself into a new life: Rosemary Streeter, skinny, dedicated mathematician, authoritative and serene, working uninterrupted for days on end in front of a blazing fire. It fit fine until the first sunset; then she got scared. She feared she'd never make it through the night alone.

"But aren't you afraid here all by yourself, with no phone or even neighbors?"

Nora stopped scooping ashes. "No," she said decisively.

Rosemary had to believe her: Nora often came out here alone to work. "Sometimes I think the height of luxury would be to live alone like this for a while. To be able to work around the clock without interruption and cook whatever I liked just for myself. Think of how much I'd get done. I envy you, Nora. I wish I could do it."

"Nonsense! You could do it if you wanted," Nora urged, hoping to inspire her friend. She was sure that in one month without that family— one month of solitary, joyous work—Rosemary too would see the light. If Nora couldn't persuade or cajole her to try herself out (for just one month!), she would try to shame her, force her, dare her to move out on her own. "Maybe you could work out a deal like mine. When I'm out here, the man who owns this place uses my apartment in the city. We guarantee each other at least three months a year, but we're very flexible, especially since we both travel a lot."

"But I don't live alone, so it wouldn't work. Unless I found someone with a family like mine who wanted to trade. But then, why bother? The whole point would be to get away from everyone. And how could I explain? Anyway, we go to the Vineyard in the summer. No," said Rosemary, shaking her head, "I don't think I could stay here all by myself even if I found the perfect swap. You must be very brave."

"Not at all. I'd be brave if I stayed here while I was afraid, but I'm not afraid. I was afraid in the hospital, I'll admit it, but I'm not afraid here."

Nora began rolling and twisting double sheets of an old Sunday *Times* and arranging them neatly side by side on the grate. She feared she sounded arrogant—anyway, smug—though it was simply true that she could build a good fire, cook a good dinner, write a good article, live by herself. "Lonely sometimes, maybe, frustrated, even angry, but not afraid. You wouldn't be either if you tried it. You'd be used to it in no time." She turned around with a sudden thought. "Would you like to use the place yourself sometime? It's at its best in the fall and empty half the winter. I always do my best work here. The silence in winter is inspiring. And if Gotham doesn't renew your contract for the fall, you could come out for a month at a time, see how you like it, get some real work done. If you were afraid to be alone, I'd lend you Buster."

Rosemary plopped down in a wing chair and placed Peter opposite her. Much better. "I could bring Peter."

Nora balanced a large log carefully on a pair of others, keeping her back to her friend to hide her disgust. "Rosemary! Haven't you ever lived alone?"

"Only once, for about two months, before I was married. . . . I'd just come home from my first trip to Europe. Since graduation from college I'd been living at home with my folks, working and saving my money for the trip, but after that summer in Europe, I felt I had to be on my own. As soon as I got back I found a job in publishing and took a sublet in the Village. It was a perfect apartment, a one-bedroom on Tenth Street—all I had to do was step outside my door and the whole world was there. But I found I couldn't stand to be alone. I'd grown up in a big noisy family sharing a room with two older sisters, and I didn't know what to do with myself. I felt too big, too tall. The world was all couples, except for me. Whenever I ate alone I got depressed; if I went to a restaurant or a movie alone, I felt everyone was looking at me." She clasped her hands tightly in her lap. "Then I met Harold. He was exciting and funny and considerate, with this promising career. He wanted to include me in his life. I moved in with him and got married as soon as I could."

Only by striking a match and lighting the blaze could Nora keep from crying out. She bit her lip and listened as Buster growled at the leaping flames.

Rosemary's Story . . .

"Where I come from, everyone married as early as they could. We had our first baby to protect Harold from the draft. I was home with the children when you were out launching your career. Not that I wasn't interested in school. There were a couple of college courses being offered on TV, but only in the mornings, at the same time as Spider's favorite programs, and of course I couldn't deprive him. But when he finally started nursery school, I turned the TV on to the college program and I felt as if I were coming back to life. That semester they were offering a course in new math. Though I'd taken my B.A. in English, I'd always loved math. This course was so stimulating I didn't miss a single program and did all the homework. One of the final lectures was on graph theory. At the end of the program, the professor, a very charming man, gave us a sophisticated problem about the pecking order of chickens, promising to mark the papers personally if we tried to solve it. Partly for the professor, partly for myself, I decided to try it. All week long I worked on the problem during the morning hours when the kids were at school, and all day Saturday. Harold and the children were very puzzled to see me holed up with this problem. By Sunday I thought I had a solution. I sent it in.

Not that I thought it was correct, but I felt that just attempting to solve it was a turning point. A week later I was told that I was one of three people who had solved the problem correctly. I was thrilled. It was like learning I'd just won the lottery. I had a wonderful, complicated dream that night about hundreds of bright yellow chickens flying north in a beautiful formation like geese that I alone had understood, and that week I decided to go back to school, in mathematics.

"If I'd known what I was getting into, I might not have had the nerve for it. But what did I know? Math seemed such a gutsy field, I'd shown some talent, and studying on my own through TV, with no one to compete against except myself, I thought the way would be clear. But when I enrolled in real classes in a real college it felt like speeding straight into a mammoth pileup on the highway. First there was my age: I wasn't that old, but since I was starting math at the beginning with basic courses, I felt like an old lady. But far worse, there was my sex. Only a handful of women were majoring in math, and most of the other students simply wouldn't acknowledge us. When I got to graduate school we were treated even worse—not only by the students, but by the professors, too. It was as if we didn't exist. And those men were so competitive; you wouldn't believe some of the outrageous remarks they made, maybe without even realizing it. I'd never been in a situation like that before. Remember, I'd gone to Vassar, where we were all women, and I'd majored in English, a pretty genteel subject. All the same, I refused to let them run me out. I knew I had talent, math really excited me, and I was absolutely determined to survive. I felt like a pioneer penetrating a hostile wilderness, but one that boasts of following the highest order of reason.

"But I'm getting ahead of my story. When I decided to return to school, Harold was encouraging, even though he was uneasy, too. I couldn't blame him. We'd already had some problems. Several years before, when Harold was in Mexico and I was in the Hamptons with Daisy, I'd had a summer affair with a piano player that Harold found out about. It was insignificant and we survived it, but you remember those days: so much turmoil in the air, no one knew what was coming next. Well, naturally, something did happen."

"What?"

"I fell in love."

"With the TV professor?"

"No. In fact, I never even got to meet him, he was at a different university. It was with another student. A young man with thick flowing hair and one of those gentle voices that men were just beginning to cultivate in those days, one of the few math students who treated me with any respect. I was so grateful, I promptly fell in love. But he was years younger than I was, which scared me. To protect myself, I acted as if we were just friends, though we were together every day. We studied together for exams, talked on the phone. He used to walk with me to pick up the children at their school on the days when Mrs. Scaggs didn't come.

"Well, of course, eventually it happened. But not right away. We were both shy. I found myself having fantasies about him—in bed after Harold fell asleep, or in the shower in the morning, the one time of day I was alone. It got so I started looking forward to those showers as my time with him. Gradually I noticed that whenever Harold was around he would disappear, and when Harold was away he'd come over and have dinner with me and the children. Then one night it happened. It doesn't matter how—maybe that part of every love story is the same. At the time, though, I could hardly believe it. I kept thinking, me? Me?

"I knew from the start I had to keep the affair absolutely secret. Look—I had two young kids, high rent, no job, no way of making a living. I was working very hard at school, and besides, I didn't want any big changes in my life. And my lover, well, he was everything I could have wanted in a lover—he was gentle, sweet, attentive—but he was a student, practically a kid himself.

"I can't believe how naive I was then. But you know how it is when you're in love. You feel as if you're invincible. You feed on crises. Soon we began to talk about living together. Openly. On what? We never said. On Harold's child-support payments, I guess. Harold's book had come out, he was getting a lot of attention, so I figured, he'll support us. I was absolutely dependent on Harold for everything, but I pretended I was free." She shook her head over her own naiveté.

"Eventually Harold found out. I still kick myself for that. If you want them not to know, they won't, especially if they don't really want to know. Well, he was wild. To punish me, he told me all about his women; we said unspeakable things to each other. We both tried to stop, but we were out of control, it kept getting worse and worse until finally we were ready to separate, though neither of us really wanted to.

"Picture it: through all of this I'm still going to school, applying to grad schools, trying to work. Studying days, fighting nights. We were all so overwrought. And then suddenly it was exam week. I was frantic. That was the week I bit off all my nails. During exams I sent the kids to Harold's mother, and I made a sort of deal with God. (I don't even believe in God!) I told God, if I do well on my exams and get into grad school, I'll stay with Harold. It wasn't a bad deal, either. If I'd left Harold for that student, I'd never have been able to continue school. My life was too hectic, and if Harold didn't come through, with two children to raise we'd be too poor.

"Not only did I get into grad school but my exams went so well that I earned distinction. At my celebration dinner, Harold and I each renounced our lovers.

"I certainly didn't intend to go on seeing him, I swear. I only wanted one last night of love. I thought, where's the harm? It's like after you've lost your virginity—why pretend you can get it back? Well, Harold followed me that night, and when he saw the student come up to me it was just too much for him. He left us then, he packed his bags and walked out. It was summer, I remember, and sometimes he'd phone to talk to the children, but he wouldn't tell us where he was or if he was coming back. His magazine had no address for him, either. It was so awful: Spider was seven. Where's Daddy? he kept asking, and I didn't know what to say.

"That's when my real punishment began. My rage was absolutely uncontainable—that he could just leave the children like that. Me, okay—but the children! I was in summer school, taking two classes every day; but seeing the children fading, withdrawn, depressed, I began to get depressed myself. Soon I couldn't work, couldn't concentrate. I couldn't bear to see the children suffering that way."

"And your lover? What about him?" asked Nora.

"He'd moved in shortly after Harold left, but it took only a few days for me to see that it wouldn't work. We'd have had to adapt to each other, accommodate, and the best thing between us, our passion, would die of dailiness. And how could he suddenly be expected to assume the responsibilities of a family man? Since he was moving into our world, which was already set, he'd be more like another child for me to take care of than another adult to help me. As soon as this became clear to me, you know what happened? I lost all my sexual feeling for him. One day it just disappeared—like that.

"And no wonder. I was so preoccupied, so distraught, for the first time in my life I understood how people can take up drinking. A drink, a joint, a movie, anything to help you forget your pain for a little while, to help you sleep, to help you get through one more agonizing night. You know that Emily Dickinson poem?

> The Heart asks Pleasure—first—
> And then—Excuse from Pain—
> And then—those little Anodynes
> That deaden suffering—

That was my love affair. But even though all I wanted was to get Harold to come back, whenever he phoned I berated him for leaving the children, I raged at him and carried on, I even hung up on him. Which was so foolish, since all I wanted was to talk to him. I couldn't help it, though. I was a mess.

"I'll leave out the details. We reproached each other, we cried, we negotiated, we wrote letters—and eventually Harold did come back home. He arrived just in time to drive the children up to camp, and then when he returned we began to have the most passionate sex of our entire marriage. Far more intense than back in the beginning. We had terrible wounds to heal. For weeks, it seemed, we could do nothing but make love. Feverish, ardent love. Words were feeble compared to our lovemaking. Though God knows we talked too. We talked and talked till we were exhausted—physically and mentally. But nothing was ever settled, we went round and round with protestations, accusations, explanations, recriminations, until we could do nothing but return to the bed again for more of that soothing balm.

"This passionate healing went on for about a month—while the children were away at camp—night and day, right up until the new semester began. It wasn't about pleasure, it was much deeper than that. It was like a great movement of troops, ending a war. And gradually peace did return to our house. Until, when school started in September and our old routines resumed, all that passion, that sexual urgency, simply vanished. We fell back into our old comfortable patterns: sex before sleep every week or two, a kiss good night, work, peace.

"And you know, I was relieved? I preferred it that way. I preferred peace to passion, by far! Peace—what a blessing! We needed, we longed for stability in our lives; I needed calm in order to do my work. And the children—they needed it too, as much as they needed us, both of us.

Regular meals, routine schedules, reactions they could count on, that's what the children needed. That's what they still need. More than anything else.

"By the time Harold and I reconciled, it was clear that some new bond had been cemented between us. After all that, I was somehow more committed to our marriage than ever—or committed in a new way. I knew then that I couldn't leave Harold for another man, at least not until after the kids were grown. But I also knew about passion. And pretty soon, after our lives returned to normal, when our house was calm and busy, now and then damned if I didn't find myself thinking again about a lover. Not that I hadn't learned my lesson. Hardly! I'd learned that separation from Harold was unbearable—too painful, too dangerous, too terrifying to bear. I knew I couldn't suffer that terror, that depression again and keep my sanity. I needed him, he needed me. Our family came first. Sex was a mere tool, coming and going as it served our needs."

Nora, who had been listening attentively with her mouth clamped firmly shut, could now no longer contain herself. She leaned forward, eyes flashing, words shooting from her lips. "How can you say that? It isn't your family that came first. It wasn't Harold you wanted back. It was your security. The cad walked out on you and your kids. How could you want him back? You acted out of fear, sheer cowardice."

Because she lived alone, Nora was able to preserve the highest standards of family life. Rosemary, because she didn't, was more inclined to preserve the family.

"Don't you see," said Rosemary, "there's no difference? The children were suffering, they wanted their father, we were all in horrible pain. The only way it would end would be if Harold came back to us. There was no other way."

Nora turned to the fire. She pitied Rosemary for her dependency, for having given herself away before she had a chance to grow up. "But that was long ago," she said. "Now your kids are grown and you have a job. Now you could learn to live alone. It's never too late. I was just as scared as you once. I couldn't make a fire or fix a flat or walk into a restaurant by myself."

Rosemary stared at her, amazed. "You?"

"Yes. The first time I was genuinely comfortable eating in a restaurant by myself wasn't till ten years ago, after I'd settled down to work. Before that, I was terrified. After that, I was free. Now I can go anywhere in the world by myself. Anywhere."

"I wish I could do it. But I know I can't."

"Can't! Don't be ridiculous!" Nora grabbed up a handful of papers and began fanning the fire. "Living alone is like anything else—like learning to read, or swim, or dive, or speak in public. At first you approach it with a great dread; you think, I'll never be able to do this, not me. But once you've mastered it, then you have the knack for life. You become a survivor. You adapt—like the dolphins, living under water. After that, it's no big deal. It's just one of your permanent skills, like riding a bike."

Or like diplomacy or compromise, thought Rosemary, whose life had taught her different skills. Empathy, accommodation. And who could say which set of skills, in the end, was needed to survive? "I still think you're very brave, Nora," said Rosemary aloud, utilizing her skills.

Nora placed a last log on the fire and stood up. She stretched, feeling her strength, trying to discharge the uncontrollable surge of pride that paraded before Rosemary's pathetic story of weakness. "Not brave. Lucky."

Though she admired Nora's strength, secretly Rosemary thought that she, not Nora, was the lucky one—lucky to have her children, a husband, a lover, a job, lucky not to have to live alone.

"What do you say we get your stuff up into my crawl space? After that we can open a bottle of wine and make some dinner. That fire's really blazing now, and we have plenty of wood to keep it going all night."

Barbara looked across the table at Harold with something between a pout and a sneer. Actually, she was smiling. But then she was always smiling; even with tears slipping down her cheeks she'd be sitting there twirling a lock of her auburn poodle fluff and smiling away. At first he thought it her sheer good nature; now that he can read her moods he thinks it designing.

"But if we're not going to Boston, then why can't we spend the same time together, only here? I don't understand," said Barbara. She wondered if he was taking another woman instead of her.

"I told you. The whole reason I canceled Boston in the first place is so I can take my kids to see Lip Service."

"I even arranged to take a day of leave time," she said.

"So, nothing's lost. Go in to work and take it later."

"Work!" She stroked her fork slowly across the leftover sauce at the bottom of her hors d'oeuvres plate, making a pattern with the cress. "It's too late now. Ginger is covering for me. We switched Fridays."

"I thought you said you were taking leave."

"I *am*. But someone has to cover the 'Morning Show' anyway." She twirled a lock of hair at the back of her neck and glanced up at him with a look he took for coy, saying, "I wouldn't mind seeing Lip Service too, you know, but in cable, only the big producers can get tickets. Not plebes. . . . Do you think you could get an extra one for me?"

"I'm taking my *kids*."

Barbara shrugged. "We wouldn't have to sit together. Besides, you promised you'd let me meet them sometime, see how kids of yours come out."

Harold went on alert. First they want to meet your kids, next they want to replace your wife—as if changing families were of no more consequence than changing banks. Every man knew that a little power, a bit of fame made you fair game for the marriage hunters. That's why he tried to let them know how he felt up front. He even sported a wedding ring. Men of real power—Kennedy, say, or FDR—never let their private lives destroy their families. ("After FDR's affair with Lucy Mercer," he'd written in a recent column, "his relation with Eleanor became more of a partnership than a marriage.") After his own wife's first affair, he no longer felt any obligation to be faithful, but that didn't mean he'd be willing to divorce her for someone else. She was mother to his kids—no one else could ever replace her at that.

"This could be the perfect chance," continued Barbara. "We could just sort of bump into each other in the lobby. Like, by accident. And then afterwards, maybe—"

"Goddammit, Barbara!" barked Harold, throwing down his napkin. "I've already gotten the goddamn tickets!"

Barbara drew her head into her neck, tried to smile, fiddled with her pearls. She'd never understand him. He'd become so jumpy lately. Not like at the beginning, when there wasn't enough he could do for her.

Softening, Harold reached a hand over the table and tried again. It was getting impossible to talk to her. She was just like a wheedling child. No matter how much he allowed her, she wanted more. No matter what he said, even if he said absolutely nothing, she was ready to jump on him.

She was never satisfied. And now, beneath her latest smile she looked as if she were going to cry. "Come on, honey. Here we are, having a nice, a possibly great, dinner together on a weekend, something we never get to do. We're going to go to a late movie and stay together the entire night just the way you said you want. We may even get to have brunch tomorrow. And you're crying over some concert weeks away."

"I am *not* crying," she cried.

"Okay, you're not crying. You're laughing. Now will you please just come back and consider what you might want to eat for your next course?"

Harold lifted the wine out of the cooler and refilled their glasses. "Okay?" he said, smiling himself. She sniffed and softened. "That's a good girl." He handed her her glass. When she had sipped, a grateful glow spread up her face, tinting her plump cheeks, lighting her green eyes, making everything seem worthwhile.

"I really don't want to bug you, Hal. Really," said Barbara when they'd finished making love. "All I want is for us to be able to talk about it."

"About what?"

"You know. Us. Sometimes I feel you're not really interested in me at all. Sometimes I think all you want is an audience."

"An audience!" Now it was Harold's turn to protest. "How can you say that? I have an audience of millions for everything I write. What do I need you for an audience for? That's the last thing I want from you. An audience!"

"What *do* you want from me, then?"

Harold reached over and lit a cigarette. "I can't believe we're having this conversation," he said. He took three rapid puffs. Wasn't it obvious what he wanted? Wasn't it obvious from the first day she sat down in the front row of his features class? He wanted the same thing he thought she wanted. He wanted her sweet face in his hands, her soft skin against his lips—"Right now I want you to snuggle up in my arms so we can go to sleep."

Barbara sat up. "That's just what I mean. When I want to talk, you want to go to sleep. You're not interested in *me*."

"Jesus. If I want to talk, I'm not interested in you, I just want an audience. If I want to go to sleep, I'm not interested in you, I just want to sleep. Jesus Christ!"

Barbara stiffened. He was doing it again. Whenever she tried to talk, he turned on her. "Hal—why are you doing this to me?"

"Doing what?"

"Acting mad."

"Don't you realize you just insulted me? Gratuitously?" he added.

"But *you* insulted *me*. You do it all the time. Not being interested in anything I say or do. Not caring what *I* want. That's why I brought it up. It's hard enough to—"

Harold felt abused. Why did she start accusing him when he was too tired to defend himself? Women. He sighed. To please Barbara, he had offered her the whole night as soon as Rosemary said she was going to the country with Nora. But if he'd known she planned to berate him, he would have spent the time working. He certainly had enough to do. His desk was awash with projects that needed everything from a few finishing touches to major effort. Not to mention the half-read investment books Bacon had urged on him and the brokerage tickets piled up unrecorded. Since his fortunes had turned so that everything he chose to write got published, seducing him to promise far more than he could deliver, his biggest task was cutting down. In everything—in love, in work, in investments—his curse was to be overextended. Sometimes he felt like Balzac, like Dickens, like Aristotle, like Abraham—lustily undertaking to fill a universe with the products of his vitality. But sometimes he felt he lived his life on margin, always anxiously awaiting the margin call. He knew other men would be content with such achievements as his: his one big book, his two fine children, his solid marriage and devoted wife. Like the gold bullion he had wisely bought, he could rely on them in a world at risk. But it was not in his nature to rest on his laurels or leave the race when he was ahead. Especially when the people he loved were counting on him.

Barbara had stopped speaking and was waiting for some response. "I'm sorry if I insulted you, honey," he intoned wearily. "I didn't mean to hurt your feelings." He snuffed out his cigarette and put a tired arm around her. "Is it better now?"

"Yes. A little better," said Barbara, accepting his kiss. But inside she rippled with dissatisfaction. Once again he had avoided listening to her. "I'm sorry too, Hal. Really," she said, cuddling up against him. "I just wish we could talk sometimes, that's all. And go see Lip Service."

26

The radio belted blues. Lex moved two small rugs into the corner, then held out his hand. "Dance?" he said. He was relieved to see Nora lay down the chopsticks with which she'd been listlessly picking at morsels, kick off her shoes, stand up, and lift her arms. Lately she'd been rejecting all his offers, things she'd always enjoyed, like sea cucumbers from Chinatown, and dancing, and even love.

He put his arm around her back and pulled her to him. But she closed her eyes and followed her arms and hips in undulating circles, curling away from him. Just the way, he thought, during her recent scare (he refused even to think the word *cancer*) she'd waited till it was over to tell him about it. Flaunting her freedom. Punishing him. Pulling away.

Behind her eyes Nora tried to think about her book. Since the surgery, she needed to make up for the time she'd lost to her body. She tried to channel the music into her feet and hips and arms, leaving her mind free.

Lex stood still and admired her. He only danced the old way, body to body, hand in hand. Moving free, she seemed lost to him, eyes closed, swaying like phlox. "What are you thinking?" he asked.

"I was thinking about the detention camps set up for dissidents under Nixon that are still in place just waiting for folks like us."

"You *were*? While you're dancing?"

"That and . . . other things." When she was going under the anesthesia Lex never entered her mind. Only afterwards, when she was helpless, did she allow herself to backslide. In those oblique twilight moments when she contemplated death, she discovered that what she wanted most was to write her book. Now that she was clean again, she didn't dare forget it.

He was sure that behind her closed eyes lurked traitorous thoughts. Since the day he brought her home from the hospital she'd been getting increasingly skittish, bringing out all her old accusations one by one. She was losing weight, too, he could tell; but when he remarked on how slim she was getting, she raised her lip in that sardonic smile of hers intended to shut him up. He wondered if she was concealing something about the biopsy, or if she was still in pain, or if it was something else entirely.

"Okay," she said without stopping her hips or opening her eyes. "I was thinking about how you're going to leave me soon. You're going to find someone else and leave me." She opened her eyes to see if he had fallen for it again, if he still believed she was worried that he would leave her when so clearly she was the one intent on leaving him. Not that she was lying—each new resolve to leave him always surfaced as a fear of being left.

"Come here, you," said Lex, catching her hand and turning her to the music. "We both know I'm not the one who will do the leaving. You are. We both acknowledged that long ago."

"Oh, that's right," said Nora, eyes flashing. "I forgot. You're a complete flop when it comes to leaving, aren't you?"

Lex stoically swallowed her reprimand. "And you?" he finally asked, turning her faster and faster as the music wound to an end.

The Supremes took over. "I hope I'm better than you," Nora sang, twirling out of his arms and away.

Harold and Rosemary climb into the marriage bed after the eleven o'clock news, he on his side, she on hers. "Seven okay?" he asks, setting the clock. Rosemary moves her feet to make room for Gorky, who has leaped onto her side of the bed. They switch off their lights, kiss good night, and turn into the positions they have gradually grown used to, she curled toward the window, he toward the door: back to back.

For years they started off the night curled together, either facing, arms entwined, her head against his chest and one leg thrown over his, or else, especially in winter, both facing the window, he pressed against her back, his arm over her arm, hand on her breast, willing to move apart only deep in the night, in sleep. But gradually comfort has come to replace contact, and as his neck started giving him trouble and he began to put on weight and then to snore, and as she developed lower back pains from sitting too long at her desk, they agreed to attribute no symbolic meaning to their growing practice of going to sleep with their backs to each other and a bit of space between them in bed.

She closes her eyes and instantly encounters the wispy outer mists of sleep, as she's done at will since childhood when she shared a room with two talkative older sisters who stayed up late. Harold reserves this hour for thinking secret thoughts, just as he did as a boy. There was something disturbing in Rosemary's voice when she answered the phone before dinner, and now he's begun searching back over the weeks and years to tones and gestures he's noticed but never tried to understand. He calls them forth—the startled looks, the lowered voice, the hands thrust into pockets—tries to chart from memory the ups and downs of her flighty enthusiasms. It was John Andrews who called at dinner, his friend John, inviting them to a party. Why was she so excited? He can't remember exactly what it was she did that troubles him now; he's as much unnerved by his own failures of attention as by Rosemary's stance at the phone. How often does she turn her back to him and speak low when she answers the phone or withdraw to an extension in another room? He has never listened in, but now— The thought of an affair between his wife and his friend is intolerable.

"Rosemary?" he says, unable to censor himself. "Rosemary."

She stirs slightly, grunts softly.

"I want to ask you something. Important."

She doesn't open her eyes, but her body rouses. Can he have discovered the missing cash? She'll ask what he was doing hiding it, demand an explanation. "Hmmm?" she hums, dissembling, as her blood pumps fast, afraid to learn the truth.

He clears his throat and blurts out his question, even as he dismisses in advance her answer. "Tell me—are you having an affair with John?"

Now she opens her eyes, astonished, alert. Their civil code, hammered out the hard way after years of pain, has always been clear:

1. ask nothing you're not prepared to know;
2. deny everything.

And here he is toying with Commandment One. Above the building across the street Rosemary sees the full moon shine down like a spotlight on this interrogation. She hopes she can disguise her jitters. "John Andrews?" she says. "Don't be ridiculous! If I were having an affair with anyone, which I'm not, it certainly wouldn't be with John! Why do you ask?"

"I don't know," says Harold, recalling the terrible question she posed on the very eve of their wedding. Another question follows in the footsteps of his first. He can't hold back. "If not John, then who?"

In the moonlight Rosemary sees the silhouette of Harold's face: the high-bridged nose, the small, deepset eyes, lank thinning hair, now streaked with gray, the thin lips in the square jaw, beginning to double and jowl. She remembers the day in the playground (Daisy was two) when he witlessly asked what a young woman sees in an older man, revealing that he had already launched his betrayals, and she wonders if his new question presages another alarming revelation.

"I'm not having an affair with anyone, believe me," assures Rosemary, heading toward the familiar high road. But something of the audacity (or is it confidence?) in Harold's question makes her reconsider the route. She slows down, signals a turn. "If I were, though—are you sure you'd want to know?"

Harold reflects. That summer when she deceived him with the piano player, he'd felt betrayed. And the other time, with the student, he'd been frightened. But now, after all these years of harmonious marriage, he thinks only of the humiliation. "I'd sure want to know if it was with one of my friends."

"Harold!" cries Rosemary, scandalized. "I would never have an affair with one of your friends. You should know that!" She reaches for his hand.

Touched and relieved, he returns, "I want you to know I wouldn't have an affair with one of your friends, either." They squeeze hands, renewing their goodwill, executing this codicil to their marriage vows.

If . . .

But now they seem to have turned up a back road, flanked by jagged hills. In the moonlight horned creatures graze in fanciful fields. Once, they would have felt frightened, lost, leaving the highway. But now they want to explore this countryside. Rosemary, excited, sits up. "Look," she says, pointing. "As long as you woke me up to ask, tell me—how would you feel if I were seeing someone unconnected with our lives? I'm not, of course. An affair is the last thing I need, with a hundred problem sets to grade every weekend. But just suppose I were. Would it matter to you, as long as you knew I wasn't in love or anything?"

"Would it matter to you if I were?" returns Harold, edging around a bend.

Rosemary holds her breath. "I don't think so. Not if I knew our marriage was really safe. . . . What about you?"

He tries to see ahead, stretches his mind. "I don't know."

"Suppose we both were," says Rosemary, in her excitement kicking the dog. Down he goes, off the bed, over the precipice. "Suppose you were having a quiet affair and I started having one too. Just suppose. What would you think?"

"If *I* were having a 'quiet affair,' as you call it—which I'm not—I know it wouldn't interfere with our marriage. I could be having half a dozen affairs," says Harold in all sincerity, "and they wouldn't make the slightest difference to our lives. You're my wife. But I'm not sure that if *you* were having one we'd be so safe. You tend to fall in love."

"But I feel the same way!" cries Rosemary, tickled by their audacity. (Who else can she talk to like this?) "If I were in love with someone—which I'm not!—you'd have nothing to worry about. I would never allow anything to threaten our family." Coasting on righteousness, she dares to ask, "Have I ever?"

When Harold doesn't reply, Rosemary wonders if maybe they're riding too far down this road for safety, teetering too close to the edge of truth, with no other protection than *if*. Yoked with him in this bed, this conversation, she supports her position by pointing out that they might have separated years ago if it hadn't been for the children.

Cautiously, Harold applies the brakes on such hypothetical suggestions by observing wryly that likewise they would probably never have married if they'd never met. And would speak Chinese if they'd grown up in China.

But the fact remains: they did meet, the children were born, this was the road they took, one on which, for better or worse, they're traveling still—together. Given the truth of their lives, each is convinced that no other mate would be half so amiable or understanding.

Rosemary clutches Harold's hand. What other husband would want just what she wants? "Can you believe we're having this conversation?" she asks.

Harold checks his safety gauge. Every other time they've faced adultery it's been with tears and vows. This time they seem to be safe. Half a tank at least and an open road. "It is astonishing. But then you've often astonished me."

Husband and wife exchange kisses, but instead of turning apart for sleep, they kiss again until, for the first time in what feels like years, Harold writes his signature inside his wife, signing anew their intimate compact, and she gives her seal. In celebration, renewal, relief. Down the hall Daisy pecks at her typewriter, and Spider's foot pounds against the floor. Harold wraps his arm loosely around his wife's shoulders. She leans her head against his chest and throws her calf over his as she did in their earliest years. They remain pressed together, even when they close their eyes in sleep, until his snoring momentarily jolts her awake. As she turns toward the window for the night, Harold mumbles, "Anyway, I'm awfully glad you're not having an affair with John."

"To tell you the truth, I think he's pompous and funny-looking," she reassures him.

In the moonlight Rosemary kisses him again, then turns, and dreams the past.

So who would like the pope's nose? asks Mama, raising her chin with an air of martyred resignation. She lifts the first plate from the stack before her. No one speaks. So who? she repeats. Sarah had it for twenty-three years, now she's gone someone else gets a chance. Mama looks down at the plate and begins scooping on potatoes and peas. Then slowly she says, No one outside this family needs to know the details. She throws a stern look at Jessica, teller of tales. That means you, Missy. It's no one's business. Father? You want it?

Okay, pass it to me, says Father.

She wants to live that kind of life, she can, continues Mama, lifting the second plate. She's a grown woman, she finished school, she can do what she likes. When the rest of you finish school you can do what you like too. It's a free country. But I hope you learn right and wrong better than Sarah did.

Jessica and Rosemary exchange a look.

If she wants to throw away a fine job, says Mama, if she wants to live in sin, that's her business. She plops a plump drumstick on the plate, spoons on gravy. Pass this to Rosemary, she says, handing the plate to Thomas.

But what are we supposed to say if someone asks? says Thomas.

Father looks up, puts down his fork, and says, Don't say anything.

But what if somebody else says something, insists Thomas.

Then say she got married and moved out.

No, cries Mama, don't say that. Suppose she comes back?

She's not coming back. Not while I'm here, says Father, setting his jaw.

You don't know what you're talking about, shouts Mama.

Oh, don't I?

A rotten man like that could walk out on her day after tomorrow. He did it to his wife, he could do it again. Or Sarah could get some sense.

Sense! Where's she going to get any sense? She always acted like she knew everything—see what happens? Well, now she's gone, good riddance.

Father! gasps Jessica.

What's the matter with *you?*

Enough! shouts Mama, pounding the table. You just tell anybody that asks, she got a better job in Chicago than she could get here. And if it doesn't work out, she'll be back. And that's enough anybody in this family has to say about Sarah.

Ever! says Father. I don't want to hear that name.

The corners of Mama's mouth turn down. She sniffs loudly, squeezes her eyes closed, blows her nose in the handkerchief she always keeps tucked up her sleeve.

Rosemary lowers her eyes and pushes peas around her plate. Father picks up the pope's nose.

Why I Am a Vegetarian

I have never been clear about why I am a vegetarian. I started by accident when I slept over with a friend who didn't eat meat. I didn't even notice the first day, and the second day I thought, okay, let's see if you can go without meat for a week. Why? As a challenge, I guess. I loved the feeling of control I had when the week was up, so I said to myself, think you can make it two weeks? Soon the weekly challenge was not enough, so I set myself a monthly one. Eighteen months later, I'm still going strong.

Why? None of the usual reasons apply for me. Although I would not go out to kill an animal, I'm not against all killing. I wear leather, eat fish, swat mosquitoes. I consume too many unhealthy foods such as fudge, pastry, ice cream, Fritos, french fries, chocolate donuts, and other empty and worse-than-empty calories to pretend that I'm driven to vegetarianism out of a concern for my health. You may wonder, is it for religious or spiritual reasons? But that's not it either. Nor can I blame my upbringing, being the only vegetarian in my family. Nor is meat particularly disgusting to me—on the contrary, a thick, rare hamburger is a frequent fantasy. [This was a lie, but Daisy liked the sound of it.] Yet I find I am as strict a vegetarian as people with all those reasons. Why? There's only one answer: because I enjoy it. And by now, when it's almost a way of life to me, because I don't want to break my record.

When I see a tempting meat dish from my past, a Thanksgiving turkey, a Christmas ham studded with cloves, or even a large rare hamburger on a platter surrounded by crispy fries, I enjoy the pleasure of resisting temptation more than I would the food itself. I know the triumph I feel will last ten times longer than the pleasure of the most delicious meat. The feeling of control I have over my body is more satisfying than any feast.

I can almost say that vegetarianism is my hobby. I can almost say that my favorite leisure-time activity is the cultivation of my will and my triumph over temptation.

Nora turned on her word processor before going to sleep, called up the Dear John file, and, with Bianca's clean bill of health, tried another approach to shedding Lex.

Dear John #6. . . . or like an all-consuming fever that has temporarily transformed me, diverting all my energy and trapping me in the sick room away from the world, making me hide from my friends, until at last, mercifully, it finally BREAKS. With a sigh of relief I ask for something delicious, something more palatable than the thin broth I've been living on. For the first time in weeks I venture to the window and open the blinds. How startled I am to see that spring has moved into the world while I was sick and is waiting outside to welcome me back. Dogs and children cavort on the grass; the shrubberies are turning green . . .

Tripping

27

THE PILOT has turned off the no-smoking sign, they've reached their cruising altitude, the flight attendants are starting to serve drinks, and now there's no going back. Rosemary hands Peter back the flight map and turns to the window.

When Spider's throat flared up the week before departure, Rosemary almost canceled the trip. Suppose something awful happened while she was gone—how would they reach her? She certainly couldn't leave behind a detailed itinerary, even if she had one. But of course, she had none: she had only a professional pretext, a fantasy, and a 21-day Eurail Pass.

"What would you two like to drink?" asks the perky flight attendant.

Until this minute, Rosemary's thoughts of food and drink have been for everyone but herself. She planned for every contingency, leaving emergency numbers taped to the phone and detailed instructions for Harold and Mrs. Scaggs affixed by magnets to the refrigerator. She stocked the freezer, put in a fresh supply of Gorky's pills, conferred with Spider's English teacher, and asked Ross to prepare a new will for her. If my plane goes down, she said cheerfully to the children, I'm leaving Spider all my Beatles albums, and Daisy, you get my clothes. Now will you both please try not to fight while I'm gone? But the real problem that sent her to the lawyer was not what to do with her worldly goods, but whom to appoint as the children's guardian in case Harold cracked up the car and died too. Everyone she considered was deficient in a different way: too flaky, too rough, too indulgent, too cold, too distant, too stern, too busy, too old; those who'd be wise about money would be wrong about discipline; and since she and Harold could never agree, the problem was never settled.

"What kind of juice do you have?" asks Rosemary.

"Juice?" says Peter, incredulous. And even though he's in debt, he orders them champagne.

Watching Peter pour, Rosemary suffers an acute attack of guilt. Families were too fragile nowadays; a marriage could shatter as easily as glass, strewing the house with shards on which the children were in danger of cutting themselves for years to come. Just before departure Harold practically had to push her out of the car, insisting he was perfectly capable of handling the home front by himself, thank you, and would be insulted if she didn't calm down and just leave. (She didn't know he had a dinner date with Barbara.) And even after the jet lifted over the Atlantic, banking away from the handsome Manhattan towers, Rosemary was pulled back down, remembering crucial neglected details: Would someone remember to water the plants? Would Harold leave money each week for Spider's music teacher?

They loosen their seat belts; Peter raises his plastic cup; they toast.

And now an amazing thing begins to happen to Rosemary. Between the bubbles and the altitude, her memory begins to blur. First Harold fades into the blue, then the children sink like cherubs behind cumulous fluff, then even guilt melts like soft cheese in the sun. With nothing but sky above, below, and to the sides, they're flying free.

"What time is it in Rome?" Rosemary asks Peter.

"Six hours later than it is here. Let's change our watches and get started."

Like a wife she hands her watch to Peter; but when he returns it fixed for their future, she keeps his hand and like a lover giddily draws it deep into her lap, between her legs.

"Look, Peter," cries Rosemary as landing music fills the 747. "Look!" She points out the window and begins to laugh. "See?"

Peter leans into his seat belt to gaze down on the splendid spread of Rome. "What?"

"Our dome!"

Rap slapped a plastic baggie onto the table and, arms folded, slid into a chair, the proud provider.

Daisy stared at the transparent bag. The buff-colored mushrooms looked very like the kind one bought at the supermarket, only bigger. Daisy was afraid. "What's it feel like?" she asked, turning the bag over slowly.

Eyes glittering, Rap leaped up and began to pace. "It can make you see things you never saw before. Things get clearer. Like, you could be sitting at the window watching the sun and you might start understanding that you're really part of it, you know?" He shrugged. "You'll see."

"But can anything bad happen? I'd hate to waste maybe the only weekend of my life my whole family is away at the same time. Even on pot I can get pretty paranoid if I have too much."

Rap rubbed his chin, considering. "No. You don't throw up like with peyote, or hallucinate like with acid. No, I never heard of a bad trip on shrooms. More like ludes in that regard. Anyway, we won't eat enough of them to get really wasted, just enough to get high. The rest of them you can hold onto for another time."

"Me? Where am I supposed to keep them?"

"Just put the bag in an envelope and hide it somewhere. It's no big deal for you. You're not on parole." He emptied the bag on the table and began sorting the larger caps into two equal piles.

Daisy's hand went up to check her earrings, the gold studs she made love in because they wouldn't scratch or fall out, earrings she had care-

fully put in her ears at the same time she had inserted her new diaphragm, so that she would be ready the minute Rap grabbed her. "And
for sex?"

"They don't give you that fast surge like coke or make your climax
explode like poppers. But"—he grinned—"they're a lot better than green
M & Ms." When he had finished sorting the caps, he began dividing up
the stems. "We could get high faster if we brewed them into a tea, but
raw, they're easier to chew. Better raw for your first time. Now if you'll
just pour us a glass of milk—"

Carefully Rap pushed one pile toward Daisy, then lifted his largest cap
to his lips. Daisy selected the daintiest cap. "What about the milk?" she
asked, wishing she didn't have to do this.

"First the shrooms. Then the milk."

The Train . . .

When the purple and royal blue lights begin to flash, Daisy is stretched
out with a blanket in front of the fire, her head resting on her hand, her
eyes focused beyond the screen and grate directly on the flames. Though
vaguely aware of Rap's warm body nestled against her naked back, she
concentrates on the flashing diorama in front of her.

Ahead is the entrance to a railway tunnel. In a moment the whistling
train, just emerging into the light from around a bend, will pull into the
station. A few men in tall hats and overcoats lounge restlessly just beyond
the grate, and several women in fur muffs and bonnets, some holding
children, wait in the shadow of the platform. A black engine hurtles
toward them, emitting great puffs of smoke and soot and fiery sparks,
coloring the snow beside the tracks a steely gray.

Riveted, Daisy watches the oncoming train, hypnotized by the huge,
powerful force. She knows that fire can leap out and harm her, but the
screen protects her; she's almost safe. The power she watches is her own.
The longer she watches, the calmer she grows.

After a long time she hears Rap calling to her from far away. "Daisy!
Daze! Come over here! Something's going on in the sky you won't believe. A real UFO, flashing lights and everything. Come on! I'm not
kidding!"

But the train is pulling into the station and she wants to see what happens. Who will get off? Who will get on? What will happen to them all? The gaslights of the station are lit with tiny flames of purple and green and gold; the long skirts of women, the black coats of men, the puffs of steam coming from their mouths as they smile and nod in the freezing air render absurd the very idea of UFOs. Beyond the station the tracks turn, leaving the fireplace, the room behind. Daisy calls back, "Later. After the train's gone . . ."

When Rap slides back under the blanket, Daisy feels her body begin to tingle, the way it sometimes does with the best pot. Her toes and fingers, her knees and thighs, the place on her hip where Rap's hand rests with the lightest touch, the spot on her buttocks where she feels the Jagger (ridiculous name!) stiffening. As the train disappears around the bend, Daisy turns over and opens her arms.

Nora has just come in from a workout at the Haven, hasn't even taken off her coat, when the doorbell rings. Panic: Keith's plane isn't due for hours, but who else can it be? Or will this be the one time this year (her luck!) that Lex finally manages to shake his family on the weekend and come to her? She picks up the intercom. "Delivery," says an unknown voice.

She opens the door to a stubbly old man holding a long florist's box. Her glee registers in a new baroque flourish on her signature. She glances at the card—from Keith—then takes off her coat, pushes the whole bagful of goodies she's just purchased into the fridge, and gets down a tall vase.

Roses, long and red. Morning-after flowers, in advance, she thinks, trying to resist her delight. Giving in, she rereads the card and inhales the scent deep down into her lungs, then plays back her phone messages.

A voice she doesn't recognize announces the date, and suddenly she realizes today is her father's birthday. The twenty-fifth: the same place in the month as His, she always said as a child, often working it into the elaborate birthday cards she made for him. A savior, a hero, who rose from the dead ("missing," her mother said) and returned to be her god on Easter Sunday, 1946. Big powerful ruddy god, in the exalted uniform of the U.S. Marines, with the deepest voice she ever heard and the longest, strongest arms. With that voice and those arms, even without her adoration he'd never have had to lay a hand on her. Only once she remembers standing at her door shouting, Try and stop me! (or was it, You can't make me?), at which he merely laughed, picked her up with one arm, and slammed her down on her bed. Living in seventeen towns in as many years—no wonder her mother left. But by then Nora had left, too.

Now he's retired. Consults for "oil" concerns in the Middle East. Computer weapons systems, she suspects—once his specialty—maybe even CIA. By the time she left home he'd become her fallen god, her anti-god. In their final battle he marched her, captive, down an aisle under a canopy of crossed, forbidding swords, forced her to her knees. But she showed him: the next day she ran away.

He had two more families after her. And her mother had two more husbands. Sometimes she suspected they were in a race. Sometimes she wonders if her father isn't the reason she finally had her tubes tied and so relentlessly opposed the war. His war. If so, she's grateful: it got her started writing. (How she loves her life!) Not that he's impressed. He considers writing a scam and asks her every chance he can when she plans to get a job.

"Nora, darling—" Her name in Keith's slightly nasal voice sets her pulse so fiercely pounding in her ears that the actual words don't register. He sounds so close, he must be calling from La Guardia.

"Nora, darling, I have stupid, depressing news. I seem to have cracked a stupid crown, and my dentist can't see me till first thing tomorrow morning. By the time he's finished, it'll practically be time to turn around and fly back, so I'm afraid I won't be coming east tonight after all. Please call me and we can—"

Nora is quite sure she hasn't heard. This is their first time together in New York. They have dinner reservations, theater tickets. Nibblies, roses. She rewinds the tape and plays it back again—incredulous, then humiliated, then angry, then depressed. It takes her a full half hour of concentrated effort before she can understand that Keith's sudden cancellation is no rejection, no disaster—may in fact be a boon, giving her an unexpected gift of time.

Earlier that week, the ideas for her book all at once began to jell into usable words. She had a powerful insight about the nature of war she needed to get down on paper before it flew away. She had seen in a flash that the essence of sin is insatiability. Lust, greed, gluttony, envy, anger, sloth, even pride were deadly precisely because they could never be satisfied, you could never get enough. No matter how much you got, you always hungered for more, more, more. And precisely *that* was your punishment. Never being satisfied, longing for more until it killed you.

So sin was its own punishment exactly as virtue was its own reward. The sins were mortal not because they were forbidden but because they would eat you up alive or hound you to death. Otherwise, if you could leave off, if you could be satisfied, lust or hunger or pride would just be healthy desires, normal human passions, hardly sins at all, certainly not killers.

As she was brooding on the stunning simplicity of her discovery, it came to her that this was the essence of the arms race too. Insatiability. No matter how many warheads either side had, they weren't enough, would never be enough to satisfy. It was a terrible deadly sin, a race to the death, already its own punishment.

So simple, so elemental. She knows she'll be open to ridicule, even dismissal, using the language of sin; but she also knows she's on to a powerful understanding that she owes the world—and herself—to pursue.

So what could be luckier, she consoles herself, than to repossess the weekend—this particular weekend? For the first time in years, she decides to call her father in D.C. to wish him a happy birthday.

Three ninety-six, three ninety-seven, three ninety-eight—Spider's eyes cross in concentration as he juggles three yellow clubs doing Chops before the mirror. His goal is to reach five hundred without a miss. Then he plans to switch to the rings as a reward.

Had you asked him before Christmas what Chops were, he would have dismissed the question with a certain withering look achieved by curling the left side of the upper lip and elevating the right eyebrow—a look carefully copied from his mother when he was eleven. Since Christmas, however, when he got his weighted clubs and dashed off to his room to begin practicing, he gratefully responds to the same question with an eager, illustrated explanation—fuller than you want to hear. Determined to master Chops by the time his mother returns from Italy in April and Backcrosses by the time school's out in June, Spider spends no less than two hours a day practicing, more on weekends. His trumpet languishes. He will never go anywhere without his juggling balls.

That's Spider. At three he was a dump truck (omnipotent, yellow, with many sets of interlocking gears) and during waking hours never without his motor running: full voice like a turbojet when unobserved, low buzz like a bee when in public, or subvocal like the whoosh of wind through a crack when someone reminded him that he was humming. At six he became a spider for one entire triumphant day, gleaning such praises for his architectural feat that he's a spider still. At nine he was a master spy, concealing himself under tables and behind doors, slipping in and out of rooms unseen, able, with the aid of fingerprint kit, magnifying glass, ingenious codes, chemicals, and a small cassette recorder, gift of his Uncle Thomas, to solve untold mysteries of his own design. At twelve—but no need to go on.

Today is Saturday; his mother's in Italy, his father's in the shower, and there stands Spider in his pajamas before the mirror, background rap song on the stereo, rhythmically counting four hundred seven, four hundred eight, determined to reach five hundred without missing before lunch. He's convinced that all this practice may enlarge not only his triceps but his organ, and that perfect Chops and Backcrosses will make him attractive to the female sex. If he misses now, he'll count it a minor tragedy, but that won't deter him from starting again at one and practicing, damn it!, till he gets it.

A life is a story that can't be interrupted. You can open any door on any Streeter at any time of day or night and know that what you see, however puzzling or perverse, is perfectly in keeping with the rest.

Now, for instance: If Spider were to open the door on his father at precisely this moment, he would be more shocked than we to discover Harold doing what Spider himself does behind his door almost every day. His father! Spider would be so amazed that he'd tiptoe quickly out the door and run up the path of disbelief as fast as his long legs would carry him. By lunchtime he would doubt the evidence of his own eyes and by dinner he would have "forgotten" the sight completely. Yet there stands Harold in the shower with his legs apart, knees slightly bent, stroking his penis slowly, lovingly, with two soapy hands, right thumb just below the ridge, concentrating on the task at hand no less ardently than his son in his room concentrates on his (four seventy-two, four seventy-three . . .)— as ardent and as blameless.

Or take Daisy. At this moment she's in her closet biting her fingernails in a panic because at four o'clock this afternoon she has an interview with one Cyrus T. Plumb, alumni representative of Williams College. She has applied under a special complicated procedure that may better her chances of getting in or may, on the other hand, worsen them. She has no idea what to say or wear. She wants her mom. With everyone looking over her shoulder to see what college she gets into, and Rap (the most thrilling thing in her life since she got to dance in *The Nutcracker*) back in the city again, no wonder she's in a state. Senioritis, plus no decent clothes, no night talks with her mother, no regular meals. No wonder she lets herself go bad on weekends. Now she fears she'll have to pay.

Spider, who never heard of senioritis, knows only that Daisy's been acting weird lately. She whispers on the phone when no one's around to overhear, stays out all night whenever she can, and last Saturday—a week ago today—forced Spider to sleep at Herschel's during her sleep-over party. Of course their father backed her, he always does, vacating the house himself for the night. That same night, Spider happens to know, Daisy and her friends used the fireplace—something they never did before. The evidence hit his nostrils the minute he walked in the door. Were they trying to destroy some evidence? He should have taped the party. Sifting the ashes for clues turned up nothing but ashes.

That whole Sunday his sister was inexplicably sweet to him, as if she'd been invaded by some benevolent body snatcher. She shared her brownies and invited him into the living room to dance. Dance! I don't know how, he told her. Then I'll teach you, she said—come on.

When he was a small boy Daisy once saved him from a murderous dog, an event of family lore fondly dragged out at dinner at least once every year. When she pushed him on the swings, he remembers, she stopped whenever he asked her to. In the plays they used to put on for grown-ups she made his costumes and let him have the roles he wanted. Even now, she only threatens to snitch on him, never follows through. In gratitude for the dancing lesson, he considered erasing one of the priceless tapes of Daisy and her friends made by him and Herschel.

But when she suddenly turned on him with her old nasty self as he tried to wake her the next morning, he changed his mind. It was Monday; their father had already left and it was getting late for school. Instead of thanking him, she began shouting, Go away! and, Leave me alone!

Okay, be late then, I don't care, he said, slamming the door. When he got home from school and found her still in bed, he began to worry. You better get up and feed Gorky his pill, 'cause he's pulling out his fur again, he told her. But she just kept repeating, Go away, go away, go away. Next, he tried mild tickles, which made her sit up and scream, I hate you!

O-KAY! said Spider, sleep through a nukular blast, see if I'll wake you!

And in his rage, instead of erasing any tapes, he put on the most damaging one, turned the volume all the way up, and triumphantly burned.

The First Tape . . .

What do you think they do together?
Larry and Jody?
Yeah.

Daisy's perplexed. She hears Diane and Carrie in the hall. How did they get in? Is it someone's birthday? A surprise? Then she hears another voice that she can't quite place saying something oddly familiar. The whole conversation sounds oddly familiar, something from long ago.

He's very cute from the front. And a great dancer. But, I don't know, he stands a little stooped over, and when he puts one hand on his hip the way he does, it ruins him, it really turns me off. What do you think of him?

I don't know anymore. In sixth grade I used to like him secretly. We walked to school together sometimes. But when we got to junior high and he got in the smart class and started going out with Kim I couldn't even talk to him anymore.

As soon as she comprehends, Daisy stands, points like a setter, and races down the hall toward the loud cascade of giggles coming from the tape.

Now, with Aaron Sampson, that's another story. He's just the opposite.
How do you mean?

In seventh grade he was really a jerk when we were in Miss Farnheld's class. But now he's got that slow sexy voice and those big brown eyes and big hands and—I don't know, I just think he's very sexy.

Yeah. And those lips. He's probably a great kisser.
Do you think so?

Spider's door is wide open. He's lying on his bed, arms behind his head, legs crossed at the knee, a queer uncertain smirk spread across his face.

They'd be soft and not too wet, and one kiss would last a long time, and maybe he'd move his mouth a little bit, slowly, back and forth, like this.
Show me.
Okay. Come over here . . .
You mean like this?
Sort of, but not so hard. Slower. Try again.

. . . Like this?

Daisy scans the room, spots the machine, lunges.

That's better. But more like this. Lean back.

Spider's off the bed and on her in a flash, but not before she's managed to raise the cassette player over her head and hurl it crashing to the floor.

Spider's stunned. No one's allowed to touch anyone else's property without permission. He looks at the broken box preparing to demand payment when he sees Daisy move for the cassette. He dives for it. "No you don't!"—and dancing away from her on his toes, he gleefully shoves the tape into his pocket.

"Give me that tape!" she shouts, chasing him down the hall into the living room, every muscle taut. Not that she cares about a stupid conversation from years ago, but if he's got this on tape what else has he got?

They circle and leap, making passes and feints. A table goes over, a chair. When he's tired of the chase Spider stands ready for her in the clear center of the room.

Until last year she could always beat him, but now they're evenly matched. She lets her rage lift her off the ground in a flying leap, then they tumble to the floor. She'd think nothing of killing him. They roll, pound, clinch, kick, bite, until they find themselves locked in an unbreakable embrace, an intimate impasse. She's angrier, therefore stronger. They clinch for a long time.

Finally, panting, she pulls away while he sits catching his breath. Once, years before, in a terrible fight she almost killed him, accidentally knocking his head against the corner of the coffee table. (That event too is dragged out and displayed like a family heirloom at least once a year.)

"Give me the tape, Spider," she orders.

"Say *please*."

Her mouth is a gash of rage. "Please. . . . Now, give me that tape!"— every word distinct.

He holds the cassette out to her. "And you get me a new player."

She spits at him.

"Okay, suit yourself. But"—he plays his trump, already sensing it's too soon—"if you want the other tapes you better get me a new one."

She turns without a word and leaves the room.

.   .   .

Rosemary is appalled at the sheets. A bunkful of Boy Scouts might have scrimmaged on the bed, and in the center it's drenched. Recently, her body has been producing strange new liquids when they make love, as if her vagina were shedding buckets of tears.

She thinks it started in Rome. Now, sometimes, after they've been making love for hours and both of them have come, sometimes when she's straddling Peter and slowly, rapturously riding him, her calves folded back at the knees and her thighs spread, a shower of fluid flows from her, wetting his body and the sheets, as if a faucet had suddenly been turned on full force. That's just how she feels inside, too—as if he had penetrated so deeply into her, through dark basement corridors, that he had somehow reached the hidden room that housed the controls to her body. At first she'd been ashamed, fearing a malfunction of her bladder. Then she hoped it might be Peter's semen flowing back out of her. Now she calls it *gushing*, so there'll be no doubt that it's love, not urine.

"God, Peter. This is really awful. What will they think?" says Rosemary, pretending to be concerned not about Peter but the chambermaids.

"They'll think we're lucky. Wittgenstein says the body is the best picture we have of the soul," says Peter. They pull the blanket over the sheets, then he walks around the bed, takes her in his arms.

Even though they're checking out of the hotel in half an hour, Rosemary places an empty glass on the table beside the bed, as if to imply that the wet is nothing but spilled water.

When he gets home from school Spider finds his tapes, once so neatly arranged, ransacked. He retaliates by raiding Daisy's drawers. A diary is what he's after, or letters—something to make her as vulnerable as he feels himself. He's scared too: they've passed from turn-taking to anarchy.

In the bottom drawer among piles of sweaters Spider finds a sealed envelope with something lumpy inside. Instinct tells him he's struck gold. He smooths the sweaters, closes the drawer, and runs to his room with his prize.

28

Lex is gone, and Nora sits at her word processor staring out the window to the east. From the moment Lex left and she sat back down to work, she grew more and more alarmed. Now that she finally knows what she wants to say, feels its urgency, her book grows increasingly elusive. Worse, it's gradually unwriting itself. This has never happened before. All the notes and numbers she carefully compiled over the past year to support her position now appear quite useless. Not wrong exactly, but irrelevant, superseded, like Spitfire fighters in a world of jets. Gestures, motives, fears, and hopes—the very substance of her book—are simply unquantifiable.

And beneath the rubble of useless numbers, she knows a deeper problem lies buried: How can you ever know what's true? Were even the most vivid memories dependable? The very facts that seemed least disputable, those that came directly out of your own firsthand experience, the ones you build your life around, were, in the end, at best, interpretations.

The one authority she has always absolutely relied upon is herself, yet in her present shaken mood, even her own views are suspect. She's begun to notice certain discrepancies. For example, each time she'd explained herself in recent months—to Lex, to Keith, to Rosemary—entirely different stories emerged, though she drew on the same fund of experience.

Her marriage and abortion—the central drama of her early life which determined all that followed—what was the truth of that? Had she bravely, defiantly aborted herself, as she liked to think, or had her body, indifferent to her will, miscarried? How can she ever be sure? Weeks before anyone else knew she was pregnant—neither Paul nor her parents—she had tried to take charge of her fate. She had skied from the highest mountain in northern California, had ridden horses, swilled ergot, filled herself daily with the foulest-smelling dark brown douche (the giveaway); and, after her mother made her confess and her father forced her to marry, she swallowed twelve bitter quinine pills in twenty-four hours—starting just before the wedding. From the burning bath she soaked in after the final dose, she rose up so high, leaving her poisoned body behind to die some hideous married death, that she felt herself triumph like a martyr, like a saint. Better death, she felt, welcoming the pain, than to give herself over at seventeen to—

To what? She didn't know. To resignation, submission, duplicity. In the very moment her blood began to flow, she felt high enough (the quinine? the bath?) to take on anyone. Like her hero-demon, her father, who had proven himself at Guam and Midway, she would rather die than submit. But unlike him, she would never follow orders. With demonic energy she packed a suitcase and, before her husband was due back from the base, fled to Berkeley, her father's enemies' high command.

But suppose she'd failed to abort (or miscarry)—what of her convictions then? Suppose she'd had Paul's baby there on the base? Useless to speculate: if she can't be sure what happened, how can she ever know what didn't? She likes to think she'd have had the guts to do everything the same, only nine months later. Give in on nothing that matters. Leave Paul anyway (never would she live with a man she didn't love!), put it up for adoption, then begin to write—

A question for her book streaks across her mind, too fast to get down: Is an insatiable lust for freedom also sin?

Nora turns from her screen and takes up the galleys of her long piece on the Colorado Rocky Flats nuclear installation, due to run next week. So much easier to polish the old than invent the new. Maybe, she thinks, after she's broken with Lex the book will come.

Dear John #7. Our affair was like a trip to another country, an exotic culture. Though I could never live there, I had a great time. Now I'm home again, back in my own place. You know how it is: while you're abroad you're transformed, inspired, supercharged; you pay attention to everything, study the language, the gestures, the dress, the maps and guides, you even imagine living there. But when you get back into your own life, you start to forget, and you realize what a strain it was having to smile all the time, never being able to express yourself with subtlety in that foreign language, having to hold back all your criticisms and doubts and questions for fear of offending your foreign hosts.

In the end, the trip, though exhausting, was worth it for the stimulation of another culture—the people, art, food, music, sex.

But as soon as you begin to wonder, What am I doing here? it's probably time to go home. Otherwise, very soon the strain and alienation of being a foreigner, even in a great metropolis, will grow tiresome. Oh then what a relief to speak your own language again at last, to be understood!

Harold, eyes closed, feet elevated on Rosemary's pillows piled at the end of the bed, had turned down his earphones and was just losing himself in a dream, when Spider burst into the room.

"You busy, Pop? Can I talk to you?"

"Come in, come in," said Harold, sitting up and moving the earphones from his ears to his neck like a doctor his stethoscope. Though he was exhausted from the day's work plus having to be mother too, he was less sorry for the interrupted nap than he was grateful for the parental opportunity, whatever it might be. "Sit down," he said, patting the bed.

But Spider stood. A person of extremes, Spider sat as infrequently as possible. Instead, he began systematically cracking his knuckles. "I have to do this report for social studies, and I need to ask you a few things, okay?"

"Of course. Ask me anything you like, son, and I'll try my best to answer."

"First," said Spider, finishing his right hand and beginning on his left, "how much is your annual income?"

Harold gulped and stared. He snapped off the tape machine, cleared his throat, then cleared it again. "Well, you see," he began, "I never know exactly. It varies considerably from year to year. Why do you want to know, anyway?"

"I told you. For my social studies report."

"What sort of report?"

"On Money. Everyone got a different topic, and my topic is Family Income. I have to make a budget for our family. I'm going to try to do it on the computer. So—what's our annual family income?"

"Unfortunately," said Harold, assuming the voice of innocence and authority suitable for addressing an investigating committee, "I'm afraid I can't answer that question." Spider waited. "As a writer, you see, I don't get much of a salary, so I never know in advance how much I'll make in a year. One year it can be a lot and the next year relatively little, since I don't know how many pieces I'll publish in a given year. That's one of the major liabilities of my profession—though don't get me wrong," he added, so as to avoid prejudicing his son against following in his footsteps should he choose, as his own father had unthinkingly prejudiced him, "I'm not complaining, I'm grateful to be able to do the work I do."

"Yeah, but what about your teaching? And Mom's? You both get salaries, don't you?"

Caught. Of course, they could never live as they did on his teaching income. And for all it cost the family in time, Rosemary's barely kept her in pocket money. No, it was the investments on his *Terror!* killing that kept them going. But, as even Rosemary agreed, their balance sheet (which she'd once had the gall to call obscene) must certainly not be divulged to the children. "True . . . but," said Harold, wriggling, "I don't consider teaching my major occupation. I'm a writer. Though God knows when I'll finish another book."

A film of perspiration was beginning to form on Harold's neck. He removed the irritating earphones and laid them on the table.

"Someone else is doing Professions, Pop. I'm just doing Income. What I need to know first is a number. How much do we make?"

"Frankly, Spider, that isn't the sort of thing I see any reason to tell your school. It's private. Besides, as I already said, it varies so much from year to year that I can't really say."

"Okay, just this year then."

Seeing his options narrowing, Harold stalled. "I won't know that till April 15."

"Then last year. Any year," said Spider, an impatient whine beginning to color his voice.

Harold ignored him. "You're probably still too young to know what that date signifies, aren't you? It's one of the most important dates of our society."

To Daisy, Rosemary, and soon enough to Spider too, April 15 was the terrible day the colleges mailed out their rejections. But Harold had other concerns. "April 15 is income tax day," he said sharply. "You'll learn that sooner than you know."

"Come on, Pop, I just need some figures to feed the computer. Then I have to make a budget. How much for rent, how much for food, for telephone, for taxes—you know, the reglear expenses."

"You mean *regular*. Reg-u-lar."

"Yeah, right. And from that, I'm going to try to write a simple program for budgeting."

"Well, then," said Harold, "for your purposes it doesn't really matter which numbers you use, does it? And since no figure I give you can possibly be accurate, why don't you just choose a figure that will be easy for you to work with and say it's approximate."

"Like what, though? I don't know anything about money. Tell me a number and I'll round it."

Harold was relieved to know that though he would have to supply a figure, and soon, at least he'd be permitted to invent it. But what figure? Sometimes, as when people were soliciting contributions from him, he wanted to give out that he made half as much as he actually did, but sometimes, as when he needed to impress, he preferred to imply he made twice as much. He was not entirely sure which conditions applied at this moment. There was the school and there was his son. Sensing that Spider's tyrannical foot was about to begin tapping out the seconds of silence now conspicuously piling up, Harold plucked from the air two round figures, one plump and reassuring, one spartan and tough, lounging on the perimeter of possibility, and presented them to Spider. "Somewhere in that range."

"Wow!" breathed Spider, rolling his eyes. "That's thousands of times my allowance."

Harold felt defeated. "Yes, but wait till you compare your expenses with ours," he said wearily.

"That's next. How much do we spend a year on rent? On food?"

Harold replaced the earphones on his head and switched the music back on. Suddenly he remembered that he had forgotten to leave money for Spider's music lesson. "That's the best I can do for now. Why don't you wait till your mother gets back and ask her to help you with the budget? She can probably fill you in on our expenses a lot better than I can. . . . Now, if you don't mind, I'm going to try to catch forty winks before dinner."

Barbara was beside herself. She couldn't tell who was crazy, she or Harold. The wheel of love was turning backwards now, coming off its axle. When she'd consoled herself to the tune of six extra pounds (almond butter and chocolate, mainly, unless she was pregnant), she called up her old boy-friend Warner Beam, now a shrink, figuring he'd be good at least for a prescription for trancs.

They met at the office he shared with a hypnotist in the basement of a town house in the East Sixties. He offered her coffee and, as he always did with friends to set them at ease and distinguish them from his patients, sat beside her on the beige sofa instead of behind his desk. Still, she's embarrassed to tell him about her affair with a famous married man, her ex-professor almost twice her age, figuring he'll disapprove—though heaven knows Warner's had his share of dubious affairs and even married a patient once.

But she's desperate. She needs something fast. "Help me," she says. She's even considered getting pregnant by Harold on the sly, that's how desperate she is. "Can you believe it? Me? A mother?" If she's ever going to do it, she thinks it might be fun to have the child of a genius. It's risky, though. He has two kids already and might just decide to dump her anyway.

Here's her problem, she explains. Harold's calls, once daily, have ta-pered off. And when he does call now, he's evasive. His wife is away for spring break, she just found out, yet he still forbids her to phone him at home. She's spent entire weekends sitting by the phone waiting, plan-ning what to say; but when she tries, ever so cautiously, to ask what's going on, he denies everything and treats her like a demanding child. In the early days, if she felt shaky about him, he'd take her out of town for a day or a night of love. But now their lovemaking, restricted to quickies, is perfunctory. She fears he's fallen in love with someone else, one of his Yale students maybe, brilliant and beautiful. Crazy is what he called her when she finally found the nerve to ask him if he'd fallen in love. "I don't know, Warner. Am I crazy? I can't work, I just cry and eat; I feel he's messing with my *reality*."

Warner offers, by way of friendship, to treat her obsession with a sure cure—something new he's been researching. "Hypnosis?" she asks, see-ing the framed diplomas on the wall, but he shakes his head. That's his suitemate's specialty; his is aversion therapy.

Abruptly she returns her cup to its saucer, spilling a few drops. "For *love?*"

"Sure," says Warner. "Why not? Love is a mental aberration particu-larly susceptible to conditioning. We have a better than seventy percent success rate with homosexuals, almost as good as we do deprogramming smokers. Love's just a compulsion. What's your boyfriend's name?"

The indignity of the word shocks her. Hal is famous and a professor. "You don't understand. This isn't some boyfriend."

"Of course not," says Warner and waits.

"Hal," she admits grudgingly, like a criminal signing a forced confession.

Warner pulls a cigarette pack out of the breast pocket of the jacket of the three-piece suit he wears to disguise his wild nature and offers it.

"No thanks," says Barbara.

The Box . . .

"See this box?" says Warner. "Looks like an ordinary pack of cigarettes in an ordinary plastic case, doesn't it? But it's special. It's so special it's going to cure you." His eyes are sparkling behind his small, round wire-rimmed spectacles, the same ones he wore in college.

Can he have discovered some smokable antilove potion, some negative of coke? Barbara shrugs and feels hysteria coming on.

"Now, I want you to think of Hal, how he turns you on. Close your eyes, get him right up there in your mind, and then open up the box."

"What is it?" Cautiously she takes the box from him. "Anyway, I've almost stopped smoking. I'm afraid."

"Go on. Don't be afraid. Think about Hal and open it."

She closes her eyes till she gets the image that arouses her—not of his face or even his naked body, but of their limbs arranged in the peculiar way they always end up. Why not try anything? Gingerly she opens the box.

A hideous sharp blue pain streaks through her, from her toes straight into her teeth. She lets out a shriek and flings the box to the floor.

Warner, a small man with yellow teeth and a few beloved strands of long black hair lying in stripes across his scalp, is smiling. "Don't worry," he says. "It's a very small shock, nothing that can hurt you." He reaches down to retrieve the box. "Really. They sell them in novelty stores over the counter."

"How could you do this?" cries Barbara, tears springing to her eyes. "I come to you desperate, as a friend, and you play horrible stupid jokes."

Warner pouts. "They may market these boxes as jokes, but they have real scientific applications. I use them all the time. . . . You want to be cured, don't you? What's love but a set of strongly conditioned neural responses? When you see this guy you associate to pleasure, and each time you go to bed with him it's reinforced. That's why it drives you crazy when you can't be with him. Now, all you have to do is reverse the positive conditioning with negative reinforcement. I guarantee you, if you shock yourself like that every time you think of him, inside of a month you'll be out of love. By two months you'll never want to see the guy again."

Barbara's crying full force now, the real thing: shoulders heaving, face in hands. Warner squirms. Tears always unnerve him. He reaches over to his desk for the Kleenex. (He keeps a whole case of Kleenex in his supply closet for his patients' tears.)

"What kind of friend are you?" she sobs, wadding a handful of tissues under her nose. "I've been living with this . . . this . . . torture for months, it's making me practically crazy, I don't know what to do with myself. And what do you do to help me? Do you give me some pills or even try to comfort me? No. You give me electric shocks! Someone should take away your license!"

In a wild attempt to turn off the tears, Warner goes to his sample drawer and pulls out half a dozen packets of pills and capsules and lays them beside her on the couch. "Look, try some of these, they're free. Read the directions, see which ones you like. They should keep you calm for a while until you decide, then I'll get you a whole supply, since that's what you seem to want. Come on now. It's only love. Cheer up." Warner puts the trancs in an envelope and quietly slips the small plastic box into his desk drawer.

They were standing in the House of the Vettii in Pompeii before a small, perfect image of ancient lovers on their hands and knees, united forever in the most intimate embrace. The guide had shown them a frieze of charming cupids, then described to them how, nineteen hundred years before, Vesuvius had suddenly without warning sent tons of lava pouring down on this fashionable Roman spa, burying the town with its twenty thousand souls in eighteen feet of ashes and lapilli, capturing even the dogs at their games for all eternity. Here a lady was preserved for posterity clutching her jewels and covering her face with a cloth, there a servant went to his death napping. Perhaps at that moment a pair of lovers like themselves might have been regarding this very image, clasping each other in that same embrace, approaching, perhaps, the very moment of climax, when the molten lava from above rolled down to take them safely out of time.

Peter leaned forward to examine the small ancient painting, and in that instant Rosemary saw how, with the beard he had lately grown, he bore an uncanny likeness to the smiling Pompeian youth forever straddling the happy maid.

It took so little to excite Rosemary now. No longer confined to a single room, her passion made all Italy an erotic field. She felt herself, too, drift out of time and imagined the rest of her life, her real life, like this. Why go back to seeing her lover only once a week in one small room if she could love him openly, freely, every day? Thousands of couples did it— why not they? In their private world of S they could replace Secrecy with Simplicity, add Sun and Sky and Sea. Why wait for Harold's car to crash on his way home from New Haven or his plane to be hijacked to Libya (where he'd choose to stay) when they could simply return on schedule, resume their lives, and announce to the family that henceforth they were a couple? Why not?

For the first time in the years since she met Peter, her fancy was not met by her ready corps of resistance fighters armed with the latest high-tech weapons; for once no tanks rolled out to protect her from the painful knowledge of everything she'd given up. The unthinkable walked freely across the ancient meadow, took up position on hands and knees in a charming immortal image that belied the shame of sex, then smiled and beckoned.

Rosemary took a step forward and whispered in Peter's ear: "Tonight?" When Peter squeezed her hand she amended, "Or, if you like, we could go back to the room right now."

29

Spider was half a block past the porn parlor on his way home from school when he saw a fat man in overalls lying on the sidewalk delivering mouth-to-mouth resuscitation to a prostrate woman. Spider slung his pack to the ground and squatted down beside them for a better look. The woman's legs stuck straight out from her short dress, the toes of her high-heeled shoes pointed rigidly up, and as he watched her, she opened her eyes and stared ahead dazedly. "I think she's conscious now, so you can stop," said Spider, who had just that week covered consciousness in his first-aid class.

The fat man wiped his brow on his sleeve. "Give me a hand," he said, reaching an arm beneath the woman's shoulders and grasping her left elbow with his free hand.

"Wait," said Spider. "The worst thing you can do is try to stand her up, in case she's in shock."

"Yeah?"

"You're supposed to give them a little salt water and then wait for a doctor. Want me to get some salt water?"

"Yeah," said the man, letting the elbow drop.

In his pack, hidden in the pages of his science notebook, were three skin magazines of Herschel's that Spider had sworn to guard with his life. But, longing to be a hero, he said, "Okay, watch my pack," and took off.

Bursting like Spider Man into the pizza parlor down the street, he spilled his story, getting a free cup of water from a clerk. He added salt, then rushed off with his prize.

Back at the scene, Spider found the fat man replaced by two policemen, a tall one squatting beside the woman, a short one standing against the building keeping guard. "Is that man a doctor?" Spider asked the standing one.

"Wise guy. Does he look like a doctor?"

At that moment, the other policeman began tugging at the woman's arms, trying to stand her up.

"That's the worst thing you can do for someone in shock," insisted Spider to the short, uniformed man beside him. "That's really stupid. You're supposed to just give them a little salt water and not lift them up. Here," he said, holding out his cup.

"Bug off, kid."

"Really," said Spider, getting agitated, "my first-aid teacher, Miss Aldridge, she's a nurse, says when someone's been unconscious—"

The short policeman grabbed Spider by the collar, thrust him up against the wall, raised his fist to his face, and said, "Keep this up and you'll be unconscious. Now get outa here."

"Okay. But you'll be sorry. If that lady dies it'll be your fault." Spider flung the paper cup on the ground in disgust.

"Pick that up or *you'll* be sorry," said his adversary.

Spider picked up the cup, crushed it, and stuffed it into his pocket. He opened his pack and took out a pencil and paper. Ostentatiously he copied down the policeman's name and badge number. It was an odd name; Spider returned to check the spelling until he was sure he had it right.

"For that I'll have to run you in, you know," said Officer Hyeena. He shoved Spider in the patrol car and locked the doors, then dropped Spider's pack in the trunk.

Spider concentrated on not crying. "How long will this take?" he called through the back window, trying to sound reasonable.

Hyeena hitched up his pants and smiled. "You'll know when it's over."

When the two policemen returned at last to the car, Spider was sitting stiffly with his arms folded, trying to remember the road map on which he had once charted his father's journeys away from them. In the front seat Hyeena lit a cigarette, then turned around and leaned into the metal grille.

"How old are you?"

Spider screwed up his nose as he routed the smoke with his hand. "Thirteen." As soon as it popped out Spider was sorry, but he was finding it hard to think.

"Thirteen years old and already a police record," said Hyeena, shaking his head.

Spider felt immensely lucky that his mother was away—this would break her heart. But his father . . . Tears welled in his eyes. Vainly he tried to think of an alias before the next question came—an alias and a story so his parents would never have to find out.

"Had to learn the hard way, didn't you," said Hyeena with a wry smile. Spider began to cry.

"Too bad for you. Now we're going to the station and find out everything there is to know about you."

Despite the raw crispness of the air, Central Park was filling up. Old people fed pigeons, Sunday fathers threw balls, vendors sold health food and complicated sugars and starches. Buster dragged Nora straight toward the distant hill where a group of dogs of varying sizes frisked and leaped without benefit of leash. Nora released him to his kind. Buoyantly he made the rounds, sniffing and submitting with canine dignity, until he was invited to join a small pack of pigeon stalkers. Nora settled back against the black railing to watch the show among a crowd of owners sipping coffee from cardboard containers and nibbling breakfast pastries from bakery bags.

A brown bag was thrust before her. She looked down: half a dozen assorted bagels. She looked up: Harold Streeter.

"Have a bagel," said Harold, rattling the bag.

The letter from Rosemary hidden in Nora's pocket proclaimed itself like a beating heart. Caught. As an officer refuses a drink from someone he intends to arrest, Nora quickly shook her head. "No thanks."

"Go ahead," insisted Harold, towering over her, "I've got lots." He shook the bag again. Accepting her fate, Nora reached for a warm, dark pumpernickel and broke it in half, returning one half to the bag. "Thank you," she said and, stalling, took a bite. Perhaps if they talked shop she could avoid betraying Rosemary.

Harold examined Nora. She was going on about some upcoming conference for imprisoned Third World writers. He wondered if he ought to inquire about her health—she'd recently been in the hospital—or if delicacy forbade it. Women's troubles, he recalled, but he didn't remember if it was breast or down below. She'd had her tubes tied, he remembered that. A tough woman. Maybe a complication. As his wife's intimate, she had a claim to be family; still, he resented a friendship that pre-empted his wife, one from which he was so conspicuously excluded. Who knew what they said behind his back? Women were like that—even Priscilla, his best friend's wife, had betrayed him once. And this one was a writer. She'd reviewed his book intelligently, despite certain uninformed reservations. Perhaps she knew Pippa, too. Harold took another bite of his sesame bagel and, fixing Nora with his most engaging gaze, confided, "We were awfully concerned about you, you know. Rosemary even considered canceling her trip. I hope you're all right now?"

That *we*, yoking husband with wife—how Nora despised it! Ordinarily she would have challenged it, but with the letter in her pocket from Italy proclaiming Rosemary's new resolve, she feared to speak. She was brave to the world, but duplicity unnerved her; and suppose her collusion showed? All the same, she was touched by Harold's concern for her, despite the intrusive *we*. Besides Lex, he was the only man who knew about her surgery; reluctant to show weakness, she hadn't even told Keith. In her pocket, she secretly folded the letter to hide the handwriting from Harold's possible X-ray vision and proclaimed herself well.

Harold smiled as if he were genuinely relieved. When he graciously invited Nora home for breakfast—"with the kids"—Nora felt trapped. Only once had she visited the Streeter apartment. She and Rosemary had left the Haven after dark, and Rosemary, reluctant to end a particularly exhilarating discussion of creativity (how much nature, how much nurture), had invited Nora home to dinner. They had gone into Rosemary's study, but no sooner had their conversation spread its wings than the interruptions began: a foolish question, a senseless complaint, a trumpet endlessly repeating the same maddening tune, the phone ringing like a siren demanding instant attention. Nora was vexed to find the atmosphere at Rosemary's quite as awful as in any other nuclear household: a dangerous installation with all its energy poised for destruction at the first malfunction. Even before they assembled in the dining room she felt a headache coming on; then, at table, the conversation was so disjointed, the subjects so inconsequential, the interruptions so chaotic, the focus so flitting, the rivalries so blatant, the dynamics so volatile, the personalities so pronounced—Harold churlish, Daisy morose, the boy nervous and noisy, and Rosemary unconscionably subservient—that Nora, pleading a headache, excused herself before coffee and fled to the liberating solitude of her own apartment.

But now, alone with Harold, the object of his singular benevolence, she saw him in a new light. Undoubtedly women found him attractive: the man, the man, the powerful man! A large friendly person whose work invoked at once the glamour of terror and the sheen of success, peering down from his superior height straight into one's eyes with such flattering, unwavering attention, exuding warmth and protection, offering food—how smoothly he belied what Nora knew. Refusing to be fooled by his charms, insisting on absolute equality, she declined his invitation and inquired about his book.

Harold slumped. Coming from another writer, such a question could not be finessed. "It's coming, but slowly," he said, feeling his stomach sink. "You know how it is—I never seem to have enough time. Even though I try to spend four hours writing every morning, between my columns and the teaching and—" He broke off. To admit defeat before a woman was unmanly—particularly this woman. And not only because of her mixed review. There was something hard and secret about her; he didn't understand his wife's devotion. Why, if they were as close as Rosemary said, did Nora never come to the house? Did she know something he didn't? "I thought I'd make some real headway over spring break," he explained, "but with Rosemary gone, I have to take care of everything. The food"—he held out his bagels—"the family. It's not easy, you know?"

Nora fingered the letter in her pocket. Just like a man—demanding credit for doing what every woman did without thanks. And another thing: he had yet to ask about *her* book.

"Well," said Harold, sensing hostility, "if you can't come home, at least take another bagel." But again Nora demurred. Diet and loyalty demanded no less. Besides, for a long time she'd deemed it prudent when possible to avoid looking a husband in the eye unless the wife was present.

A large black-and-white mongrel with a pink nose bounded up to Harold, ears flopping. As Harold bent down to fondle the creature and engage Gorky's leash, Nora clapped for Buster. When the two dogs, aping their masters, circled each other like rivals, Nora relented, allowing her sympathy to flow. After all, she noted, Harold walked the dog, bought the breakfast, and would soon enough be wifeless—deprived of man's most precious possession. She smiled and offered her right hand, which Harold used to pull her to him for a full-bodied embrace.

Nora was proud of how convincingly she reached up to kiss Harold on the cheek as they parted, he to the east, she to the west, pulled by their large respective dogs.

· · ·

They are kneeling on a blanket on the weedy dirt floor of an abandoned barn, smoking a joint, unbuttoning their shirts. It's chilly, early spring. An ancient orchard with its delicate veil of new green shade and a peeling hex sign on the side of the barn protect them from the curse of last year's condoms strewn on the ground.

Daisy sighs. She feels defeated, ashamed. It's not the drugs or the record—which, after all, have their exotic appeal—that keep her hiding Rap. It's something worse, something not about him but about herself: Who wouldn't see after five minutes' talk exactly what she sees in him? It's so obvious, she feels naked sitting in the same room with him. Her shame and her passion are exactly equal, are one.

"I don't know why we do this," she says.

He looks at her and laughs; then with an abrupt thrust of his hands, he pushes his pants off his hips. "You don't?" he says, as the Jagger springs up to point at her. "Want me to remind you?"

Reminded, she gasps. Already, she's someone else.

His right hand waves his helmet in front of his organ while his left helps trombone sounds to issue from his lips. (She doesn't laugh.) Then, tossing his helmet on top of hers, he falls forward from his knees and rolls her into his arms. His tongue circles the inside of her lips; her tongue probes the empty places in his gum. The strangers depart; the lovers move into the pleasure cave.

When they've accomplished everything they know, he takes a reading of the sky, calculates the time, and says, "Okay, girl, now I want you to lie back and dream while I eat your pussy."

And here's Pippa in a fetching silk kimono, lips moist and ready, cheeks glowing, eyes melting in the aftermath of afternoon love, as Harold emerges from the bathroom zipping up his fly. "Do you really have to go now?" she asks, reaching her arms up to circle Harold's long neck. The wide sleeves of her kimono fall back to her shoulders, revealing the side curves of her white breasts.

Harold slips his hands inside—only partly to placate her. At parting time, they always want more of him than he can give.

Pippa nuzzles his neck. "Today especially I hoped you could stay, since Mark's keeping Lolly till tomorrow."

But Harold's late. What with traffic and parking and conflicting commitments, he's been late all day. All week. All his married life. In five minutes a star student will appear at Harold's door for his thesis conference, and Harold will still be half an hour plus parking time away from his office. If he doesn't catch up, how will he ever pick up Barbara in time to take her someplace nice for dinner in time to meet his kids at the ticket window in time to fabricate a spontaneous meeting of all three in the lobby in time to pull off the introductions and still find their seats? Timing is critical—as always. Harold feels the clock running, the rack tightening: love against pleasure against duty—and he can't even tell which is which!

"I wish I could stay. You know I do. But I can't now. I can't." He retrieves his hands to run his fingers around her face tracing a perfect heart.

Pippa tilts her head on her neck and looks at him expectantly with her big round eyes. Awaiting details. Though beset by the stop signs of family life that have long barred him from the freewheeling open road of his youth, Harold can't accuse her of accusing him. Unlike Barbara, who's always after him, attributing his tardiness to selfishness and God knows what, Pippa's never yet accused him of anything. Her tactic is to prolong their partings. Here she goes:

"Don't you want a cup of tea before you rush off?"

"Wish I could, but I've gotta run."

Since he never knows when a woman might unexpectedly pounce on him for some inadvertent admission, he pays out as few details as possible. He can't fathom their responses. They seem always to be laying hidden traps for him, springing secret tests; and if he fails to notice, they might suddenly turn on him with their disappointment, vindication, and tears.

Pippa pouts. "Then when will I see you again?" Imperceptibly she increases her pressure on his neck.

Harold places his hands over Pippa's and, positioning his wrist, over her shoulder sneaks a surreptitious glance at his watch. Would it be faster to leave the car in the parking space he fought for and take a taxi to his office? Drivers are crazy, especially toward rush hour. One rush hour he was forced to sit down in the middle of 86th Street traffic to preserve his parking space and prove a principle, costing him an hour and a near arrest.

"I'll call you tomorrow," says Harold, stalling. "We'll figure something out." Gently he pulls Pippa's arms away from his neck and kisses her wrists and palms. Probably already too late to get a taxi. Got to move. His student is waiting for his comments. Barbara is waiting for his call. Kids are waiting for their tickets. Pippa's waiting for a promise.

"In the morning? Will you give me a wake-up call?"

"Mmmm," assents Harold behind his lips while he contemplates canceling dinner. Should have left the tickets for the kids at the box office, so it wouldn't matter if he showed up late, and then seen Barbara after the concert. Now they'll start getting antsy half an hour early, checking their watches like their mother, as if the paucity of Manhattan parking were all his fault.

"I'll be here alone until noon, when Mark's bringing Lolly home, so try to call me early, okay? The earlier the better. I'm up at seven." Pippa smiles brightly. "I can make us breakfast if you like."

Harold drops Pippa's hand. Tomorrow's schedule is denser than today's. With Rosemary gone, he'd hoped to have the leisure to satisfy all the competing demands on his time and love—to get to know his kids, make it up to Barbara, get it on with Pippa, see the students he'd been putting off all year for lack of time—and still make headway on his book. But all he's done is fill up his schedule and whip up desire.

"I'll try," he says—generous, hopeful, deluded.

"Please don't be late."

The word grazes his ear; he draws back in a huff. He's never late on purpose, so why the *please?* That his desires outstrip his capacities seems to him a virtue, not a vice. Zest for Life.

"Careful," says Pippa, picking up a broken truck and kicking Lolly's Raggedy Ann out of Harold's path as he moves toward the door. She catches his wrist and warns, "Remember, you better be nice to me, 'cause you're going into my next novel." Then she dimples and adds breathily, "Tomorrow."

This is his formula for happiness: At any given moment, someone else must need him more; however much he's getting, more is waiting.

Half an hour before Lex is due, Nora checks her mailbox. Santa Fe mail she'll lock back in. She flips through the haul like a deck of cards, looking for an ace. Nothing to fear: not even a postcard from her jack of hearts. She walks upstairs, sorting by class, and, inside, dumps everything less than first class into the trash. She considers the invitations, scans the magazines, and reads through the following letter:

THIS IS A CHAIN LETTER FOR LIBERATED WOMEN.
DON'T PANIC—YOU'LL LOVE IT!

Dear Friend:

This letter was started by a woman like yourself in the hopes of bringing relief to other tired and discontented women. Unlike most chain letters, this one does not cost anything. Just send a copy of this letter to five of your friends who are equally tired and discontented. Then bundle up your husband or boyfriend and send him to the woman whose name appears at the top of the list.

When your name comes to the top of the list, you will receive 14,762 men and one of them is bound to be a helluva lot better than the one you already have.

DO NOT BREAK THE CHAIN!

HAVE FAITH!

One woman broke the chain and got her own S.O.B. back. At this writing, a friend of mine had already received 184 men.

Signed,

Alita Kicks (A liberated woman)

Remember, add your name to the bottom of this list and send it on to a friend . . .

Precious Patsy
Mary McNasty
Lisa Lush
Rita Rotten

Nora sits down at her desk to make a list. At the top she writes *Rosemary Streeter*.

Harold honks his horn louder and louder, triumphantly. A killer Doberman in the car ahead leaps at the back window with bared fangs. All around Harold people shake their fists and stomp their feet from neighboring cars. He lets off honking till the next corner, where, stopped by gridlock, he hits the horn again. Can't let them get away with this shit! Now there are five dogs attacking the windows of his car. Ten. He's surrounded, horns are screaming, sirens join, the crowd swells, they're after him, he's late. The light changes: red, green, red, green. Motors stall; nothing moves. Finally, a huge glittering green light descends from above and Harold tears away, tires screeching, leaving the dogs and cars behind. A long straight roll down Park, twenty blocks, thirty, forty—a trombone slide, smooth as a waltz, through a glittering tunnel of lights. He's euphoric again, ascendant, triumphant, even though the lights are red.

Harold's searching for a parking space. Everything's taken. He cruises over the hoods of minicars, under the wheels of pickup trucks, in and out of dark alleys, weaving through vast crowded lots. No matter how quickly he spots a car pulling out, another is always there before him to beat him out. He circles and circles; his head bobs, his eyes close, stubble grows on his cheeks, he's running out of gas. He knows that if his eyes begin to close he'll never find a space.

Suddenly he's awakened by the roar of motors. The panel truck he crouches beneath tears away, leaving him safely, miraculously parked. The space is his! But as soon as he turns off his lights he sees cars of every type zoom toward his and surround him. Five bikers in black leather carrying chains dismount and approach him. Snarling dogs strain on their leashes and piss against his tires. Now he's outside, pinned against the door of his car, surrounded by leather, metal, fangs, and flesh. He scrambles up to the roof of his car and impulsively swallows the key. There, unyielding, he sits, on principle: arms folded, legs crossed. Mine! he shouts, Mine!—the triumphant word strangling in his throat.

"Daddy!" hisses Daisy, elbowing him in the ribs.

The hall is throbbing with music and motion and glittering stars when Harold opens his eyes. Spider, beside him, is a blur of leaps.

Daisy pokes him again. "You're snoring again. First you're late, and then you fall asleep. *God*, Daddy!"

Not his fault: another overloaded day. He has to be mother and father both. Harold checks his pocket for his parking ticket, looks around groggily. "Where's Barbara?" he asks, until a jolt of adrenaline reminds him that she canceled the concert when he canceled dinner.

"Who?"

He locks his eyeballs in place and stares at the stage, determined to stay awake. "No one," he says, "nothing. Never mind."

.   .   .

This time it's wild boar and polenta at Casa Della Mare. But how can she concentrate on food? Rosemary strains across the table.

"When I'm fifty you'll just be forty-three," she says, testing him again, as she sees all her advantages turn to liabilities. In three years, she and Peter have never once quarreled. What was there to quarrel about? If the compact balls that were their hardened wills had ever collided, they'd have pushed apart, rolling out of each other's orbits, each one sliding off separately into the future. But now, everything might change. Their passion could easily evolve into something else if they let it. All they'd need would be a few witnesses, a circle of common friends, and there they'd be: making duty visits, disturbed about money, rushing home late, checking off lists, taking turns with the phone, closing their eyes exhausted.

"Don't be silly. You're younger than I am," says Peter.

She's still young, it's true, buoyed by the wild size and shape of the complicated cake she's chosen to bake, younger than draggy women half her age who lack her manic will to beat the batter and make it rise. But in five years? In ten? Will Peter open his eyes one day to see beside him on the pillow one of the evicted hags of Shangri La and turn her into his enemy? Can one only desire but never possess?

"Yes, but I'm talking about a very long time."

"So am I. When I'm ninety-three," says Peter, "you'll be a hundred and taking care of *me*."

An extended family of fifteen ducks and ducklings bob near the shore like live models for the graceful sailboats farther out, each trailing its small dinghy. And still Rosemary overlooks the children.

Not Peter. "I've won you," he says as they skip their fears one by one over the shimmering water of the cove until they drop from sight. He'll take the children to Coney and have her in his bed every night, though he has yet to find a decent gallery. "I've won you," he says, drawing charming pictures in the sand of their never-ending simple life. Gently he caresses her forearm with the tips of his nails as they move toward home, forgetting where they're going, what awaits them.

"I've finally won you," he repeats. And every time he thinks of how he hung in and persisted until he won, his penis gets hard.

Trouble

30

THE GATES of Customs part, and it all returns. There's Harold waiting to greet her with smiles and complicity. Usually he's the one returning with gifts, insisting that nothing's changed; this time she's the one. Instantly, Rosemary wavers. "Where are the kids?" she asks. "How was your trip?" he asks—each of them grateful for the consideration with which the other asks only conventional questions, easing them gently around their treacheries.

Not until they reach the parking lot does Harold approach the quick, admitting that during her absence there was "a little trouble. But don't worry, I've got the whole thing under control."

Some things escaped Rosemary even after eighteen years of marriage, but not that affected nonchalance. The children! "Spider?" she asks, as Harold piles her bags in the trunk. Then he slips into the driver's seat and starts the car with a great show of concern over the motor.

Rosemary rolls down her window to let in spring. It has to be Spider. Starting back when she asked the baby-sitter to give that fat, happy three-month-old the first bottle of his life, it was their joint destiny that he be the instrument of her punishment. She'd returned to find a mysterious rash all over his body and their pediatrician out of town. I'm going to be absolutely frank with you, Mrs. Streeter, said the pinch-hitting doctor. The origins of this rash are uncertain. If it's meningo toxemia, as my colleague Dr. McFerson believes, then it's very serious. Too late to arm, she listened helplessly as he pummeled her with information. Meningo toxemia is a form of encephalitis, inflammation of the lining of the brain, which can be fatal within twenty-four hours. On the other hand, there's a fifty percent chance your baby has nothing more than one of a great number of atypical, nonspecific rashes that will simply disappear by itself in its own good time. However, we don't want to take any chances. So I'm afraid it's the hospital for now. She was ashamed to admit, in the face of such punishment, that she'd left her baby with a stranger and a bottle. But I'm nursing him, she offered feebly in self-defense. That's okay, said the doctor. We'll arrange for you both to go in.

"Oh my God," moans Rosemary, as Harold backs out of the parking space. "Was it a car accident? Tell me. Quick. What happened?"

"No, no. He's okay. Nothing like that." Harold hands his ticket and a bill to the parking attendant, then zooms down the ramp wishing he'd waited to begin this saga at least till they're on the highway. She'll want details; he'll be inadequate. "Just a little run-in with the police."

"The police!" When Rosemary pulls out her security mints, she's shocked to notice they're Italian. A family is a creature, an organism, a living colony with an ecology of its own. You can't withdraw one crucial element without affecting the whole. She always knew she'd be punished for going away. "Where is he? He's not in jail, is he?"

"Not that I'm aware of."

She wants to smack her husband for making jokes. "Harold!" she cries. "Where is he!"

"Calm down and I'll tell you. Right now he's waiting in line for tickets to the next Lip Service concert, I expect. He took his sleeping bag and plans to stay there all night if necessary."

She tries to control herself while Harold summarizes what's happened, but when he gets to the part about how the police grilled Spider in the station house till he broke down and cried, her own eyes fill with tears. "I should have been here," she whimpers. "He's just a baby, he doesn't know how to act with cops. He doesn't know kids have no rights."

Harold pulls a neatly folded handkerchief out of his back pocket and hands it to her. "To tell the truth, I'm pretty proud of him for taking down the guy's number. Got to hand it to the kid. Next time I hope he'll get the names of some witnesses, too."

"Next time! God forbid!" cries Rosemary, her eyes now streaming.

Harold pats her thigh, secretly glad she was away. The boy had to grow up. "Anyway," he says proudly, taking a long banked curve past a green pickup, "as soon as I found out what happened I got right on the case. I had Ross send a letter. We've started Civilian Complaint proceedings. Can't let them get away with this shit."

Rosemary reaches for Harold's arm and holds it in silent gratitude that he is there for Spider and for herself. How comforting this uncorrupted bond. How much deeper than the erotic. When they'd finally brought Spider home from the hospital knowing he was out of danger, sex was the last thing they wanted. Clinging to each other while the baby slept, they knew it would be sacrilege to make love then.

Around the curve traffic suddenly stops.

"If only I'd been here," repeats Rosemary, dabbing at her eyes with Harold's handkerchief. "My poor baby."

"Baby nothing." Harold comes to a halt and plans his strategy while Rosemary twists the handkerchief in her hands as if any expense of energy could somehow help.

"I should never have gone away."

Harold feels accused. "It wouldn't have made a damn bit of difference if you'd been here. By the time I got wind of the thing it was all over. Spider, that cocky imbecile, tried to keep it secret; I didn't learn about it till a few days ago. So you wouldn't have been able to do a thing, either."

Even before the words were out, Harold knew they were a mistake.

"What do you mean? Didn't the police call you? Didn't Spider?"

She was too quick for him. She must suspect he wasn't reachable by phone. To divert suspicion, Harold honks his horn at the car in front of him and launches a tight maneuver out of his own lane up onto the shoulder, trying to flee the question.

"Where are you going, Harold, for God's sake!"

"Shit!" says Harold as each car he passes honks a protest at him. Like most of the guilty, he assumes his accuser has secret information. "Shit!" he repeats strategically.

Rosemary, oblivious of traffic as usual, is getting annoyed. Harold possesses all the crucial information, yet he's making her drag it out of him, bit by bit, turning her into an inquisitor. "Then how did you find out?"

"Find out what?"

"About Spider!"

He squeezes back into the slow lane between a Bug and a Buick. "I got an official notice in the mail from the Youth Aid Division. That's when I called Ross." He leans over Rosemary to search the glove compartment. "Can't let them do this to defenseless kids. Ah, here it is," he says, handing Rosemary an envelope.

Police Department, City of New York

Dear Parent,

Your child, <u>Maximilian Streeter,</u> has been brought to the attention of the Youth Aid Division for reasons indicated below. Though he has not been convicted of a crime, a report of this incident will be kept on file until your child reaches the age of 17 years, at which time it will be destroyed. However, if your child continues to engage in this type of behavior, Juvenile Court process will become necessary.

Legally, parents or guardians are expected to be reasonably diligent in the supervision of their children to prevent neglect, delinquency, or conduct that may prove harmful to the child or the public's safety. We are informing you of this matter so that you may discuss it with your child and possibly prevent any more serious problems from developing in the future.

You may request a further investigation if you believe that the alleged offense, as described below, is not accurate.

Alleged Offense: Interfering with the Officer at the scene of an aided case. Refusing to leave and throwing paper at the Officer.

Reporting Officer: Hyeena, Joseph

Very truly yours,

Lt. Bryan Flanagan

Unit Supervisor, Youth Aid Unit

"I should never have gone away," Rosemary repeats helplessly.

Rap whacked the strings of his guitar ferociously—ostensibly for the sake of the music, which he'd built up to a fierce crescendo, but really because after the divorce, his mother had finally kicked him out of the house, then his father's girlfriend had come to live with them, he had no idea how he would ever make a living, and anyway, the whole world was going to burn.

"The way I see it," he said, laying his guitar on the living room floor to light a joint, "we know we're all going to be blown away anyway. Fifty years at the most, probably sooner. So what's the point worrying about school and grades and shit like that?"

Daisy felt Rap's assault on higher education as a personal attack; she should never have opened the subject. According to him, all colleges were basically fraudulent, the courses a racket, the professors a joke. Why sit around in classes with a bunch of robots and idiots handing in busy-work papers on useless subjects no one, not even the professors, cared about? To help you get a job as a zombie in a society of zombies? To get to be a lawyer, a computer, a shrink? No thanks. He would rather space out on dope than help the world destroy itself.

"If you're so worried we're going to be blown up, why don't you do something about it?" said Daisy, who was soaking her foot in a pan of hot water and epsom salts.

"You mean like march around singing songs? Shit like that? Don't be an asshole!"

"Maybe if enough people did it . . ." Skeptical, Daisy let her voice trail off as she examined her swollen toe.

"Come on," said Rap impatiently. "What do they care how many people are singing as long as they've got all the weapons?"

His anger was a powerful cleanser, like carbon tet, with one swipe stripping away from common opinion layers of obfuscating scum, leaving the truth exposed beneath, but at the same time destroying anything it touched that happened to be made of the wrong material. Sometimes Daisy felt she was made of the wrong material. Too flimsy for his honesty, she didn't even know what she wanted to major in.

"Put down you want to major in languages," Rap counseled. "They're your best bet. Because for languages, unlike all the bullshit courses, you can use a good teacher. They're the only courses that aren't a total waste of time. That's what I'm going to study. I figure, I'll learn lots of languages and then take my time looking over the world. And maybe someday I'll find a place I can stand to live. Australia, or maybe Japan, I don't know. Most of your radioactive winds never get to the southern hemisphere."

As usual, when they started out discussing her life they wound up discussing his. "How come you want to go back to school at all, the way you feel?" she asked.

"My dad says, school or the street. He's crazy—I'd be a lot better off if he stood me to a year of just figuring things out. But the people with the money have the power, so okay, I'll do school, I'll go through the motions and get the degree. But nothing says I've got to like it, right?"

He sucked in a full mouthful of smoke, then, placing his lips over hers, exhaled into her. She felt the rush from the back of her throat to her loins as she inhaled and blew the smoke back to him. Back and forth, until there was no smoke left. "Don't," she said afterwards.

"No, I've thought about it, and I'll tell you the truth," he said. "I can only see one possible way to save the world. There aren't that many people who stand to gain from having nuclear weapons. So if a bunch of really dedicated guys formed a secret terrorist organization to wipe them out—get all the powerful leaders in the world, all the bankers and industrialists and heads of state who've got itchy fingers for that button, not only here but in Russia too, I mean all over the world, man, everywhere, including every dinky little country that's got the bomb"—he swept his hand across the air in an arc, taking in the universe—"then kill all of them, all at once. Very fast and secret, before anybody knows what's happening. K-Day. And then take all the nuclear weapons and get rid of them, bury them maybe or send them into outer space or something. Then, maybe it would work. That's the only kind of organization I can see joining." He looked off toward the ceiling and exhaled slowly. "Sometimes I can see myself joining something like that."

Daisy stared at him, amazed. "You'd get killed too, you know."

"Probably. But it's the only way that has any chance of working."

Daisy tried to think about selective killings all over the world. Like evening lights coming on all over the city. She could visualize one, two, even three or four, but as soon as she tried to imagine a fifth, she lost the first and second. After a bit she gave up and said, "It would never work."

"Of course," said Rap, "it would all have to be very carefully planned and coordinated. Better than the best-rehearsed band."

"You'd all be killed. You can't fight violence with violence," she added, appropriating her mother's phrase.

He took her hand and pulled her toward him. Water slopping over the rim of the pan onto the maroon carpet deepened the color to spilled wine. "Now see what you've done!" cried Daisy.

He dropped her hand. "Okay, okay. But Christ, why are you so uptight? There's no one here."

She spread the towel on the rug, the pan on top of the towel. "I told you—the plane could be early; they could be home any minute." She looked at his face: like an angel's—till he smiled. He wouldn't do. "You better go."

"Come with me."

"No, Rap! I haven't seen Mom in a month."

He lowered his voice. "And I haven't tasted that pussy in half a week." He leaned forward and put his hand on the back of her neck. "Want to know what I'll do if you come out with me?"

She looked at the clock on the mantel. "Not now."

"I'm only talking. If you don't want me to, I won't touch you at all." He slipped a hand under her skirt.

"How many times do I have to tell you? Not *now!*"

He shot up and plunged his hands into his pockets. "I don't get it with you, Daze. You're so uptight. You think your parents don't do it themselves? I remember, me and my sister thought the same thing once, before we knew anything. Mom was always such a demon about what we did—always after us about what time we got home, who we hung out with, Tina's boyfriends, the whole bit. Then just before the divorce the whole thing blew up. Dad told us the trouble with Mom was she hated sex. She got so mad, she decided to set us straight. She sat us down and started and she couldn't stop. She said she'd always tried real hard to keep us out of it, but since Dad was dragging us into it, she better tell us her side. Boy, did she pop some surprises."

It always made Daisy uncomfortable when Rap talked about his family; it was never long before he got around to guilt-tripping her for not despising her parents as he despised his. "What did she tell you?"

"She was out to prove it wasn't her problem at all. She said it was only with Dad that she hated sex because of what he made her do. She said she'd made it with lots of guys and loved it with all of them except Dad. She was so mad, she started giving us every little detail about their sex life. And Dad's girlfriends. Tina had to leave in the middle of Mom's rap to throw up or something. Finally, I said, Mom, stop. Can't you see you're making Tina sick? But nothing was going to stop her."

"That's awful."

"Yeah?" Rap narrowed his eyes and smiled. "How come you're so sure your family's different?"

"For one thing," said Daisy, "my parents have been married for more than eighteen years." She knocked surreptitiously on the bottom of her chair.

"As if that ever stopped anyone."

Sometimes Daisy wished she could stuff something in Rap's mouth to shut him up. Instead, she dried her foot on a corner of the towel and told him to leave. "Right now. You can call me tomorrow."

Rap put his guitar in its case and took out a sealed envelope that he handed to her.

"What's this?"

"It's our free ticket. Hold onto it."

"What am I supposed to do with it?"

"Just keep it with the shrooms I gave you."

"But what if someone finds it?"

"Christ, you're not starting *that* again, are you?"

Before she could answer, they both heard the elevator arrive at their floor. "Quick!" cried Daisy, as the gears ground to a stop. "Quick!" She pressed the envelope back into his hand.

He took precious seconds trying to kiss her good-bye, but she pushed him away. He grabbed his guitar and got out the kitchen door just as the front door opened. As she emptied the pan of water and epsom salts into the sink she saw the envelope lying on the counter and quickly hid it in her shirt.

31

"What do I smell?" said Harold, sniffing the air.

"Sweetheart," called Rosemary, "I'm home."

Gorky, whimpering like a baby, leaped at Rosemary until she dropped her bags and squatted for him. "There, there, there," she crooned as he licked her face with his rough tongue. He pinned her shoulders with his paws and kept her so busy stretching her neck this way and that to keep his tongue from scouring the full front of her face that it was a few moments before she noticed his denuded flank. "Oh my God, what happened to Gorky? Didn't anyone give him his pills?"

"That was Daisy's job," said Harold. "She feeds him, Spider walks him."

Daisy hopped down the hall holding up one puckered foot, a green-striped sock in her hand. "I couldn't help it, Mom. I gave him his pill every single day, I swear, but he'd just spit it right out."

"Then you didn't give it to him."

"Yes I did!"

Rosemary decided to start again. She approached her daughter smiling, arms wide open, to deliver as fervent an embrace as she dared give someone standing on one foot. "Sweetheart! Mmmm, mmmm." She breathed in Daisy's cozy familiar scent. "Wait till you see the wonderful things I brought you. What's the matter with your foot?"

"Nothing much. I stepped on a rusty nail and got blood poisoning."

"Daisy!" said Harold, picking fur off the hall rug. For the first time since she'd left, he began to see things through Rosemary's eyes. They looked mostly fuzzy and uncertain. "She got stomped at ballet. I called the doctor. Then I told Daisy she had to stay in and soak that toe like the doctor said."

Rosemary was stooping, easing the sock over the moist puckered foot, when the phone rang. She picked up, afraid that Peter might be claiming his new rights prematurely or that a crisis-ridden student might somehow know she was back.

It was Nora. "Thank heavens you're home. I've got to talk to you right away. Can I see you tonight?"

Seeing it wasn't for her, Daisy limped off to her room on a heel and a foot to dispose of the envelope.

"But I just walked in," said Rosemary, observing the puffs of fur lining the hall like dandelion fluff.

"I know, but I thought for just a little while . . . I have a big favor to ask you. It's important."

When Daisy opened her bottom drawer, she saw that the shrooms were gone. The old envelope was missing. That Spider!

"I should really be with my family tonight," said Rosemary. Even though she knew she was right, she felt guilty admitting it to Nora. Like the time she'd referred to Harold as *my husband*, and Nora, exasperated, had shot back, Why do you call him *that*? Nora's question was absurd. Also unfair: had not Rosemary herself long since consigned her wedding ring to a drawer and cut off the tops of the old blue stationery printed with Mr. and Mrs. Harold Streeter and truly regretted having automatically dropped her own last name in favor of Harold's, leaving her children without a sign of her half of their heritage? What shall I call him then? she'd pleaded. The father of my children? The co-owner of my goods and chattels? My fallback? The co-signer of the joint return? The principal beneficiary of my life insurance? My legal next-of-kin?

"If not tonight, how about tomorrow? I really need you," Nora insisted, articulating each word. "You could come to my place for breakfast. Or any time you say. Just for a little while."

Rosemary had never before been invited to Nora's apartment; they always met in public places. There was something urgent in Nora's voice she couldn't refuse. Abandoning all hope of devoting one last morning to her proof before classes resumed, she promised, "I'll try."

Daisy locked herself in the bathroom and opened the envelope. Strange tiny hard bluish balls, maybe a couple hundred of them. She had half a mind to flush them and be done with it, but instead she wrapped them in toilet paper, returned them to the envelope, carried them back to her room, and hid them at the back of her jewelry box.

In the living room Rosemary recognized Gorky's white undercoat distributed gaily on the club chairs and the maroon rug, which now also sported a fresh wine-colored stain.

"It's only water," said Daisy, coming back in, "with epsom salts."

Harold stared at the fur. For the first time he became aware that fur might respond to suction. But dammit, cleaning was Mrs. Scaggs' bailiwick, though she wasn't due back again until Tuesday.

Rosemary clamped her lips, determined not to criticize. She'd give Gorky double dosage till the problem was under control. It was only after she opened the barren refrigerator and found her eight-quart pot filled almost to the brim with enough Five-Alarm Chile to feed a summer camp that she accepted the impossibility of escape. "What have you been eating?"

Daisy shrugged. "Oh, you know—pizza, Spider's spaghetti sauce, you know."

"And Daddy's chile," added Rosemary.

Daisy screws up her nose. "It's way too hot. And every time we tell him, he makes more, trying to dilute it. Oh, Mommy," she cries, limping to her mother and throwing her arms around her neck.

"Darling. Tell me." Rosemary pats Daisy's back, trying for cheer. The needier those around her, the more cheerful she tries to be.

From her pocket, Daisy pulls out a letter. "Look." Then she turns away to the window, wanting no part of this reading.

Rosemary's forgotten how relentlessly nature speeds along events. Not two hours after landing, she faces another crisis. In less time than she's been away larvae hatch into flies, branches burst into bloom, streams flood into swollen rivers and break through dams; in a mere seven days the flu runs its course from sniffle to misery to radiance again; tides make islands of isthmuses in seven short hours, berries ripen overnight, creatures pop from the womb or gulp their last breath in a matter of minutes; temperatures drop, frosts kill, stocks rise and fall, buildings yield to the wrecker's ball, cars crash in an *Augenblick*. Had she expected to come back to the world she left? *A life is a story that can't be interrupted.*

We are writing to inform you that only a small number of the 485 First Choice applicants are being offered a place in our Freshman Class at this time. We regret that, due to the complex requisites of our Freshman profile. . .

For Daisy, events have been occurring at precisely their usual rate; it's Rosemary who must scramble to catch up. In her own life, of course, she's right on schedule, smack in the next chapter, Italy left behind. What was the story there? Maybe the sirocco was blowing without her knowing, or it was that time of month. Never mind: now nothing matters more than these dire official communiqués.

This one is embossed with Latin words embedded in a fancy seal. The salutation has been rendered deceptively, shamelessly personal by silicon chips. The college that threatens to "ruin" Daisy's life is one she never heard of until six months ago. Rosemary purses her lips and shakes her head like a popcorn pan, starting a host of consolations popping in her mind. By the time she's done reading the letter she hopes they'll be ready to butter and serve.

Unexpected luck! After a moment, Rosemary is able to dish up an unctuous, encouraging response. "But this is fine, sweetheart. They haven't rejected you at all, they've just deferred you to their Priority Waiting List. That's why you applied First Choice, to get a double chance. Now you've made it through the first round. Till May first you're still in the running. Why aren't you happy?"

In a few more years Daisy will wince at this question, taking it for an accusation, but right now she offers her mother a path to her heart through her widening eyes. "They accepted Aaron Sampson and Lisa Holliday on this round," she says.

"That's them; you're you. All I know is, if they didn't want you they'd have turned you down. Come," she says, putting an arm around Daisy's sad shoulders. "Come to the table, I'll cheer you up. This isn't something to be upset about. It's nothing compared to Spider's arrest."

Alongside the herbal teas, multivitamins, wheat germ, and Gorky's pills, Rosemary keeps a tall jarful of reasons to be happy that she distributes as bedtime snacks. She purrs and smiles. The unfortunates are people who want more out of life than it has to offer; Rosemary preaches contentment and scrupulously tries to practice it. *Amor fati,* says Nietzsche: Love what is. For better or worse, this is the daughter, that the son given to her.

"Arrest?" says Daisy. Her heart flips, her stomach sinks, everything tumbles on top of her. The missing shrooms: Spider must be taking the rap for Rap. "What arrest?"

"You don't know? It happened a few days ago. He tried to keep it secret until the police got in touch with Daddy." At the mention of the police, Rosemary's eyes fill up again. "He's got a J.D. record now till he's seventeen."

"No one tells me anything," moans Daisy. "Oh, Mom," she cries, throwing herself into her mother's arms.

Turnabout . . .

"Come," says Rosemary, master consoler, "let's go to your room. I want you to try on the clothes I brought you." One thing leads to another until there are three piles of clothes on Daisy's bed—the brand-new, the still usable, the abandoned—and Daisy is happy again. After all, it's spring: time to retire the woolens and try on the cottons to see what still fits.

"I'm so glad I splurged in Italy," says Rosemary, planning to give her daughter some of the frivolous Italian tops she bought for herself. She measures blouse against Daisy against blouse. "You've outgrown practically everything you own and you're still growing. Maybe I can wear some of your tops myself—wouldn't *that* be strange?"

Now, at seventeen, Daisy's breasts are fuller than her mother's and still immature, the nipples, pale pink, barely distinguishable from the surrounding flesh. Her waist is narrow, her thighs strong and slim in preparation for the rangy woman about to inhabit her body.

When they've finished viewing the new clothes and reviewing Daisy's wardrobe, Rosemary says, "Let's go down to my room and see what else I have for you. There's one dress I bought in Florence maybe we can share, and I bet some of my other good dresses will finally fit you this year."

The Good Dresses—the soft jerseys and satiny silks hanging in the closet in garment bags—are the Streeters' ticket to love. Even Spider, who couldn't care less about clothes and hates having T-shirt after T-shirt yanked over his head in the semiannual dress rehearsal for the coming season, appreciates the power of the Good Dresses.

"Oh let's!" shouts Daisy. Half her life she's been waiting for this. There was hardly a rainy day of her childhood when she didn't find her way to her parents' room and delve into the bureau drawers ready to find anew their treasures. The jewelry and handkerchiefs in the top drawer, the mysterious, silky underwear in the second. And from the bureau she crossed to the closet, where, standing on tiptoe, she could pull the bell-shaped tip of a shiny chain to light a dim bulb in a cage. To her left on a long pole were her father's somber clothes, a row of dark, forbidding suits of gray and navy, pinstripe and tweed, hanging over black polished wing-tipped shoes filled with ugly shoe trees—mouths with tongues. But from the pole to the right hung a rainbow of dresses over an array of pumps—leather, suede, silk—each with its matching bag on the shelf above. The gap between the back of the shoe and Daisy's heel when she teetered toward the mirror was a measure of the distance to be crossed before she could attain her mother's grace.

Recently Daisy's feet have leaped two sizes past Rosemary's, leaving behind for her mother several pairs of almost new sneakers which, though sneakers aren't her style, Rosemary adopts for the country as readily as she eats all leftovers and turns discarded T-shirts into polishing rags.

Daisy trips to the closet, reaches into the dark recess of her mother's side, and pulls out a clear plastic garment bag, housing certain dresses from the past too good to give away—dresses that, when new, her mother wore only at night with her hair drawn back and her garnets hanging like chandeliers from her pierced ears, dresses that stopped Harold in his tracks: "Well, well, look at you!"

"Ah, that one," says Rosemary dreamily as Daisy slips one out of the bag. "That's always been one of my favorites. Try it on."

The cloth is a heavy blue-black silk. A few impressionistic roses of deep magenta shading down to pale pink, in full bloom or in bud, are scattered sparsely in the field. The lining is also blue-black silk but of a fine, tissue weave. The seam where the lining meets the neck is stitched by hand. A low, classic neck and gently flared skirt cleverly nipped at the waist are timeless; only the fabric and the unusual shape of the gathered sleeves draw attention from the wearer to the dress itself. "I always thought it was the most flattering dress I ever owned," says Rosemary, unzipping it for Daisy and holding it ready.

Daisy hears the skirt flowing over her mother's thighs like milk and swishing silkily against her stockings; she recalls the tops of her mother's breasts on those rare occasions when she leaned into the mirror to color lips spread taut against her teeth. . . .

"Look how it's made, though. Every inch lined, and with these tiny tabs to hide your bra straps, and the hidden zipper. Isn't it splendid?" She fingers the sleeve while Daisy strokes the skirt lightly with open palm as if it were an animal. "I never wear it now . . . my life's so different. . . . You know, with one of those wide belts they're wearing and the right jewelry, it could pass for new this season. Except they don't use fabric as fine as this anymore."

Daisy slips the dress over her head, hears the silk slide past her ears with a rich rustle, feels its coolness envelop her arms, her ribs. "Hold up your arm," says Rosemary, starting the zipper. As the zipper closes, Daisy's breasts fill the bodice.

"Darling!" cries Rosemary, standing back and clapping her hands. "It fits!"

"Does it?"

"Even the length is right for someone your age. I couldn't get away with that length, but you—it could have been made for you. . . . Come. Look."

In the mirror, Daisy sees at once her old self in the new dress and her new self in the old dress. Like their dog Gorky before the mirror, she's not quite certain whom she sees.

Rosemary watches her daughter turn like a dancer making her debut. From the wings she joins her. Together they stand before the mirror, arms around each other's waist in a familiar pose. One flesh, but different too: the daughter's cheeks glow rosy, her neck is smooth, the bridge of her nose and her fine silken hair are definitely her father's, her brown eyes are less confident, though in this dress she looks almost womanly.

Rosemary kicks off her shoes. "Look, sweetheart," she cries, "look! The last time we stood here like this you came up to here on me. But now—now I can't tell which of us is taller anymore. Can you?"

"Excuse me," says Harold, opening the door. "Sorry to interrupt, but has either of you two ladies seen last week's *Report?* I know I brought it home, but I can't seem to find it."

Daisy sends him a mean glare. She's embarrassed to be seen trying on dresses, as if she really were the frivolous adolescent he enjoys teasing. Sometimes she thinks she has two fathers: one, the confident, glamorous man who has taken her to lunch on her birthday every year since she was nine, the one whom her friends hold in awe: big, handsome, slightly famous, a man she always regarded as knowing everything until just last year when the whole thing began to topple; and this other, who enters without knocking and forgets the names of her friends, who gives lectures instead of answers, who falls asleep at concerts, and, worst of all, makes light of everything.

"Have you looked in the bathroom?" asks Rosemary.

"I've looked everywhere. I don't suppose you could stop dressing up for a minute and help me look?"

Daisy curls her lip. If he knew what she planned to do in these clothes and with whom— She has half a mind to tell him. But she can't stand the thought of her other father's disappointed face as he discovers Rap's record and missing teeth.

"Oh, hell," grumbles Harold, picking through the papers on the night table.

"In a little while, Harold. Now we're doing something important," says Rosemary with the little pout that unrolls like a window shade to shut him out, and suddenly, as Harold leaves, Daisy winces for her father (the good one).

As soon as he's gone, Rosemary says, "Let's measure."

Back to back, mother and daughter feel the tops of their heads. Side by side, they test the lines of their shoulders. They take off their outer clothes, lay them on the bed, and search the bones in the mirror for a verdict or a clue. One minute one seems taller, the next minute the other. "Stand up straight," says one. "Feet flat on the ground," says the other. They stretch their necks, thrust back their shoulders, straighten their spines and stare into the mirror. Neither can discover who is taller.

Rosemary presses hard on the top of Daisy's head. "Down!" But Daisy doesn't budge. Their eyes meet in the mirror. "At this moment," says Rosemary solemnly, "I think we are exactly the same height. In another month or two, though, you'll shoot right past me. And then—"

"Mommy!" Daisy's face crumples. Turning her back on their reflection she throws both arms around Rosemary's neck and presses her cheek against her mother's.

"Sweetheart."

They stand hugging until Daisy sneaks another look and pulls away. "And there's another dress you have I like just as much."

"Really? Which one?"

"The white silk jersey with the tiny black dots."

"That one? Good. Try it on."

As soon as she hears the door open Rosemary slips out of bed and scoots barefoot down the dark hall. "Spider? That you?" She runs forward to meet him, gives him a tentative squeeze, and pecks at his cheeks, unsure of his response. Thirteen can go either way.

"Hey! Mom! When'd you get home?" When he hugs her back she lets herself go, crushing him to her.

"Shhhh," she cautions. "Didn't you know I was coming tonight?"

"I guess so, but I forgot."

"Come into the kitchen where I can look at you. I'll make us some cocoa, okay?"

"Yeah, great. But first let me go brush my teeth."

"Honey, don't you want to brush your teeth *after* the cocoa?"

"Naah. I've got an awful taste in my mouth from the onions and stuff."

When Spider reappears wrapped in a striped terry towel, Rosemary is knocked out by how handsome he's grown. All his limbs have stretched several inches longer; his eyebrows, already thick, are creeping, manly, toward each other; and the baby cheeks she remembers have quite disappeared. "Honey! Look at you! You've grown!"

"Yeah? Really?" Spider looks down at himself, not displeased. "Maybe 'cause I'm juggling clubs now," he says proudly.

"Could be." Then she adds, she can't help it, "You've gotten so handsome while I was away. Honestly."

Now that she's home, she looks beautiful to him, too, but he hasn't the slightest idea of how to tell her. He rolls his eyes toward the ceiling in feigned disgust and plops into a chair. Grinning, Rosemary places two mugs on the table. As she fills them with steaming chocolate, she asks after the computer.

"Remember, I told you when Bobby Biddle deleted my Rogue file? Well, Mr. Gundy said he wasn't going to do anything about it because we weren't supposed to copy game files to begin with, which isn't true, so now Herschel's figured out how to break Bobby's security, and as soon as the Center opens I'm going to access his account and start a rabbit job. That should fix him for a while."

Rosemary stares at him. The fractiousness and the sudden absence of baby fat remind her of certain boys in her classes. She checks her disapproval (Harold's department) but can't help saying, "After that awful thing with the police, you'd think you'd want to stay out of trouble for a while."

"Oh, Mom!" says Spider with his most patronizing sneer. "This isn't illegal or anything." His mouth is a slit of disdain.

"Neither was trying to help that poor woman on the street. But you saw what happened." She sips cocoa till she's sure her voice won't wobble, then leans forward, lays a hand gently on Spider's arm, and says,

"Tell me, honey, were you terribly frightened when they took you to the station?"

"Let's skip it, okay?"

"I couldn't believe it when Daddy told me." She checks her voice again. "How awful for you."

"If you come to my room I'll show you my Backcrosses. I can usually do them perfect with the balls, and now I'm working on the clubs. Herschel says I do them better than the Gimp, even. We're working on this double—"

"I'd love to, Spider. But first, just one thing, okay? I left you all those numbers. You had them in your pocket. Why didn't you call someone? Even if you couldn't reach Daddy, any one of those people—Ross, Jessica, Thomas, Arianne—any of them would have been very glad to come and get you out. You didn't have to submit to that horrible grilling for three hours!"

"Two hours."

She knows her voice seems to be issuing accusations, when all she wants in the world is to reassure him and win his forgiveness. But she can't stop.

Spider shrugs, shrinks, pulls back from her why, why, why. Once he lived for her. It was for her beaming smile that he learned the right way to carry scissors, brush his teeth, do cat's cradle, construct a house of cards. For her praises he practiced his scales, mixed exquisite poisons, drew winged monsters with electronic talons and horny beaks, sent rockets to the moon, studied fractions and maps and stars. Yet here she is yelling at him again. He looks for a way to withdraw his offer as fast as he can.

She knows this boy. Every gesture, word. She can still name each of the first ten words he learned from someone other than herself. And now—she sees it in his eyes—she's losing him, he's slipping away. His feet are fidgeting; his brow furrows like a man's—her baby, her second chance, her only boy. The tears she's straining to hold back will finally wash him away. With a valiant effort she breaks free. She hugs him hard. "Sorry," she says. "Jet lag. I'll fix you some pancakes and then let's go to your room so you can show me your stuff with the pins."

"Clubs, Mom. Not pins; clubs. Honestly . . ."

Not My Mother . . .

All eight teachers of science and mathematics who make up Rosemary's department were annoyed and finally outraged at the suggestion that their mothers had affairs. Maybe their fathers—once—but not their mothers. They readily conceded that most men did; it was documented in all the epics and novels, ancient and new. They themselves had affairs, had them before they were married and since; their friends, colleagues, students, and spouses were having affairs right and left, barely bothering to cover their tracks; sex hung in the air like low-lying clouds always threatening to burst forth in showers or violent storms— how could their mothers alone have escaped the universal torrent? Yet the eight members of Rosemary's department, trained though they were to honor reason and evidence, huffily insisted that while everyone else might be guilty, their own mothers were exempt. This amazing opinion gave rise to Rosemary's first Corollary to Streeter's Theorem of Association, by which anything can go with anything. *Corollary #1: There exists no limit to the contradictory views that can occupy separate compartments of the same head at the same time.*

As Rosemary slips the last pancake she's rustled together out of odds and ends onto Spider's plate, she realizes that her children, like her colleagues, will never believe that a comforting kitchen person like herself could admit an alien lover to her heart or alien semen to her womb. *Their* womb. Impossible.

32

Nora's apartment, with its questionable location and stabilized rent, was one of the things she always mentioned first in her litany of luck. Her address was famous in their circles. She had moved there a decade back, before the entire block had been designated a historic landmark, and had remained there through several real estate booms and gentrifications. That particular tree-lined block was one of the architectural gems of the city, and Nora's particular apartment was on the top floor of one of the most picturesque and oldest of the houses.

Climbing the stairs, Rosemary remembered one of their more flippant exchanges.

ROSEMARY: Yes, it's true. I'm sure we would have separated years ago if we hadn't had children.
NORA: That's a good reason not to have children.
ROSEMARY: Are you kidding? That's a good reason to get married. The children are the best thing in my life.
NORA: Really! My apartment is the best thing in mine.

Nora opened the door holding a wadded tissue to her nose. Her eyes were red and sunken, ringed by black shadows; her cheeks were streaked with makeup, like ski trails on a mountainside; and though she somehow managed to look elegant even in a plaid flannel shirt over old jeans, her face was gaunt, her mouth drawn, her brow creased. "Come in," she said sniffling. "Don't mind me."

"Nora! What happened? You look like death."

"You got it. Death is what I look like. Death is what it is." Nora put her face in her hands and began to sob.

"Forgive me," cried Rosemary, wrapping her arms around Nora. "How stupid of me. What a way to greet you. I'm so sorry. What's the favor you want? What happened?"

"Wait." Nora blew her nose into her fast disintegrating tissue and led Rosemary into the living room.

Rosemary regretted the gasp that escaped her lips at the sight of the scrupulously tended room. How differently the childless, the single, were able to live! Any New Yorker would surely admire the historic charm of wide plank floors becomingly decked out with several small, artful scatter rugs; the ornately carved fireplace in which a demure fire flickered; a low slanted beamed ceiling pierced by two leaded skylights giving onto a reddening late-afternoon sky; and the old shuttered windows through which Rosemary saw the blunt bronze tops of distant towers; but most particularly would a mother wonder at floor-to-ceiling bookcases in which fragile treasures were interspersed among the books on even the lowest shelves, cut-glass vases filled with dry autumn bouquets adorning tiny tables with delicately turned legs, tapered candles here and there, even white upholstery. The antique table piled with papers and surrounded by open books bespoke a household in which everything might remain forever exactly where it was put.

Nora disappeared beneath a narrow arch and returned with a tray bearing two delicate coffee cups and a plate of lace cookies. A smile was superimposed on her expression like a pressed flower over a bleak poem. "Just because I look like this doesn't mean I neglect my hospitality. Sugar? Cream?"

"Black, thanks." Rosemary sat back. "Now. Tell me."

Nora's Second Story . . .

"I suppose I should start way back when I began seeing Keith, that man in Santa Fe, remember? Not that I thought anything would come of that—he's quite inappropriate for me. Still, after all those years of my not being able to break it off with Lex, Keith made me feel the time had finally come to do it, even though it took me till just a few weeks ago to really get up the nerve.

"Lex and I hadn't quarreled or anything; in fact the day it started was one of our better days. It was a Friday—one of those early spring days you always remember, the first warm day of the year, after a rather miserable cold spell. The crocuses and irises were in all the flower shops and I heard they were beginning to come up in Central Park, and the ailanthus trees outside my window had suddenly begun to bud. It promised to be a gorgeous weekend—though of course *we* never saw each other on weekends, he spent his weekends with his family. The news reported that the polar bears had come out of their caves and the youngest bear was on exhibit for the first time. So when I was about to sit down to work, instead, on an impulse, I called Lex at his office and convinced him to take off a couple of hours of work and meet me for brunch at the zoo—one of the few outdoor places where we ever risked meeting because it's mostly families with young kids who go there, no one we know. A weekday morning seemed safe enough. It turned out a lot of people had the same idea—mostly kids cutting school and lovers like us. Who wouldn't want to be outside on a day like that?

"We sat on the cafeteria terrace drinking coffee for a while and watching the seals sun themselves; then we strolled over to the bird house just like any other couple, and then we fed the does and watched the bears frisking and playing after their long sleep. Finally, it was time to eat, so we went back into the cafeteria, ordered cheese omelets and corn muffins, and carried them out onto the terrace. I had brought a thermos full of Muscadet; I poured it into coffee cups. We hardly said a word, we were so happy just sitting there in the sun looking at each other."

Nora sniffed loudly and blew her nose.

"Now, it's true, my happiness was mixed, knowing that for us such pleasures had to be sneaked into stolen moments, and even those weren't really free. When we walked around the zoo we couldn't hold hands like other people, and every time someone came out onto the terrace we had to stop what we were doing while one of us checked them out. But I was used to it, and that morning I wasn't particularly thinking about breaking up.

"But then something awful happened. We heard shots. It was a little after twelve—the clock had just chimed. There was a great commotion over behind the cafeteria in the direction of the polar bears. People left their tables and started to run toward the sound. I didn't stir; I was mainly annoyed at the interruption. But Lex's sense of drama won out and he got up from the table to go see what happened. I must have had a premonition about how awful it was because I asked him not to go—come to think of it, I practically begged him. But he went anyway.

"He came back looking grim and told me that a guard had shot one of the polar bears. I asked, which one?

"The mother, I'm afraid, he said. Then he told me not to go, he said it wasn't something I'd want to see. The whole city saw it on the evening news, but not me.

"Did he kill her? I asked. Lex nodded. Then he sat down and told me what he knew.

"Evidently, some teenage boys had got past the moat and climbed over the outer bars. They were poking sticks through the inner bars, teasing the bears. Maybe they were showing off to each other or maybe they were just trying to attract the baby bear's attention, not trying to be mean at all. Who knows. But one boy put his arm through the bars and the mother grabbed it and started to pull. The boys all started hollering, people screamed, the guard was there in a second with his gun. At first the guard tried distracting the mother with food, with noise, by going for the baby—but she wouldn't let go of the boy's arm. People were screaming, and soon it was clear the guard had no choice but to shoot her. One shot, through the head, Lex said.

"I made some angry crack about teenage boys, and then I started to cry. When I was finally able to stop, I asked, What about the boy? Lex said, in this snide voice I'd never heard before—he said, I was wondering if you'd ever get around to asking. He's still got his arm.

"I stared at him. I couldn't believe he'd said that. His remark stunned me like the gunshot I'd just heard. I felt I was hearing what he really thought of me for the first time. He was no different from anyone else. Just because I don't have children, the world assumes I'm either pathetic or a monster."

Rosemary nodded. And just because I do have children, the world assumes I'm a drudge or a prude, she thought but didn't say.

"It was so cruel. In that single remark the one person in the whole world I assumed understood me revealed that he hadn't any idea of who I really was. And worse, he had turned against me, attacking me in my most vulnerable spot. I thought he'd known all along the sacrifice I was making to his awful, clinging family, living a double life, compromising the one thing that matters most, my integrity, because of my love for him; I thought he knew and was grateful and at least respected me for it. And here I discover instead that all along he's despised me for it. He's never even recognized it as a sacrifice. Like every cliché-ridden unconscious philistine stranger, he thought that I was your standard selfish brute for not wanting children. And this discovery was so hurtful that I broke down and started crying and carrying on right there in the park. I turned on Lex and began accusing him of every cruelty and insensitivity he had ever committed against me from the beginning. I went completely out of control, crying that he didn't love me, that he had never loved me, that he had taken my best years and used me up and given nothing back. I told him I was finished with him, I never wanted to see him again. Right there and then I started emptying my purse of everything he had ever given me, anything connected with him, and threw them at him across the table. My cigarette case, his picture, everything.

"Well, he was squirming. People were watching us. He tried to calm me down, but I wouldn't be calmed. I was out of my mind. I know it had something to do with that dead bear, though I can't say exactly what. The waste of it, of her life, and the pain—and all because some boys carelessly toyed with her for their own amusement. I don't know—I was a mad-woman, one who sees everything perfectly clearly.

"Finally he induced me to leave the terrace and walk in the park. By then it was afternoon, and the benches and paths were starting to crowd up, but I didn't even notice.

"All those years of being careful, of secrecy and caution, just rolled away; I said anything I felt as loudly as I wanted, convinced this was the last time I'd ever be with Lex. It felt so great to be coming clean at last. *And another thing*, I kept saying, *and another thing*. Such a stream of words! I told him exactly how I felt cheated, how he'd hobbled me, how I wanted a normal open life like other people and he'd prevented it. I told him what I thought of his cowardice and his marriage and his hypocrisy and his forcing me to live out his hypocrisy. We came to the small lake where kids sail model boats—you know the one?—and there, surrounded by a dozen little boys, I couldn't help it, I started sobbing again.

"Lex didn't know what to do. I could see he was feeling awful—guilty, scared. He'd never heard me talk like this; he'd seen me hurl my nasty barbs and little witticisms or complain bitchily, but he'd never seen me wounded by him like this. I guess he never had any idea how I really felt, that what I crave is a unified life, or that I was prepared to stop seeing him. I hardly knew it myself. But there, by the model sailboat pond, he could see that I meant it.

"After a while he took me by the shoulders and turned me around to face him and said in this new, low, deathlike voice, Do you want me to leave her? Is that what you want? I nodded. Okay, he said, then I will.

"I couldn't believe it. I looked at his face. It was deadly white and deadly serious. When? I asked. As soon as you say, he said. Immediately. I'll tell her this weekend.

"All I saw was how there was nothing joyful in his face. Then I asked, What about the boy?—meaning his son, of course—and then I smiled, because I had just asked the same question, in the same words, that had started everything, and he smiled too. *What about the boy?* You see? We knew each other so well in some ways, not at all in other ways.

"He told me that of course he'd try to get custody and have him live with us."

Nora walked to the fireplace and folded her arms against the mantel and leaned her head upon them.

"It feels as if I haven't stopped crying since that day in the park, as if maybe," she said, turning around, "I had a nervous breakdown at the zoo and haven't yet begun to recover."

"Have you thought of seeing a doctor?" asked Rosemary, watching the tears flow in runnels down Nora's cheeks. She remembered how, some months before, one of her favorite students, Amanda, had sat in her office crying nonstop, just like Nora, and within a week had withdrawn from school. "If one of my kids cried like that for even just a couple of days, I'd call the doctor."

"Wait. You haven't even heard the whole story. When you hear the rest, you may have a different opinion. Where was I? Oh, yes. He's leaving his wife and little David's coming to live with us, right?"

"Right."

"Wrong, actually. Wrong. . . . So we get into a taxi and come up here and make love. So full of import and pain—different from all our other lovemaking. Almost as if we were saying good-bye. Tortured and ex- hausting. We outdid ourselves.

"After he finally leaves me, all fired up to go and tell her, I start thinking. Where am I going to put his son in this apartment? Will I have to move? This place is me, I've lived here longer than I ever lived any- where in my life. This apartment is the best thing in my life. So I decide, no, I'll keep my apartment, and we'll get another apartment nearby where we can all three live together. And so it begins. Pretty soon I'm thinking I want Lex but not his son. I've never actually talked to the kid, I've only seen him twice, and I've heard he's quite a handful. But how will I ever tell Lex now? Especially since it was my feelings about children, my claim to have been misunderstood, that started off this whole crisis in the first place. And now I'm feeling doubly misunderstood, and panicked be- sides. The truth is, I've always resented Lex's son for keeping Lex from me. Whenever Lex talked about him I always tensed up, guarded myself. I don't know, it was all crazy—because Lex used the boy against me, I know he did. I could make remarks about his wife, but about the son it was impermissible. And now I'm imagining him up there at home, telling his wife, or already having told her, after years of secrecy. All over in a minute, with one sentence—poof. And me—the evil stepmother all of a sudden, at thirty-eight years old? Now I really start to panic. If I say I don't want the kid after he's told his wife he's leaving her, I'll lose him for sure."

"But Nora," said Rosemary, "let's be practical. If his wife wants their son she'll probably get to keep him. She *is* the mother."

"But an incompetent mother. She's crazy."

"Oh, that's what the husbands always say. That's their justification.

For leaving or for staying around. But the boy's in his teens? He'll probably get to choose which one he lives with." Rosemary couldn't help it, she was pulling for the mother.

"Well, it doesn't matter anymore," continued Nora, "it's all over. . . ." Distractedly, she poured more coffee into their cups.

"So I finally decided to call him at home, to stop him before he says anything to her, if it isn't too late, to tell him we have to talk more first. But calling his house is absolutely forbidden; if he hasn't told her, it could bring on the crisis, and if he has . . . But I have to call. I pray he answers. If she answers and he's already told her . . . But I needn't have worried. No one answers. I call again and again, I call at all hours, Friday, Saturday, Sunday—but no one answers all weekend long. Where can they be? I try to imagine. . . . Wherever they are, the whole weekend is lost to me. I can't work, can't sleep. I work myself up into a real state. Has he told her yet? Is it too late to stop him? If he has, how can I ever tell him about my own reservations? Or, how can I *not?* Round and round, trying to work, tossing in bed, giving up, until the sun comes up a second time, and not one single minute of sleep. Exhausted, weepy, all shaky in the knees."

Nora lights a cigarette, sniffs, and smiles at Rosemary. "You see? It all fits: nervous breakdown, all the clinical symptoms. Sleeplessness, obsession, crying, loss of appetite, hopelessness. On the other hand, though, who could sleep with a burden like that? Who wouldn't feel hopeless?"

"That's what I love about you, Nora," says Rosemary. "The way you can step in and out of your plight as if it were a pair of jeans. Go on."

"There was hardly any doubt in my mind that he'd told her and they'd had it out. I thought maybe he'd kidnapped the boy and driven away— you read about such things. Or maybe she'd killed herself the way she always threatened. By Sunday night I was a wreck. I didn't know what to think. So when I called him at the office first thing Monday morning I wasn't prepared for his cheery business-as-usual hello, as if it were no different from any other Monday morning. I waited for him to say something, but he didn't. So finally I asked, Well? Did you tell her? Not yet, he said, there was no opportunity.

"No opportunity? I was flabbergasted. I know, you're probably thinking I must have felt relieved, right? But I didn't. After what I'd suffered over the weekend, I felt betrayed again. All the feelings I'd had at the zoo came flooding back, as if the polar bear had just been shot again. Nervous breakdown, right? You think it was a crazy reaction!" She turned her back to Rosemary and wept into her open hands.

"That was the beginning of a week of the most agonizing indecision and anxiety I've ever known. A week of madness. You know you're acting against yourself but you can't help it? I still don't understand those awful days. Before, we'd always known how we stood. Now, everything was uncertain and we were both torn up with the most agonizing conflict and guilt. Lex—toward me, his wife, his son. And me too—toward Lex. I wanted him to leave her more than anything, I'd always wanted it, and it was a matter of principle, but I didn't want his son to live with us and I couldn't bring myself to tell him so. Instead of coming out with the truth, I kept hedging, talking about the living arrangements, about this apartment—as if it were all just a matter of space and convenience, of real estate. And all the time, terrified of what was happening. You see, every outcome I could imagine was impossible for at least one of us. I don't know what drove me. Was it injured pride? Lust? Rage? Revenge? All I know is I wanted him to leave her, and at the same time, I knew it would be disaster for us if he left her.

"Now I know what hell is. Hell is perfect ambivalence. For five years I accepted our arrangement without much fuss, even though it tore me up to live a disgusting lie. But once I really imagined another possibility, everything changed. I had always hated most the moments approaching five when he would look at his watch, and then punctually at five, get ready to leave me, no matter what we were doing. But I had accepted it. Now it was no longer acceptable. And the weekends. God, I didn't want to spend another weekend all alone. So before he left here, as he was getting dressed, I said I couldn't live this way anymore. I said, tell her by Friday or we're through. I said, I won't bring it up again, not one word, but I swear to you, after Friday I don't want to see or speak to you except openly. I was prepared to go through with it, too, I really was—I had to have it settled one way or the other. I couldn't stand the uncertainty anymore. And I thought it would be better for him too—after all, I was the one he loved, he didn't even pretend to love her, he only stayed with her out of cowardice, because he was weak."

"And because of his son," added Rosemary.

"That's ridiculous. His son is fourteen years old. That's already grown up."

Rosemary clapped her hand over her mouth and listened. She knew better than to point out that fourteen is needy, or that nothing, not even marriage, could dent uncertainty.

"I waited. I didn't ask him anything, I didn't even hint. I just waited, as I said I would. And you know what? I really didn't care what happened.

"Finally Friday arrived. He came over in the afternoon, as usual. I could tell instantly by his manner that he hadn't told her."

"What did you do?"

"You would have been proud of me, Rosemary. I didn't carry on, I didn't make a scene, I just walked around the apartment very calmly collecting everything that belonged to him—his toothbrush and shaving equipment from the bathroom, his clothes, his pipes and tobacco, pictures of us, books he'd brought me, his big skillet and his coffee mug, that beautiful painted wooden panel from the back of a Sicilian donkey cart hanging over there, letters—everything I could lay my hands on from our years together, and I put them in a pile right there next to the door, and I told him to get them out by that night or they were going into the trash. And I told him to get together everything he had of mine and return it all to me. And he could start with my key, I said, at once.

"He came toward me to kiss me, but I backed off fast and held out my hand for the key. After he gave it to me, I went into my bedroom and closed the door. And I didn't come out until I heard him leave. And then, only then, did I cry."

"Did he take his things with him?"

"No. I cried and cried. And I hated myself because before he even had a chance to get home I knew I would call him up and tell him to come back."

"Maybe he planned to anyway if he didn't take his things."

"Yes, I thought so too for a moment, and that gave me hope. But then I realized there was just too big a pile for one trip.

"I held off as long as I could, but finally I couldn't stand it. I called him at home and gave our signal—one ring—then hung up and waited for him to call me back."

"That's our signal too," said Rosemary. "Maybe it's everybody's signal."

"When he didn't call, I did it again. Still nothing. I thought, fuck him, can't he tell I'm desperate to talk to him? So I rang through. I know it was terrible, but I didn't care. A man answered. I was confused. I thought I must have misdialed. I asked for Lex as if I were legitimate—the man didn't know my voice. He asked who was calling. I gave our code name. The man hesitated, and then he said, I'm sorry to have to tell you this, but Lex passed away last night."

Rosemary stopped her cup midway to her lips and cried, "No!"

"I didn't believe it either. Then the man told me he'd had a heart attack in the night and died in his sleep."

"Is that really what happened?"

"He'd had a bad heart for years, evidently. He was taking medicine for it. The way he smoked, I'd never have suspected heart trouble. That was only one of the things he never told me. The strange thing was, the man told me Lex wasn't sleeping in his own bed, he was sleeping on the hide-a-bed in the living room. If he'd been in their bedroom she might have known he was having a heart attack and maybe she could have saved him. But he was sleeping in the living room."

"Poor, poor Nora."

"I still can't believe it. I talk to him every night." Nora threatened the ceiling with her clenched fist. "I say to him: you dirty bastard, you coward, you weak-willed, passive, servile, craven weakling! . . . But I loved him."

Rosemary moved to the loveseat beside Nora and held her in her arms. "No wonder," she crooned, "no wonder."

"So now—what do you think? A nervous breakdown or not?"

Rosemary squeezed her again.

"Why do you suppose he was sleeping in the hide-a-bed? Do you think he finally told her? Or was he just upset and restless and didn't want to disturb her? I ask him that every night now, but he won't tell me a goddamn thing."

Rosemary looked at her watch. Nora carried the tray to the kitchen with Rosemary trailing her. "I was the one he loved, we'd been together for five years; he might already have been on his way back to me. And if not, I know he would have left her for me when his kid grew up. But I couldn't even attend his funeral."

Rosemary didn't trust herself to speak. Her heart went out to Nora, but also to the widow and child. On safer ground, she asked, "What's the favor you wanted to ask me?"

"Will you get my letters back for me?"

"You wrote him letters?"

"Sure. Love letters, hate letters, panic letters. Dozens. Maybe hundreds. I wrote him at least once a week."

"Where are they?"

"She has them."

Rosemary gasped. "Then she knows about you?"

"Now—everything. After years of insisting on the most crippling, humiliating sort of caution, he blew the whole thing by leaving all the evidence neatly packed up in a Macy's box beneath his desk. He must have got it all ready to return to me, only instead, at the last minute, he finked out with a timely heart attack, the bastard, and left her sitting on all my letters!"

"How do you know this?"

"A spy told me."

"I'd never put anything in writing, not one incriminating word," said Rosemary, shaking her head.

"Oh, *you!*" snapped Nora. "You see love as nothing but a game."

"No I don't. Not a game."

"A hype, then; you call it a hype."

"All I mean by that," explained Rosemary, "is it's a state of mind. It depends on imagination, on will. You have to want it to feel it. And keep on wanting it."

"You think so? Well, I didn't want it. Not this. I was stuck with it. And I'll tell you another thing. No more married men. Never."

Rosemary knew it was the wrong time to pursue the debate. She wanted to say, Good, then we won't be rivals, because I'm coming to think the only safe lover for me is a family man, thoroughly married, plenty of children, with no desire to leave them. Instead, she asked, "How am I supposed to get these letters?"

At last Nora smiled. "You're the big strategist. You've met Lex's wife. I leave it all up to you."

33

"What'd you say?"

"Nothing."

"I hate when you do that. Tell me."

"I told you. Nothing."

"It's so irritating. Just because I didn't hear you, do I have to beg you to tell me what you said?"

For the hundredth time Rosemary vows that the next time Harold misses something she says she'll pull the same thing on him. And for the hundredth time she knows she'll never bring it off. She can never exact a punishment, never stay angry overnight, never even remember what angered her. No more than she can refuse a student who needs her help.

All the same, she makes a try. She stands up, picks up her cup, and threatens, "Just wait till *you* want to know something *I* said. In fact, forget I even spoke to you today." She straightens her spine, stretching to her full height, and with the cup balanced in her hand sweeps toward the door.

"Christ," says Harold, raising his voice, "why must you always—"

At the door, Rosemary almost bumps into Daisy, long-faced and bewildered, looking from one angry face to the other. "Am I interrupting something?" she asks.

"No!" barks Harold, clutching his cigarettes in his pocket.

Rosemary sends Harold a warning look, then sprouts a smile for Daisy. She hopes Harold will put aside his anger as she has already forgotten hers. She hates to fight in front of the children. "We were just having a discussion."

"Good, 'cause there's something I need to talk to you about."

"Me or him?"

Daisy gulps. How can she choose? Her mother will swallow the sex, gag on the drugs, her father the opposite. And the prison record she fears will kill them both. Damn her brother for forcing her into this crushing confession, especially now, but what else can she do? Guiltily she twirls a lock of hair and answers, "Both of you."

Rosemary returns her cup to the table and sits down, feeling her heart thump double-time, as if everything is about to be revealed. Quickly she runs down every possible slip since her return, then every oversight of the last year: the phone, a note, the souvenirs she brought back home. . . . Hearing the gravity in Daisy's voice, her fingers grow cold as blood rushes up to her defense.

"I'd give anything not to have to tell you this," says Daisy, tossing an envelope in the center of the dining table. "Just please listen till I'm done, okay?"

Rosemary squints. One of her letters? Maybe she carelessly wrote something that gave her away?

"What's that?" asks Harold.

Only when Daisy looks pleadingly at her mother with the terrified eyes of a student sitting down to an exam does Rosemary surmise it's Daisy who's in trouble, not her. In fact, she can tell from Daisy's eyes that nothing less than her best is required of her now. More than her best if Harold withholds his. She fills her eyes with sympathy and beams it at her daughter. "Of course, sweetheart," she says. "Tell us."

Harold has no doubt that the envelope holds the missing money from the fireside lamps. So she's the one who took it. Daisy! He rests his chin in his hands, closes his eyes.

Daisy sees her parents waiting there like lambs. She wants not to hurt them, but even more she wants not to cry. She takes several deep breaths and imagines herself calmly doing yoga, pulling the breath from deep down below her diaphragm. She'll start with the missing drugs and work backwards through Spider to Rap, the hardest part to tell. Exhaling slowly, she counts to ten, then takes a final breath, and begins.

"Wait. Stop right there. Do you mean you shot up with him? Is that what you're saying?" asked Harold.

Rosemary threw him a frantic look, hoping he'd be still. Otherwise, how would they ever get the whole story? Drugs, police—she was beside herself. Maybe if she hadn't gone away . . .

"Daddy! Do you think I'm *stupid*? All we ever did besides pot was shrooms. These," she said, pouring the contents of the envelope into Rosemary's favorite ashtray from Italy, the one made of genuine Vesuvian lava, "are morning glory seeds."

Harold leaned forward to examine the tiny blue spheres, relieved that she didn't take the money. "Mushrooms I've heard of," he said, "but morning glory seeds? Really? What on earth can you do with morning glory seeds?"

"Come on, Harold," said Rosemary excitedly. "Does it really matter what you do with them? You get high with them, right, sweetie? Same as with the mushrooms."

"Not exactly," said Daisy. "They're different. Rap says most people chew them up, but he puts them in the blender."

"Then what?" persisted Harold. "What happens then?"

"Rap says you throw up a little, like a mild sneeze, and then your body gets ethereal for about an hour, and then you have wonderful flowing thoughts for the rest of the night. Anyway, that's what Rap says."

Rosemary watched Daisy, speechless. How could she not have guessed? She flipped frantically back through the past for clues but found none.

"Rap says. Rap says. What do *you* say?" asked Harold.

"All I got was nauseated."

"Oh, poor sweetheart," said Rosemary, reaching out a hand. In a mere three weeks her children had broken loose, were picking up speed; in a minute they would be gone. Gone!

"Criminal," muttered Harold. "How old is this person?"

Daisy picked listlessly at her cuticle. Soon she would have to tell them the part about prison. "It's really not his fault. If Spider hadn't raided my drawers and stolen my things, then nothing would have happened."

"Come now," said Harold. "When you choose to commit a crime and deal in contraband you have to be prepared for the consequences. Spider would never have found them if that man hadn't brought them into this house and made you keep them."

"He didn't make me. I *volunteered*."

"But why, sweetheart?" asked Rosemary, wondering how she had failed her child. All the troubled students she'd ever helped paraded before her in mockery. "Why?"

Daisy couldn't bear the bewilderment in her mother's face, her trusting innocence. She could tell her anything except what hurt her. Now, after so carefully protecting her parents from the world, she must let them down in order to protect Spider, whose danger was worse. "Because he . . . because I'm . . . in love with him!"

"Love!" cried Rosemary.

"Nonsense!" said Harold.

"*In* love," corrected Daisy. Then, lifting her chin to try out the word for the first time: "He's my lover."

Harold watched the alien phrase issue from his daughter's lips as if she were a child actress. The young Elizabeth Taylor, say, or a chastened Brooke Shields. She opened her eyes wide at the appropriate moments, showed nervousness, touchingly tossed back her hair, and let her voice catch at key words. A child, a child. He filled with disgust; he could kill the yahoo who'd done this to her.

"Really!" said Rosemary. "Why didn't you tell us? Why haven't we met him?"

Harold looked at Rosemary involving herself in the whole sordid business. Next she'd be on the telephone boasting to her female friends: Guess what? Daisy's got a lover.

"You met him, Mom. The same day I did. At your friend's Thanksgiving party. He was there with his father, that doctor with the beard."

Harold folded his arms in satisfaction. "You see?" he said, pinning everything on Rosemary.

Rosemary tried to remember, but her mind, like her feet, was turning numb. "And you've been seeing him ever since?"

"Not really. He left town a few days later and didn't come back till a few weeks ago, when you were in Italy."

Rosemary gasped with guilt. She was quite sure that had she been here instead of Harold, nothing would have happened. Or if it had, Daisy would have come to her for help. But she wasn't here. She was off with a lover of her own. And this was her punishment. When she was able to breathe again she leaned forward and asked, "If he really loves you, why did he ask you to keep these drugs?"

"Because I can't be prosecuted, I'm too young. But if they found them on him, they could ship him straight to prison."

"Serve him right," said Harold. "Keep him off the streets. Save me the trouble."

"Oh Daddy, *must* you?" said Daisy in the diminishing voice that goeth before tears.

"Really, Harold, do you have to always make jokes?" said Rosemary to the rescue. "You know your father doesn't mean anything. Go on. Try to explain what you're afraid of."

"Okay, I'll tell you." Daisy sat up in her chair to play her dubious trump. "He's been serving time. In fact, he's on parole. Now, because of those shrooms, they'll pick him up and send him back. And he'll know it was all my fault."

Rosemary and Harold Streeter leaned across the table to stare at their daughter with their mouths open. She might have just handed them a report card covered with F's. Rosemary's eyes widened. Doubt leaped on her chest, inflicting a host of short multiple wounds. Although she'd always prided herself on her refusal to bow to convention or honor the double standard, fiercely defending her children's freedom as if it were her own, at the same time she'd secretly counted herself lucky that her children had never got into trouble, grateful her principles had never been put to the test. It was to avoid taking chances that she had always cared for them herself, refusing to turn them over to surrogates, taking her share of play dates when they were little, and keeping their confidences as they grew. But now, the first time she leaves them, everything that can happen does. Drugs, sexual blackmail, crime . . . "Prison?" mouthed Rosemary, as if the meaning of the word escaped her. This time, Harold was speechless.

How Daisy wished she could save her parents from these brutal shocks. Her father looked like a great, sad, disappointed collie, and her mother, smiling through tears, like a heartbroken clown. Two clowns: top-heavy, massive heads on wobbly necks, shocked innocents ready to topple. And no one but her to keep them from crashing to the floor and shattering.

"What'd they catch him at," said Harold, "corrupting minors?"

"Oh, what's the use," wailed Daisy at last, pulling the plug on her tear ducts as if they were life-support systems of a hopeless case she'd finally given up on.

The Rally . . .

Rosemary runs over to Daisy, squats beside her, and puts her arm around her shoulders with a there-there-there. "Just who is this *they* you're worried about?"

"The police. The ones who arrested Spider."

"*You* told her that," says Harold. "I didn't. I didn't tell one soul except

Ross." He walks around the table and squats on Daisy's left. "Here," he says, holding out his handkerchief.

"He was *questioned*, and then given a *summons*," says Rosemary calmly, "but not for drugs, sweetheart."

Daisy looks up through teary eyes. "For what then? And how do you know?"

"Because," says Harold, "they sent me a letter, saying Interfering with an Officer, but nothing about any kind of drugs. Not one word. Believe me, they'd say so if they had something else on him. I'll show you. Rosemary—where's that letter?"

"Probably still in the car."

"Want me to go down to the garage and get it for you? That make you feel any better?" Gently Harold lifts Daisy's chin with an index finger, wipes the tears from her cheeks.

Daisy takes the handkerchief and blows. "You're not mad?" she whispers.

"At you? Why should we be mad at you?" He pinches her cheek. "You're just a kid. What do you know about mushrooms and morning glories? *He's* the one. I'm going to inform his father, let him know what kind of business his son's up to. A doctor, eh?"

"Daddy! Don't you *dare!*" cries Daisy.

Rosemary, joining Daisy, throws Harold her most ferocious look. She has always valued Harold for being a family man, reliable, energetic, ready to do whatever is required; but left to himself, his judgment seems to her dubious. How relieved she is to be home at last—she only hopes she's not too late.

Harold pats Daisy's knee, tapping out reassurances. "Okay, whatever you say. I just want to do what helps you, honey. That's all. Whatever you tell me to do, that's what I'll do."

"It's all right," says Rosemary, taking Daisy's hand. Then she reaches a hand out to Harold, who accepts it and with his other arm encircles Daisy's waist. "You see? We're not such ogres after all, are we?" he asks his daughter, squeezing.

"Look out!" shouts Spider, chasing five airborne balls into the room.

"Spider!" cries Daisy. "Come here, you rat."

He lets the balls cascade home to his hands, tosses them on the sofa one at a time, then slips inside the family circle. "What's going on, anyway?" he says, turning. "No kidding, what is this, a dancing lesson or something?"

Over Daisy's head Harold winks at his wife, who, though misty-eyed, is smiling again.

34

Dressed somberly in brown wool—black would have been pretentious, she barely knew the deceased, and gray might have passed unnoticed— Rosemary sipped her Dubonnet, a drink she considered equally somber, and waited at the bar for the widow. Pairs of lovers at the small tables punctuated the indelicacy of her mission. Not a week since Lex's death, here she was, interceding with his widow on behalf of his mistress.

When Sheila Levy finally appeared inside the doorway she resembled a celebrant more than a mourner. Resplendent even in black, glittering like jet, far more attractive than the wife Rosemary remembered, she surveyed the room like a stage star used to attention.

Rosemary stood up and reached out a hand. "I'm awfully sorry about your husband," she said sheepishly, hoping her guilt over this unsavory mission might pass for regret.

"Thanks. It's a terrible time for me, a terrible loss," said Sheila. Her face assumed the even deeper beauty of suffering. "So—you were in love with him too?" she asked when they'd moved to a table.

"Me? No! I barely knew Lex, though of course I followed his work. I don't think I've ever seen him when he wasn't with you."

"Really? Then what did you mean by a 'private matter'?" Sheila called over the waiter with a finger and ordered a Scotch sour. "Maybe I had you wrong."

Rosemary avoided her eyes. "There are some letters to him written by a friend of mine that she'd like to have back."

"Ah," crowed Sheila. "So it *is* about his love life. It had to be, you know; he was so careless with it, like a naughty boy." She shook her head and clicked her tongue against her teeth three times. "He was a genius in his work but a clod in his private life, you know? I was always having to rescue him from some entanglement or other. One of them even had the nerve to show up at the funeral—and in mourning, if you can imagine!" She lit a cigarette. "Well, what about these letters? Who is your unhappy friend?"

Rosemary didn't know whether she was more shocked by Sheila's insouciance or by Lex's philandering. She had expected to pity Sheila, but now she pitied Nora too. In fact, Sheila almost seemed to be enjoying herself while Rosemary was doing the suffering. Sheila's eyes were too bright, her color too high, her voice too brittle, her smile too grand for a new widow; the only hint of her bereavement was a slight edge of hysteria—or was it bitterness?—in her tone. Rosemary lowered her voice almost to a whisper as she mentioned Nora's name.

"So you're a friend of *hers?* I'm surprised at you, Rosemary. How does that feel?" Sheila swallowed half her drink in a gulp, but her eyes and voice remained steady. "Look, if you're feeling sorry for me because of *her*, you're wasting your time."

Widow's Story . . .

"You think you can tell me something I don't know? Not a chance. I know all about him. I was his wife. I know what was important and what wasn't. His work and his family were important. The rest wasn't. My job was to see to it that he took care of his family and did his work and behaved like a decent father till our son grew up. And now . . ."

Her voice broke off as her eyes closed and her lip trembled, but after a moment she recovered herself and began again.

"You think I didn't know about his women? I knew. Of course I knew, just the way you know. You're a journalist's wife. Every little budding actress and reporter in town was after Lex, all the ambitious little climbers thinking only of their careers and their good times. What do they care about the man and his family? They smelled his weakness and went after him. I knew all about it—I didn't even care. No, that's not quite true. I cared. But I knew those women were insignificant.

"Let me tell you something. My husband was a great man, a terrifically talented man, some say a genius. But he wouldn't have got anywhere without me. On his own he didn't have ambition, or direction, or discipline. He needed me and he knew it. When I found him he didn't have any idea of what he was going to do. He was in love with the theater then; he knew he wanted to write, but he was nowhere. I recognized his potential back when he couldn't get a line he wrote published. He was working as a waiter and was losing his confidence, but I had faith in him.

I told him to keep writing. For years I supported him while he got his career off the ground.

"He was very talented, but a weak man, too. Aren't they all? Like babies. He was weak, he had a weakness for women. He didn't know how to say no to them. A man like that needs to be protected. He was no match for those young wily girls who come on all sugar and principle. But then, they're no match for me, either. They're ignorant. They have no idea what real life, family life, is about.

"And he appreciated what I did for him, protecting him from your Noras and your Kimberlies. He counted on it. For two decades I made that man's home. I don't mean cooking his meals and washing his underwear; a maid could do that. I bore his son and raised that child. I arranged his calendar, kept the lions away, saw to it that he had sharp pencils every morning. I balanced his checkbook for him, I ordered his clothes. I kept him safe. And after his heart attack six years ago, I watched his cholesterol—on his own he'd have eaten nothing but eggs, butter, and cheese, I swear!—and made him stop smoking those terrible pipes, gave them all away."

Rosemary remembered the meerschaum pipe carved like a mermaid that she and Nora had seen together in a shop window on Hudson Street and Nora had promptly bought for Lex for Christmas. But if he'd stopped smoking years before . . . ? Or had he never stopped? Did those other women precede Nora, or was he seeing them all along, or were they only Sheila's fantasy? Rosemary felt a bit woozy from the hail of new evidence that anything can go with anything, that nothing can ever finally be known. Or maybe from the Dubonnet.

"You think it was a picnic for me, always covering for him to our son? Seeing him give in to his weakness again and again, when his work was waiting? Sometimes I was impatient—why couldn't he learn? But I would have cut my tongue out before I'd have let David know about his father. Sure, it hurt. But all I cared was that he be a responsible father to our son. If that meant letting him have his flings, even if people talked— well, I pride myself on being above all that. I'm not the weak one. Thank God."

While Sheila hailed the passing waiter and ordered two more drinks, Rosemary tried to penetrate Sheila's bewildering bravura. Was it simply an act to edify her husband's lover's friend, or was it what she really felt? Maybe it was both. If it was an act, she was turning in a star performance.

"Let me tell you something," she continued. "Sometimes I hated what that man put me through, sure, I admit it. Sometimes I wished he wasn't so attractive or such a hopeless weakling, prey to every little 'liberated' gal who came sniffing by his office door.

"Don't get me wrong; it wasn't jealousy I felt. For them? Hardly. Sometimes, though, I did resent the effort I had to put out, all that work, the exhaustion. But then, you get out of something what you put into it, you know? From the very beginning, when I first met him, I decided that he was worth it. If I hadn't, I would never have married him, because from the start I saw his weakness and knew what I was taking on. Christ, when I was in the hospital giving birth to our son, Lex was having dinner with some actress.

"These 'liberated' females with their new ideas, your Noras and Debbies and Kimberlies, they think they're different and don't have to follow the rules. But these gals aren't new at all. They're as old as Jezebel. They're just your plain, old-fashioned homebreakers; the only difference is they don't know it, that's all. They don't have the slightest idea that you have to work for what you get, you get what you deserve, when you're wicked you get punished."

Rosemary sipped her drink. She'd expected to find pitiable this deceived widow, victimized even by a corpse, but now it's clear that any message Rosemary carried from Nora, Sheila could fit neatly into her martyrdom. How convenient the silence of the dead. Alone in the bright light of center stage, at last Sheila's beauty is secure, her performance accomplished, her life justified.

"I worked hard for Lex. And he appreciated me. Just as much as I appreciated him. We were one of those rare couples . . . a rare family," she repeated, drawing breath for her final, triumphant speech.

"So you can take your friend's letters back to her. What do I want with them? Who is she to me? Just one of the people he didn't know how to refuse, someone who played to his weakness. Her letters mean nothing to me. You want to know the truth? I never even looked at them. I know without reading them what they say. They're trash. Teasing, self-promoting, begging, sycophantic trash. Your friend is nothing to him but a weakness he indulged, partly because he couldn't say no, partly because he still liked to play the naughty boy. He knew it, I knew it. Every wife knows it. I knew the man inside out. This is where he lived and this is where he died."

Her index finger thumped her breast.

"Right here where he belonged. With his family."

Rosemary ran down her excuses as she parked the shopping cart and ducked into the phone booth. She had waited too long to call him, scandalously long, but she was still afraid to talk to him. She looked furtively up and down the block as she dialed, half hoping he wouldn't answer.

Peter put down his brush and picked up the phone. All day, waiting for her call, he'd built up a case against her, filling his canvas with menacing reds, taking off from the Caravaggios they'd seen in Rome. But at the sound of her voice, he imagined again his triumphal descent into her ancestral lands: a processional, bugles, ring bearers, red carpet, maybe even a wedding banquet. "It's you," he said, giving her the benefit of the doubt.

"Barely," said Rosemary. She felt accused. "I tried to call you yesterday, but I couldn't get through. *So* much has happened. What is it, two days since we talked? Three? I'm terrible at transitions."

"Closer to three," he said, grudgingly.

But she only laughed and tried to jolly him. "And how many hours?" Peter had always been their official record keeper. Not that her memory was faulty, but her frequent need to deny the affair led her to falsify the evidence, leaving the historical task to him. Week by week, then month by month, event by event, he'd marked their progress and survival (as she had marked her children's), until three years had come and gone. He could recite the date of their first meeting, the subjects of their first misunderstandings. He remembered every setting: each hotel, restaurant, coffee shop of their beginning phase; the borrowed rooms; finally their sublet. Their rituals, their secret lexicon, their shy assaults on the polite boundaries of sex, their increasingly risky practices, Pompeii . . . And now, she had a sickening premonition, he would record the end.

Peter's doodle resembled an intricate enclosed garden. "I don't know. Too many. Since we came back it's been hard to settle down. What about you?" What he meant was, Have you told him yet?, but he didn't want to come right out and ask.

Rosemary watched the shoppers laden with parcels restlessly waiting for the light to turn. A mother yanked her child back up on the curb and began yelling. "Peter," she began, seeing her dream of freedom in a downtown loft flattened under the passing cars, "you can't imagine what I walked into here. You just won't believe it. Jove really decided to punish me this time."

"For what?"

"For going to Italy with you."

"Come on, baby," he said, an edge building in his voice despite himself. "Shoot."

"Okay. Youngest first: Spider got arrested for helping an old lady on the street. Daisy's in love with a drug addict. Nora's lover died. My—"

"Died? Did you say *died?*"

"Yes. Alexander Levy. A heart attack. Nora thinks it was revenge."

Peter couldn't help it, he dropped his voice and asked, "Have you told him?"

"Not yet," confessed Rosemary, her voice high and anxious. "Look, I've got to talk to you." She looked at her watch. She had to get the groceries home. "Can you meet me at our place in an hour and a half?" An ambulance, siren screaming, raced by. She pressed her palm to one ear. "I can't hear you. . . . Peter?" she shouted.

"I said, When are you going to tell him?"

"I can hardly hear you, there's so much traffic here. Can't you meet me? We've really got to talk."

"You mean," said Peter, rapidly filling in space until the garden was choked with weeds, "you're not going to do it? Is that what you mean?"

Rosemary sighed. "Oh, Peter. Honey. Listen. It was crazy to ever think I could. The gods—"

Peter snapped the pencil in half. "Cut it out with the gods." He felt himself losing it, but anger wasn't permitted, they'd never once quarreled.

"Please. Let me meet you. I want to see you. . . . Peter?"

Peter closed one eye and aimed the pencil like a dart at the red part of the canvas across the room. He should have known she'd never do it. He'd been a model of patience, forbearing for years while she hid behind her children, thinking only of herself. How many times had he said nothing while she aired her qualms? How patiently he had soothed her guilt, absorbed her slights. But now, still bloated from their rich Italian binge, he couldn't swallow any more. "Why don't you say what you have to say right now."

Rosemary shrank into herself. There was no way out. Whatever she did, she'd be wrong. But she had to do what she had to do. "Peter. Listen. It was a mistake. We were under a spell. It was Italy. But that doesn't mean—"

Peter picked up a palette knife, slapped it against his thigh. A fool, he was a fool.

"They need me," said Rosemary, starting again.

"Oh, yeah?" He whacked a passing cockroach with the palette knife, then stomped it underfoot. "What about me?" he said. "Doesn't it matter that I need you too?" When the roach was nothing but smear he held the phone out at arm's length and shouted into it, "What about me for a change? *Me?*"

Rosemary cringed. She'd never heard him so excited before. She'd always thought he understood. "But darling," she said, trying to soothe him, "nothing has to change." They'd managed for three years. Why not three more? "We can go back to the way it was before."

She sounded strangled and distant, like a voice from the depths. If she surfaced now he'd try to save her, give her one more chance, but she'd better come up fast. "You can, maybe. I can't." He didn't care that he was still shouting.

"Why not?"

His studio was dingy and plain. She'd visited him here only twice. How could he ever have thought she'd trade in that life of hers? He'd been blind. And what was more farcical, more absurd than a blind painter? "Because I've had it."

Rosemary's hands began to shake. If they hadn't gone to Italy, she thought, none of this would be happening. She'd overstepped her bounds. "But Peter," she whimpered, "we've still got four more months on the sublet." How ridiculous she sounded, even to herself.

"I think maybe we'd better just cool it for a while," said Peter. As every stroke of his brush limited and spoiled the picture in his mind, so now each word they said befouled their love. Love? He felt the edge of the word in his throat like a bone. *Love.* What was love? An image? A habit? Out of habit he added before hanging up, "If you change your mind you can give me a call. But don't count on me, Rosemary."

The tremor in Rosemary's hands spread to her knees when she heard Peter put down the phone. What should she do? She knew she deserved whatever he dished out, but all the same, when the dial tone cut in with its low, cruel buzz, she reached in her pocket for a coin and dialed again.

Peter walked across the room and examined his canvas. It was awful. Pretensions and lies. He'd just have to scrap it and start again.

Rosemary let the phone ring a long time, begging Peter to answer; but as she counted the rings, she kept thinking of how, when she was fifty, he'd only be forty-three, and then where would she be? Even if she could convince him to keep on seeing her, they'd never make it to her fiftieth. They might not even be able to finish out the sublet.

She looked out at her shopping cart. In the brown bags the ice cream was melting, the greens wilting, the bacteria in the meat reproducing at an alarming rate. The thought of the meat made her sick; her shaking hands were clammy and she had an urge to throw up. She hung up and dialed again.

When the phone resumed its ringing, Peter picked up his brush and slashed at his canvas with every ring.

> *One* worm in the apple
> *Two* teenaged brats
> *Three* years down the drain
> *Four* months of sublet wasted
> *Five* feet of ruined canvas
> *Six* hundred dollars' debt
> *Seven* years too young
> *Eight*—what was eight?

Worst of all, Rosemary couldn't figure out if she was being brave or cowardly, strong or weak. Probably weak, she decided, since no doubt Nora would be appalled by what she was doing. But then Nora had no children.

Peter stopped counting on eight. The picture was wiped out now. He walked to the door. He'd try to clear his head and start again.

Judging by her discomfort (she was too numb to call it pain), Rosemary guessed she was being strong. After the twelfth ring she gave up and went home.

35

Though Daisy was ready to pounce on him, Harold could hardly pretend to be sorry that Rap had been picked up for dealing and was now back in prison, safely out of the picture. The best he could do was carry his telltale smile into another room. One jailed Rap meant ten worries less. Let the women shed their tears while he kept the dangers from their door. Let them weep for the halt and poor, the junkies and felons while he paid the bills, took them to the ballet, transported them here and there, filed Civilian Complaints, had letters sent to admissions committees, saw to the doormen's tips at Christmas, held down two jobs, sent roses on appropriate occasions. And what more appropriate occasion than this? His beautiful, talented daughter, his pride, had just been admitted to her first-choice college. As should she be. He excused himself to call the florist and make a reservation for seven thirty for four at the Odeon.

"You see?" said Rosemary, exulting. "It was only a matter of time, just as I said. Williams is a very lucky college." As for the other news, she took Daisy's hand and bowed her head, pitying Rap, and Daisy, and herself. Now she would probably never get to know her daughter's first love. As her children would never know Peter. "In just a few months, you'll be meeting all sorts of fascinating new people," she promised, consoling herself as much as Daisy, sadly wondering if anyone could ever replace anyone.

Daisy stares at the two letters, one in her left hand, one in her right. It seems to her no accident that on the very day Williams College accepted her Rap should write to her from prison. Somehow the two events seem deeply connected: as if she'd made a pact with the devil and not her soul but Rap's was the price. It was absurd, of course—Williams knew nothing of Rap, nor Rap of Williams, both independent agents who didn't listen to her. But how convenient to be set free of Rap just as the next phase was beginning. The train was pulling into the station, dropping the old passengers, picking up the new. She knows she will write to him once, no more. That her happiness will forever be tainted by guilt is the price she must pay for all that awaits her. Yes, even in this most triumphant moment, as she dials Carrie's number to tell her the incredible news, beneath the hum of the wire she hears her father's cautionary nay and Rap's sardonic sneer.

"Guess what?" she cries into the phone. "I got into Williams. Finally! And I was all ready to mail my acceptance off to Wheaton. Now all we have to do is get through the next few weeks till graduation, and after that—real life. Can you believe it?"

Daisy's pulses throb, her blood pounds in her ears as she imagines real life. The difficult, the unknown. Physics, linguistics, anthropology, ecology, maybe even animal husbandry (Williams is in the country, after all)—who can tell? She will learn to think and act and drive. She will learn all the skills to make her free.

Daisy triple-knotted the twine over Rosemary's finger. Federal Express was picking up the trunk at four, Harold would load the car after dinner, and early in the morning they would set off for Massachusetts.

She knew that with all the classes she planned to take she was packing more records than she'd ever have time to listen to, more than her share: all the Vivaldi, half the Mozart, most of Bach, even some of her father's precious opera albums. But no matter how many boxes she packed, she would still be alone, while the family would have each other.

Rosemary stacked records in another box as Daisy handed them to her. During the excitement of the past month, when she and Daisy had pored over the course catalogue, shopped together for good shoes and winter clothes, made detailed lists of what to take, right up to that very afternoon when they began packing underwear into the bottom of the trunk, Rosemary had barely imagined Daisy gone. But now, seeing the black holes in the shelves gaping before her like Daisy's looming absence, she took up pencil and paper and began writing down the titles and composers of the records she might want to replace.

Daisy watched, horrified. Oh, how easy for them to do without her, to make a list, pick up a phone, and place an order to repair all the damage her departure might inflict. How convenient it would be if she too could so effortlessly replace all she must now give up. When Rosemary asked her to read off the record numbers to her as she packed them, she lost control. She pushed up her sleeves, faced her mother, and, hands on hips, cried: "All you have to do is pick up a pencil and make a list and you can replace anything in this world that's missing from your life, can't you?" Then she hid her face in her hands and began to sob.

Rosemary dropped the pencil, put her arms around Daisy and held her. "Sweetheart, sweetheart," she said in a choked voice, "I'm sorry." She stroked the soft, sweet-smelling hair she had so often washed and braided and adorned but would probably never get to brush again. Always, she had put devotion first, hoping to make her children strong through love; suddenly she wondered if she ought not to have concentrated instead on trying to make them independent. It was useless: whatever compromise you chose, whatever you did, something else was always required, frequently the opposite. She pulled back until she had Daisy's eyes in hers and said, "Don't you know you're sweeter to me than all the music in the world? Nothing will ever replace you."

Daisy, now taller than her mother by an inch, wiped her eyes on the back of her wrists. They smiled, they kissed. Neither knows why the smiles that cover their pain are suddenly tinged with embarrassment. Until this moment, neither one has truly understood that henceforth they will live apart. When they resume packing, Daisy turns away from the records back to the trunk, and Rosemary lets the pencil lie.

The Blessing . . .

When everything was packed and they were ready to close the trunk, Rosemary, hoping there might still be time, turned to Daisy to offer a last-minute maternal blessing. She wanted for her daughter all the possibilities of experience she had seized for herself and more. She wanted her to grow, to flourish, to be free, to have her share of everything. But she also knew that a share of everything was not everything, that seizing your rightful share was more difficult than people let on, that every gain involved a costly sacrifice. Maybe in time it would be easier; perhaps the price per share would be coming down as people clamored for their due—though her instinct told her that, as with most things that mattered, from bread to clean air, prices seemed always to be going up.

She cleared her throat, trying to temper the caution bred of knowing that you leave the baby unguarded for a single instant only at the risk of death. She formed her words with the hope that Daisy, of another generation, might be able to take certain risks she hadn't (though not, she prayed, at the price of losing all!), and with new, trembling courage turned to her daughter and said:

"At this moment you've got everything going for you. You're curious, talented, sensitive, resourceful, determined, kind, and free. Though sometimes you may get discouraged and confused, and often you'll find your way difficult, I think you're one of those people who can make of your life anything you choose. I only want you to promise me one thing before you leave."

Daisy, who'd been standing, embarrassed, with her hands clasped and her head bowed, looked up. "What?"

"That after college, before you even consider getting married, you'll live on your own for at least a year, preferably two."

"Married?" cried Daisy. "Mom! You can relax right now. I'll probably never get married."

"You won't?" asked Rosemary, surprised. "Really? When did you decide that?"

Daisy shrugged. It was not that she'd decided but only that she hardly thought of it. Nowadays marriage seemed old-fashioned, a waste. What she wanted now was to taste the world, chew it, swallow it all. And afterwards, leave her mark. "None of us are going to get married," she explained. "Why should we? We can do anything we want without it. It's just not necessary anymore."

"Don't you want to have children, though?" asked Rosemary in a very small voice.

"I don't know. Maybe. I want to do everything there is to do, so, sure, someday I might want to have a child, too. But you don't need to be married to have children anymore. Things are different now, Mom."

Daisy turned away. Across the bulging pile of clothes and books and mementos in the steamer trunk she laid Aunt Jessica's newest hand-knit sweater, a wide-shouldered, intricately patterned graduation present of deep tawny wool. She had intended not to take it because the neck was funny, but at the last minute she decided the color was too rich and becoming to leave behind.

When she tried to close the trunk by sitting on the lid, the latch wouldn't catch. She rested. "When I think of the future," she said, leaning back on her strong arms and turning her rosy face to the window, "I try to picture myself an old lady, looking back. I'm sixty years old, tough, wrinkled, and satisfied that whatever else may have happened, at least I chose my own life and did what I wanted to do and never gave up and just got married."

Rosemary was amazed to hear Nora's voice rise from the trunk and exit through the mouth of her very own child, especially since, as far as she could remember, they had never actually discussed this question together. Not that she was disappointed; she wouldn't dream of predicting what course her children's lives would take (*Corollary #2: everything, everything, must be possible*), much less what course was for the best. One could do a lot worse than turn out like Nora. But she did wonder where the voice had come from and how it had entered Daisy.

"You may be right," she said vaguely, upholding her first commitment to give support no matter what; "but don't be disappointed, sweetheart," she added cautiously, "if someday you find you've changed your mind."

The house phone buzzer blasts. "I'll get it!" shouts Spider from another room. In a moment a door slams and footsteps gallop down the hall.

"Oh my God, they're coming up for the trunk, and we're not even ready. Quick, Mom, please—help me sit on this."

Spider leads a brawny Federal Express man into the box-strewn living room to find his mother and sister bouncing on the trunk in unison. "Jesus," says Spider, whacking his head, "this place is a reglear circus."

"Regular," corrects Daisy. "How come," she muses, turning to her mother, "he says *reglear* instead of *regular*, but he can't say *nuclear* instead of *nukular*? It doesn't make any sense."

"We all," says Rosemary protectively, "do a lot of things that don't make sense."

Spider's lips begin forming words subvocally, lighting a gleam of sudden comprehension behind his sparkling, widening eyes. *Nukular. Regular.*

When the Federal Express man shifts his weight from one foot to the other, Daisy, remembering the trunk, begins bouncing again. "Come on, Spider," she calls, "don't just stand there like a dope. Help us."

Spider elbows his way between the two women and sits down hard.

"Ready?" says Rosemary, raising a finger. "Okay. Uh-one, uh-two, uh-three—" But before they can force closed the overflowing trunk, they're all doubled over, laughing.

Next

36

DAISY TURNED the handle and pushed, but the door wouldn't give. When she'd lived at home, they'd always left it unlatched, but now it was locked. How quickly things change. She felt spurned, forgotten—until she remembered that they weren't expecting her plane to land for four more hours.

She lowered her pack to the floor, checked her lipstick in the hall mirror, and rang the bell. Spider opened the door with a big black beard.

"My God!" cried Daisy, peering up into the familiar face. Behind the new glasses and the beard was Spider. With—Daisy saw it for the first time—their father in his face.

A satisfied smirk spread across Spider's lips. He crossed his arms and tilted his chin, giving her a three-quarter Abe Lincoln pose. "What do you think?"

Daisy took in her little brother, inches taller than everyone, looking grown-up, solid, suddenly dark. Junior, going on Senior. Still stretched and skinny, but now . . . substantial, like someone to be reckoned with. The beard: there was something immodest about it, something embarrassing. The way it differed from his familiar, appropriate head hair. The way it called attention to itself. It didn't go. It wasn't brown but black— or rather, with its perverse smattering of shockingly orange-tinted hairs, off-black. It was big, bushy, and obscene.

"I expected punk, maybe. Not this. You look like Daddy."

Spider scowled. "How? He never had a beard."

Daisy smiled a message but added, "Aren't you going to trim it?"

"I thought I'd let it just grow for a while, see what develops before I decide what to do. What about you?" he said, feigning a punch to her chest. "Aren't you going to trim that?" He ducked and ran up the hall.

"Everything's changed!" cried Daisy in the living room, clapping her hands to her cheeks.

"Yeah. Mom took a bunch of stuff to her apartment. Ages ago."

Tears flooded Daisy's eyes. "Everything's changed!" she repeated. She knew as well as anyone of her generation that marriage doesn't last forever. In California everyone's parents were divorced. Half her college housemates had married after graduation, and half of them were already divorced. But she'd always felt her family was different. Her mother had been proud of their closeness, and her father too, she could tell, they were in love right up to the day she left for school. She blinked hard and looked at the empty shelves. "Where are the books?"

"This is nothing. Wait till you see the dining room. If there's stuff you want, you better get it now, before everything goes."

"Even *my* things?"

"You think they sent you an airline ticket just because my school's playing in Carnegie Hall? Unh unh. Dad says this week is the week we have to go through our stuff and save what we want. After New Year's everything gets thrown out."

"Out!" In California, where, to ensure her freedom, she'd taken a job after graduation as far from home as possible, she had one sunny room in a share. Where could she put everything? Unless she moved in with Michael. And even then . . . If she has a baby . . .

"And they're selling the piano."

"Why?"

"Same reason they got rid of Gorky. Too big, no place to put it anymore." He moves toward the kitchen. "You want a beer?"

In California, she'd grown all her fingernails but one and given up fish and finally learned to like coffee; but she still dislikes beer. "No thanks," she threw back as she lifted her pack and hurried down the hall toward her childhood room.

Nora brushed her fingers through her hair, sending a cascade of bracelets jingling up her slender arm. She wore twice as many bracelets as before she went to Paris and a fraction of the hair, now cropped close to her shapely head, revealing a minor collection of tiny earrings.

Rosemary was nervous to be sitting in a restaurant when Daisy was coming home that very afternoon. With some last-minute shopping still to do and dinner to cook, she'd have preferred to meet Nora the next day, when Mrs. Scaggs was coming in and Spider's concert was over, even though she hasn't seen her friend in a year. But Nora insisted on today, saying she had two free hours before she had to leave for the airport, otherwise they'd have to wait another week. Nora's flying to Denver, where someone has promised to give her documented evidence of a mountainful of untended nuclear waste—evidence she's spent years searching for. A tremendous story if it's true. "I think I've hit a lucky streak. If this stuff is what I think it is, and if I handle it right, who knows? It might even force a major policy change. I'm very excited—this could be really big. In fact, I probably shouldn't even discuss it in case I jinx it." Her eyes glittered as she looked around for ears. "First I finish my book, then I come back to this. And you too, Rosemary, you seem to have gotten lucky too. A full-time job teaching courses you really like, and your own apartment. At last! I tell you, the night I read your letter I rode up the Eiffel Tower and toasted you in champagne. How'd it all happen?"

"All it took was a new dean. That, and having stuck around long enough. This one cares about teaching. He's appointed a committee on gender discrimination in the sciences, and besides me, he's looking to hire two more women."

"Tell me honestly," said Nora, lighting a clove cigarette and leaning forward, "now that you know what it's like to belong to yourself, aren't you sorry you waited so long to make the break?"

"Not at all."

Suppressing her guffaw, Nora swallowed smoke. It was inconceivable to her that anyone pressed into domestic service for twenty-some years could finally escape without regretting the wasted years—certainly not an intelligent, spirited woman like Rosemary, restricted to chancy jobs and secret affairs, and that husband—but she'd never get her to admit it. When she'd finished coughing, she fixed Rosemary with her famous stare and asked, "Why not?"

"Because raising my children was the very best thing in my life. We were a good family. While they were growing up I was doing just what I wanted to be doing."

Nora tried to invoke her principle that people believe in the points of view they express. All the same, she had to think Rosemary was lying, if only to herself. "And math? Didn't you want to be doing that?"

"Yes, but I didn't have time then. Now I'll probably go back for my Ph.D."

"Great!" cheered Nora, though she couldn't resist adding, "but think of all the time you lost."

Now it was Rosemary's turn to laugh. When she was married and had her family to oversee, Rosemary was secretly proud of everything she accomplished that was extra; she'd pitied her single friends, with their opposite agendas, wasting so much time in their endless search for mates. "I didn't lose time," she explained. "If anything, I gained it. I wasn't ready to be free till my kids grew up."

"But in the end, your marriage failed anyway."

"Not at all. I consider my marriage one of the more successful specimens around."

"Rosemary! How can you say that? You're getting divorced!"

"Only legally." Rosemary squeezed out her rose-spice teabag and laid it in her saucer. "Harold and I have a very strong tie. We're family. That can't ever end. We have children together, it's an indissoluble bond. For us, divorce is simply marriage by other means."

Nora put on a face intended to shame, eyebrow up, mouth puckered, the one she turned on corruption, hypocrisy, and sentiment. But Rosemary, far from being sorry or ashamed, was proud she'd waited to divorce. In fact, the more difficult her marriage, the greater her pride in having found a way to stick it out.

Daisy gets her hairbrush out of her pack and returns to the living room. She brushes her hair in long, even strokes, looking out the window, waiting for her mother.

Spider fiddles with the stereo. He wants to tell Daisy it's really their mother's fault that they have to break up their home and move, but he knows she'll take her side. Sure they should get divorced if that's what they want to do, it doesn't matter to him, but where's he supposed to go over his vacations? He can't see why, if they managed to stay together for twenty-three years, they can't at least wait till he graduates, the way they did for Daisy. They split up once and got back together, they could do it again if they wanted to. At least for a couple more years. He tunes in jazz from Newark, New Jersey, turns up the volume, and sits down with his beer.

"That's the same beer Michael drinks," says Daisy. "It's Mexican."

"Who's Michael?"

"A very good friend."

Daisy wishes she could tell Spider she's pregnant and watch his beard drop. But till she decides what she's going to do, she can't tell anyone. Especially not her family, who would pepper her with abortionists. No. This decision is hers alone. She thinks she might like to have the baby, but she doesn't think she wants to get married, she'd be too ashamed. That's why she hasn't even told Michael. Her friends all swore they'd never marry, began defecting one by one, and one by one have gotten divorced. Not that she believes you have to be married to have a baby; for herself, she'd like to have it alone and show the world. But would it really be fair to the baby? How would she support it alone? Her great job counseling at the Child Abuse Center in San Jose is threatened by funding cuts, and if she loses her job, how can she risk having a baby? Her work, though intense, sustains her; she intends to go on working as some sort of advocate forever. But how, if she has a baby? Everything's possible! shouts her mother's voice in her head, routing each vacillation. Maybe if she takes a year-long maternity leave while Michael supports them, they won't be able to lay her off. If she could only find good, cheap day care.

She looks at Spider drumming on his bony legs. His head bonks from side to side, keeping the main beat; his right foot pounds the floor while his hands blur on his thighs. "Since when have you been into jazz?" she asks, laying her hairbrush on the mantel.

"One of my roommates freshman year played tenor, and sometimes we fooled around. Then he got a couple of guys in the orchestra to jam with us." Spider can't tell Daisy how jazz, like road maps, can make you forget; he barely knows it himself. "Did you know Dad's got a really great collection of jazz records?"

"Yeah? I bet *they're* not getting thrown out." Surveying the barren room, she swears that when and if she decides to get married it will be forever. Otherwise, as her mother always said, what's the point? Now her mother too has abandoned her.

One thing she knows for sure: she'll never risk having a baby without a job.

"I'd have thought Paris would be nothing but distractions," said Rosemary, "but you found the time to write a book."

"Yes, and with a month to spare. It feels as if I got more done in one year in France than in five years before at home."

"I'm afraid all I managed to do while you were away was kick coffee," said Rosemary.

"What do you mean? You're finally teaching full-time and you're getting divorced. That's quite an achievement."

"But I still haven't proven a single new mathematical principle. That's why I'm going back to school. You, on the other hand, just keep on outdoing yourself."

"That's because the French took me seriously. They were interested in my work. Not like here. Here, no one cares what I think, only if my stuff will sell, the rest is hype—so I have to spend half my time hustling. In France it was the opposite. They wanted to know what I think. So I thought. And I told them. And they loved me for it. I worked all week, played all weekend. Work and love. It was glorious."

"So there's a man?"

"Was," said Nora, lighting another cigarette. "That man I wrote you about when I first got there, the actor with the Comédie-Française."

"What happened?"

"Ah," said Nora, blowing a smoke ring, "what happened. The unanswerable question. But I'll try. He was wonderful to me at first. Very charming, very gallant. We spent a lot of weekends together going all over Paris, the restaurants, the opera, dancing, the galleries—he showed me the whole artistic life of the city. He was the perfect man to be with there, and the sex was remarkable. I thought, after Lex died and Keith dropped out of the picture, I was finally getting what I needed. But since I was working hard day and night on my book I mainly saw him on weekends. Well, can't you guess what happened?"

"Tell me."

"I discovered that he had another woman—and she was living at his apartment!"

"Not another married man!"

"No, but he might as well have been. At first I didn't believe it when I found out. I just couldn't understand it. When I confronted him, he told me she didn't mean nearly as much to him as I did. Then why is she living with you? I asked. I would have accepted almost any answer, believe me. I refuse to be possessive, and I really liked that man. But you know what he said?"

Rosemary shook her head.

"He said, You can only be with me on weekends, and what am I supposed to do the other five nights of the week?"

When the meaning finally registered, Rosemary burst out laughing. They both whooped with laughter till the tears came. When they stopped to catch their breath, Nora repeated, "What was I supposed to do the other five nights of the week?" and they rocked the table with their laughter again.

Nora raised her chin and soberly blew a set of concentric smoke rings. "I'm beginning to see that if you're not with them on their terms, sooner or later you won't be with them at all. It was the same with Keith, too, when you come right down to it, just a different time frame."

"How do you mean?"

"There we were, together for three years, commuting between Santa Fe and New York, talking every other day, taking vacations together, everything. I thought we had a pretty good arrangement since we each had an independent life and at the same time we had each other. I thought we were a new kind of couple. What a relief it was after the torment of sneaking around with Lex. Then, when I got the invitation to go to France for a year and I said I was going to accept, he started to withdraw from me. He warned me that we wouldn't survive that kind of separation. It was as if he were saying, what am I supposed to do the other twelve months of the year? You see? So . . . one minute we're like this, and the next he stops answering my letters. Well, what was *I* supposed to do—not go to France? I'm just glad I was in a place where I could work and not think about him."

Rosemary shook her head. "I don't understand men."

"Neither do I. They *can't* be as simple as they seem," said Nora.

"I'm afraid they can. Or rather, they're only as interesting as we make them by the hard work of drawing them out."

"And then listening," added Nora caustically. "If I weren't such a dummy maybe I could have figured it out. Of course he met someone else. He wasn't a man to be alone. When I got back I called him up—just to see what he'd say. A woman answered. The old story. One person's meat is another one's mate."

Once again, Rosemary was amazed and somewhat awed by Nora's intractable innocence that saw weakness in every compromise. She herself would certainly have known the price of leaving an attractive man alone for a year. Though she couldn't help admiring her friend, even more she pitied her.

Seeing the old pity in Rosemary's eyes, Nora snuffed out her cigarette, ran her fingers through her cropped hair, lifted her head proudly, and said, "No, Rosemary, don't worry about me. He may have got himself another woman, but I've got my life. My integrity."

"Of course you have," said Rosemary, rushing in with support. "It's just too bad it always has to be such a struggle."

Nora took in Rosemary and slowly shook her head. Even after five years of intimacy Rosemary still didn't seem to get it. Would probably never get it. For Nora, integrity was its own reward, and the greater the struggle to maintain it, the more rewarded she felt. "Struggle is what I thrive on," she tried to explain. "It's what keeps me alive. When I stop struggling to preserve my integrity, that's when you'll know I've sold out. Then you can pity me, even write me off, anything. But not yet."

"Of course, Nora. But still—you, of all people, deserve—"

"No," Nora interrupted. She waited to catch Rosemary's eye, then insistently repeated, "No. I have what I deserve." A satisfied smile spread over her face until it began to glow. "The important thing is I finished my book."

37

Harold huddles in his overcoat in a phone booth on the highway and dials. He's forgotten his travel code so he calls collect.

When the telephone rings, Daisy and Spider look at each other and race to the hall. Spider slides to the desk and, pressing his forearm sharply against his middle, jackknifes himself in a gallant bow, allowing Daisy to pick up the phone.

"Go on, Daisy," says Harold, "tell her you'll accept the call. It's me."

"Yes, operator. Daddy!"

"So you made it home!" shouts Harold into the receiver over a caravan of long-distance vans. "Aren't you early? Lucky I didn't plan to meet your plane. Look, I'm still in Connecticut. I'm going to try to get home for dinner, but just in case, you better go ahead without me. Tell your mother if I don't make it I'll join you at the hall, I've got my ticket. Can't wait to see you, honey."

Daisy hides her disappointment as she faces Spider. "That was Daddy, saying he'll be late."

"It figures. He'll be late for his own funeral." As Spider looks at his watch, Harold looks at his, retrieves his quarter, and walks back to his car. "I hope he makes the concert," says Spider. "I've got a six-bar solo in our first piece."

"He was calling from the road, so he'll probably make it," reassures Daisy.

"Listen, I've got to pick up my tux on Forty-ninth Street. You want to come with me?"

"When's Mom getting here?"

"Come with me. We'll walk. Then she'll be here when we get back."

. . .

With his knee guiding the wheel, Harold wiggles out of his coat, throws it in the backseat, refastens his seat belt, adjusts the speakers, and opens up. Having warned them to start dinner without him, he feels easy about the time—in fact, virtuous: Rosemary always swore she wouldn't mind his being late as long as he called to let her know. Now that traffic's finally moving along at sixty-five, leaving him plenty of time to spare, he decides to treat himself to another cup of coffee.

Since his first advanced Yale seminar five years before, Harold has driven this road at least a hundred times. As the distance between his class-room and home is eighty-four miles, he persists in believing the driving time is one and a half hours, the optimum, despite its having taken almost twice as long as that more than thirty percent of the time. If he were to drive straight through instead of stopping, he would easily pass a certain forty-foot-long, blue-striped trailer, now half a mile ahead of him, before it comes uncoupled from its cab. But having thrown down two silver bullets at his Press Club lunch before leaving New Haven, Harold wants that coffee. (Nothing more, not even a slice of pie, since Rosemary's doing a special dinner.) He pulls into the next turnoff, a truck stop.

At the first curve, cab and blue-striped trailer part company. The un-fortunate trailer, with its full cargo of lumber, rolls to a spectacular stop, spilling two-by-fours like Pic-Up Stix all over the highway. Luckily, the driver of the cab, which rolls free of the wreck, will sustain only minor injuries, but traffic will halt completely for over an hour while medics stream forth from ambulances and troopers with radios swarm around till another truck and crew arrive to remove the lumber. Thirty minutes will pass before the State Highway Patrol can even get a man to the Milford Exit to divert traffic to the Merritt Parkway, where it will creep along bumper to bumper all the way into Manhattan.

While he's flipping through magazines at the turnoff, Harold is com-pletely unsuspecting that the trailer rolling fatefully to a halt three miles ahead can have anything to do with him. He, like the unfortunate driver who had expected to collect his pay at the end of the run and spend the night with his girl friend in Brooklyn, will consider this accident a major disaster, one of a kind, though in fact, this heavily trafficked highway supports an average of ten disasters every week. Harold sucks his teeth, pays, picks up two toothpicks, and returns to the car.

. . .

Rosemary unwraps the peonies, and immediately the scent begins to brighten the kitchen, just as if most of the dishes, including the tall vase suitable for long-stemmed flowers, weren't packed in boxes stacked against the north wall of the dining room. With her chef's knife she cuts an inch off the stems and arranges the giant blooms in a gallon apple-juice jar.

She inserts slivers of garlic in the lamb, Spider's favorite, puts it in the oven to roast, then assembles an artichoke quiche for Daisy and tries not to think of her own life as it might have been. If she'd traded that pressing safety for a flight of freedom . . . Sometimes, when she least expects it, an image of the possible past, of all her lost opportunities, assaults her with such sudden force that she has to bury her head in her arms to shield herself from the violent blow. If she and Harold had been divorced even after Italy instead of now, if she'd stayed with Peter . . . But she knows better than to regret.

After fifteen years in this apartment most of the everyday dishes are marred or chipped. That's life. (She's taking the silver and the copper pots, Harold's keeping the good dishes.) She's pleased to see that the four dinner plates left unpacked are perfect ones. As she sets the table she sends up a tribute to Mrs. Scaggs—or whichever one of Harold's girl friends is helping him pack. Only when she discovers the children's handmade tiles and trivets gone from the bottom drawer where they belong does she feel herself sinking again. Harold *can't* have thrown them out!—yet nothing else in that drawer has been disturbed. This is the man she stayed with all those years? But this breach only proves the more how her children needed her. No regrets: she couldn't have borne her life if she'd put her pleasure ahead of them. She sets a potholder on the table for the peonies.

Now, seeing she's alone, she decides to search inside the fireside lamps one final time. Her pulse races, but this time she's less worried than curious, and, recalling the enormities of married life, even amused. (Once a marriage ends, how easily the parties slip over to the other side, where truths become lies and lies become truths: from *Always* to *Never!* and back again—almost as simple as *I do.* How quickly the honored web gets whisked away.) Once this divorce is over, Rosemary thinks her own secrets will no longer need to be kept—except maybe from the children. She lifts the tops off the kerosene chambers—first the left one, then the right—and peers inside.

Both empty. No trace of riches or loss, sorrow or guilt. Not even an outraged note.

Suddenly she notices Daisy's hairbrush on the mantel. She's home! But where?

Rosemary's heart contracts. Daisy!

"Shit!" cries Spider, as an evil mote invades his right eye.

"Don't rub it," says Daisy.

Spider stops walking, removes his glasses, and carefully pulls the top eyelid over the bottom one. "The whole city's fucking polluted," he says.

"Don't say that," says Daisy. "Michael, my friend in Santa Cruz, says you shouldn't go around insulting the world, calling it polluted. He says that's blasphemy. Want me to take a look?"

With pure Rosemary care she looks in his eye. Mysterious, moist sphere in a milky, green-flecked universe. Precious protoplasm.

"I don't see a thing, Spider."

"Anyway, I think it's out now."

They zip up their jackets and proceed down Third Avenue. To Daisy the air is exhilarating, especially when gusts go whipping through the cross streets. The great array of faces, styles, and body types gives her a nervous high. If she moved back here, her fingernails would probably go in a week. Every block a movie, a deli, a newsstand, a grocer, a bar. How come she never noticed before? She checks the headlines, the marquees. Housewives fondle fruit while their babies bawl. Everyone says it's dangerous to raise a baby in New York City. If she could talk it over with her mother—but why upset her or invite advice?

"You should see Dad," says Spider. "He started smoking again. He's up to a pack a day. This divorce—I think it's getting to him."

"What are you talking about? He always smoked a pack a day."

"You're crazy. He stopped for years."

"Only in front of you."

"How do you know?"

Daisy looks at him. "Everybody knew except you."

Rosemary walks nervously to the window. Where is everyone? This apartment, no longer home, feels cold. Clutter of decades is neatly boxed against the walls. Soon it will be gone. With Peter it was a fast, clean good-bye, but Harold was her mate of more than twenty years! There's no wood for a fire, and not even the smell of roasting lamb can disguise the obvious. The children will know everything as soon as they walk in the room, if they don't already know.

Still, she's glad they decided to sell while the market's high, sweep everything clean; glad Harold is moving away. After all these years, her own money will be enough and she'll have empty drawers to fill again. She turns on the stereo and finds Bach. Then she pours herself a glass of wine and walks back to the window to wait for her children.

Below, a small, yappy terrier bounds behind a couple pulling a sledful of toddlers down the middle of the street. And suddenly she recalls the exact shocking moment fifteen years before at Beaver Hill Park when she first understood how ineluctable, how uncontrollable, how finally unstoppable is the unfolding of a life.

Spider was cranky all through the trip, provoking Harold twice to slam on his brakes, pull over, and roar at Daisy in the backseat.

Taking her baby in her lap, Rosemary sings to him, wipes his nose, kisses his cheeks, plays one-potato-two-potato, feeds him quartered apples and animal crackers. Still Spider fusses and whines.

At last they reach Beaver Hill. Harold parks, gets out the sleds. Daisy, with Harold beside her, lugs her new Red Rider across the snowy lot toward the path while Rosemary stays behind, helping Spider on with his mittens. When she's tied his red scarf around his chin, she sets him on the toboggan and begins the long trudge up. Halfway to the top, she stops beside a lone fir tree. Sun lights the snow. Rosemary sits on the toboggan and takes Spider in her lap, facing down. "Ready?" she says. He continues to sulk. "Then here we go!" she cries, pushing off.

Down they start. She holds him tight, stealing hopeful glances at his awakening face. The toboggan grazes the ground, picks up speed, hops lightly over bumps, flies. Spider's curious grunts become wild joyous shouts, terror-edged, as they whip along. She catches it—pure joy.

When they reach the bottom, where she digs in her heels and stops, she grins into his astonished face, echoing his giddy laugh.

"More, Mommy," he shouts. He sits on the toboggan, feet straight out, and folds his small arms imperiously across his chest shouting, "More! More! MORE!"

. . .

Three bearded Spiders in tuxes stare awkwardly out of the three-way mirror. Spider makes faces while Daisy chooses his studs and tie. He squints at his shoes, frowns at his cuffs. "How are the sleeves?" he asks skeptically, imagining the flirtatious cellist in the row in front of him whom he'd like to impress. "You think they're long enough?"

Daisy looks him up and down. "I have to admit, Spider," she says, smiling, "you do clean up well."

Spider loses his frown. When he's back in his jeans he fills in Harold's signed check with the rental fee plus twenty dollars he takes back as cash.

They stop for a cone before turning uptown. "Spider," says Daisy, despite herself, wiping ice cream from her brother's mustache, "if you're going to go to all the trouble of renting a tux for this concert, don't you think maybe you should trim your beard?"

38

At the last possible moment Rosemary carries in the lamb and sets it at Harold's empty place. She sharpens the carving knife, closing her ears to the whine of steel on steel, hoping he may still appear. Daisy brings in the quiche, Spider the salad.

"I knew he'd be late," says Spider, dropping into his seat.

"It's nothing. He's always late," consoles Daisy.

"You can't tell, he still might get here," says Rosemary, shining her best possible smile on everything. "But even if he doesn't, you mustn't feel bad, honey. Traffic can be fierce." (Traffic indeed! Not for a minute does she believe he's caught in traffic. All the same, she covers for Harold, though she's no longer obliged to.) "Anyway, better he misses dinner than the concert."

The more cheer Rosemary aims for, the edgier everyone feels, even though they don't yet realize that this is the last dinner together in their family home the Streeters will ever get to eat. Tomorrow Spider's orchestra leaves on tour for the Midwest, and by the time he returns Daisy will be back in California. Then the movers will disperse their worldly goods like birds spreading seeds, and the secrets hidden behind mirrors or tucked away in books (some now earmarked for charity) will return to dust. Those in the Streeters' hearts will follow each of them home, never to meet again, and no Streeter will benefit from the knowledge the others have so carefully laid by. As in every family before them, Daisy will bring forth her children in pain and learn about marriage the hard way; Spider will earn his bread by the sweat of his brow and the corruption of his convictions. Rosemary will act as if no one suffers for the family's sake, not even herself; and Harold, arriving late, will shake his head, wondering how it all happened.

The Last Dinner . . .

Spider cuts an oversized piece of Daisy's quiche for himself while Daisy circulates, pouring wine. Seeing her quiche on Spider's plate, Daisy retaliates by brimming his glass. "Just a drop for me, thanks," says Rosemary, two glasses down already. "I want to hear every note of this concert. Spider, are you sure you ought to have wine tonight?"

"You should see what Herschel slipped me last night and I didn't get drunk," says Spider.

"Frankie Herschel?" asks Daisy, sitting down. "Whatever happened to him?"

"He went to Bennington. I mean, he started at Bennington, but he's taking time off. Right now he's a waiter at the West End. Which is great for me 'cause he can get me into the Jazz Room free."

Daisy rolls her eyes toward her mother. "What an obnoxious little kid he was."

"He couldn't stand you, either."

Now, children, please don't fight, Rosemary wants to say, though they're both of age. Instead, she goes along. "Wasn't he the one who used to leave those pictures of eyeballs with fishhooks sticking through them around the house?"

"To scare me," says Daisy. "He was so gross. I feel sorry for his wife. If anyone ever marries him."

"Jesus!" says Spider, spearing a piece of lamb. "That's all you and your friends ever thought about. Getting married."

"How would you know?"

Spider smiles. "I've got it on tape."

During the main course and second helpings the conversation trips through gossip, slides over insults, as if this were any other meal. Spider gobbles his lamb without spilling a drop of resentment; Daisy, slightly nauseated, picks at her food, concealing her newest appetites. And Rosemary, hoping to set an example by pretending anyone can lose a home with jovial equanimity—you see?—lets slip away their last crucial chance to examine the past before they're forced to leave this garden.

Not until dessert do they finally understand:

"So tell us, Spider," says Rosemary, serving their all-time favorite fudge cake from the Budapest Bakery, "what cities are you going to?"

"Tomorrow night we play Pittsburgh. Then Cleveland, then Chicago for two days, then St. Paul—"

Daisy puts down her fork. "You mean you're leaving *tomorrow?*"

"Yes. When are you leaving?"

"Monday."

"Too bad, sweetheart," cries Rosemary, reaching out a hand. She looks at Harold's empty chair. The peonies nod like Pagliaccis. "Here I thought you were going to try to take some vacation time. It is Christmas, after all, and you get home so seldom." (No one questions her use of *home*.) "We've hardly begun to visit."

"Look, I'm missing two days of work as it is," defends Daisy, as if her job were the reason she must leave. For a moment she imagines coming clean—showing the clock ticking, the cells dividing. She's sure her mother would love Michael, with his artistic nature and his M.A., and Spider would be absolutely flabbergasted. But this is one decision she must make entirely by herself.

"So then I guess I won't be seeing you for a while," says Spider, suddenly sorry. Now he'll have no one to help him through this smiley divorce. "Unless maybe we get to play the Coast over spring break. . . . Too bad about Daddy. . . ."

"Oh, darling, I'm sure he'll be at the concert," reassures Rosemary, checking her watch.

But now it's late! Now, when the truth might out, it's time to rush. Spider's due backstage in twenty-five minutes. Since Harold has the car, they'll have to grab a taxi—if they can find one, now that it's begun to snow. "Do you have the tickets?" asks Daisy as she begins clearing the table. "Call us if you need help with the studs," says Rosemary. Spider eats his last bite of cake standing, then dashes to his room to dress.

The Second Tape . . .

He's so self-centered, he'd make an awful husband. He'd never talk about anything but himself and his great ideas. It'd be so boring.

But he is good-looking.

Very.

Do you think some poor girl would fall in love with him without knowing, just because of his looks?

Yeah, and if he loved her back, maybe it wouldn't be so bad.

Oh, come on! It'd be awful! I'd feel really sorry for his poor wife. He'd never listen to a word she said. And if she ever had kids, God, she'd be stuck with him.

They'd be awfully pretty kids, though.

That wouldn't help.

But now, Kenny, he's going to make someone a great husband.

Why?

He always does what he says he's going to do. And he wouldn't go out drinking every night, and he'd pay attention to his wife and try to understand her.

It's true. I can talk about anything with Kenny.

Yeah, sometimes when we're talking I think of him almost like one of us.

Me too.

Would you want to marry him though?

No, I could never.

Why not?

He's too fat.

When Harold finally crawls onto the Merritt, he hears his family reproach him for being late. Always the same: accusations or suspicions whenever he comes home—starting the day he got married. How come they're so willing to blame the victim? For God's sake, there was an accident. How could he possibly have done anything about it? He was drinking a cup of coffee at the time, he didn't even order a piece of pie, that's how sure he was he'd make it home to dinner. How can they blame him for a disaster that was completely beyond his control? No wonder they're getting divorced!

. . .

The conductor strides in from the wings and the applause begins.

"Oh dear, he didn't make it, he's going to miss Spider's solo," says Rosemary, searching the aisles for Harold. She squelches the triumphant *You see?* that lies lurking behind her disappointment.

"If he just gets here before the end, maybe Spider won't even have to know," offers Daisy. "Look, Mom"—Daisy pulls her mother's sleeve and muffles a guffaw—"Spider's foot."

Spider feels his irritation in his feet. It's his night, still his mother and sister are giggling, in cahoots, and his father's not there. He feels his blood rise to his face as the conductor raises his baton, commanding the perfect attention of sixty-some eyes. Spider licks his lips, taps his foot, raises his horn to his hirsute mouth.

Rosemary watches him, holding her breath. By concentrating all her attention on his face, she will be able to beam his instrument straight to her ears.

Spider glues his eyes to the eyes of the conductor, expands his focus to the pursed mouth, the elevated eyebrows, the expectant body, the raised baton. Maybe he'll be a conductor himself one day. Twelve opening bars, a trill from the strings, then the conductor looks at him, lowers his arm, and a long, uplifting note, sweet as grapes, rises out of Spider's horn to fill Carnegie Hall.

Rosemary's eyes lock on her son. She forgets that over Christmas half the college orchestras in the East have their shot at fame, remembers only that it's Spider Streeter soloing in Carnegie Hall.

Harold hurries up the stairs into the lobby, carrying his coat. Faint strains of music echo around him. It bursts forth, sonorous and rich, as he slips inside the doors and waits along the back wall for his eyes to adjust to the dark. The orchestra is playing something atonal, mournful, that resonates through the half-empty hall.

As soon as he's able to see, he takes the first aisle seat he comes to and scans the front rows for his women. He mops his brow. Sets of heads in twos and threes come into focus, but no Rosemary, no Daisy. Satisfied, he turns his eyes to the stage, zeroes in on the brass, focuses down on the trumpets, until he finds the dark curly crown and winter beard of his only son.

39

Continental Divide . . .

Halfway across the continent, Nora stuffs the brown hotel bath mat with its beige-lettered *Continental* into her suitcase, then rides the elevator down to the main dining room to re-enact one central moment in the drama of her life.

As it's still early, she asks for a table in the very center of the room. She takes her time with the menu, selecting the most delicious meal she can in honor of that banner day a decade before. Not the day her first story was published, nor the day her first by-line appeared, not the day she signed her first book contract, or gave her first public lecture, or was cited in the *Congressional Record,* or even the day the Petersen Prize was announced, for each of those triumphs turned on someone else's decision. No, the event she considers her watershed depended on nothing and no one but herself.

She had come to the hotel to do her first interview with a general, a man in charge of a big nuclear installation. It was an assignment she'd schemed for, and she'd allowed herself an extra day to rest up and do some last-minute homework before meeting the big man the next morning. She disguised the discomfort she always felt alone in hotels, like the beginnings of a mild headache, by gazing at the famous stained-glass sky-lit ceiling above the lobby, surveying the wallpapers and mahogany paneling, running her fingers over the plump period furniture—as if to assure the world she had some legitimate reason for being in the lobby alone at cocktail hour among all those tall, convivial, booted western couples. But after a quick tour she fled to her room to work. A good room: she was pleased with the large picture of an American Indian, blanket-clad and dignified, above her bed and the tastefully draped window framing a spacious Colorado sky over jagged mountain peaks.

She hung up her clothes and unpacked her papers. But when it came to dinner, though the hotel boasted five dining rooms, she decided, with the trepidation she had felt all her life at eating alone in public, to skip it. Instead, she filled the tub to steaming, added a packet of the hotel's pine bath oil, soaked herself bright pink, and climbed into bed with a pile of notes.

When she woke some hours later, she was ravenous. The room was dark; out the window the cerulean sky had deepened to midnight blue, and only the snowy caps of the highest peaks of the continental divide were visible beneath the moon. She studied it, that hulking nonnegotiable mass where all the waters of the continent divided to flow to one great ocean or the other. She shivered. Perhaps she'd work better if she ordered up a snack. But as she perused the room-service menu, the picture of the dining room with its green banquettes and bright chandeliers caught her eye. Okay: she'd stand herself a trip downstairs, taking her research with her.

She'd forgotten it was Saturday night. She made her way through the lobby crowded with carousing weekenders to the main dining room and waited to be seated behind parties of couples and foursomes. Beyond the entrance arch she saw a well-proportioned room, high-ceilinged but cozy, filled with buoyant diners. Fresh flowers brightened every table; busy waiters carried trays aloft to the rhythms of live blues drifting in from the bar. How many? asked the captain, and Nora replied for the first time in her life without a trace of apology: Just one.

That was it. Just one.

The captain led her to a small round table in the center of the room. When he pulled out her chair, she felt neither patronized nor pitied. She needn't even have brought along her notes; her magazine was paying her to be here. She let her eyes roam unashamedly over the room and linger wherever they happened to light. She lay her room key on top of the superfluous notebook. When the waiter had removed the extra place setting and left her the menu, instead of ordering her habitual fast sandwich and coffee that would spring her more quickly from scrutiny, she flipped slowly through the leather-bound offerings, taking her time.

She deliberated; she asked for the wine list. It was one thing to grab a sandwich alone in a New York deli, quite another to occupy a center table solo in a land of couples. But what did she care if everyone in the dining room stared at her? They were mistaken. That night it happened she had every reason to be there, better reasons than they; if they knew, they would no doubt envy her her assignment. Her confidence surged, as if she suddenly knew how to breathe under water. She rejoiced in her power. She studied the menu. She chose carefully, ordering all the courses for herself, all the specialties, and a split of Saint-Estèphe. As the waiters delivered new dishes to her table and departed with the old, she knew she would never again dread eating alone. And the food—never had food tasted better.

The next morning the general—brass polished, pate gleaming, nails buffed—leaned eagerly into her mike to tell her all.

As the players drifted in from backstage, euphoria bubbled through the room like air through seltzer. On the bar side of the room, proud parents, suppressing for an hour their secret anxieties, inflated their children's accomplishments to one another, while on the stage side the young people, feeling the inadequacy of their own achievements (despite their formal clothes), vied to top each other's anxieties. The males looked half like penguins, half like bridegrooms, while the females, with their long black skirts, shining eyes, and flowing Pre-Raphaelite hair, played their costumes along with their instruments for all they were worth.

"Harold!" said Rosemary from behind him. "We were so afraid you wouldn't even make the concert. We looked for you at intermission. What in the world kept you?"

She wasn't his wife anymore, he didn't have to say. "I made it though, didn't I?"

"You did," she conceded.

He pressed his advantage. "Don't I always?"

She smiled charmingly. "Not quite always."

"It happens," he said, raising his chin officiously, "that there was a big pileup near Milford. A truck turned over. Several people may have been killed, I was damn lucky to escape. As it was, I had to take the Merritt. It was backed up all the way to the bridge." Taken in by his own embellishments, he extends himself all the sympathy his wife and the world withhold.

"Well, at least you made the reception. Spider will be so relieved. Have you seen him yet?"

Spider saw his father crossing over to his side of the room carrying a tall glass. He wondered how to shed quickly, without offending, the petite cellist listening rapt at his side whom he'd just as soon not introduce to his family. For sure they'd foul it up. With an astute half-turn and a timely opinion, he slipped into a nearby conversation, leaving Elizabeth Ann looking around surprised.

At the hors d'oeuvres table, Rosemary was listening to Elizabeth Ann's father deplore the difficulties facing women musicians. "You'd think that in a field where talent really counts, they would have stopped discriminating by now," he said peevishly. Rosemary was astonished at the man's naiveté, though she had once been as naive herself. Growing animated, she assured him it was the same for women mathematicians, thinking more of her students than of herself. "Well sure, in mathematics," he said, "you'd expect that. But the cello!" Over the man's shoulder Rosemary located Spider in the center of a small circle. In a tux and beard. He seemed to be explaining something. He gesticulated emphatically with the familiar expression on his face (excited, earnest, pedagogical) that he'd worn all his life when explaining things, from the logic of Dr. Seuss to the secrets of road maps—an expression that would soon, she realized with troubled pleasure, pass for authority in the world. Since he'd added the beard, which he was at that moment stroking with professional aplomb, it probably already did.

Over near the window she saw Daisy casting the light of her radiant, California smile on a pair of flushed violinists, one short, low-browed, and dark, one skinny and blond, as if they had been the undisputed stars of the night's performance. Maybe no one else could tell what Daisy was up to, but Rosemary could tell.

". . . No," said Harold to Spider, wiping his mouth. "I was there the whole time. I sat near the back, where the sound's better, so maybe you didn't see me. But I was there. I'm here, see?"

Spider's unconscious stared at the map on which he'd once tracked his father's progress west the year he was seven. "I was afraid you'd miss the overture and just get here for the Berg. Which would have been awful, because I had a six-bar solo in the overture, and the strings really fucked up the Berg."

Harold ignored *fucked* and drew back. How could Spider doubt him? He'd sat through fifty miles of bumper-to-bumper traffic, he'd missed his dinner, and at that very moment he was risking a thirty-five-dollar parking ticket to be here. "You think I would have missed my son's Carnegie debut? Come on," he said, feigning a punch to Spider's cheek. "I wouldn't miss one note. You were terrific, the whole bunch of you."

Spider lowered his head and voice to approach his father's ear. "See that guy with the red mustache? That's Dennis Moglen. It was his fault, mostly. The asshole. If you don't know the notes you should just fake it and at least not mess up the sound. Nobody'll know you're not really playing."

Elizabeth Ann approached them with a camera. "Would you like me to take your picture?"

Embarrassed, Spider shook his head. "Naah, that's okay."

"Wait a minute," said Harold. "If this nice young lady wants to take our picture I think it would be a fine thing to have. And then we can take yours if you like."

Inside his shoe Spider's toes began frantically drumming. "Pop . . ."

"If you don't mind just waiting a sec till I get Spider's mother and sister?" Harold scans the room, then waves his arms till Daisy and Rosemary respond. "What do you think? With the trumpet or without?"

"Pop . . . please . . ."

But here they come. Harold makes the introductions. "Okay? Maybe we should do it boy-girl-boy-girl," he says, directing. "Thank you very much, Elizabeth. We really appreciate this. . . . A little closer in, Daisy, that's right. . . ."

Elizabeth Ann smiles and presses the button. The flash connects. The Polaroid goes to work while she turns it over and begins counting seconds.

"Should we all go out for dessert, or what?" asks Rosemary.

"No!" snaps Spider, terrified his mother will invite Elizabeth Ann, standing there holding her camera. "I can't," he stalls, while he thinks up something. "Herschel promised to sneak me into the eleven o'clock show at the West End. Dizzy's playing."

The mere thought of food gives Daisy that nauseous feeling again. She shakes her head. "No thanks, I'm still full," she fibs, patting her increasingly interesting belly.

"Dizzy Gillespie? Really? Maybe I'll drop in later myself," threatens Harold, longing to ingratiate himself with his son. He won't go, though. Since he's started dating again he's come to hate dark, loud, smoky clubs dominated by noisy youth who eye his women and make him feel old.

"How would you like to come back to my apartment, then?" Rosemary asks Daisy. "You haven't seen it yet."

But Daisy's afraid that once they're alone together she might break down and tell her mother everything. "Maybe tomorrow," she demurs, asserting herself. "Tonight I think I'll go home." Back to her room, her drawers, her closet to sort through her things before strangers put their hands on them. She has only two more days.

Daisy's demurrer leaps on Rosemary from behind in a stranglehold and whispers in her ear, *home*. And her own apartment, which Daisy has never seen? Her assailant's grip tightens until she feels herself beginning to choke. When her eyes blur, she turns around, waiting till she can trust her smile.

Out comes the picture. Elizabeth Ann carefully tears off the backing, looks, grins. . .

And now: Here are the Streeters—tall, handsome, growing older; Spider, frowning, in beard and tux; Daisy and Rosemary with a single smile; Harold, drink in hand, taking charge—caught forever.

40

In every woman's life a time must come to think about marriage. And now it has come for Daisy Streeter. Though she often secretly thinks of herself as still a child (her friends are *girls*, not *women*, and the males she knows have progressed from *boys* only up as far as *guys*), her second trimester is rapidly approaching.

Lately she's begun to read her dreams as portents, and this morning she woke in the grip of an anxiety dream. She was swimming in deep water when someone, a man, began ducking her under. . . . And then? . . . She can't quite remember the rest. But she knows that whatever her dream, very soon, before the second trimester, she must decide what to do.

Like everyone, Daisy wants everything, all the pleasures and rewards of existence: safety and freedom, trust and passion, family and work and love. Who wouldn't? But how can she pull it off?

Most people marry. Some do it blindly: they step out to the end of the rocks, hold their noses, squeeze their eyes closed, count to three and leap. Others go slowly, one step at a time—the courtship, the affair, the shared apartment, the engagement, perhaps a pregnancy—until they feel they have no choice left. Some make flamboyant promises, pretending they'll do it just as soon as they graduate, get the promotion, placate the family, finish analysis, sign their divorce—then temporize for up to a lifetime. Some choose chastity, some fidelity, some adultery, some polygamy. But all settle for less than all.

Once, the choice seemed simple. No question of *if*, only *who*. When your time came to marry, you searched the available waters for the strongest swimmer and then you plunged in as if you had fallen, crying to be saved. He saved you or you sank: simple. But now the rules have changed. It's free swim for everyone. No guards blowing whistles. It's shameful to need a savior, but the water's as deep as ever, and if you're reckless you can drown.

Daisy is unprepared for these waters, despite all the advantages life has showered on her. Anxiously, she sits on the beach at Santa Cruz watching her choices fan out around her like the branchings of a complicated seaweed newly risen from the depths. Mysterious and strange they appear, with sinister nodules and fronds and blades. Are they nourishing or poisonous? How shall she choose? She lets the sand sift through her fingers as the child inside her turns and dreams.

Though Daisy's conscientious mother tried to teach her children the facts of life, she has confused them with abundant possibilities. Renouncing the strict, censorious ways of her own mother, Rosemary tried to condemn nothing. Instead, she discreetly concealed her shames, tucking her secrets in the crevices of her life, hoping they would not, like winter ice, tear treacherous holes in the surface of things. Now, those very secrets, shocking and real, are what Daisy most needs to know. She needs a map of the potholes. And her father's secrets too, the secrets of men, in place of his fusty advice. Without them, how can she surmount the confusions and hypocrisies of her own generation, who disparage marriage as ardently as they seek it? She watches the surfers spin flashy wakes as she tries to divine what to do.

She can marry like her mother and her mother's mother and all her ancestors. (No, not all: not dashing Aunt Sarah, her mother's favorite, whom Grandpa denied from the day she left home—and how many more?) There, in that comfortable house with the good kitchen and the good Michael returning every night, she could be a good, could be the best of, mothers. But one child of hers, her own unbounded spirit, born

out of wedlock, would be missing. And after a sufficient time, declared
dead. A hero, but dead. A dead hero. And then every time she gazed out
a certain window of her cozy life she'd see the gold star hanging there and
remember her missing child—daring, dashing, dead. But, for the sake of
the living children, she would not permit herself to mourn.

Or she can refuse the bondage of the past and go her own way, making
of herself an exception, an example. (A spectacle, her father would call it,
shaking his head and counseling prudence, as she stood naked in the
window flagging her ears at the neighbors' sons.) But then she'd have
only one child, whom she'd carry through the world in a pack on her
back. Gypsies together, they'd sing for their supper. Anesthetized, she'd
tie her tubes to be free.

Or she could marry Michael in every sense but the legal. Have a party
to prove it, clap three times to undo it. A fairy tale. (But who would
believe it?) Daisy piles little heaps of sand around her like reasons, but try
as she may, she can't figure out if such an arrangement would have the
benefits of marriage without the penalties, or the penalties without the
benefits. She thinks she'd enjoy having people look at them like a married
couple as long as they're not, but if they really were, she probably couldn't
stand it. She will *not* be addressed as *Mrs.* or described as *wife!* Her
mother would say you were tied forever to the father of your children,
legally or not; but her father would make a great to-do about the documents. (Whatever they said on the matter, Daisy noted, they'd made sure
to have the document themselves—and she was glad.)

But there was another, a fourth, possibility. Born of prudence coupled
with defiance, it seemed to Daisy to embody her birthright: her patrimony
and her matrimony. She sensed that it was no less absurd than her other
choices, but it appealed to her sense of drama (and there was the baby to
consider):

A secret marriage, then, like Romeo and Juliet's. She'll marry Michael—
for the baby's sake—but only in the strictest secrecy. No one, not even
their parents, will know.

Daisy pulls off her sweat shirt, drops her jeans, and walks down to the
water. How quickly everything changes. Even in this new loose swimsuit
her belly no longer looks flat, and does she only imagine as she plunges
into the ocean that her body is more buoyant?

Dreamily she floats on her back, watching the huge blue sky. Suddenly
she remembers her morning dream. She was swimming. Then a man

began pushing her head under water. Terrified, she began to struggle—until she gradually discovered she was able to breathe under water.

Yes, like her parents and ancestors before her, she will marry; and no one, she consoles herself, need ever be the wiser.

Wedding . . .

"Surrogate for what? For God?" queried Michael, to whom their official marriage in the surrogate court didn't count anyway, since he'd fudged both his height and religion on the marriage license application. But so what?—he believed in the state no more than Daisy claimed to believe in marriage. What he believed in was their son.

Afterwards, to counteract the weight of the dry, official ceremony, they bought a good bottle of zinfandel and drove high into the mountains for a secret ceremony of their own. Daisy picked a nosegay of wildflowers for her wedding bouquet—red gaillardia, blue alfalfa, yellow daisies, scarlet penstemon, Indian paintbrush, and a spray of small white evening primroses. For Michael's boutonniere she pulled a pink hollyhock through the top buttonhole of his striped shirt, then kissed him on the nose. He was slightly shorter than she was, which bothered her only when she thought of what others would think—especially her mother, who had such a thing about height. Though she'd never have admitted it even to him, secretly, she found his height something of a turn-on—perhaps because it was taboo. Of course, picking wild flowers in Echo Canyon was also taboo, but she was drawn to the forbidden as a nun is drawn to prayer. Besides: a wedding, even a secret one, ought to override ordinary rules.

They waited until the noisy family from Iowa were on their way back to the car park and they were sure they were alone before they solemnly joined hands. "Ready?" they asked each other, then walked up the path toward the spot from which each echo was said to reverberate forever.

"I don't know what to say."

"Me neither."

"You go first."

"No, you."

When Daisy, embarrassed, began to giggle, Michael, soon to be a father, assumed responsibility. "Will you marry me?" he shouted, and the echo came back, *me*.

Daisy lifted her head and yelled, "Yes!" *Yes!* returned her voice, softer but no less certain. "And you?" whispered Daisy, as if they had not already done it at city hall, as if there could be no certainty, "Will you marry me?"

"Yes," shouted Michael to the mountain, followed by, *Yes.* "Hey, this is really cool," he said.

Daisy returned to the business at hand: "I love you." But when only the *you* came back to her, she started to feel a little silly. (What could be sillier than a secret marriage?)

"You've got to keep them short," observed Michael. "One or two syllables. Try again."

Daisy tried again. "I do!" she shouted, leaning forward toward the towering wall of rock. "Me too!" boomed Michael.

I do! Me too! came the echo, and they both began to laugh and shout at once. *I do! Me too! Me too! I do! I do! Me too!*—and soon it was impossible to know which of the words came from inside themselves and which fell back upon them from the world.

All during Rosemary's talk ("The Pecking Order of Chickens: Gender Bias in College Math") her eyes kept returning for reassurance to a certain man in the front row with thick movie-star hair who sat stroking his chin and nodding (encouragingly, she thought) and afterwards was the first on his feet with intelligent questions. He reminded Rosemary of someone, of a lover from her past.

The name tag on his jacket said Bradley, Erie, PA Bd of Ed. "Is that your first name or your last name?" she asked, underlining *Bradley* with the long nail of her index finger, her first caress. They slipped off under the pines with their box lunches.

By the time of the afternoon workshops he told her he'd never met a woman quite like her. It wasn't her urbanity only; he had once lived in a big city himself for seven years. It was her combination of masculine confidence and womanly attentiveness. She'd presented her subject with authority, yet when he spoke, she listened not only with her ears and eyes but with her entire body, affirming everything he said. When the workshops broke for tea and punch, he confessed he found her bewitching, and she, recognizing his sincerity, returned the compliment.

At the plenary, they sat together. "I'd like to invite you to Erie to give a talk," he said. "We have a small enrichment program. Our students could get a lot from you."

"I'd love to be invited to Erie. See you in your natural habitat. Thank you." She restrained herself from reaching out to touch his lush black hair.

"I might be able to arrange it very soon. My wife happens to be co-chairman of the Educational Lecture Series for this semester."

Rosemary looked up at him through her lashes as if she were wearing a particularly dashing wide-brimmed hat. Her years had taught her that the moment had come to make her move. "But, you know," she said, lowering her voice though not her eyes, "if you and I are going to be lovers, I couldn't possibly accept such an invitation."

His smile froze on his lips. "Why?" he asked at last. "Because you'd feel guilty?"

"Guilty?"

"You know. Adultery. The Seventh Commandment."

"No," she said, slowly smoothing the folds from her skirt. "As a matter of fact, personally I've always found adultery one of the more appealing aspects of marriage." Since her children had grown up and left home, she'd become quite shameless.

That night, waiting for Bradley's knock, Rosemary tried to recall who it was he reminded her of. She started way back at the beginning, but all she could remember were her two kinds of men, those you fall in love with and those you marry.

But remembering the painters (one Parisian, one Basque) she'd taken turns with that first week in Paris, and the dark-eyed guide from Venice who courted her in a gondola, she thought, no, there are three kinds of men: those you fall in love with, those you can marry, and those you only want to sleep with. But then she recalled the lifeguard at the bus stop she'd met at seventeen and her piano player that summer in the Hamptons, the kind for whom you instantly conceive a great infatuation only to discover very soon that your passion is misconceived, and she thought, actually there are no fewer than four kinds of men. And there was a fifth kind, too, like Peter, whom she might have lived with happily if only she'd been free. . . .

(But Rosemary knew better than to gather regrets, which, with the right fuel, might ignite her entire past and burn her happiness to the ground.)

And the more carefully she tried to define the categories, the more the categories proliferated, until she began to suspect there might be as many kinds as she'd had lovers, real and imagined. Grand passions, one-nighters, comrades, conquests, rivals, friends; those she loved for their likeness to her, those for their difference; those who brought her news from another country, or culture, or generation, or gender, or style; the well-spoken, the silent; the shy, the bold; the cads, the wimps; the reliable, the unpredictable; the sweet, the outrageous.

In fact, she had lately come to believe that there is no one she could not, if the circumstances were right, take as a lover or love as a friend, no one on earth without a full share of the divine.

Divertimento . . .

After they had drunk his bottle of liebfraumilch and taken off their clothes, and they were stretched out on the bed in the violet light of deep dusk kissing to the accompaniment of a Mozart divertimento playing softly on the radio, Bradley said to her shyly, "There's something I keep wanting to ask you, but I'm afraid you might take it the wrong way."

Rosemary's heart beat a little faster, anticipating the unknown. "Try me," she said, rising up on an elbow so that her breasts could arrange themselves in a more attractive, reassuring pose.

He ran his hand from her cheek down her shoulder over her right breast to her hip where he rested it gingerly. Then he said, "You talk about your grown children. But your face, your body seem younger than that." He glanced up to see the expression on her face and was relieved to find her calm. "Not that I care how old you are. If anything, the older you are the more impressed I'll be. The truth is, I've always been attracted to older women. But . . . I'm terribly curious. How old are you, anyway? Do you mind?"

Rosemary felt trapped. She sucked in her stomach, crossed her arms over her stretch marks, arranged her smile. Back when she was married, the years passed easily; but now she's as vulnerable as any single woman and dares not reveal the truth. She has two ways to go: she can conceal her age or flaunt it. But to shave off even five years, she must deny Daisy. Prudently, she chooses the other path.

"I don't mind as long as you don't. Actually, my age is one of the things I'm rather vain about. This year I turned fifty," she says—though in fact she'd just turned forty-five.

"Fifty! You don't look anything like it. I'm impressed," says Bradley proudly, and a bit surprised, as if he'd just won a prize at a fair.

Now Rosemary, excited as a flasher, dares more and more. "Thank you. Yes, it really is quite a good age. It has advantages you probably haven't even considered."

"Like what?"

She smiles puckishly, glancing up through her lashes again. "Well, for instance, if you go home and tell your wife that your friend from the conference is fifty, she'll never give us a moment's trouble."

Outrageous! Only yesterday she was the wife, but now she seems barely aware of how shamelessly she's switched allegiance. She moves her hand down Bradley's body. "You—with a fifty-year-old lover!"

As he pulls her down beside him on the bed she sees her sister Sarah (*slut! homebreaker! whore!*), then remembers a remark of Nora's she had once considered quite scandalous but, being single again herself, now brazenly adopts as her own. *What do I care if he's married? I don't want to marry him. I only want to love him for a month.* And invoking her own most original work, Streeter's powerful Theorem of Possibilities with its newest proven Corollary, that *everyone is capable of everything*, she wonders if at this very moment Nora herself might not be taking marriage vows and looking into adoption. Suppressing a wicked laugh, Rosemary at last runs her fingers through Bradley's lush black hair. "And you?" she says. "How old are you?"

"Thirty-five," he acknowledges sadly, with downcast eyes.

"Ah, yes, thirty-five. A difficult age for some people. But don't worry. It could get a lot better as you go along."

He began by kissing her lips—soft, slow kisses, just the way she liked them. How sweet love could be. An attentive lover, he seemed to be watching her for cues, as she watched him. After a while, very gently, with her hand in his wonderful hair, she moved his mouth to her breast. "Yes," she whispered, grateful that it was almost dark, "there." And for a long time they lay together just like that, slowly touching each other's body, getting deeply acquainted, while he sucked her nipples and she felt the quiver of his breath upon her breast and his smooth satin penis pressing against the secret skin of her inner thigh.

. . .

Michael leans over and lightly pats Daisy's belly. That very week the baby has begun fluttering inside Daisy, but he has yet to feel it move. "My son," he says—or something like it. Paterfamilias.

Daisy remembered the smell of musk in a dank sandy room, the sense that she was stuck in a corner where she could never fully comprehend the pattern, that she would always be alone. Ardently she vowed not to repeat the mistakes of her parents, grandparents, or ancestors; and Michael beside her took a similar vow.

"If we both hope for a boy, maybe it'll help. I really want a son," says Michael (naturally). "Don't you?"

Daisy hesitates. This was all so new to her; she has nothing to go by, no experience. The only hope she ever dared express was that her baby be normal and she be adequate to raise it, since, whenever she thought about it, she felt overwhelmed by the task. She fears she knows nothing, can know nothing. Therefore, she hopes her baby is a girlchild. A girl, whose feelings she can check against her own, she might possibly be able to teach, as her own mother had taught her—how to listen and speak, how to smile and lie, how to want and sing. But a boy—how could she know what to teach a boy? Michael will know, perhaps—but . . . dare she count on him?

Michael is gazing at her belly with an expression more intense than any she's ever seen. She brushes aside the anxious thought. Wishing to banish from their new life all disharmony before it can take root, she is tempted to smile sweetly and answer, "Yes. Me too. A boy." It seems to her a small and harmless lie—for harmony, for her baby's sake. Not only to please Michael, but because, if it's a girl, she'll have what she desires and it won't matter what she said, but if it's a boy, the lie might help her to believe she got what she wanted.

She opens her mouth, but, like some of her clients at the Center, she's unable to speak. The compromising words stick on her tongue.

Daisy knows that the baby is already formed, beyond wishing, the person and gender given; knows with each flutter that her freedom is beginning to erode. But at this moment she still has her integrity. Later, she thinks, after she's split in two, there'll be time to adapt.

She takes Michael's hand and places it over their child, where he may feel the living life. Daisy tilts her head as if she's listening while Michael, concentrating all his attention, lets her guide his hand.

Before long, the baby rewards them with an incontestable kick. The mother's eyes gleam; the father draws back his hand as from a flame and then, taking a new breath, presses it on again. Their hands touch, their eyes meet, they hope.

> What is milk. Milk is a mouth. What is a mouth.
> Sweet. What is sweet. Baby.
> A lesson for baby.
> What is a mixture. Good all the time.
> Who is good all the time. I wonder.
> A lesson for baby.
> What is a melon. A little round.
> Who is a little round. Baby.
> Sweetly Sweetly sweetly sweetly.
> In me baby baby baby
> Smiling for me tenderly tenderly.
> Tenderly sweetly baby baby.
> Tenderly tenderly tenderly tenderly.

A NOTE ON THE TYPE

The text of this book was composed in a digitized
version of Palatino, a type face designed by the noted
German typographer Hermann Zapf. Named after
Giovanbattista Palatino, a writing master of Renaissance
Italy, Palatino was the first of Zapf's type faces to be
introduced in America. The first designs for the face
were made in 1948, and the fonts for the complete face
were issued between 1950 and 1952. Like all Zapf-designed
type faces, Palatino is beautifully balanced and
exceedingly readable.

Composed by American–Stratford Graphic Services,
Brattleboro, Vermont
Printed and bound by The Haddon Craftsmen, Inc.,
Scranton, Pennsylvania
Typography and binding design by Iris Weinstein